I'LL BE
WAITING

Also by Kelley Armstrong

Rip Through Time

A Rip Through Time   *The Poisoner's Ring*   *Disturbing the Dead*

Haven's Rock

The Boy Who Cried Bear
Murder at Haven's Rock

Rockton

The Deepest of Secrets   *Watcher in the Woods*
A Stranger in Town   *This Fallen Prey*
Alone in the Wild   *A Darkness Absolute*
City of the Lost

Cainsville

Rituals   *Deceptions*
Betrayals   *Visions*
Omens

Age of Legends

Forest of Ruin
Empire of Night
Sea of Shadows

The Blackwell Pages (co-written with Melissa Marr)

Thor's Serpents
Odin's Ravens
Loki's Wolves

Otherworld

Thirteen   *Living with the Dead*   *Industrial Magic*
Spell Bound   *Personal Demon*   *Dime Store Magic*
Waking the Witch   *No Humans Involved*   *Stolen*
Frostbitten   *Broken*   *Bitten*
Haunted

Darkest Powers & Darkness Rising

The Rising   *The Reckoning*
The Calling   *The Awakening*
The Gathering   *The Summoning*

Nadia Stafford

Wild Justice
Made to Be Broken
Exit Strategy

Standalone novels

Wherever She Goes   *The Masked Truth*
Aftermath   *Missing*
The Life She Had   *Every Step She Takes*
Hemlock Island

I'll Be Waiting

A NOVEL

Kelley Armstrong

ST. MARTIN'S PRESS
NEW YORK

First published in the United States by St. Martin's Press, an imprint of St. Martin's Publishing Group

I'LL BE WAITING. Copyright © 2024 by Kelley Armstrong. All rights reserved. Printed in the United States of America. For information, address St. Martin's Publishing Group, 120 Broadway, New York, NY 10271.

www.stmartins.com

The Library of Congress Cataloging-in-Publication Data is available upon request.

ISBN 978-1-250-28421–1 (hardcover)
ISBN 978-1-250-37481-3 (Canadian Edition)
ISBN 978-1-250-28422-8 (ebook)

Our books may be purchased in bulk for promotional, educational, or business use. Please contact your local bookseller or the Macmillan Corporate and Premium Sales Department at 1-800-221-7945, extension 5442, or by email at MacmillanSpecialMarkets@macmillan.com.

First Edition: 2024

10 9 8 7 6 5 4 3 2 1

I'll Be Waiting

ONE

Snow drives into the windshield, turning an evening ride home into a theme-park spaceship ride, launching us into orbit, light streaking past, making me feel as if we're hurtling forward instead of inching along the highway.

"I'm thinking . . . Iceland," Anton says from the driver's seat.

I shake my head. "It's a freak fall storm. By tomorrow, it'll be gone. Wait until February. *Then* you can start complaining about the snow."

"I mean I'm thinking about going to Iceland. The two of us. On a cruise into the midnight sun."

I glance over at him. Headlights from the opposite lane catch his face, green eyes under dark hair falling over his forehead. He's overdue for a haircut, but I'll never be the one to remind him. I long to reach up and push the hair back, uncover the hidden strands of gray, run my fingers over the scar at his temple, maybe lean in to kiss his stubbled cheek. Yes, we've been married for two years, but I'm still ridiculously in love with my husband.

"Did you hear me, Nic?" he says.

"Mmm, no. I'm busy staring at you."

His color rises, which is adorable. I resist the urge to reach out and touch his thigh, tickle my fingers over it. None of that while driving in a snowstorm.

"Fine," I say, "you were saying something about a cruise to . . . Iceland?"

His gaze doesn't leave the road. "I know cruises aren't your thing, but this is an intimate one, with an emphasis on adventure and education. I'm quoting the pamphlet. Can you tell?"

I smile. "I can. I like the sound of 'intimate,' though."

"And your brain stopped there. *Small* cruise, I mean. Fifty people. Lectures and sea kayaks. Glaciers and whale watching. That sort of thing."

"I would love that. Seriously. It sounds amazing, but I'm not sure . . . Well, we'd need to see whether it's doable. For me."

He takes his eyes from the road just long enough to fix me with a look.

"Which you have already done," I murmur. "You wouldn't mention it unless you were already sure they could accommodate someone with CF. Because you are amazing and perfect."

"Can I get that in writing? For the next time I burn breakfast? Yes, I found a travel blog from someone with CF who took the cruise, and I checked with Dr. Mendes. She thinks it would be fine, with all the usual precautions."

Which means taking along my shitload of medical supplies—bottles of enzymes and my vest and my nebulizer—and a backup power supply. But it can be done, and that's the important thing.

"I would love to see Iceland," I murmur.

"Excellent, and if you want to test out cruising first, I found another small one that sails through the Great Lakes. Would you like that?"

"Yes, please."

I smile and lean back against the headrest. Iceland. My parents would be proud of me, as if I were doing it at eighteen instead of thirty-eight. But I know, despite their boundless support, that they'd always worried I wouldn't live to thirty-eight. When I'd been diagnosed as a baby, my life expectancy ended a decade ago. But a lifetime of advances mean I'm still here, even when my parents aren't around to see it.

Thirty-eight years old, married, heading off on cruises with my husband. I spent my life being told that none of that was possible. Not by my parents, of course, or my brother or my doctors. But it felt like everyone else who heard I had cystic fibrosis put limits on me.

You won't live past twenty, thirty if you're lucky. You can't play sports. You won't marry. You won't go to university.

I can still hear the guidance counselor telling me I could skip career-planning day because, well, that wasn't for me, was it? No point in a career I won't live long enough to need.

I ended up with a master's in software engineering. At university I was part of the running club and ran three half-marathons. A decade ago, I started my own company. And then, just when I was certain marriage was no longer in the cards, Anton came back into my life.

I won't say I'm running marathons these days. I know what's in my future. I can feel it in my lungs. But for now, I am healthy enough to go on cruises and more, and we're doing it all while I still can.

It helps that I'm on a new medication. A groundbreaking one that has me more hopeful than I've ever been. The fact that—as of last month—it's covered by Canada's health plan means we have the money to do those cruises.

"I want the best cabin they've got," I say.

Anton smiles. "Do you now?"

"Yep. We are splurging. First-class airfare, best cabin on the ship."

"Champagne every night?"

"Damn straight."

He laughs and—

And then—

And then—

The rest comes in lightbulb flashes that illuminate a single scene before darkness falls.

Flash.

Headlights, closer than they should ever be, shining through Anton's window. We rocket sideways, and there's a crash, the sound coming on a delay, just as my brain screams *What the hell is happening?*

Flash.

The car has stopped. People are shouting. I'm . . . upside down? Sideways? I can only tell that I'm suspended somehow, the airbag in my face, seat belt cutting into my chest. I yank at it, panic making me struggle to breathe until I'm sure I can.

"Nic?"

Anton's voice is a groan. I turn my head, but all I see is my airbag. And blood. I see blood.

Flash.

Hands pulling me out of the car. A man's voice, pitched high.

"My truck hit ice. I lost control."

A woman's voice, snapping. "You were driving too fast. I told you to slow down."

"They're okay, right? They're going to be okay?"

"Does he *look* okay?"

Anton . . .

Flash.

So many voices. Everyone talking. Shouting for a doctor. Asking whether anyone's called 911.

"We've all called."

"Where the hell's the ambulance?"

"On its way. The storm . . ."

Flash.

I'm kneeling on grass. Slush soaks through my jeans. Blood drips down my face. Anton lies on a blanket someone has dragged from their trunk.

Anton, his breath wheezing, his chest caved in, blood streaming from his head, one eye fixed on me, the other off to the side, unable to focus.

"The airbag," a woman whispers. "Why didn't his airbag go off?"

Someone else shushes her. Strangers all around, pacing and whispering and keeping their distance, as if they're witnesses at a vigil.

"The ambulance is coming," I say, as I squeeze Anton's hand.

"I love you," he says.

"Shh. The ambulance—"

"Stay with me."

"I'm right here, baby."

"No, stay . . ." He struggles for breath, that awful wheezing sucking sound bubbling up. "It's okay. Just stay with me. Focus on me."

A noise comes out of my throat, an almost hysterical yip. "That's supposed to be my line."

"Nic?"

I squeeze his hand tighter. "I'm right here. I'm not going anywhere. Can you see me?"

His lips quirk. "I always saw you."

I squeeze his hand.

"Even when we were kids," he says. "You might not have seen me, but I saw you."

"I saw you, too."

Another quirk. "But not in a good way. I was a jerk."

"Your friends were jerks. You were just a guy with really bad taste in friends."

A soft laugh. "Maybe, but I had very good taste in girls. I always saw you, Nic. I always . . ." His voice catches. "I need to tell you something. A secret."

Something in me flails, a wild and unreasonable urge to stop him. Whatever he's about to say, don't say it. Just—

"Remember how I said I accidentally found your company when I went looking for a coder?" He's wheezing, struggling to get the words out. I try to stop him, tell him to rest, but he plows on. "It wasn't an accident. I recognized you in an article, and I had to reach out, take a chance." His fingers flutter in a weak squeeze on mine. "Best damn chance I ever took."

I lean over, pressing my lips to his. "I'm glad you did."

His mouth twists in a wry smile. "I don't think I'm going to Iceland, Nic."

"Don't say—"

"Wherever I do go, though?" His fingers tighten on mine, startling me with their sudden strength. "I'll be waiting for you. But . . ." His lips form the next word, but nothing comes out, and his eyes roll back, and his fingers release mine and, with a soft exhale . . .

Anton is gone.

TWO

Seven Months Later

"This way," says the woman. She flaps her arms in what I presume is a welcoming gesture, but with her voluminous black robe she looks like a vulture about to take flight, red talons flashing.

As soon as Shania and I step into the hall, the reek of incense hits and my insides twist.

Fake. You know this is fake, so what the hell are you doing here?

Even as my brain screams that, a little voice whispers that I know it's *not* always fake. It is possible to reach beyond this world into the next.

Of all people, I know that.

I also know what can happen if you do.

An image flashes. Blood sprayed across a bush—

I shove that aside. That was two decades ago. This séance is about Anton, and I am not the least bit concerned about summoning my husband's spirit.

I follow the medium down the dim hall. Beside me, Shania fairly vibrates with excitement. Tiny and dark-haired, Shania has kohl-liner cat eyes that make her look much younger than her twenty-five years. So does the hope shining in her face.

I met Shania two months ago, at grief counseling, where I'd been assigned as a mentor to help her mourn the loss of her sister.

I can say I'm here for her. She desperately wants proof of an afterlife. But that's a lie, and I won't give in to it.

I'm here for me. Because I'm a damn coward who can't accept that her husband is gone.

As the medium—*call me Leilani*—herds us toward the room, Shania whispers, "This time we'll reach him. I know we will." She squeezes my hand, her skin hot against my clammy fingers.

We enter a tiny, windowless room. It looks like the den in my grandparents' house, complete with wood paneling and a stucco ceiling. Mystical abstract art on the walls seems to all be painted by the same amateur, maybe Leilani herself.

Two women and a man sit at an old table draped in a black cloth. All three are middle-aged, white, and nondescript enough that they could be related. Three pairs of eyes stare at me. Leilani introduces them as spirit helpers, but I know why they're really here. To gape at me. Nicola Laughton. The woman from the news. The woman from a viral story that rises from the grave every few weeks, which I know by the sudden surge of messages with titles like "Have you seen him yet?" and "I can help you contact him."

My life changed in one night. A winter storm, not even that bad, just earlier than usual. An asshole who wasn't letting a little snow slow him down. Faulty airbags in a nearly new car. Between the three, I went from giddy newlywed to grieving widow in twenty minutes flat. A private tragedy that should have damn well remained private.

Except it didn't.

One of those strangers milling around that night had recognized a story unfolding before them. Was it one of the Good Samaritans who helped get us out of the car, wrapped us in blankets, called 911? Or one of the ghouls who only stopped to gape?

It doesn't matter. Someone overheard me telling the paramedics that I had cystic fibrosis, just warning them as you would with any chronic condition, and suddenly, a back-page "One Dead in Highway Accident" became a front-page "Terminally Ill Newlywed Widowed in Horrific Winter Crash."

I'm not sure what enraged me more: the idea that having CF made me "terminally ill" or that the headline centered around me, when Anton was the one who'd lost his life.

"Man Dies in Crash" isn't a story. Not until someone hears that he married a woman in the late stages of a chronic illness and—plot twist!—*she's* the one now planning *his* funeral. I'm not even in the late stages of CF, but given my age, someone apparently decided I was.

That story would have made the front page, but it wouldn't have gone viral. It's the other one that counted. That night, when I'd said goodbye to Anton, people had overheard us talking. They'd heard his last words to me.

I'll be waiting.

One witness swore that after he said that, his spirit flowed from his body and bent to kiss the top of my head. They even took a damn photo—because that's what you do when you unintentionally eavesdrop on a stranger's dying words. You get out your phone for a picture.

In the photo, a white blur hangs over me. It's some kind of optical illusion—from the snow and the night and the headlights—but people see what they want to see. And what they want to see is the ghost of a dead man, standing over his "terminally ill" wife, reassuring her that he'll be waiting on the other side. For, you know, when she dies. Which will be soon. Aww. How sweet.

That's the story that went viral. That's also the story that brought every medium to my virtual—and sometimes actual—doorstep. I'm the perfect client, grief-stricken and financially comfortable enough to fork over cash for a séance, pathetically hopeful after that photo, and also minor-league social-media famous, guaranteeing publicity if they can contact my husband.

Do I sound angry? I *am* angry. I'm pissed off at that driver, at the car manufacturer, at whoever shared those stories, at whoever took that picture, at the phony mediums preying on my grief. But the person I'm angry at the most?

Me.

Because I keep falling for the con artists. Because I am smarter than this, stronger than this, wiser than this. Or I should be. Yet here I am in another medium's house, paying to be tricked and gaped at by strangers.

Worse, I'm here after swearing to everyone that I won't do this again. I'm like a junkie sneaking away for her fix, and I am ashamed.

I am so damned ashamed of myself.

I've never been what you'd call meek. Dad always said I plow through life, and there may have been some mention of a bull and a china shop, implying that my "plowing" comes with the strong possibility of destruction. But when I enter Leilani's lair, I am as meek as can be. Gaze downcast, greetings murmured, praying my face isn't bright red with shame and embarrassment. I'm sure it is—the perils of being the pale and freckled kind of redhead.

I take my seat, and Shania slides in beside me. I offer her a smile that I try—really try—to make genuine. She deserves better. She deserves a mentor who can help her move past her sister's death. But how am I supposed to help her do something I can't do myself?

I know all the platitudes. Cherish the memories. Be thankful for the time you had with them. They would want you to be happy. All true. Anton would be horrified to see me in this room. But this is where I am.

Leilani lights candles and lowers the lights. She doesn't turn them off. The candles aren't strong enough for that. But the illusion of a séance by candlelight is all that matters. The illusion of the whole thing is all that matters. A proper séance must look as if we wandered into a nineties movie-set séance, complete with candles, incense, a black-clad medium, and a Ouija board. Don't forget the Ouija board.

What do you mean Ouija boards aren't traditional spiritualism? You're saying they were created by a novelty company for parlor games? Fie on you and your easily confirmable data.

Once the candles are lit, we hold hands and Leilani sends out an invitation for Anton to join us. It's a very pretty invitation, all curlicues of words, verbal calligraphy that would have Anton scratching his head: Does she mean me? What does she want me to do? I don't get it, Nic.

Just say something, damn it. Tell a joke and get the punch line wrong, as usual. Whistle Green Day and My Chemical Romance songs so off-key that only I recognize them.

Just say hi.

That's all, Anton.

Say hello.

Tell me you are out there, somewhere.

Tell me your last words weren't blind and empty reassurances.

Tell me you are waiting.

As Leilani continues, I let the sarcasm and cynicism roll off me. There's no point in asking for help contacting Anton if I refuse to listen.

Find my breath. Clear my mind. Focus on the sound of Leilani's voice. Forget what she's saying and focus on her voice, low and rhythmic.

It only takes a few moments, and then I am where I need to be. Calm and just slightly outside of myself. Aware of the heat of Shania's hand, of the smell of candle wax cutting through the incense, the tick-tick-tick of . . .

Is that a metronome? I peek. Yes, there's an antique metronome by Leilani's elbow. That makes me smile and relax a little more. Anton had a metronome on his desk. It was his form of meditation, for times when his work as a mathematician got too stressful.

I loved to sit in his office and start up the metronome while I waited for him to solve whatever problem gripped his mind.

Tick-tick-tick.

I can see him hunched over his pages, scribbling furiously, reading glasses on.

Reading glasses before forty? I say. That's what you get for straining to read teeny-tiny numbers without good lighting.

That's a myth, Nic.

Mmm, not so sure.

He's writing and frowning and writing more. There's a laptop and a desktop computer nearby, but he likes to work by hand.

Luddite.

Tick-tick-tick.

Hair falls over his broad forehead. I catch a few silver hairs and smile smugly. About time. I've had them since I was twenty-five. Never dyed them out. I'm too damn proud of having lived to see gray hair.

Anton rests the tip of his pencil in his mouth.

Going to get lead poisoning, I say.

The amount of lead absorbed—

Don't math on me, Novak.

I smile and keep reaching for that image of him, constructing it until I see the whole of his office, right down to—

"Janica."

The name whispers up from my left, and I stiffen. That's not my name. It used to be, once upon a time, but it's not now, and no one in this room knows me as anything but Nicola.

I look at Leilani, but she's still invoking Anton.

I imagined it. Imagined hearing my old name. Imagined hearing it in Anton's voice, because he knew it, though he never called me that. Only my mom called me Janica, while sighing that everyone ignored the lovely name she'd picked for me, in favor of the boyish diminutive, Nic.

But might Anton use that name if he reached out? So I know it's really him?

I shake it off, making Shania glance over, worry clouding her brown eyes. I smile reassuringly and focus on the metronome again.

Tick-tick-tick.

Anton in his office, working out a problem. Finally, with a start, he realizes I'm there.

What time is it? he says.

Finish up.

Sorry. I lost track of—

Finish. We have time.

All the time in the world.

"Janica," the voice whispers. "Careful . . ."

The hair on my neck rises. I seem to hear Anton. Isn't that what I'm here for? So why am I stiffening, my heart picking up speed, panic rising?

Because it can't be him. Because I'm imagining—

Something moves, a shape caught just in the corner of my eye. I startle, and Leilani's soothing voice stops.

"Nicola?" she says.

There's nothing there, and I'm not even sure what I thought I saw. A sensation of movement. I sensed . . .

I blink hard.

"Continue," I say, my voice croaking.

"I don't think I need to," Leilani says. "He's here. I sense him."

A soft whisper has Shania jumping and one of the observers gasping softly.

"Nic . . ." The name swirls around me. The voice says something else, but it's garbled, indistinct.

"Anton?" Leilani says. "Am I addressing Anton Novak, husband of Nicola Laughton, who is here with me today?"

"Yes . . ." The word comes as a hiss. Then more, still garbled like two radio stations coming in at once.

"Anton? We're having trouble—"

Cold air snakes over my bare calves.

Shania jumps and squeaks. "Did anyone else . . . ?" She claps a hand to her mouth. "Sorry."

"Did you experience something, dear?" Leilani asks.

"Cold air. I felt—"

"I did, too," the male observer says.

"There!" one of the women says. "Did you see that?"

"The candle flames wavered." Shania's hand tightens painfully hard on mine. "Nic, he's here. Anton's really here."

I look at Shania's shining face, and I want to smile at her and say that yes, Anton's here. If he's here, that's proof of an afterlife, proof that her sister is somewhere and Shania can move on with her own life, confident in the knowledge that she will see her sister again.

Part of me wants to be the person who can do that.

The person who can lie to make others feel better.

The person who doesn't have to face the truth. Always.

I extricate my hand from Shania's. Then I stand and walk to where the candle flames had flickered. They're on a small cabinet, nestled between two statuettes of Egyptian deities. I lift one statuette.

"What are you doing?" Leilani says, stumbling to her feet.

The statuette only moves a couple of inches. Enough to reveal the tube running into it. An air tube that runs out the side, right at the level to make the candles flicker. Then I bend, hiking my skirt past my knees to get low enough. Another tube runs along the bottom shelf of the cabinet. That's where the blast of cold air came from.

I don't say anything. I just look at Leilani, and she flinches before setting her jaw.

"I don't know what you think you've found," she says.

"Shall I say it out loud?"

I walk back to the table. Then I pause, remembering which direction the voice had come from. The one that called me Nic.

There's another yard-sale-quality cabinet right behind the chair where I'd been sitting. Where I'd been *told* to sit. I find the speaker hidden in a picture frame. I turn the frame around so everyone can see the small speaker. I don't say anything, and no one else does either.

The other voice, the one that called me Janica, came from my left, right at my ear. I look around that area, but I don't see where a speaker would hide and, honestly, I don't expect to. No one in this room knows me by that name. That voice, then, I must have imagined.

I tap the picture-frame speaker as my gaze meets Leilani's. I still don't say anything. I could sneer that I know my husband's voice. I could roll my eyes at her for using tricks I've seen a half-dozen times. I could even rage at her for preying on my grief.

Instead, I just look at her and say, "I expect a refund."

When I glance at Shania, I falter. The disappointment on her face stings, but the resignation is worse. She's accompanied me to three séances, and she already knows this is what she can expect. The decent mediums admit they can't make contact. The charlatans pull this shit. And most of them are charlatans.

I can feel bad for not letting Shania believe in this one, but that would be patronizing. She isn't a child. She'd seen through the last one before I did. She might have been fooled here temporarily, but that would have passed, and she'd have been rightfully pissed off with me for playing along.

When I look over, she's already on her feet, her glare fixed on Leilani.

"I trusted you," Shania says to Leilani. "I let you convince me to bring Nicola. If you haven't transferred back her money before we reach the door, you'll have one-star reviews on every site by sundown."

That's my Shania. I smile at her, and she mouths an apology. I wave it off and put my hand against her back, guiding her from the room. No one tries to follow us. We walk through the tiny house . . . and make a wrong turn at the kitchen.

"Kinda ruins the whole storming-out thing when we can't find the exit," I whisper.

Shania gives a strained laugh. Then she whispers back, "I am *so* sorry, Nic. I know you were trying to quit, and I talked you into it."

"I'm a grown-up, Shania, and part of being a grown-up is, sadly, that no one else gets the blame for my shitty choices. Oh, there's the front door. Whew. What do you say to a midafternoon sugar splurge? I saw one of those fancy artisanal ice cream places on the drive in."

I pull open the door. "My treat, but only if you promise not to apologize . . ."

I trail off. There's a pickup parked in front of the small house. Parked illegally, which is why I didn't take the spot. A blond woman in jeans and a pullover perches on the truck's front bumper, while a dark-haired guy in a sport jacket leans against the front panel, arms crossed over his chest.

"Shit," Shania whispers.

"Yep."

Shania surges forward, boot heels clicking down the concrete steps. "Libby. Jin. I am so sorry. This is my fault. I talked her into it."

"No one talks Nic into anything," Libby says, straightening. "Trust me. We've all tried. If she agrees, it's because she already wanted to do it. Like visiting another spiritualist after promising she'd quit."

"How'd you find me?" I ask as I walk over.

Jin lifts his cell phone with the Find My Friends app displayed. "Forgot to turn it off this time, Nic. You're slipping."

"Or she wants to get caught," Libby says, using her psychologist-in-session voice.

I roll my eyes at her. No, I do *not* want to be caught. I might seem calm, but inside, I'm cringing like I'm eight again and Mom found chocolate-bar wrappers in my pocket after I'd forgotten—again—to take my enzyme pills with me. And after I swore I *never* had snacks if I forgot the pills.

I look from Jin to Libby. From my one best friend to the other.

From my brother's husband to his ex-wife. And, yep, that's as complicated as it sounds, but Keith has good taste in partners. It's probably his one redeeming quality.

Okay, fine, Keith has lots of redeeming qualities. I just happen to prefer hanging out with his spouses. And I definitely prefer having *them* show up, because they know the shame is punishment enough. If Keith were here . . . Well, my older brother has a knack for making me feel like I really am eight again, sneaking those chocolate bars.

"I *am* sorry," Shania says.

I wag my index finger at her. "No more of that. I messed up, and I'll take my licks, which apparently won't come with ice cream." I look at them. "I suppose it's Nicola-intervention time?"

"It is," Libby says. "If you want to meet us after your ice cream, that's fine. I'd just need to ask Keith to pick up the kids at school and look after them for an hour. Which is not a bad idea. Hayden is in a mood. Twelve years old and already sulking like a teen." She takes out her phone. "Yep, I'm definitely calling Keith, whatever you decide. Then we can hold the intervention over drinks."

"You go on," Shania says. "I'll catch a cab and see you at group tomorrow."

"No, I'm driving you home." I turn to Jin. "Meet me at my place. You can drive Libby and me to the bar, so I can have a couple of drinks. I have a feeling I'm going to need them."

THREE

I take Shania home, then I go to my place, where Libby and Jin will be waiting. Anton and I have a condo in downtown Toronto. It was stage one of "the plan" when we got married. We'd both owned condos in less central—and more affordable—neighborhoods. We sold them for a down payment on this because I dreamed of living right in the heart of the city, where I could walk everywhere, including along the shores of Lake Ontario. We planned to live here for a few years and then flip the condo and buy a house in the country, because I'd dreamed of that, too—rural living within easy driving distance to a CF center.

We'd been on the verge of selling last fall, as the housing-market bubble seemed prepared to burst. Sell at a profit, and then rent for a few months before taking advantage of the housing dip to buy. So smart, right? Yep, it was. And now the bubble has burst, and I'm still in this condo, barely able to face getting up in the morning much less moving.

I arrive at my door to find Jin and Libby in the hall.

"You have keys," I say with a sigh. "*Both* of you."

They don't comment. While Libby and Jin are very different, my brother does have a type, and it's the sort of person who'll happily take my condo key for emergencies or house-sitting, but will politely wait at the door instead of letting themselves in.

They are also the type who don't comment on the boxes in the front hall, dropped off by Anton's colleagues two weeks after his death. They've each separately offered once to help me deal with that, and they won't mention it again, knowing I'll accept that offer if and when I'm ready to unpack those boxes . . . and empty his closet and move the coffee cup he left on the counter that morning before work, the one he'd always only rinse out because he'd want a coffee when he got home. It sits there, gathering dust, waiting for him to need it.

Jin pauses by the hall table and silently scans the growing table-cloth of unopened mail. He knows there will be nothing urgent—I'm responsible enough to deal with all that. I mentally recite the contents of that pile as I pass it. Two cruise ship brochures I don't need. Three subscription magazines I can't read. And eight letters addressed to Anton. It's the last that Jin's looking for.

He spreads them and takes a photo, saying, "We'll deal with these."

He means he and Keith will notify the senders that Anton has died. I want to say I'll handle it. I want to be able to handle it. I tried, but even cutting and pasting a prewritten blurb into an email felt like being at that roadside again.

I regret to inform you that Anton Novak has died.

I could have handled that. What I couldn't handle were the replies that demanded additional proof. Additional proof? My husband is dead. Dead. You really think I'd lie about that?

Oh, I know people do lie about it, but that was the part I couldn't handle—demands to prove Anton was dead, as if I wouldn't give my right arm to say "Ha! No, I was just trying to scam you. He's fine."

Jin is walking away when Libby says, "Nic?"

I turn around to see her at that table, holding a letter to me. I march back, take it, and head straight into my office, where I feed it, unopened, into the shredder.

"Good riddance," Jin mutters from the doorway.

"He shouldn't be contacting you," Libby says.

I don't answer. What can I say? That I agree, but I lack the energy—or the will—to take more concrete action?

The letter is from the guy who hit us. After I blocked his email, he resorted to old-fashioned letter writing, which I suppose is also better than laying on my buzzer at two in the morning.

I've read a couple of the letters. He alternates between begging forgiveness and blaming me for ruining his life. After all, he hadn't been driving drunk or high. He'd just been going too fast, typical twenty-four-year-old guy confident in his skills, not about to be slowed down by a little snow.

Now his life is ruined because of a momentary lapse of judgment. And was it really his fault? Couldn't my husband have veered out of the way? What about the airbags? That's the real villain here—the airbags that didn't go off. I'm suing the company, right? Suing for millions, that's what he's heard. So what right do I have to complain? I'll be rich.

Anton didn't have time to veer. That was never questioned. Yes, I am suing the automaker, at Keith's urging, and it's not for millions, and that money will go to charity because I have enough and what we really wanted was the recall, which has been issued. But the kid who hit us isn't the only one who snarks about that.

Did you hear the widow is suing the car company, too—first that story about ghosts and now this. She's such an attention whore. Probably doesn't even have CF.

It doesn't stop. None of it stops.

Prove that your husband is dead.

Forgive the guy who killed him.

Don't you want to contact your husband's ghost? He's right there, waiting for you, like he said.

I turn sharply and brush past Libby and Jin. "Let me comb my hair and we'll go."

J in drives to our favorite pub on Queen West. It's a little dive bar, the interior so dark you'd never know it's only late afternoon. Also dark enough that you can barely see the decor, which is a blessing. At this time of day, it's practically empty. We order at the bar, get our drinks, and take our usual table in the back.

"So . . ." Jin says. "Another séance."

I sink into the booth, cracked vinyl squeaking under me. "I screwed up."

"That depends," Libby says, folding her hands on the scarred table. "Do you really want to quit? Then yes, you screwed up. But is it possible you don't want to quit, and you're only saying that to get Keith off your back?"

I sigh. "I wouldn't do that to you guys. If I say I want help quitting, I really do. I don't know why I keep sabotaging myself. It's humiliating. I know they're all con artists. I just can't help . . ."

"Hoping," Libby murmurs.

I slump into my seat. "God, I'm pathetic."

"*No.* You're grieving, and they're taking advantage of that. I know you want to be stronger, Nic, but no one blames you. What happened was . . ." She sucks in breath. "The worst. Horrible and unfair. To both of you. You guys got married knowing you might not have much time left. Then you got on that new medicine, and suddenly, that timeline is shifting, giving you more of a future. But it's always been *your* timeline. That's the shittiest part of it. You and Anton were on *your* timeline. That's what counted."

How much more time I had left.

How much more time I had to be healthy.

How much more time I had to be alive.

I knock back my shot, and then make a face. "That'd be way more impressive if it wasn't a shooter."

"We know you're hard-core, Nic," Jin says. "Even if you drink like you're still in college."

"What's that one called again?" Libby says.

Jin grins. "Redheaded Slut. It's her favorite."

"Damn straight." I slam back a second test tube of Jägermeister, peach schnapps, and cranberry juice. Then I hold out the shot glass. "Hit me again, bartender."

Jin sets it aside and shakes his head. Then he leans forward. "Look, I know what Keith thinks about this spiritualist stuff. It freaks him out."

For good reason. But Jin doesn't know that part. Neither does Libby. It's my secret. My family's secret.

Jin continues, "Keith is the one making you feel ashamed of what you're doing. I love the guy, but he can be judgy, and he's judging all over the place here, even if we know he's only worried about you."

"He's being overprotective," Libby says. "But yes, it feels like judgment, and it's driving you to hide what you're doing. Driving you to get help from Shania, who's a sweet kid but . . ."

"She wants to make contact even more than I do."

Both of us blinkered by our losses. Smart people doing things that our brains know are foolish, but when you're lost in the darkness of grief, the light of emotion is the one that guides you.

"Okay," I say. "So what's the solution? Keep blowing money on mediums until I get the answer I'm looking for? I'm already that old definition of insanity—doing the same damn thing over and over and expecting a different result."

"Which is why we're suggesting one last attempt," Libby says. "You agree to try one more time and *only* one more time, and we do it right. We find a good spiritualist who might actually be legit. We take every step to do this exactly right."

We're talking about a séance, not a dinner party. You can't plan something like that "exactly right" any more than you can plan a unicorn hunt exactly right.

Except this isn't like a unicorn hunt, because I don't believe in unicorns. I might not want to believe in ghosts either—and some days I don't, convinced I'd misinterpreted everything that happened twenty-two years ago. But deep down, I know there is something out there, and if it's contacted, things can go horribly, unspeakably wrong. Only this is Anton, who would never hurt me.

That voice from earlier whispers up from my memory.

Janica. Careful.

"Nic?" Jin says.

I shake myself. I imagined it. Imagined Anton warning me that I was being tricked because deep down, I already knew it.

I look from Jin to Libby. I don't think either of them believes in ghosts. Hell, they never thought I would either, and if asked, they'd say it's my grief opening me up to the possibility. I need ghosts to exist, so I believe they do.

Libby and Jin want to do this for me. Not because they really think I can contact Anton but because they know I need to try. That is friendship, and I am grateful for theirs, and even if a séance isn't the kind of thing you can do "exactly right," I need to let them try because I need to end this.

One last time. A time where I haven't half-assed it, allowing a medium to convince me to hire them rather than actually finding one I consider legitimate.

Get everything right. Then, when it fails, I can't seize on an oversight as an excuse to try again.

"And Keith?" I say.

Jin straightens. "We don't tell him. Libby and I will arrange everything. You can help if you like, but as far as Keith knows, we're arranging a much-needed getaway for the three of us. All he has to do is take the kids for a few days."

"So we lie to him? How's that going to make me less ashamed of what I'm doing?"

They glance at each other.

"Nic's right," Libby murmurs. She looks at me. "What do you suggest?"

"I tell him I'm doing this. You guys don't need to get involved. I say it's like having one last blowout party before embracing sobriety. He might not like it, but it's my life and my money."

Jin shakes his head. "No, *we* tell him *we're* doing this."

"You don't have to."

"I will. He'll understand, eventually, and he'd rather we were there with you." He looks from me to Libby. "Settled then?"

We nod.

Jin takes out his phone. "So where do we start?"

When someone knocks on my condo door that evening, I don't need to check through the peephole. There are a very limited number of people with my downstairs access code, and I know exactly which one this is.

I open the door. Keith stands there, looking like he rolled out of bed still dressed in his Bay Street banking exec suit. His top button is undone, his tie is askew, his hair is rumpled. Is it possible for a face to be rumpled, too? Then his is.

He looks like he's been up for three nights straight, and I'd feel terrible about that, if my brother hasn't looked like he missed a night of sleep since he was a teenager. That's just Keith, always slightly tired, slightly disheveled, and when he sees me, he sighs and leans on the doorframe, as if I'm responsible for his exhaustion. Which, to be fair, is usually accurate.

I used to envy Keith. Despite that perpetually tired look, he's obnoxiously healthy. He doesn't need to spend two hours a day in treatment for a chronic illness. He doesn't need to take pills before he eats. He didn't grow up needing to be hospitalized for infections once a year.

What I realize now is that it's not easy to be the healthy sibling of a chronically ill child. My parents were very careful to give Keith an equal share of their attention, but of course, there were the little things they didn't consider, the responsibilities they gave him from a young age.

Look out for your little sister. Make sure she's taking her enzyme pills at school. Keep her amused during her daily treatments. Entertain her when she's bedridden with an infection.

Even their will favored me. They wanted to be sure I had money for all possible care when my health failed. The bulk of their estate was to be held in trust, and whatever I don't need for my health will pass to Keith when I die.

Our father died of a stroke six years ago. Cancer claimed Mom almost exactly a year later. When the will was read, I wanted to give Keith half, no matter what our parents intended. Of course, Keith refused. So if he gives that long-suffering sigh at my doorstep, he's kinda earned the right to it.

My brother has spent his life playing a role thrust on him, however inadvertently. He learned to subsume his own needs and do what was expected. Which is why, even though I'd always suspected he was gay, he did what was expected. Found a woman he cared about, married her, and had two kids.

It was Libby who realized the truth and tugged him from the closet. That doesn't mean the breakup was easy on her. It can't be, under those circumstances. But they figured it out, and four years ago, she introduced him to Jin, a radiologist at the hospital where she's a psychologist.

Keith may not have been born onto the easiest path, but life has made up for it by giving him a loving husband, two amazing kids, and an ex-wife who still talks to him. So I won't feel too bad for the guy.

"Jin spoke to you, I presume," I say.

He sighs again.

"Oh, cut that out," I mutter. "Come in and have a beer. Or should I make it a coffee? You look like shit."

"I can always count on you to make me feel better."

"No, you can count on me to be honest. You're working too hard for corporate assholes who don't appreciate you."

"They pay me, though."

"Not enough. Coffee? Knowing you'll be leaving here and going home to work for another three hours?"

"Please and thank you."

I start the machine. I know I'm deflecting by bitching about his job. Doesn't stop me from doing it, though. Just like feeling guilty about dragging him into my madness doesn't stop me from saying, "I'm doing this last séance. I know you don't want me to, but I am."

He sighs again, and I resist the urge to whip a dish towel at his head and settle for wrapping it around my hand.

"Preparing for battle?" he says.

I look down to see that the dish towel does indeed make me look like a boxer taping up for a bout. I unwind it.

"I don't want to fight about this, Keith."

"Neither do I." He pulls out a table from the breakfast bar and sits. "Which is why I'm not going to try to talk you out of it. I'm just . . ." He rubs a hand over his mouth.

"Worried," I say.

"I don't want you to be disappointed, Nic. If I thought you could contact Anton, I'd have helped as soon as you started hiring these people."

He lowers his voice, as if we aren't alone in the condo. "I'm worried that you keep trying because of what happened the last time. You realize you girls didn't actually contact a ghost, right? Patrice just . . . She had problems, and those problems led to . . ." He trails off, unwilling to fill in the rest.

"That's not why I expect it to work," I say.

Liar.

"I don't even really know why I'm doing it."

Liar.

"It just feels like something I need to get past. I know that probably doesn't make sense."

"No, it does. Losing Anton was . . ." He sucks in a breath. "Devastating. But all that viral-story nonsense?"

"It messed me up?"

A quirked smile. "Nah, you were always messed up."

"You like sugar in your coffee, right?" I lift the bowl. "Lots and lots of sugar?"

He ignores the threat. "Yes, it messed you up. Interfered with the grieving process."

"You've been talking to Libby, haven't you?"

"The point is that I'm trying to accept that you need to do this. I trust Jin, and I trust Libby, and if they say this is the way to handle it, then maybe it is. I'm an economist. I don't know anything about how the mind works."

But you know how grieving works, Keith. You grieved for the end of your marriage to Libby, and we both grieved for our parents. We're still grieving for them, in our way. It felt as if I'd just buried my parents, and then I was burying my husband, too.

Keith continues, "Jin says he and Libby are setting this up, and Jin is going to be with you." They'd originally both wanted to be there, but Libby finally admitted that her skepticism would get in the way. "I'd like to be there, too."

"I don't think—"

"Please, Nic. I just . . . I want to watch out for you. I know Jin can do that, but he doesn't know what happened with Patrice, and I don't think you want to tell him, right?"

I tense instinctively. "No."

"I agree. So can I be there? Please?"

"All right."

FOUR

A month has passed since we agreed to do this. We found a medium with a stellar reputation. He's a parapsychologist and a university professor, a scientist who started his career as a skeptic, which is exactly what we want. Dr. Cirillo lives in Chicago, but he agreed to come for half his usual fee, in return for being able to document the event—using aliases in a purely written narrative account with no video or audio recordings.

We asked Dr. Cirillo how we could provide the ideal environment, and he said it should be a quiet spot that would invoke good memories for Anton. That made the choice a simple one.

Anton and I both grew up in Alberta, but his grandmother lived here in Ontario, where she had a huge rambling house on the shores of Lake Erie. When she died, fifteen years ago, the house was sold and turned into a bed-and-breakfast. It's now a short-term vacation rental, and we'd gone there for our first couple getaway.

That makes it the perfect place for the séance. Anton had nothing but good memories of staying there as a child, and we'd built our own good memories there with three visits over the years. I worried it'd be too late to rent, but being ahead of the beach vacation season, we were able to get it on short notice.

Next we need a participant who didn't know Anton. Dr. Cirillo says it's easy for everyone to get caught up in our memories of Anton—his voice, his image, even his scent. Having an outsider there, in addition to Dr. Cirillo himself, helps eliminate a false positive. I don't even need to look for someone. When Shania catches wind of this final séance, it's obvious that she'd love to come, so I invite her.

I'm also supposed to bring items from Anton's life, and that's easily done, too, since I haven't gotten rid of anything. Shania also suggests that I tell Dr. Cirillo I have one particular thing: Anton's ashes.

Anton wanted to be cremated. He gave no instructions for spreading his ashes anywhere. That's usually illegal, and he'd never have put that pressure on me. He expected they'd go in a memorial garden, but I want to do more.

No, that's half a lie. I'm not ready to let them go, so they're in an ornate wooden box on my dresser. I'm reluctant to ask Dr. Cirillo if I should bring them—it seems a little macabre—but I finally do, and he says yes, absolutely.

Everything is settled. There's just one problem.

Keith.

I agreed he could join us, and he's done nothing but interfere. He micromanaged, as he always does, except we aren't his office interns and he's not the expert here. Every step of the way has been a battle.

A house on the lake, Nic? Are you sure? They get a lot of windstorms this time of year, and your CF equipment needs reliable electricity.

Do you really want to take that Shania girl? Isn't she the one who found that last quack?

Are you sure you want to fly someone in from the States? There must be local experts.

You're taking Anton's ashes? Is that a good idea? What if something happens to them?

A week before we leave, Libby calls.

"I've been offered a chance to attend a conference in Vancouver next week," she says.

"That's great," I say. Then I pause. "Which means you'd need Keith to look after the kids. When he's supposed to be at the séance with me."

"Right." She clears her throat. "I don't have to go to this conference. Only I was thinking . . . maybe you'd like me to?"

Maybe I'd like an excuse to do the séance without Keith. That's what she means.

"I'd be a coward if I said yes, wouldn't I?" I say.

She's quiet for a moment. Then she says, "I really hate getting between you and Keith. I always have. He's being a pain in the ass. It's only because he loves you, but if we're trying for the perfect setup, everything just right . . ."

"Having Keith there is going to mess it up. He'll interfere, and we'll fight, and Jin will get caught in the middle, and after it's done, I'll have an excuse to say *that's* why the séance went wrong."

"I *do* have a conference invitation, and it *is* unexpected. If Keith strongly objects, we can revisit it. But I think, while he'll fret, he trusts Jin to be there for you. You just might have to tolerate daily phone check-ins."

"Okay, give him a call. If he will stay home, I'd rather he did."

Keith is staying in Toronto with his kids. He'd done exactly as Libby expected. He grumbled, but gave in on the understanding that there would be daily phone calls and, when the séance was over, he'd bring Hayden and Lucy to join Jin and me for a weekend at the lake.

While Jin had offered to drive, I feel more comfortable with my own car. Since starting on the new meds, I haven't needed to be hospitalized for an infection, or even have a nurse come to dump antibiotics through the shunt permanently embedded in my arm. I still don't like being an hour from the nearest major hospital without feeling free to hop into my car at 2 A.M. if I need to. I also have a lot of stuff to bring—my airway-clearance vest alone comes in its own carry-on-sized wheelie bag. Yep, I don't travel light. But I do travel, and that's the important thing.

Before we leave, I do my daily half hour with the vest and my forty minutes with the nebulizer. I also do my workout in the condo gym.

When people hear I have CF, they offer me car rides for short distances or help carrying bags. I appreciate that, because I know they mean well. It's true that, with my shitty lungs, exercise-induced asthma is a concern, and I'm no longer running the half-marathons of my university days. But exercise has always been an important part of my treatment. I might even be a touch neurotic about it, and knowing I won't have a gym at the beach house, I'm getting in an hour before we leave. Once there, I'll make a point to rise early for long walks.

I'm in decent shape. Weight is often a concern in CF—our difficulty absorbing nutrients and processing food can lead to us being underweight and even malnourished. Heading into my thirties, I got a lot of "Oh, you're still so slender" and "No middle-age spread for you, huh?" Again, I understand the sentiment, and I only smile and don't explain. My focus is on keeping up a healthy weight and staying as strong as I can for as long as I can.

I pick up Shania and Jin and then start the trek to Lake Erie. Toronto is on Lake Ontario. Erie is to the west, which means an hour drive along the highway and then another hour south through farm country until we reach the shore.

There are no major cities along the Canadian shore—they're all at least a thirty-minute drive north. Halfway across Lake Erie it becomes the United States, with Buffalo at one end, Detroit at the other, and Cleveland in the middle. Where we're going is across the lake from Ohio, only visible as a glow of nuclear plants at night. Okay, that's not true. Sometimes you can also see smoke from the plants during the day.

The town nearest the lake house is big enough to have a name but too small to have much else. There's a beachside stand for fries, a couple of bait shops, a pier, and a half-dozen small RV parks, just starting to fill as we've passed the Victoria Day long weekend.

Our destination is lakefront but not beachfront. Along this shore, Lake Erie is mostly cliffside viewing, and that cliff is eroding fast. When we pull onto the road leading to the house, Shania gasps.

"Look at that view," she says. "Can we get down to the water?"

"There's a path if it's still safe," I say. "We can do that later, maybe at sunset. It looks like we'll have one today, and they're stunning."

I pull into the semicircular drive in front of the two-story red-brick house.

Jin rolls down his window to gape up. "Okay, when you said 'lake house,' I expected a cottage. Do I even want to know how much this place cost to rent?"

"It was cheaper in the off-season, when Anton and I always came." I stop the car in front of the steps. "But the price isn't bad, mostly because it's five years overdue for a touch-up and ten years overdue for a renovation. In other words, expect dated furniture and a toilet you might need to flush twice."

"I don't care," Shania says. "It looks amazing."

The house is two stories of Georgian-style brickwork, a red rectangle of perfect symmetry, like the way a child would draw a house, the windows all just so. Ivy covers the entire front of it. It had been in Anton's family for generations, built at the turn of the twentieth century as a summer home for his great-great-grandfather, who'd made his fortune in textiles.

Eventide Manor—as it was once called—was designed in the pre-air-conditioning days when well-off families had a summer house. Dad would stay in the humid and sweltering city for business while Mom and the kids retired to the lake, with Dad joining them on weekends. Anton remembered his grandmother telling him stories of her parents doing that—her father staying in Toronto while her mother brought the kids to the lake house once school ended.

By the time Anton's grandmother inherited it, the family no longer had the money for a summer residence, so she'd retired here following the death of her husband. Even then, there hadn't been money to keep it up, and Anton remembered summers spent helping his father lay bricks and his mother clear the overgrown gardens.

These days, the house and gardens still have a slightly disheveled look, as if someone's really trying to keep them up, but never quite manages. If it reminds me a bit of my brother—solid, reliable, and a bit down-at-heel—maybe that's part of its charm.

The gardens are mostly stone and statuary, with some bushes and perennials in need of pruning. There's a wild look to them, one that reminds me of Victorian children's novels with overgrown English gardens. When Anton and I had been here last, it'd been too cold to sit outside for long, but I'd like to do that this time. Find a spot in this wild place and curl up with a book.

We walk in, and I toss my luggage down in the front hall.

"I'm taking the Monroe bedroom," I say. "You can't miss it."

"Let me guess," Jin says. "It's the one full of photos and busts of James Monroe, fifth president of the United States?"

I smile. "That would be interesting. It's Marilyn Monroe. Very sixties glam. The decor is from when the place was a bed-and-breakfast, with themed rooms. When Anton was little, it was the room he stayed in with his brother, so that's where we always stayed. . . ." I clear my throat. "Anyway, Dr. Cirillo said I should use that one, if it's not too hard on me."

"Speaking of Dr. Cirillo, have you heard from him?" Shania asks as she carries in her duffel.

I check my phone. "Seems he texted an hour ago. He landed in Detroit safely. It might take a while to get through the border, but he expects to be here by seven. He said he'll grab dinner on the way, so don't wait for him."

"We're getting dinner delivered, right?" Jin says. "A neighbor?"

"Yep." I run a hand through my hair, shaking it out after the drive. "Lunch and dinner will be provided by Mrs. Kilmer. She lives at the end of the road. We passed her place. She has a standing arrangement with the latest owner. Anton and I had her cook for us the last time we were here, and I was glad to hear she was still doing it."

We head back outside to grab more stuff. Besides my CF supplies, I also brought groceries, for breakfast and snacks. And cocktail hour. Dr. Cirillo asked us not to drink past dinner—so we weren't tipsy for the séances—but cocktails at five were fine.

After we take that all in, I go back out for Anton's ashes. I'd tucked the box into a nook in the trunk, so no one would pull it out accidentally. As I shut the trunk, I glance toward the house, where Jin and Shania are talking in the open doorway.

I'm not eager to brush past them with this box. It feels macabre to bring it, but it also feels . . . private.

I call that I'm going to check around back. Then I slip to the side, where a wrought-iron fence stretches along the front of the gardens. The fence is a bit of a conceit when there's nothing except that front section. Anton said it'd stretched around the gardens when he was young, but the sides had been in disrepair, and at some point the back toppled over the eroding cliff edge. One of the subsequent owners removed the sides and left the front section up, including the gate.

While the fence doesn't actually fence anything in, I still close the gate behind me. Cobblestones carve paths into the overgrown gardens, and I tread with care, those stones being uneven from frost upheaval. I soon find my footing and keep going until I reach the caution tape that's been strung along the cliff edge.

My gaze goes left, to a spot where the tape dips down. That's the path Anton showed me, and that dip in the tape suggests others have found it, pushing down the flimsy barrier to climb over.

I step up to the cliff and look out. Waves lap at the bottom. The water is calm, no whitecaps in sight.

I stand there, holding the box in both hands.

"No boats today," I murmur. "Sunny and gorgeous. It's going to be one hell of a sunset."

I lift the box, as if I'm showing Anton the view. I remember the first time I stood here with him, his arm around my waist, as we gazed out over the lake. We'd just gotten together as a couple, and I'd been so damned happy. Happy and in a bit of shock.

Anton and I attended the same high school, but only for a year before my family moved to Toronto. Then Anton came to Toronto for work, and we'd met through what I presumed was an accident, though at his death he'd confessed otherwise.

When he asked me to coffee, I expected it'd be an awkward reunion, both of us spitting out names as prompts to joint memories. Then we'd go our separate ways and vow to "keep in touch," which neither of us would until we bumped into each other again.

Except the reunion hadn't been awkward. And we *had* kept in touch.

One coffee date became two and then three and finally actual dates, which brought us to his family's old lake house, at the point in our relationship where we were both feeling like it was something.

"It was," I whisper, clutching the box. "It was a big something. I love you so damn much, Anton, and—"

A frisson tingles down my arms, almost like a shock, and I fumble the box. My heart leaps into my throat, my brain imagining the box tumbling over the cliff, me jumping after it before I realize what I've done. But I only fumble it.

I step back from the edge, holding the box in one hand as I shake the other. The memory of that electrical shock returns, and I glance down, as if half expecting to see I'd stepped on a fallen live wire.

Nothing.

I rub my arm. My brain wants to jump on that jolt as a sign that Anton is here, but that was no lover's touch. It was a shock, the unpleasantness of it lingering long after the physical sensation faded.

I lift the box. It happened while I was holding it in both hands. Did I conduct a jolt of energy? Yeah, no. My degree might be in software engineering, but I know enough about science to realize that a wooden box is not a conductor.

Whatever it was—

"Looks like a storm's coming," a voice says behind me.

I jump so fast my feet tangle. Shania lets out a squeak and lunges, as if I'm about to topple off the cliff.

Waving her off with a laugh, I gesture to the three feet between me and the edge. "Even I can't stumble that far. What's that about a storm?"

I look out, the water calm and sun-dappled, the sky bright blue and cloudless. I can't imagine anything less likely than a storm, but when she points, I notice a black cloud off to our right. It almost looks like a funnel, swirling around on itself. That makes no sense. It's a clear day—

My phone rings. I glance down and sigh.

"My brother," I say. "I've been here an entire twenty minutes and haven't called yet." I glance back at the funnel-shaped cloud. "Can you check the forecast while I answer this?"

"Sure."

We're in the house. Shania looked up the weather forecast and found no mention of a storm, much less a tornado. We must have been seeing smoke. One of the nuclear plants? We check that, but the directionality is wrong and that smoke wouldn't be black. Hopefully it's not a boat on fire. The cloud seems to be gone now, though, so I put it out of my mind and focus on settling into my room.

As I told Jin, it's the Monroe room, which is less Marilyn-specific and more sixties glam, with bright colors, curved furniture, and semi-tasteful gold leaf on the plaster ceiling.

When I step in, time ripples, and I'm with Anton again on our first visit, us approaching the bedroom door.

"And here is where Viktor and I slept when we were kids. Well, until he was sixteen and stayed back home to work for the summer, and I got the whole room to myself. Baba let us decorate it, and I'm really hoping it's changed, or I'm totally blaming the pinups on Viktor."

He throws open the door and waves me through.

I step in and sputter. "Never knew your teen crushes were quite so retro, but I'm digging it."

He walks in and his face . . .

I laugh until my sides hurt. "Childhood memories ruined again."

"It's very . . ." He looks around at the glitz. "Sparkly. And gold. Very gold. I'm guessing you'd like us to take another room?"

"Never. It's a round bed with silk sheets under a boudoir photo of Marilyn Monroe." I hop onto the bed. "You wanna play horny honeymooners?"

He grins and tosses his bag down. "Nah, I wanna play horny teen who dreamed of getting a girl in my bed here."

"Well, come on then. I'm here to make all your teenage dreams come true."

I smile and shake my head as I put down my bag. As Anton said later, there was nothing of his old room here. The furnishings are strictly thrift-shop fare, with sticking drawers, loose knobs, and water marks, but they are immaculately clean, and the bedding is brand-new.

There's an entire bookcase filled with reading material, and I glance over to see whether there's anything recent. Nope. More thrift-shop finds, with nothing published in the last twenty years. Luckily, I brought my own reading material. I set two novels on my nightstand. Then I take a third from my bag. It's a space opera with a bookmark three-quarters of the way through. The spine is bent at that same spot, from having sat open to that same page since October.

I take the novel to the right side of the bed. Anton's side. Then I remove the bookmark and lay it open, just as it had been the night he died.

Do I feel a little foolish doing that? Yes. Mostly, though, I feel relieved, as if I can sleep in here now. If it helps, then it's fine. Or so says my therapist.

The bed is circular, with white satin sheets, and I imagine pulling them back and sliding in. Just for a few minutes.

Just for a few minutes.

Which will turn into hours, lying there, paralyzed by grief, crying into the pillows.

Yep, none of that today. I pull the folded comforter tight, as if it's a shield that'll keep me out of bed until nightfall.

A knock at the door makes me jump.

"Nic?" Jin calls. "Once you're settled, it's cocktail hour."

"Be right there!" I call before fleeing the bedroom and the memories there.

FIVE

I'm in charge of tonight's drinks. Each of us has a day when we'll serve our signature cocktail. Yes, we're here for a very serious purpose, but that won't stop us from treating it like a holiday. Dr. Cirillo says that's exactly what we should do. We aren't going to spend all of our waking hours trying to contact Anton. We need to relax, and in relaxing we're making the environment welcoming and reminding the dead of the best parts of life, spending time with family and friends.

My signature cocktail is, yep, shooters. Jin and Libby can tease me about it—and Anton thought it was adorable—but drinking is as much about ritual as the actual consumption of alcohol. University is the first taste of independent life for most kids, but when you have a chronic illness, that independence can be even slower coming. There's someone watching and monitoring and fretting long after the age when other kids slip from under parental eyes.

It wasn't just my parents. It was me, too. After we left behind the trauma of my junior year, I was the perfect little CF patient. Part of it was an apology for uprooting my family and part of it was knowing that those events would make my parents even warier of letting me attend any postsecondary-education institution that couldn't be reached on the Toronto transit system. My goal was software engineering at Waterloo, which was only an hour's drive, but I really wanted to live on campus like a normal student.

Drinking age in Ontario is nineteen, and I was that weird kid who didn't actually drink until she was of age . . . which was also my first year in university. Then it was all shooters, all the time. Okay, not *all* the time. But when I went to parties, I didn't want beer or vodka or, god forbid, wine. I wanted sweet liqueurs, layered in pretty colors, knocked back fast for that delicious buzz.

So my drink for our cocktail hour is shooters. A shooter buffet, to be exact. I've brought test tubes, so we can sample without getting wasted. Because my choices are mostly liqueurs, my food offerings are also sweet—homemade caramel corn and spiced nuts.

Jin, Shania, and I enjoy our cocktail hour, chatting away as the buzz settles in. When we're finishing up, Shania walks to the fireplace and peers at the portrait overtop. It's a very old painting of a Victorian couple's wedding day.

"Relatives of Anton's?" Jin says, waving his shooter at the portrait.

I laugh. "Uh, no. Something the owners found in an estate sale, I bet."

"Is it just me," Shania says, "or does she look like she wants to escape?"

Jin shakes his head. "They *both* look like they were led to the altar by a shotgun."

"It's the time period," I say. "Smiling for portraits wasn't really a thing—"

Jin cuts me off with a jabbed finger. "None of that. We're here for a séance. Get in the spirit."

"Fine. They're clearly a miserable couple, forced to wed at gunpoint. They spent their first night together, and when he woke, she was gone."

"Never to be seen again," Shania chimes in.

"Until years later," Jin says. "When her spirit began haunting the honeymoon suite. Then, one day, while playing hide-and-seek, someone opened an old chest in the attic . . . and out fell her body, still in her wedding gown."

"Nice." Shania glances at me. "Are there any weird stories about this house? It's so old and so big that there must be some."

I munch some caramel corn. "Nope."

"No, it doesn't have any or no, you don't know any?"

"According to Anton, it doesn't have any. I'm sure some relative died here in the distant past but if so, their spirit moved on. There's never even been a hint of a ghost."

"Well, we are about to change that," Jin says. Then he makes a face. "Sorry. One too many shots. That was inconsiderate."

I lean over and lay my head on his shoulder. "It wasn't. I do hope to make contact with Anton, but a haunting is a very different thing, and this house has no history of them. Dr. Cirillo actually asked about that, and he was happy to hear there aren't any stories. We're hosting an intimate gathering, not a wild party. Our invitation is extended to a very select audience of one."

I rise from the sofa. "Okay, let's not get maudlin. I should take you two on the tour of this weird and wacky—if boringly ghost-free—estate."

"Oh!" Shania says, zipping ahead of us. "There's a locked door. I wanted to show you that."

She leads us down the hall. At the end is a door. The antique knob has been removed and replaced with a modern lock.

"So what's behind the door?" she says, waggling her brows. "Any guesses?"

"One vacuum cleaner," I say, "two mops, and three Costco megapacks—toilet paper, paper towels, and tissues."

She mock-glares at me. "You are terrible at this game, Nic."

"No, I've just rented enough places to know there's always a locked room. That's where they keep the cleaning supplies, and sometimes stuff the owner doesn't want us touching."

"Such as the bodies of the last renters," Jin says. "Stacked like cordwood."

"We'd smell them," I say.

He shakes his head. "You really *are* bad at this."

He looks up and down the hall. "I bet this place has plenty of secret rooms and passages."

"Nope," I say. "Anton poked in every nook and cranny. There's nothing."

Both turn on me with looks of clear disapproval.

"Oh!" I say. "There *is* a dumbwaiter shaft."

Jin grins. "Now we just need to wait to hear it creaking up to the top floor, as if pulled by an unseen hand."

"The actual dumbwaiter is long gone. It's just the shaft. And before you say anything, it's not big enough to fall down. Or to stuff bodies in. Again, you'd smell them. However, if you are determined to find something creepy, follow me."

They do. On the way through the living room, Shania sneaks the last shooter from the table, sliding me a grin like she's snatching something she shouldn't.

I smile at her and take another handful of caramel corn for myself. Then we continue to the sitting room, which is not where we'd actually been sitting, and they are about to see why.

"Damn . . ." Jin says.

"Is this . . . a joke?" Shania says as she steps into the tiny room. "Ironic creepy decorating?"

"I'd like to think so, but I suspect not."

The room is barely ten feet by ten feet, with no windows, which makes it a terrible sitting room. I can only guess that whoever designated it as such thought the small size and claustrophobic feel made it cozy. Anton said that when he was young, this was his grandfather's den—a place where he could retire with his newspaper or book when the house full of grandkids got a little too rowdy.

Back then, the room held only a sofa, which would have made it nicely spacious. Now it's crammed full with a couch, a love seat, and two recliners. If you used it as a sitting room, you'd be *sitting* on top of everyone else. But the truly creepy part is the dolls.

The room is ringed with bookcases and every shelf holds a motley collection of books plus three or four antique porcelain dolls, all attired in colorful starched dresses, all scrubbed and clean, all retouched and repainted. And all staring at us with vacant eyes.

"I don't get it," Shania says, staying in the doorway as Jin and I walk in. "How does anyone *not* find porcelain dolls creepy? I can see getting some in an ironic way, where you're being creepy on purpose. But who looks at this room and thinks it'd be a great place to curl up with a book?"

"Under the watchful eyes of the damned," Jin says.

"This is actually an improvement over the dolls' last residence," I say. "Before Anton and I rented this place, we read the reviews. Apparently, when it opened as a bed-and-breakfast, the smallest bedroom was called the Doll Room, and these were displayed in there."

"Where people slept?" Shania says. "Probably children?"

"Yep. The dolls were quickly moved down here and that became the Disney-themed room. Whenever we stayed here . . ."

I trail off because I find myself smiling. I'm thinking back to when Anton and I stayed here, and when I smile, it feels like laughing at his funeral. I struggle with that. I know I *should* smile at memories of our life together. Being able to smile at them is part of the process. But when I do, I feel as if I'm moving too fast. I might not be an old-time widow, draped in a black dress and jet jewelry, but internally, I feel as if I should be in continual mourning, and when I'm not, I'm stricken with guilt.

I smack that guilt away. This is a good memory, and I'm sharing it.

I walk farther into the tiny room. "Whenever Anton and I stayed here, he kept moving the damn dolls."

"Freaking you out?" Shania says. "If I woke to find one of those things on my bedside table, I'd grab the keys and run. Let him find his own way home."

"Nothing like that," I say. "Just moving them around. I'd flop down on the sofa in the living room, and ten minutes later, I'd notice a doll on the shelf. Or on top of the fridge."

I walk to one, with a gingham dress and bonnet, red braids, and painted eyes with a little too much white around the iris, giving her a demented stare. "This was our favorite. We named her Laura. Pioneer zombie girl. We were thinking of finding one for Lucy, to add to her collection of American Girl dolls."

"Lucy's outgrown her doll stage," Jin says. "She's moved into the preteen phase where she'd actually love that creepy thing." Jin looks at Laura and shudders.

We continue our exploration of the house. I show them the dumb-waiter shaft. I'm honestly surprised the owners haven't sealed it up. I guess it's safe enough, and it's something people find cool.

As I poke my head into the shaft, I remember a story Anton told, about his brother scaring the shit out of him as a kid, insisting that you could hear the dumbwaiter at night. I'm about to withdraw and tell the others when a sound stops me. A low moan from below.

I back out fast. "Did you—?"

"Another locked door," Jin says, his voice distant.

I turn to see him over at the basement door with Shania. I glance back at the dumbwaiter. What was the story Anton told me? That his brother claimed to hear the dumbwaiter moving? No, that's what Jin had just joked about. Viktor scared Anton . . . by making noises from below.

I shake my head. Apparently, I might be good at ruining Jin and Shania's haunted-house fun, but it seems my imagination is having a little of that with me.

Jin jiggles the door handle as I walk over. "Now don't tell me the entire basement is filled with mops and tissue boxes, Nic."

I frown and walk back to it. I try the knob myself, but it's clearly locked and there's a keyhole in that knob.

"That's where the washer and dryer were," I say. "Anton and I stuck our heads down there, but since we only stayed for weekends, we didn't need to wash clothing."

"So they blocked access to the washer and dryer?" Jin says. "That's not suspicious at all."

"They put compact stackables in the bathroom right there." I point.

"Because they needed to block off the basement to hide the bodies."

"There are definitely bodies down there," Shania says. "And secret tunnels."

I shake my head. "It was your typical damp old basement, with framed-up walls and a concrete floor. I'm not surprised they've blocked it off."

Jin looks at Shania. "She really is bad at this."

"The worst," Shania says.

"Fine," I say. "The basement isn't very creepy, but that's just the part we saw. When we went exploring, Anton wanted to show me the furnace, if it was still there—it was a monster of a thing. But the door was locked. Two doors, in fact. Both locked."

Shania is about to comment when a floorboard creaks, and she goes still. "Did you hear that?"

"Sounds like someone on the front porch," I say. Then I lift fingers and count down. "Three . . . two . . ."

The doorbell dings. They both sigh as I head to answer it.

Dinner has arrived, along with our cook. Mrs. Kilmer is the type of woman I always feel a little sorry for, and then chastise myself for jumping to conclusions based on appearances. She's slight and faintly stooped, despite being only a decade older than me. Her face already shows stress lines around her mouth and worry lines on her forehead, and there's a hesitancy about her, as if she always expects she's doing something wrong and is ready to apologize for it.

"Mrs. Kilmer," I say, smiling. "It's good to see you again." Before

I can put her on the spot, I say, "I was here last year, and I was hoping you'd still be cooking for the house."

I don't say "my husband and I" were here. That's another thing I feel guilty for, as if I've already excised him from my life. But I know that if I say my husband and I stayed here, she might presume he's with me, and I'll need to explain, and she'll feel bad for mentioning it. . . .

Yep, best to just stick with the singular. *I was here.*

Mrs. Kilmer does the customary "Oh, yes, of course I remember you," which probably means she doesn't, and that's for the best.

"Would you like me to put this inside?" she says, indicating the rolling cooler she's brought. "It's today's dinner and tomorrow's lunch, along with some fresh muffins for breakfast."

"Thank you, and I know this is going to sound incredibly rude, but I'll need to empty that inside and give it back. This week . . . Well, it's not actually a vacation, unfortunately." I lean against the doorjamb. "I'm here with some other scientists, working, and the person in charge has asked that no one else come into the house."

That *does* sound rude, and also weird. But I can't exactly say that we're doing a séance and the medium has insisted the house be kept clear of "other auras."

Technically, it's not a lie either. Dr. Cirillo is a scientist conducting an experiment. I'm an engineer, Shania is a nurse, and Jin is a radiologist, so we all work in STEM fields, right?

"Oh, isn't that interesting," she says, without any hint that she's insulted. "Certainly. I understand."

She rolls the cooler to me. I take it inside, unload it as fast as I can, and bring it back out, where she gives me instructions for cooking the meals. I thank her, and she trundles off down the lane, pulling the empty cooler behind her.

We're enjoying lemon-meringue pie and coffee on the back porch when a voice says, "Hello?"

A man's head pops past the corner of the deck, and I scramble up, wiping my mouth with my napkin.

"Hello," I say.

The man is in his early forties, with graying dark hair and a close-trimmed beard. His bright blue eyes crease in a smile. He's dressed in a golf shirt and chinos, with a jacket over his arm, sunglasses on his head, looking like . . .

Looking like a guy on vacation.

Shit. I've heard of this happening, where you rent a place and it turns out to be double-booked.

"Ms. Laughton?" he says as I hurry over.

I slow. "Yes?"

He extends a hand. "Davos Cirillo."

"Dr. Cirillo," I say, shaking his hand.

I'd been so engrossed in the conversation that I'd forgotten we were expecting him after dinner. I also should have looked up a photo of the guy. Stereotypes again. I'm accustomed to mediums like Leilani, with her jangling bracelets and flowing dresses. This guy looks like a doctor or lawyer or . . . college professor? Yep, because that's what he is.

"Glad you could make it, Dr. Cirillo," Jin says as he comes forward.

"Davos, please."

Jin smiles. "I'm Jin, Nic's brother-in-law. And this is Shania, our 'outsider' for the week."

"Thanks," Shania says.

"Hey, that's your role, right? The designated outsider." Jin grins at her and then turns to Cirillo. "Come join us. We're having pie and waiting for the sunset."

SIX

We sit on the porch with the propane heater taking the chill off as the sun sets, and it is a spectacular sight, pastel blues and pinks darkening as the sun disappears into the lake.

We ask Dr. Cirillo about his work. That seems a safe topic. It's a bit of an odd situation, with him spending three days in a house with strangers. It's supposed to give him time to settle and get to know us, rather than ushering us into a room for an hour-long séance. It does mean, though, that he's here as a professional, and we can't treat him like a fellow houseguest. I don't want to ask anything personal, so we stick to work questions.

His actual degree is in psychology. As a discipline, parapsychology is considered fringe science, even junk science. One professor at his college had specialized in an offshoot of parapsychology called anomalistic psychology. It wasn't what Cirillo imagined studying, but he found himself intrigued.

Anomalistic psychology examines common paranormal experiences and attempts to explain them. I know a bit about it from my spiritualist research, as I girded myself against the predators. As a scientist, I found the explanations fascinating. Like the one that explains the common phenomenon of seeing a dead loved one at your bed-side, watching over you. I remember a friend telling me she'd seen her dead grandmother and I will fully admit that, at thirteen, I was a little bit horrified by the thought of my grandmother in my bedroom at night, catching me doing . . . whatever I was doing while awake in bed at thirteen.

Seeing a dead loved one in your room might be the most common ghostly experience. The scientific explanation is that when we're falling asleep, we sometimes drift into a hypnagogic state, where we're still transitioning to sleep and think we're awake. In that state, we dream of seeing a loved one and mistakenly believe we're awake.

I remember one time when Anton was away at a conference. Shortly after I went to bed I swore I heard him come home early—open the door, take off his shoes, walk into the kitchen. I'd gone to sneak up and surprise him and found myself alone in the condo. I texted and discovered he was still in Montreal. He'd wanted me to call the police, certain we had an intruder. But the door was locked and the alarm on. I understand now that I'd had a hypnagogic hallucination.

That's the sort of thing Dr. Cirillo studied under his advisor. Scientific debunking, though he winces at the term when Jin says it. Debunking suggests you're on a mission to prove people wrong. What Dr. Cirillo's advisor did was accept people's experiences and look for the explanation beyond the paranormal.

Many supernatural experiences *do* have a natural explanation. But our brains are wired for story, and we try to create it where none exists. Our sports team won twice while we were wearing our blue shirt and lost when we wore our green one? The blue shirt is lucky. We notice an ad for a vacation to Cuba, and suddenly we're seeing ads for Cuba everywhere? It must be a sign. We hear voices in our empty condo? It's ghosts, not real conversation conducted through the vents. Creaking boards upstairs? Ghosts, not the plumbing system. We want to believe that luck exists, that signs exist, that ghosts exist, and so we find proof.

Dr. Cirillo had been happily pursuing his doctorate, investigating paranormal phenomena and leaping on scientific explanations like a detective solving crimes. At first, they all did have explanations. Then came a few where the explanation felt like jamming an octagonal peg into a round hole. It almost fit . . . but not quite. That didn't bother him much. Science doesn't always perfectly explain everything.

"Then, I had an experience myself," he says. "One that I couldn't explain away."

"Story time?" Jin says.

"If you want it."

"We absolutely want it," Shania says.

Jin's gaze shoots to me, suddenly cautious. "If it's okay with Nic."

"Fine with me. I like ghost stories." I flash a smile that sells the lie and turn to Dr. Cirillo. "Please continue."

Dr. Cirillo settles deeper into his wicker chair. "I was investigating a haunting at a recently purchased home. The new owners claimed to hear crying and the sound of someone pacing in the attic. They discovered that the former owner had ended his life, quite violently, in that attic."

"They discovered that *after* hearing noises?" Jin asks.

"That was the question. They said they definitely heard the sounds first, but I went into it knowing that might not be true. It would be understandable to learn about a violent death and then imagine sounds from that part of the house. Also, it was a very old house, with all the attendant creaks and odd noises. On the first night, I heard nothing. The second night, the whispers and crying came. On the third, the pacing started. That's when I went into full detective mode. These clearly weren't the creaks of an old house. Therefore someone was faking a haunting."

He takes a pause to sip his tea, and I have to give him credit for knowing how to play his audience.

"I tried everything to catch someone in the attic," he says. "I set up video. I checked for alternate entrances. I positioned myself right below the hatch. Still the noises continued. When I cleaned up the recording, I clearly heard a woman's voice pleading to be let out. Promising she wouldn't tell."

Shania rubs her arms and shifts in her seat. Even I feel hairs prickling.

Cirillo's gaze goes to Shania. "I could stop there."

She twists a smile. "Then I'd only imagine the worst. Go on."

"Well, I don't have a definitive answer for what I experienced, only a theory. It turned out that the man who'd ended his life had a niece who disappeared a few years earlier. The story went that he was supposed to pick her up at college and drive her home for the summer break. Only he was late to the meetup spot, and she was already gone. The police suspected she'd accepted a ride with someone else when her uncle was late. The family believed the uncle blamed himself for it, and that's why he ended his life. But . . . given what I heard in that house, I see another explanation."

"He did pick her up," Shania whispers. "And locked her in the attic. After she died, he kept hearing her there. So he went into the attic and . . ." She shudders.

"I believe so," Cirillo says. "That experience obviously unsettled me. Not only was it disturbing, but I had no rational, non-paranormal explanation for what I experienced. I told my advisor I needed a break. I thought I was getting too deep into the work. He argued that to properly investigate these phenomena, we had to accept the possibility that there *could* be something out there. That shook me. I thought I knew what I was doing, and then I didn't. But I went back to it. Nineteen times out of twenty, I found an explanation. But every now and then . . ."

"You found one that couldn't be explained away," Shania says.

"Yes. I finished my doctorate and decided to stay in the field. Over time, those exceptions to the rule increasingly seized my attention, and my studies evolved to where they are today. I still investigate phenomena with an eye toward scientific explanations, but I also actively try to communicate with the dead, because I believe, sometimes, they are there and want to communicate, as that poor girl in the attic did."

"So you're not a medium?" Shania says. "I mean, in the sense of having the Sight or being attuned to the other world."

"I don't believe in the Sight, as they call it, nor in the idea of some people being naturally attuned to the spirit world. I *am* more attuned, but purely through practice. And still, as I explained to Ms. Laughton, ninety-five percent of the time, I find nothing."

"Nicola, please," I say. "Or just Nic. Your research is the reason we chose you. I don't want guaranteed contact, because I know that's bullshit, pardon my language."

His eyes warm with a smile. "No need to pardon any language. I'm a professor, not a priest. What I believe is that some spirits are right on the other side, waiting to communicate. Most of them, though, are not. They've crossed over."

"And Anton might have stayed," Shania says, "because of what he said before he died."

Dr. Cirillo answers carefully, "It's possible, but more than that, I think Ms.—Nicola is in a particular situation where what I offer might be what she needs. Not necessarily contact, but answers, even if that answer is that I don't sense him."

I nod. "I won't lie and pretend I don't care whether I make contact or not. Of course I want to know he's somewhere and he's okay. But mostly, I just . . ." My hands find each other, clutched on my lap even as I try to relax. "Mostly, I want to be done with this. I tell myself that the person who claimed to see Anton's ghost just wanted attention. But I feel as if . . . as if Anton disappeared and someone said they saw him, and I ignored it."

"A missed opportunity," Dr. Cirillo says.

"More than that."

Jin looks over at me. "Like he's trying to call, and you aren't picking up the phone. One of those nightmares, where you can't answer it."

My eyes fill. "Exactly. As if he's trying to get in touch, and I'm not answering the phone. As if he's right there, waving his arms, and I'm ignoring him. As if . . . I've moved on."

Jin reaches out to squeeze my hand.

I squeeze my eyes shut against welling tears. "I'm going to do this now and then. I know it's been eight months but . . . I'm not getting past it."

"Your husband died," Jin says softly. "No one expects you to get past it."

"No one expects anything of you this week, Nicola," Dr. Cirillo says.

But *I* do. I don't expect to get over Anton. That's never going to happen. But I expect to be able to put on a good face in public and save my tears for private. Months of therapy, group and individual, and I've barely progressed beyond where I was at his funeral.

No, my therapist would say that isn't true. At his funeral, I didn't cry. I know people judged me for that, but those who knew me— Keith, Libby, Jin, and others—realized the truth of my stony silence. I was locked behind that facade, screaming at the top of my lungs that this was all wrong, that Anton wasn't gone, that someone had made a terrible mistake.

Reaching the point of being able to cry was an improvement, even if it meant nights of sobbing so bad that I'd rented a house for a week because my neighbors complained about the noise.

I *am* making progress. It's just not where I personally want to be. I want to keep my grief as private as I'd kept my love.

Everyone knew I loved Anton. They just didn't know how much. I want the same for my grief. They can know I'm still hurting . . . just not how much.

I take a deep breath. "Okay, so let's talk about tonight. You said you'd explain the process when you got here."

That sounds accusatory, as if I've been waiting and he's failed to deliver.

I rub my mouth. "That came out wrong. I'm just . . . not good with spontaneity. I like plans, and if I can't be the one making them, I'm eager to know them."

"Eager." That's a good word, a positive word. Much better than admitting I've been anxious, not knowing what's coming.

I grew up planning my days around my CF. It wasn't intrusive; it just required planning so it didn't *feel* intrusive. My insistence on scheduling worked well for day-to-day life. It worked less well when an infection exploded my schedule.

And it really, really did not work well when the universe stole my husband in the blink of an eye, ripping up my entire future, incinerating all our plans.

I realize Dr. Cirillo is talking, and I don't know how long he has been while my thoughts swept me away.

"—making a place for Anton," he says. "That's our focus tonight. We will make no attempt to actually contact him."

"We're rolling out the welcome mat," Jin says.

Dr. Cirillo smiles. "Yes. Think of the séance tomorrow as the arrival of a guest. Tonight, we're preparing. We want him to feel welcome here, comfortable here."

"If I were expecting a guest," I say, "I'd get out the good towels and change the sheets on the spare bed. I'm guessing this is different."

"Not entirely. If you were expecting a guest, is there anything else you'd do?"

I consider the question. We didn't have a lot of guests at the condo—while we did have two bedrooms, the second was an office with a pullout bed. We'd had the kids—Hayden and Lucy—over about a dozen times, though.

"Clear my schedule," I say. "Figure out a meal plan. Buy foods they like. Decide what we're going to do while they're here."

"Good. It's something like that, then. We clear our mental schedule to fully focus on the séance. We spend some time getting comfortable ourselves. We set out food and drink that Anton would associate with a party. And we relax, as much as possible. Maybe it's better to think of it less as entertaining a guest and more as inviting Anton to join the gathering."

"Nothing tonight then?" Jin says. "No ritual or whatever?"

"I do a small welcoming ceremony. It's a little woo-woo, but it sets the tone. We can have that whenever you're ready."

Shania and Jin both look at me.

I rise. "Let's do it."

Dr. Cirillo had asked whether there was a place in this house Anton liked best, especially one from our visits here together. My first thought had been "the bedroom." We had just gotten together, after all. But the honest truth is that his favorite spot—and mine—hadn't been in the house at all. It was the cliffside.

Anton had even carried out chairs from the deck for us, which was an absolute violation of the rental agreement. We'd sat there, bundled up, watching the lake and feeling as if we were at the edge of the world. Some postapocalyptic drama where the last two people on earth dragged chairs to the edge of a cliff and enjoyed the view in the silence of a dying world.

Holding Cirillo's welcome ritual outside is not an option. So we move to Anton's next-favorite spot—the breakfast nook that overlooks the rear garden.

We keep the door into the rest of the house open. I even light a fire in the living room. It's cool enough for that, and it's one of my favorite memories of this place, with its three fireplaces.

While we have the living room fire going nearby, we also open the breakfast-nook windows. Anton always loved throwing them open to hear the sounds of his childhood here—the lapping of waves, the cry of cliff swallows, the chirps of tree frogs. That's one reason we'd planned to move into the countryside. Get our fill of the city and then escape to a place where we could have the windows open and drink in the smells and sounds.

I'd wanted that, too. It'd been part of my "someday" list for as long as I can remember. Live in the heart of the city until I was sick of it and then move into the country. When I reunited with Anton, I hadn't even completed the first part of that plan.

I tend to postpone things I want, as if I haven't earned them yet. I must endure life in the suburbs to save money for living in the city. I can't take vacation time until I've banked enough time for a big trip. I must get through the chocolates I don't care for before I indulge in the ones I like.

Anton taught me to eat my favorite chocolates first . . . and discard the ones I didn't want. He converted my "someday" list to an actual plan. He didn't remind me that I was unlikely to live past forty-five, but that's the truth, and I didn't want to be housebound, waiting for a lung transplant that might never come, thinking of all the things I'd wanted to do.

There's a reason why I didn't buy a downtown condo even when I could afford it. Fiscal responsibility. I don't know how long I can work, and so I must be prepared for that eventuality, along with in-creased health expenses. While my parents left me money for that, guilt made me lock it all up, in hopes the lion's share will pass to Keith.

Anton didn't advocate for spending my inheritance. Yes, when the new medication made a huge difference—and wasn't completely covered by my plan—Anton and Keith convinced me to dip into that money, but otherwise, Anton respected my decision. He brought his own "professional with zero dependents" earnings to our marriage, though, and he showed me the joy of splurging. The trick is to keep them as splurges. Fly business class on every trip and it soon becomes just part of travel.

Anton pulled that "someday" list out of my brain and handed it to the part of me that loves to plan. We came up with a list of things we'd do in the next five years, and if I was still healthy—the medication gave me honest hope of that—then we'd make another five-year list.

Only we never got through the first one. Now, between my savings and his savings and his life insurance, I have enough money to do everything we planned twice over . . . and none of it matters if he's not here to do it with me.

And there I go again, getting sidetracked by grief and anger and a discomfiting amount of self-pity, all triggered by opening the damn windows and hearing the chirps of tiny frogs.

We're in the nook, sitting around the table with cups of chamomile tea, because that's what Anton liked when he was here. It was a ritual that pulled in memories of his childhood visits, when he'd get to stay up until his grandmother served tea and shortbread fingers. He'd curl up with his very adult treats and listen to the very adult conversation and feel very adult.

I brought the tea and the shortbread, and we enjoy them ourselves. Drinking and eating. Inviting him to join us. Invoking fond memories.

And then I have to do the hard part. I have to do more than invoke memories. I have to share them. As if this were an evening with friends, telling stories.

Dr. Cirillo is explaining when my attention drifts to the window. I'm sitting right beside it, the chill of the night air making me consider going for a sweater. It's dark out, and I can't see the lake. The cliff seems to drop away to nothing. The edge of the world.

I'm still staring out when I pick up something and tilt my head, frowning.

"Nicola?" Dr. Cirillo says.

"Sorry. I just . . . Do you guys hear that?"

Shania perks up. "Anton?"

"No, it's a buzzing." I lower my head to the opening, ear almost against the screen. "I hear a buzzing."

"All I can hear are the damn tree frogs," Jin says.

"There's that, but there's also a buzzing."

The others listen, only to shake their heads.

"Nic has great hearing," Jin says. "Keith always says never talk about her when she's in the house or she'll hear." He grins. "Not that we ever talk about you."

I roll my eyes. Then I shake off the odd noise. "I'm supposed to share a memory, right?"

"Tell me about the first time you met Anton," Dr. Cirillo says.

I smile. "He filled out the contact form on my website, if you count that as 'meeting.'"

"Before that, though. You knew him in school, right?"

Shania looks over, frowning, and I realize she doesn't know about that. It was a small part of our story.

No, that's a lie. It was an important part of our story, one that I wanted to gloss over because of what it dragged behind it.

I look at Shania. "We went to high school together. Briefly—less than a year before my family moved east. And I didn't really know him. He was just a guy in a few of my classes."

"But he noticed you," Jin says, his brown eyes dancing. "Don't leave out that part."

I try not to wince. I'd have preferred that my final conversation with Anton stayed private, but that's not what happens when your husband dies at the side of a busy highway, with people all around, at least one of whom stood close enough to report every word to the point where I wonder whether they'd recorded it. If so, I guess I should just be glad they didn't post the video of my husband's death. Or I'll tell myself they didn't, which will keep me from searching, in case it's hidden in some dark corner of the Web.

I mask my wince by pulling a face, as if I'm just embarrassed to be talking about this. Although, now that I think of it, the fact that Shania didn't know Anton and I were classmates means she never went looking through those online stories, and I'm grateful for that.

I explain Anton's "secret" for Dr. Cirillo and Shania.

"Oh, that's so sweet," Shania says. "He had a crush on you."

I try not to make another face. "I don't think it was like that. He just meant that he noticed me, and then he sought me out after seeing that article. Which is still very sweet."

"But you never noticed him?" Shania says, her voice rising with hope. She wants this to be a romantic story, two teens with secret crushes who reunited twenty years later.

I answer carefully, because it's not that kind of story, but to say I never noticed Anton is a lie. I just . . . didn't notice him in a good way.

While Anton himself had seemed decent, his two friends were assholes, which had made me wonder whether he was secretly one himself. And if he wasn't, what the hell was he doing with those losers? The answer was simple. They were popular, and he'd been flattered by their attention.

Anton was easygoing, with his own gentle form of popularity. Even teachers liked him, which bought his friends a certain degree of immunity.

"I noticed him," I say. "He was cute and popular and . . ." I shrug. "I was the new girl. We'd been living in a small city. When the local CF clinic closed, my parents moved us to Edmonton. Anton and I didn't travel in the same circles." *Understatement of the year.* "So we didn't have much to do with one another."

That isn't strictly a lie. Anton and I only had brief exchanges. But our groups had interacted, in the way popular asshole guys sometimes interact with geeky awkward girls. Which is to say that the interaction was not, by any means, a positive one. That wasn't Anton's fault, though. Both he and I were on the periphery of our groups and the drama between them.

"Would you rather tell me about when you first reunited?" Dr. Cirillo asks.

I shake my head. "No, let's do the first time I noticed him. If he's someplace he can hear me . . ." My throat constricts. "I didn't get a chance to tell him at the end, to reciprocate. I'll do that now."

I take a deep breath. "Okay then. First time I noticed Anton. I was sixteen. Grade eleven. My parents had hoped to stay in our small city until I finished high school, but the CF clinic closing plus Dad getting a job offer in Edmonton meant we moved the summer before I entered grade eleven. . . ."

I close my eyes and let my mind slide back to high school. It starts tapping around at first, feeling its way, touching things that set me flinching before I redirect.

Back. Go back.

Back to the beginning.

SEVEN

An empty classroom. The smell of whiteboard marker. I've lost one of my earrings. I have a habit of twisting them when I'm focusing, as if they're radio dials to tune my brain. The most likely place for me to lose one is here, in math class, which I left about ten minutes ago.

I walk in, and there's a boy at the whiteboard, staring at an equation. He has an eraser brush in one hand and a marker in the other, and he's too lost in concentration to notice me enter.

I know him. That is, I know him as the guy to beat in my AP math class. Not that I'd personally try to beat him. I might be in advanced math, but I'll never be competition for . . .

What's his name?

Andrew? Alan?

He's an inch or two taller than me, meaning slightly below average for a guy. Lean bordering on skinny. Tan skin. Dark hair that curls over his ears and the back of his neck. His nose is the most prominent thing about him, and it reminds me of a phrase I've seen in books. A Roman nose. I never understood what that meant, but seeing him in profile, I get it—his nose looks like it belongs on a Roman statue.

He's cute, which is why I may have been going out of my way to not notice him. A cute guy who's also a STEM nerd? That should be my catnip, but instead it makes me want to ignore him. Otherwise I might find him attractive and start staring at him and trying to talk to him and— Yep, best to just keep it like this, where I'm not even sure of his name.

I slip in as quietly as I can. I was sitting in the second row, at the back, making it easy to slide past his notice. He's too engrossed in his work to look up anyway.

What's he doing?

Don't look. Don't try to figure it out. Maybe he's having trouble with that equation and came back to work on it.

There's my earring. Under the desk. I crouch to pick it up—

"Hey."

I jump, like I've been caught stealing.

"Janica, right?" he says.

When I nod, he grins like he guessed the right answer on a pop quiz.

"Anton," he says.

"I lost my earring," I say. "Found it."

Yep, I was smooth at sixteen. So smooth.

"Good," he says.

I glance at the board. Then I see what he's done, and before I can help myself, I say, "You came back to correct the equation?"

His cheeks flush. "Nah. I just thought there was another way of doing it, so I came back to try." He makes a face. "Weird, right?"

I shrug. "I don't think so, but I spend hours fussing with computer programs to see if I can do it in fewer lines of code."

He grins, and maybe I should say my heart gives a little flutter, but it doesn't. It's my stomach that reacts, twisting in a sudden need to flee. He's too smart, too cute, too tempting, and nothing good would come of that.

"That's right," he says. "Computers are your thing. My parents sent me to coding camp when I was a kid, hoping I'd find a science that pays a little better than . . ." He motions to the board with a smile. "But I couldn't wrap my brain around it."

I could say something to keep the conversation going. Mention that math can make you money—my older brother is at university, applying his own math skills to finance and economics. But I just want to get out of there before this turns into an actual conversation and I start to think he's interested in what I'm saying, and then I realize he's just being nice or, worse, setting me up for mockery. I know who he hangs around with.

"I should go," I say. "My friends are in the caf. Lunch."

Yes, because clearly, if they are in the cafeteria during lunch break, I need to clarify why they're there. So smooth.

I mumble something and flee.

What would have happened if I stayed? Knowing what I know now—that Anton was making conversation, that he wasn't an asshole, that he'd noticed me.

What if I stayed, Anton?

If I'd stayed, would we have had twenty-two years together instead of three?

No, because what happened six months later would have ended it. I'd have been gone, my family whisking me to Toronto under a new name.

Any relationship Anton and I developed back then wouldn't have survived what happened that spring. The séance. The aftermath. The trial.

Blood splashed through a forest clearing. The only sound the chirping of tree frogs.

"Janica."

I jump out of my seat. I've been telling the story to Dr. Cirillo and the others, speaking on autopilot as I relive those memories. Now that name yanks me back, and it's not the soft whisper I'd imagined at the séance with Leilani. It's harsh, spat with a sneer.

"Nic?" Jin reaches to lay his hand on mine.

I blink hard and look around. Clearly no one here said my old name . . . or heard it.

Because it never happened. I imagined it because I'd been thinking of that old life, when I bore that name.

"Did something happen?" Dr. Cirillo asks.

I shake my head. "I was just . . . just thinking of how things might have been different if I'd stayed and talked to Anton. But we were sixteen, and my family moved again that spring—Dad got a job transfer to Toronto." *Because he requested it.* "So maybe, if anything happened then, Anton wouldn't have sought me out later. We'd have already had our shot."

"He sounded sweet," Shania says wistfully. "A cute, sweet math geek." She sighs. "I need to find one of those."

I smile at her. I could say something. Like that, if she wants to find someone, she needs to get out and look. Shania is a nurse who also works part-time as a personal support worker to pay off her student debt. That doesn't leave much time for socializing, and her sister's death seems to have made an already introverted young woman fold deeper into herself.

Shania may have found me through our grief therapy, but it's become more than that. Friendship? Not in the traditional sense. I acutely feel our thirteen-year age difference.

Am I filling her big-sister void? Maybe, a little.

Am I okay with that?

I . . . I'm not sure. I'm fond of Shania, and she certainly isn't thrusting me into that role. I balk at the idea because I have too much going on in my life to be anyone's big sister. I'm very, very busy. With work and grieving, and more grieving.

It's not that I don't have time to be a big sister. It's that I don't have the bandwidth. And maybe I should find it, but I'm afraid of seeing Shania as a project to distract me from my grief.

I'm drifting again. I gather my thoughts like an armful of clothing

I keep dropping, forever losing a sock or shirt on my way from the laundry.

"Anton was sweet," I say. "I wish I'd kept talking to him, but if we could only have had a few months together, then I'm glad I waited. What we had later . . ." My throat tightens and my eyes tear up.

God how I love you, Anton.

"Shh, Nic," a voice whispers. "It's okay."

I stiffen. The words come from a distance, as if from deep in the house, so soft that my ears wouldn't have picked them up if I weren't already halfway zoned out, lost in memories of Anton.

I glance over my shoulder, toward the door. The voice came from over there.

"Nicola?" Dr. Cirillo says.

I want to shake it off, but I keep staring over my shoulder. That snapped "Janica" was easy to dismiss. It hadn't even sounded like anyone. But this had been Anton's voice. Undeniably Anton's voice.

I pull myself back. "I'm sorry. I thought I heard something."

"Anton?" Dr. Cirillo says gently.

"I'm hearing what I want to hear, and if no one else does, then it's just me."

"What did you—?"

"I was imagining it," I cut in, a little too sharply. "That happens sometimes at séances. It's just wishful thinking."

Dr. Cirillo meets my gaze. "You're engaging in what I call blocking behavior. You're worried about seeming foolish, right? Being the grieving widow who leaps on any curtain flutter as a sign that her husband is in the room."

My face heats. That's exactly what I'm afraid of. At séances, people expect the grieving widow to be desperate—hell, it's what the charlatans count on.

Dr. Cirillo continues, "If you—or anyone else—experiences something, I want you to share it, please, without qualifications or apologies. We accept that there will be misreadings, so to speak. Now, did the voice sound like Anton?"

I nod.

"Could you tell what it seemed to say?"

My throat closes, but I force the words out. "He said it's okay. Which is trivial, but also what I'm hoping for and—" I take a deep breath. "That's qualifying, isn't it?"

He smiles. "It'll take time to get used to this degree of openness, particularly after you've been taken advantage of so many times."

"But Nic's really good at seeing through the scams," Shania says, and then shoots me an apologetic look. "I don't mean to cut in, but you spot the snake oil before I do."

"And Nicola recognizes that if she hears Anton, it could be wishful thinking," Dr. Cirillo says. "With all those caveats in place, would you like to return to the welcoming? Or investigate the voice?"

"Return to the welcoming, please," I say.

"All right. Jin? You knew Anton, didn't you?"

Jin nods. "He got together with Nic not long after Libby introduced me to Keith. We joked that we joined the family together."

"Would you feel comfortable sharing a memory?"

"Sure. First time we met?"

"Please, if that works."

Jin gets comfortable in his chair. "It was the first time I met Nic, too. I knew about her. Actually, I knew about her before I knew about Keith. Libby would talk about going out with Nic, and I thought it was really cool that she'd stayed friends with her former sister-in-law. Then when I started dating Keith, he'd also talked about Nic. So I felt like I knew her already. Anton was just some guy she was seeing that both Libby and Keith really liked."

Jin takes off his sweater and hangs it on the back of his chair. "So, that sets the stage. I'm going to dinner with my new boyfriend and his sister and her relatively new boyfriend. Last thing I want to be is late, right? So of course I was late. Got held up at work, and I'd texted Keith, but he hadn't answered. I thought I'd pissed him off. Turned out he just didn't see the text."

Jin slants a look my way. "Typical, right?"

"It is," I say.

"Anyway, I'm freaked out, and I get to the restaurant, back into a spot, throw open my door . . . and smack into the door of a guy climbing out of his car. My fault—his door was already open. Now there's a nice crease in the door of his little Beemer, and I look like the pickup-driving asshole who throws open his door without looking. I apologize, say I'm late to meet my partner's sister, can we exchange info and I'll cover the damage. I'm babbling, flustered and very aware I'm getting later by the second. Then he says 'Oh, you must be Jin. I'm Anton. Nic's boyfriend.' Great. First time meeting Keith's sister, and I make a bad impression on her boyfriend—a *literal* impression in his car door. But he just laughs about us both being late and in such a hurry that our doors collided, and what's the chance, right? Starts joking that we should make it a bigger story like someone sideswiped him on the highway and—" He stops short. "Shit. I'm sorry."

"Go on," I say with a reassuring smile. "I knew about the doors, but I'd like to hear the whole story."

I'd like to hear it because it's an angle Anton would never have given, where he's the decent guy who tried to make a stranger feel better about an accident. It's not that Anton didn't want to be seen as a decent guy. Just that he'd never have taken credit. To him, it would sound like boasting.

I prompt, "Anton joked about pretending he'd been sideswiped on the highway."

"And that I'd stopped to help him, which is why we were late."

Even in his joking suggestion, Anton made someone else the hero. As much as I loved his humility, I love this even more—seeing him through the eyes of others.

Jin continues, "Of course, he just said our doors collided and joked about us both running late and being flustered. Then I met Nic, and she was everything Libby said, and I decided I wanted to be part of this family, and if I had to marry Keith, then that seemed a relatively small price to pay for it."

Jin glances at me with a smile that doesn't quite reach his misted eyes. "That was my first glimpse of Anton, and it showed me who he was. I never got to know him as well as I did Nic, but I always expected there'd be time for that."

He turns away, fingers drumming the table. When he looks back, he says, "Is that okay, as a memory? It's a good one, but being a good one means it brings up . . ."

"The pain that he's gone," I murmur. "I still like hearing them and—"

Jin's head swings left, and I stop short. He stares toward the living room before looking back at us.

"You didn't hear that?" he says.

We all shake our heads.

"What was it, Jin?" Dr. Cirillo asks.

"I . . ." Jin's gaze goes to me. "I thought I heard Anton. His laugh. But distant. Maybe just someone walking past outside?"

"That's easy to check," Dr. Cirillo says. "Let's do that."

We walk all the way to the lane, which ends at the house. "No one's out here," Shania says. "And I doubt we'd have heard them anyway, with all the front windows shut. You said it was a laugh, Jin?"

"Anton's laugh. It came from . . ."

Jin heads back inside to the breakfast nook, stands behind his chair, and shuts his eyes. Then he opens them and walks as if following an invisible trail. He ends up in the living room, near the sofa across from the fireplace.

"Over here," he says. "Or this direction, at least. As if Anton were on the sofa, laughing at something."

"Nicola?" Dr. Cirillo says. "Can you tell us where you think the earlier voice came from?"

This is exactly where it seemed to come from. This side of the room, on the sofa where Anton and I had curled up together every night, talking and . . . laughing.

"Could we be hearing echoes?" I say. Then I make a face. "Okay, that sounds even more far-fetched than ghosts. I was just thinking that Anton and I sat here a lot when we'd visit. Especially at night, with the fire going. Sharing a drink and talking and laughing."

Dr. Cirillo rubs his short beard. "People talk about echoes. Sounds permeating a place. I'd call them memories, because they're usually experienced by those who knew the deceased."

"Like me." I touch the back of the sofa. "Remembering that we used to sit here and talk, and then hearing him talking from here."

"Only that doesn't explain Jin's experience," Dr. Cirillo says. "Did you ever mention sitting here with Anton?"

Jin shakes his head. "She didn't."

"If Anton's here, we should communicate, right?" Shania says. "Do a proper summoning?"

"No," Dr. Cirillo says. "If Anton is here, he'll stay, and it gives everyone—including Anton—time to settle in and relax for tomorrow." He looks at me. "Is that all right, Nicola?"

"It is."

EIGHT

I fall asleep faster than I ever imagined, especially since my sleep cycles have been dictated by pills for the last eight months. I go off them for a while, only to give up after a week of restless sleep endangers my deadlines.

After Anton died, I'd taken a month off work. That's hard when I run my own business. It's also hard when my staff are support workers hired through a co-op, which provides self-employed coders with a pool of people who handle the nontechnical parts of the business. That's a huge help, but it also means I don't have a dedicated PA who would understand what I'm going through, explain the situation to clients, and rearrange my deadlines. Nor do I have coders working under me whom I could off-load some of my work on. So a month was all I could take, which then meant I had a month of work to catch up on. Since then, I've reduced my workload, knowing that lack of decent sleep means I put in full days but only manage half the work.

Dr. Cirillo had asked us to forgo sleep aids. I was nervous about going cold turkey, so I'd weaned off them last week. Tonight I expected to be staring at the ceiling. Or curled up, hugging a tear-drenched pillow and wishing it was Anton, thinking of all the nights

I'd rolled away from him—the man was a hot-water bottle when he slept—and wishing I'd cuddled close each and every night, no matter how warm it got.

Instead, I go to bed hugging a pillow, and my mind drifts to that semi-dream state where it becomes Anton, radiating imaginary heat, and I snuggle in and fall asleep . . . only to tumble back twenty-two years, part of my mind still spinning there from reliving that high-school memory at the welcoming séance.

When the dream starts, March break has just ended, and my family had enjoyed a few days in Vancouver, which was easy and safe travel for me. I'd spent the rest of the week studying. I was eyeing two of the country's top software-engineering programs, which meant I needed to nudge my grades up.

I'd made two good friends at school—Patrice and Heather—but both had gone south with their families for a little sun and sand, so I immersed myself in schoolwork, and by the time Monday comes, I'm dying to talk to anyone under the age of forty.

My bus drops me off at school just before first period, so I don't get more than a "Hey!" from Patrice, shouted across the crowded hall. Neither of my friends are in my morning classes. We might all be considered geeks, but we're different strains of the variety. I'm the computer geek, Heather is the art geek, and Patrice is all about drama, mostly the theatrical kind, but sometimes the personal kind, too.

Mom once called Patrice "high-strung." I gave her shit for that. No one calls *boys* high-strung. They're volatile or energetic. Mom accepted the criticism and apologized. I got what she meant, though. Patrice gives off an energy, and sometimes it's raucous and exhilarating and other times, it feels like nervous tension.

Heather is the opposite, focused and even-tempered, always assessing a situation to see how it can be improved. I'd once made the mistake of joking that she had a coder's personality—analytical and logical. I'd meant it as a compliment, but it stung because Heather gets a lot of feedback that her art is too perfect, too constrained. She longs for a little of Patrice's drama or my recklessness.

When I find them at lunch, they're at our usual table, sitting side by side, leaning together in rapt conversation. I slow. While they welcomed me into their friendship last term, I respect that they were best friends long before I came along.

Patrice sees me and perks up, waving me over with an expression that has me quickening my pace. Whatever they're discussing, it's something they're eager to share. Gossip? Good news? Either promises a little excitement in a dull school day.

I slide in across the table and take out my water bottle and enzyme pills.

"Heather was telling me what she did on break," Patrice says.

"You were in Cuba, right?" I say. "Did you do a lot of sightseeing?"

Heather makes a face. "No. I was hoping to see the art and the architecture, but we weren't supposed to leave our resort except on guided trips, and when we took one, it was really uncomfortable, like we were rich tourists who needed to be guided past the areas where real people live." She inhales. "I didn't like it."

At the time, I didn't quite understand her point. I was a sheltered white girl from an upper-middle-class family. But even at that age, Heather would have seen and felt the economic disparity.

"Which is not what we were talking about," Patrice prompts.

"Yes. So because we barely left the resort, I got to know a couple girls our age. Cousins. From Cambridge."

"Massachusetts?" Patrice says.

Heather and I exchange a smile, like older siblings rolling their eyes at a younger one.

"It's Cuba," I say, and yep, that's a little rude, but at sixteen, I could be insufferable. Okay, at thirty-eight I can also be insufferable, but as a teen I had an excuse.

"Oh, right," Patrice says. "Duh." Her tone suggests she doesn't understand, but she's not saying so. I won't call her on it by explaining that Americans can't visit Cuba. She can look it up later. The internet makes that a lot easier than it was when we were little and had to pull out an encyclopedia.

"Cambridge in England," Heather says. "One night, they ask me to slip out and meet them for something fun. I'm thinking skinny-dipping. Maybe meeting up with some of the boys."

"*For* skinny-dipping?" I waggle my brows.

Heather's cheeks pink, and Patrice's grin says she already knows what Heather did—and it's good. I lean forward, ready for the big reveal. *Was* it skinny-dipping with boys? I'd totally do that. Hell, if *that* was on the table, I'd be trying to talk my parents into a Cuban vacation myself.

Let's just say that at sixteen, my dating experience sorely under-served my curiosity. I wasn't sure whether I wanted a boyfriend. That seemed like a lot of work. But if I could go to a foreign country and have a safe hookup, I'd be writing my parents a thousand-word essay on why Cuba would be an important cultural experience for me. I am all about culture.

So when Heather leans in my way, I really am thinking something happened with a boy. Or maybe a girl. I'm never quite sure where Heather's interests lie, or whether she's decided, which is her business unless she wants to tell me. Either way, sex is sex, and if Heather got some, her glowing eyes tell me it was a positive experience, which is the important thing.

"A séance," she whispers.

I nod, my mind racing. Was there something sexy about the séance? I've read a couple of novels where magic led to some steamy situations, including one with a ritual that turned into an orgy.

By no stretch of the imagination can I imagine Heather partici-pating in a magical sex orgy, though. Even I'd be out of there—too much, too soon, and not my style. Maybe everyone got naked for the séance?

When I don't react, waiting for the rest, she says, "We had a séance."

"Uh-huh."

"We summoned the *dead,* Nic."

"Okay."

Still waiting for the rest of the story.

As they both stare at me like I'm a little thick, I realize this *is* the story. A séance.

Is that not something kids do in Edmonton? They sure did where I grew up. I'd been twelve when my parents first agreed to let me attend a sleepover, and there'd been a séance. I'd known there would be, because girls always talked about having them, and I'd felt I was missing out on that experience even more than the actual sleepover part.

That first time, we'd started by watching *The Craft,* and then we summoned the spirits . . . and I'd realized séances weren't actually all that exciting.

We didn't summon actual spirits, obviously. There was a Ouija board and a candle and a whole lot of giggling. The planchette moved—because Alice Lee was guiding it—and someone felt a cold chill and someone heard a whisper, and I'd been sorely disappointed. I could see through all of these "signs" without even trying.

I soon discovered that most of the girls realized it was a game. A delicious and forbidden game that was even more fun because some girls *did* believe. That sounds cruel, as if we were mocking our friends. But it felt more like putting on a performance for them. Even if they shrieked and swore they had nightmares, they couldn't wait for the next sleepover and never so much as hinted for us to stop.

I say "us" because after that first one, my problem-solving-oriented brain had a new challenge. I wanted to be in on the game, and I wanted to do better than the others. I wanted to create the signs even the other actors in this drama wouldn't see.

I came up with ways to move the planchette without anyone holding it, ways to tug at a blanket so someone swore they'd felt a touch.

No one ever knew it was me, and they loved that. Someone else was playing the game. Someone else was *mastering* it.

So when Heather says she participated in a séance, I'm confused by their excitement. They're practically vibrating. I could understand that reaction at twelve, but at sixteen?

"We contacted the *dead*," Heather repeats.

So she really believes they did, which means she must not have played those games in middle school. I'm about to explain what she actually experienced—how it's done—when I bite my tongue. Yep, I could be insufferable and a bit of a know-it-all, but I was learning that sometimes people don't want to hear how their sausage is made.

So how do I play this? Patrice is the drama kid. I suck at fake enthusiasm. I try, because I don't want to hurt anyone's feelings, but my mother told me years ago to tone down my Christmas-gift gushing because it was obvious that if I seemed really excited, I hated it.

I opt for a neutral diversion, one that allows me to focus on facts rather than an emotional response. "What did you do at this séance?"

Heather explains, and I'm glad I asked because I don't remember when I've seen her glow like this. It reminds me of those childhood séances, when the girls who'd been the most scared had the best stories to tell afterward, as if that was the point. They'd had the strongest experiences, and they came away with the best stories.

"And then the next night," she says, "we were doing it again when this woman came along. We freaked out, thinking we'd be in trouble for leaving the building at night, but she was really cool. One of the cousins said she was high on something."

"Drugs?" Patrice says.

Another shared look between Heather and me.

"Yes, drugs," Heather says patiently. "Anyway, she talked to us, and then the next day, she gave us something and said if we wanted to do a proper séance, we should use it."

"What was it?" I ask.

She shrugs. "Some kind of mushroom. She said if we made a tea of it, we'd be able to see across the veil into the world of the dead."

"So you took it?" Patrice says, her eyes bugging.

"Of course not. I liked the cousins, but I didn't know them well enough to drink weird mushroom tea around them. I brought mine home."

"You—you brought drugs on a plane?" I say.

Now I'm the one getting the eye roll. "They're just mushrooms," she says.

I bite my tongue. Hard.

"Anyway, the cousins used theirs in a tea before our séance that night, and it didn't affect the one, but the other one had this incredible experience. She says she saw—"

Someone yanks my ponytail, jerking my head back. I turn to glare up at a blond guy. Cody, with his buddy Mike right beside him. Anton is about ten feet away, pausing to talk to someone before joining his friends.

"Hey, Red," Cody says. "Got a question for you."

"And the answer hasn't changed," I say, because he asks this question at least once a week, as if it's the most hilarious—and original—thing ever. As if guys haven't been asking me it since I was in a training bra.

My friends cast me sympathetic looks. They don't say anything. Like my daily CF therapy, this is just something to get through, a lesson most teen girls learn, even if we later realize we shouldn't have needed to.

"Does that red go all the way down?" Cody says with a leer, his gaze lasering in on my crotch.

"And, once again, the answer is . . ." I nod to my friends, who say in unison, "You're never going to find out, asshole."

"I don't want to. That's why I asked."

"Hey!"

Anton has caught up and he gives Cody a shove, paired with an apologetic look at me.

Part of me wants to give Anton credit for that, and part wishes he'd react more strongly. But guys never did. At worst, they laughed along. At best, they did this show of protest.

The boys move on, Anton herding them away. And I move on, too. That's what you do when boys remind you that the only thing you're good for is fucking, and you personally fail to even interest them that way. You accept it as part of teen-girl life, as unpleasant but predictable as menstrual cramps.

I lean over the table. "So the one cousin had an experience."

"Janica?"

The voice startles me far more than the ponytail yank. I knew the yank was coming because even asleep, I recognized this as a memory, like a play I'd seen before and could predict every line of. But this isn't part of the script.

I glance over my shoulder. Anton's there, one corner of his mouth quirked in a half smile, a little self-conscious.

He bends down, voice lowered to a whisper. "I'm really sorry about that. You're right. He's an asshole. He has no idea how to treat girls." His face is right in front of mine now, that tentative smile hovering on his lips. "But I do."

He leans in closer, and my eyes half shut, my lips parting, the adult me seeing past teen Anton to *my* Anton, my face rising for a kiss as he leans in, hands braced on the back of my chair—

Anton yanks my chair backward, and it hits the floor with a slam loud enough that I bolt upright in bed, gasping.

I lie there, catching my breath, coverlet bunched in one shaking hand.

Then the door rattles.

I turn fast, tangling in the bedsheets, heart jammed in my throat. Across the room, I can just make out the closed door. Everything is still and silent—

The door rattles again, enough to make me jump.

I clutch the covers and curse at myself. It's a rattling door. Someone's there, trying to get my attention. In my dream, Anton yanked my chair over, which never happened. What I remember is that crash. Is that what I heard in real life, and my brain did something weird with it? Was the "crash" just a knock at the door?

I take a deep breath. "Hello?"

No answer. I slide one foot from bed. My bare toes touch down on the cool hardwood—

Another rattle has me yanking my foot back into bed as I twist to watch the door.

"Is someone there?" I say. "If you're goofing around, this isn't funny. . . ."

I trail off as I stare at the door. My door is shut. Yes, that should be obvious, but *why* is it shut? I always sleep with it open—old habit from childhood, when my parents wanted to hear me if I had trouble breathing. Eventually they realized that if something happened, it wouldn't be that sudden, but by then, I couldn't sleep with it shut. Last night, I'd left it about half open.

Again, I remember the dream. The crash of my chair didn't sound like a knock. It sounded like a door slamming shut.

The door rattles again, and my gaze swivels to my window, which is open, because I wanted the night air. Open window plus spring breeze equals a slamming door that turned into an overturned chair in my dream. And now that breeze is rattling the closed door.

I get up, shut the window, and the rattling stops. Then I crawl back in bed, firmly shut my eyes, and focus on getting back to sleep.

NINE

Miraculously, I do fall asleep . . . and drop straight into the same damn memories.

I'm not in the cafeteria anymore. After the guys left, I'd been uncomfortable with the séance talk, so I'd "remembered" something I needed to do before next class.

The séance idea doesn't die there. Suddenly, it's all my friends can talk about. In retrospect, I understand it wasn't about teenagers wanting to contact the dead. It was about teenagers dealing with their curiosities and their insecurities.

Patrice wanted to try the mushrooms. Drug experimentation was an area of interest and frustration for her, with two best friends who wouldn't even try pot. For me, it was the ingrained warnings about smoking in general—with my lungs—plus a discomfort with ingesting anything that might interact with my medications. For Heather, a lifetime of "don't do drugs" messaging had done its job. Patrice, though, was curious, but being a girl who really only had two friends, if they wouldn't experiment, she was stuck, being smart enough not to try anything without supervision.

The other dynamic at play here was Heather and Patrice's relationship. There had always been a clear leader and follower. Heather might have refused Patrice's drug-experimentation hints, but she felt guilty about it. Didn't her art teachers always tell her that she needed to relax and let the creativity flow?

Patrice wasn't dropping the séance idea because it involved drugs. Heather wasn't dropping it because for once, Patrice wanted something only she could deliver.

That Friday, as I'm waiting for the bus, Patrice marches over, with Heather in tow, and announces, "We're doing it with or without you. Tonight. In the woods behind the school."

"You don't need to take the mushrooms," Heather says. "One of us shouldn't, and that can be you."

I bristle at the emotional blackmail. She's saying I can watch out for them. I can make sure they do this safely. And if I'm not there? Who knows what will happen, and it'll be my fault.

"Fine," I mutter.

Patrice grins and hugs me. "You're the best."

I turn away to hide my annoyance. As I do, I spot Anton, a few feet away with Cody and Mike.

Cody is leaning toward Anton, saying something with a smirk, and Anton's gaze is on me, his expression unreadable.

Cody socks Anton in the arm, pulling his attention back. Mike leans in then to say something. Anton makes a face. Whatever they're talking about, he doesn't like it. But he glances my way, and then he nods.

The sound of footsteps tugs me from the dream. I listen, but it's only someone up and about, probably using the bathroom.

I refocus on the dream. I'd forgotten about the guys being there. It was a tidbit that had seemed meaningless, just Anton talking to his friends. Even admitting I'd noticed would be embarrassing, because it meant I was paying more attention to Anton than I wanted. But in retrospect, knowing what I do from Anton, it's significant because—

The creak of a footstep breaks my concentration. I glare toward the hall. I understand needing to use the shared bathroom or even going downstairs for a glass of water, but why do I keep hearing footsteps right outside. . . .

My thoughts trail off as I track the slow, deliberate steps. My face turns up to the ceiling.

Thump. Thump. Thump.

I swallow and inch back in the bed.

Those footsteps aren't down here. They're in the attic.

No, I'm hearing things. Another trick of my treacherous mind.

Sorry, there isn't any history of hauntings with this house. It is one hundred percent ghost free.

You think so? Here's a moaning voice in the dumbwaiter shaft and rattling doors in your bedroom and footsteps in the attic. How's that for a not-at-all-haunted house?

I shake my head. The voice in the dumbwaiter was just me remembering Anton's story about his brother spooking him. The rattling door was the wind—I proved that.

And the attic?

The steps pace back and forth. Then, with a scuffling sound, they stop right over my head, and I swear I hear a soft sob.

Someone is crying in the attic.

Someone is trapped—

Goddamn it. That was the story Cirillo told tonight. Ghost in the attic, moving around, crying.

I rub my face.

Coming here was a bad idea. A phenomenally bad idea.

Sure, let's hold a séance in Anton's grandmother's old lake house, with its creepy dolls and empty dumbwaiter and locked basement and a million creaks and groans to prey on my fractured mind.

As soon as I think the word "fractured," everything in me rebels. Fractured? Damaged? Me? Of course not. I'm grieving, yes, but otherwise . . .

Otherwise I'm fine? Fuck no. Otherwise I'm a goddamn train wreck, plowing through my days, pretending nothing is wrong.

Unable to sleep without drugs. Unable to function without therapy and exercise and endless stern self-talk. I'm gliding across thin ice with a smile plastered on my face as I pretend I'm dancing over a slab three feet thick.

Thump. Thump. Thump.

I clench my fists, glare up at the ceiling, and say through gritted teeth, "You're not there."

The footsteps continue. I press my hands to my ears and squeeze my eyes shut. Not there, not there, not—

The steps stop above me again, and I hold my breath, heart racing. Then they resume.

Thump. Thump. Thump.

I'm not imagining it. I definitely hear footsteps—

Because there's a door to the attic. It'd been locked when I'd been here with Anton, but he'd told me all about it. It was a walk-up attic where he'd once had a play fort. The last time we'd been here, he'd been talking to the owner, who said it was a mess but she was hoping to renovate it into a children's suite. I hadn't thought to see whether it was open and finished.

I hear footsteps in the attic? Yes, because someone else can't sleep and has gone exploring.

I roll out of bed and grab my wrapper. Cinching it around me, I head into the hall.

There's enough moonlight coming from a window that I can leave the lights off. I make my way toward the attic door, hands out to feel along the walls. I reach it and—

It's still padlocked.

I try the lock and the door itself. Both are firmly shut.

I turn, putting my back to the door and tilting my head to listen. Nothing.

I stay there a few minutes. When no sound comes, I slowly make my way back to the bedroom, slip inside, and stare up at the ceiling.

Still silent. I climb onto the bed and carefully balance as I stand, shut my eyes, and focus on listening.

It's so quiet I can hear the ticking of the cheap alarm clock.

Because I imagined the footsteps. I'd been dreaming and thought I woke up, but I might not have.

I exhale. Of course. Earlier, Cirillo told that story about the ghost in the attic, and then I fell into memories of Patrice and Heather, only to be woken by my door slamming and rattling in the wind. My brain was chock-full of ghost stories, and so what did I imagine, in my state of half-sleep? Footsteps and crying from the attic.

I had a hypnagogic hallucination.

I'm settling back into bed when something thuds downstairs, and instead of jumping, I only groan.

Really? More noises? Forget sleeping pills—I need earplugs.

When another thud follows a minute later, it pokes a memory of my first childhood home, out on the prairies. Our old house had storm shutters, and occasionally one would come loose and thump in the wind, just like that.

Does this house have shutters? It might. I know from my visits that—like the prairies—Lake Erie can get some incredible winds.

I should ignore it, but after my door slamming and rattling, and then my footsteps-in-the-attic hallucination, I am *not* sleeping until I know what's making this latest weird noise.

Yep, I definitely need to pick up earplugs. This is the loudest "quiet house in the country" ever.

I grab my phone a pad from my room and pause at the top of the steps. Everything below is still. I haven't heard any more of those thuds.

Again, I consider going back to bed, but I'm sure I know what this is, and it's easy to check. Better than startling awake every time a shutter smacks against the house.

I'm halfway down when something plucks at my nightshirt.

I jump, feet tangling as I stumble. The only reason I don't fall is because my mother taught us to use the railing. She'd had a friend who suffered a serious accident on stairs, and here I must send up a whisper of thanks to her spirit, because her teachings just saved me from the same fate.

That's when I remember why I stumbled, and my breath catches. Someone had grabbed my nightshirt, startling me and nearly sending me tumbling down the steps.

Hand tight on the railing, I look up the stairs. No one's there. I sprint back up, as if I can catch the culprit, but the hall is empty. I listen. Silence.

So if no one grabbed me, what happened?

I go back to where I stumbled, peer down at the railing, and spot the culprit—a splinter coming off the underside. It must have caught on my nightshirt—one of Anton's old tees, billowing around me.

Could a sliver do that? From the underside of the railing? There's no lint caught on the splinter or prick mark on the shirt.

Another thump from below. I dismiss the splinter and stride down the rest of the steps. I'm looking for a loose shutter. I head to the front door—

A sound stops me.

That wasn't the thud I've been hearing. I don't know what it was. A hollow noise. That's all I can say, and I'm not even sure what that means. I only know I heard something, and it sounded distant, but it definitely came from behind me.

I head straight for the most obvious spot: that dumbwaiter shaft. I unlatch and open the door. No, the dumbwaiter itself has not somehow re-formed from the ether, a grinning porcelain doll going along for a ride. The shaft is, as always, empty. I carefully poke my head in and shine my cell phone light up and then down. Yep, empty. No moaning voice from below, either.

I walk while mentally replaying the sound, trying to pinpoint the direction, like Jin had with the laugh. It leads me near the kitchen, and I'm heading that way, certain that's my destination, when I stop to stare at a closed door.

The locked room.

I shake my head. The sound did *not* come from a locked storage room, because that would be as ridiculous as footsteps in a locked attic. The door is very clearly still locked, and I know what's in there. Cleaning supplies.

But there's a whole locked basement to store supplies in now. Why not open up this room?

Because according to Anton, this is just a walk-in pantry.

Isn't that all the more reason for them to reopen it? The kitchen cupboards are stuffed so full of dishes that all our groceries are on the counter—

A creak.

I jump and spin.

That did *not* come from the locked room.

But the other sounds . . . ? The thumps? That hollow *something*? Could they have come from in here?

It's a *cleaning closet*. At most, it holds stuff for special bookings. Champagne fountains for weddings. Extra glasses for parties. Hell, maybe high chairs and cribs for little ones. Something in there shifted or fell.

But I heard more than one noise down here.

What if a high chair began to topple, sliding until it clunked over. Or a bunch of brooms and mops, one falling after the other.

Did that sound like what I heard?

I have no idea what—

"Nic?"

I wheel and stumble back against the locked-room door as Jin hurries over to steady me.

"Shit," he says. "I'm sorry."

I run my hands through my hair, as if raking out sleep tangles while I let my heartbeat slow.

"Were you down here?" I ask when I recover.

His brow furrows. "Huh?"

"I heard someone down here a few minutes ago. Was that you?"

"No, I just came down."

The creak. That'd been the stairs.

He continues, "That buzzing was freaking me out. Is that what you heard earlier?"

My brain takes a moment to engage. Buzzing? Right. I heard buzzing earlier this evening.

"So it wasn't my imagination?" I say.

"Nope. Like I said, you have good hearing. What is it anyway? It seems to be outside." He looks at the locked room. "You think it's in there?"

"No, I heard a thump that seemed to come from in there." I start to relax, sliding back into myself. "I think one of those stacked bodies woke up."

He jabs me in the side. "Sure. *Now* you play along . . . when it's the middle of the night and I'm freaked out by weird buzzing. You don't want me getting any more sleep tonight, do you?"

"I just know the proper time and place to tell spooky stories. Which is now, in a strange house, in the middle of the night. So where's the buzzing coming from?"

"Outside."

I roll my eyes. "Obviously."

"Hey, you asked."

"Come on then, let's go check it out."

When I open a window, I can hear the buzzing. I flip on the rear hall light and we move to the back door, where it seems loudest. When I peer out, I can only see darkness.

"Where's the outdoor-light switch?" Jin says, scanning the wall.

"Somewhere I don't see it."

"So we open the door?"

"Seems like it. Got your baseball bat?"

He gives me a hard look. "You jest, but if I saw one, I'd grab it. It's pitch black out there. We could be opening the door to a killer luring us out."

"With weird buzzing noises?"

"The fact it's weird is our downfall. It doesn't sound scary or threatening. Just odd. So we open the door and he's right there, waiting."

"He? That's a little sexist."

Jin shakes his head and grabs the doorknob.

"On the count of three," I say. Then I meet his eyes. "I gotchu, boo."

"Fuck off."

I bite back a laugh as he pulls the door oh-so-casually. It swings open and—

Bugs rush at us.

"Holy shit!" I say, lunging to grab the knob in his hands even as he shoves the door shut.

We both lean against it, as if we have indeed just slammed it on a serial killer. I lift my head toward the hall light, where a dozen bugs circle. Then I burst into a snickering, choking laugh.

"So . . . killer bugs?" I say.

"How do you know they're not?"

"Because they're attacking the light instead of us."

That's not exactly true. While the hall light drew them in, they aren't buzzing around it. Some have landed on the wall, and I peer at one. It looks like a mosquito, with the narrow thorax and long legs, but it's obviously not, since they aren't bothering with us.

"Guess *we're* going to be the killers tonight," I say as I take a tissue from a nearby table. I smush the bug, and it almost disintegrates, leaving an oily smear. When I rub at the smear, it stays on the wallpaper.

"Well, shit," I say. "This is going to take a little more finesse. What are they anyway?"

"Ugly." He swats at one as it bumps into his face, as if it didn't see him there. "Also stupid."

"Hey, no insect shaming." I shut off the hall light and pull back the curtain on the door window. Still nothing but darkness. "I think the light brought them in. We should be fine with it off. I'm going to open this again."

"I'll be right behind you."

"Uh-huh."

I carefully open the door. When it seems safe enough, I ease outside onto the porch. The buzzing is louder, but I still can't see the yard. Everything is dark. I move toward the railing and—

"Holy *shit*," I say. I step forward and grip the railing. "Are you seeing this?"

"If you mean a giant cloud of flying insects filling the entire freaking yard? Yes, I'm seeing that, and I'd really like to get back—" He swats a hand. "Fuck. They're—" Another swat. "Fuck!"

Bugs float past. They're flying, but it looks more like floating, that aimless, lazy flight as they bump into us. I open my mouth . . . and one sails in. I back up fast, spitting as we retreat into the house and quickly close the door. I may even turn the lock for good measure.

Jin bends over, coughing as he runs his hands through his hair. I pluck at my nightshirt and shake off bugs.

"What the hell are those?" he says. "You can't tell me that's normal."

"Not being an entomologist, I cannot tell you anything about them. Except that, while creepy as hell, they don't seem to be biting. I'll contact the owner in the morning and ask."

"You do realize you're being unnaturally calm about an entire yard full of buzzing insects."

I shrug. "Shania and I saw a black cloud over the lake under clear skies. I heard buzzing last night when no one else did. I'm just happy to have a logical explanation. It's bugs. Lots and lots of bugs, which don't seem to be biting or attacking. They just leave stains on the walls, so kill them carefully, keep the windows shut, and I'll get answers in the morning."

He exhales. "Fine. Yes. It's creepy but probably not a sign of the apocalypse. *Probably.*" He looks at me. "I am not going back to bed, though. Not for a while anyway. Drink?"

I smile. "I will definitely have a drink."

TEN

We take our drinks to the strange little sitting room, mostly because the lack of windows means we can close the door and not hear any buzzing. I stretch out on the sofa under the glass-eyed dolls while Jin takes the recliner and grumbles when the footrest smacks into the love seat.

"Are we sure this is actually a sitting room?" he says. "And not just the place where they store all the extra furniture and stuff no one wants to see, like freaky dolls?"

I tap a book. "We could call it the reading room instead."

"Yeah, I hate to break it to you, Nic, but for some people, books are as unappealing as those dolls."

I sigh. "Poor Jin. You just need to find the right one."

He reaches over to kick my foot. "I don't mean *me*. But I read this article a few months back about redecorating your apartment so it doesn't turn off potential lovers. Removing visible books was high on the list."

"The fuck you say."

"I do say. Apparently, it's a huge turnoff."

"The turnoff would be going into a guy's apartment and not finding *any* books." I peer at him. "Why are you reading those articles? If you're dumping my brother, I want my wedding gift back."

He tosses a throw pillow at me. "I read the article because I saw it going around online, mostly for that 'get rid of books' bullshit. Now, personally, if a guy didn't have any books, I'd stay . . . I'd just be gone by morning. One night does not require intelligent conversation. In fact, it can kinda get in the way." He waggles his brows.

"True," I say. "Long-term, though, I want to see books." I lean back into the sofa. "And books that look read. I dated a guy once who had this really impressive bookcase. Turned out it came—already filled—with the apartment."

"Ouch."

"Anton had books," I say. "Not a lot, because they were mostly fiction, and his apartment was tiny so he'd donate them after he was done. I pointed out the existence of libraries, but he liked new books. New paperbacks. Not hardcovers. Definitely not ebooks. Paperbacks he could read on the subway. And, to completely shut down that bullshit article, he got a lot of attention for his subway reading. People were always trying to strike up conversations about what he was reading, completely ignoring the fact that, for most of us, reading means we don't *want* conversation. But you know Anton. He was always polite, and always amazed by how many women wanted to talk books."

Jin lets out a snorting laugh. "Because that's really why they were talking to him on the subway."

"Why else? So many fellow book lovers in the world."

Jin shakes his head. A happy quiet settles, as that memory washes over me, but then it starts dragging along the reminder that I'm never again going to hear Anton telling me about the book a fellow subway rider recommended, writing down the title on the back of her business card.

I clear my throat. "So, how is married life? Everything you expected?"

He barks a laugh and then slaps a hand over his mouth, gaze shooting up toward those sleeping overhead. "If it was everything I expected, I really would be looking at those articles."

"So it has surpassed your very low expectations?"

"It has." He settles in, legs outstretched until his feet are on the love seat. "I never thought I'd get married. I mean, I knew I legally *could*. It's been an option since before I went on my first date. But my parents—as much as I love them—did not set a good example for marriage. Have you ever had two friends who just didn't get along? They only hung out together because of you?"

"Mmm, yeah. If it wasn't for me, you and Libby wouldn't be caught in the same room together." I smile over at him. "But yes, I understand the principle and the analogy. Your parents are good people, and you love them both, but you didn't want to be the reason for them staying together."

"Exactly. When they finally split, it was a relief, and they went on to happy and fulfilling lives apart, while my siblings and I learned that marriage might not be the can't-miss life experience the world says it is. I wasn't dead set against it, but if I did settle in with one guy, it would definitely not be a man with an ex-wife, two kids, and one foot still in the closet. I don't have time for that shit. And then along comes Keith and . . ." He shakes his head. "And suddenly I'm ready to make time for that shit."

"I'm glad you did. Keith is probably glad, too."

"Probably. Hard to tell sometimes. You know your brother."

"I do, and I know exactly how he feels about you, which you should never question even if I joke about it."

Jin shifts on his seat, the fake leather squeaking under his sweatpants. "I don't. That's the thing with Keith. He might have a toe in the closet even now, but that's just his nature."

"Takes him twenty minutes to wade past his knees in the lake, too."

"If he even goes that far, because first he has to check for pollution flags and undertow warnings, and where are the kids? Are they safe? Is anyone in too deep? Has he left anyone behind?"

I make a face. "Growing up with a chronically ill younger sibling can do that."

"Oh, don't blame the CF. The problem is growing up with a younger sibling who'd be running into that water, ignoring the pollution and undertow warnings, swimming past the buoys before anyone notices."

"And Keith was always there, pulling me back and giving me shit. Such a spoilsport."

"Which is why he's not here this week. We can love the guy while still not wanting him around sometimes."

He lifts his glass, and I lean over to clink mine against it.

Jin and I both fall asleep downstairs. I drift off first and wake first. He's sleeping so sweetly in the recliner that I can't help but smile . . . right before I arrange the dolls in a ritualistic circle around him and then I head to the kitchen.

It's almost eight, but the only person up is Dr. Cirillo, already working in the breakfast nook. I slip past unnoticed and brew a coffee. Then I do my nebulizer therapy, sitting and taking in medication through an inhaler while I read emails and type responses one-handed.

After that, I put on my vest. Having CF means daily airway clearance. That does not, thankfully, involve tubes down my throat or anything so invasive. When I was young, it did mean sitting in a chair for forty-five minutes a day, which might be how I came to love both reading and coding. People who know me marvel that I have a desk job. But books and code fully engage me, and if I'm fully engaged, I can indeed sit for hours.

Those old airway-clearance systems had to be plugged in, which kept me in one spot. I say "old" but they're still in use for children and those who can't afford my current vest, which cost more than my first car—and my second.

When Anton saw my vest, he said I looked ready to play laser tag. From the front it's like a black life jacket with a small plastic box and attached wires. The back is one big box—like a mini backpack—that holds the rechargeable battery and some of the mechanical parts that send high-frequency oscillations through my chest wall, thinning the secretions in my lungs and helping them keep moving along.

The vest weighs about twelve pounds, meaning I definitely know it's there. It's advertised as being suitable for walking and even jogging, but even I don't have the personal comfort level to wear it in public. At least not in Toronto. Here, though? I'm looking forward to combining two of my daily activities. A brisk five-kilometer walk before breakfast should give me my exercise and vest time.

I suit up, start my vest app, and pour my coffee into my travel mug. Then I swing open the back door and—

And jump back as a swarm of bugs rush at me.

Right. I forgot about the bugs.

I check my watch. It's still too early to text the owner. The bugs seem to be mostly out back, near the lake. Going out front should be fine.

I head through the house, step onto the front porch, and . . .

Okay, this isn't so bad. Fewer bugs, and they're only in the shade. When I walk into the morning sun, only a few float past.

I can do this. It's just bugs. Nonbiting flying insects. A mere annoyance that will not impede my enjoyment of this gorgeous spring morning.

I set out. I can feel the vest vibrating, but I'm used to it. As secretions move from my small airways to the large ones, I have to cough it out. I've preprogrammed the vest with cough pauses for that.

I walk briskly as I usually do to get my heart rate into the zone, but today I feel as if I'm marching to show the bugs that I'm not afraid of them.

The low drone of the vest does not, sadly, drown out the buzzing. It's kind of surreal. I've seen insect swarms before, but this is next level. The swarm has moved farther over the cliff and hovers there, where it swirls like a funnel cloud.

Are those more swarms over the lake?

My fingers itch to take out my phone and do some research, but I am walking in the beautiful May sunlight, on a peaceful morning by the lake, and I am damn well not going to be that city person with her gaze glued to her phone.

I'm training my gaze on the non-bug-infested portion of the scenery when I spot a distant figure. My hands fall self-consciously to my vest, but I stop myself.

As the figure draws closer, I realize it's Mrs. Kilmer. She's carrying a box, and the only place she could be heading is Eventide Manor.

I have the urge to veer off onto a path on my right. That urge brings a wave of guilt, as if I want to avoid Mrs. Kilmer herself, when I really just don't want to stop and chat to anyone. But when a bug bumps into me, I'm reminded that I have something to ask her about.

"Hello!" I call.

She smiles as she walks up, her gaze firmly on my face and avoiding my vest.

"Ignore this." I tap the vest. "I'm just heading out cliff-diving."

Her eyes widen in such horror that I feel terrible for the joke. "Kidding. It's a medical device. I have cystic fibrosis."

"Oh?" That same look returns as she stops short. "Oh! You have CF."

"You don't need to stay six feet away," I say, smiling. "If you've heard that, it only applies to me with other CF patients."

"I saw a movie about that," she says. "Two young people with CF who had to stay six feet apart."

I wrinkle my nose. "Mostly Hollywood nonsense. Basically, the rule is meant to guard against inhaling lung cultures other CF folks might be carrying. Precautions could be taken. As for the vest, it keeps me breathing. While I look like I'm ready to go boating, I don't think I'd be doing that today with these bugs."

She gives a soft laugh. "I'll bet that was a bit of a shock to wake up to. I thought I'd stop by with these." She lifts the box. "And also to make sure you knew about the midges."

"So it's not a sign of the apocalypse?"

Another laugh as she relaxes. "Oh, it might be, but it's a very short and regular apocalypse on Lake Erie. Every spring and fall, the lake flies invade. They mate and then return to the lake. Well, the females do. The males die, which is a whole other mess. The birds appreciate the feast, though."

"I bet they do. So this is a regular occurrence?"

She nods. "I thought I saw a swarm over the lake yesterday, and I considered mentioning it, but I didn't want to worry you, in case it turned out to be nothing. We really can't predict when—or even if—they'll arrive."

"How rude of them," I say.

"Very rude. But with any luck, this is the worst it will get. Walks are best in the sunlight. They don't bite, but they'll crawl over you and get in your mouth and nose."

I shudder. "As I discovered."

"Deeply unpleasant, but not dangerous. Keep the porch lights off at night. And if they get inside, try to scoop them in a tissue rather than crushing them. They leave a nasty stain."

Mrs. Kilmer peers over the lake. "Those swarms will hopefully land farther up or down the coast. Then these ones will be gone in a day or two."

"Thank you. For the bug intel and for . . ." I look at the box.

She hesitates, and I play back what she said. Did she not plan to give us whatever was in there? That would be incredibly awkward.

She holds out the box. "Yes, it's cookies. Chocolate chip and sugar. No nuts, in case that's an issue."

"It's not, but thank you."

She keeps her hold on the box even as I reach for it. "One other thing. My son seems to have stepped out last night, maybe for a walk. You haven't seen him, have you?"

I pause to process that. "You have a missing child?"

"Oh, no." A laugh that doesn't sell itself. At all. "Brodie is twenty-four. He came back home a few months ago. You know what it's like. Hard for young people these days to find steady work that pays the bills. He just wasn't home this morning, and his car's still in the garage, which means he went for a walk. He does that. He likes to come this way at night."

Last night? With the bugs?

Also, even at twenty-four, if I wasn't home by morning, Mom would have been calling in the search dogs.

To judge that, though, would be to judge Mrs. Kilmer as a parent, which is a shitty thing to do. Maybe her son has a hookup in town and doesn't always get back by morning.

That boy just loves his walks. Sleeps out under the stars and a layer of lake flies for a cozy blanket.

"I haven't seen anyone," I say. "If I do, though, I'll tell him you're looking for him."

"Brodie," she says. "His name is Brodie. He's five foot ten and a hundred and sixty pounds. Short light brown hair and blue eyes. He's probably wearing a ball cap and his plaid jacket."

That's . . . very specific. It sounds as if she'd given this information before, possibly to the authorities.

Is Brodie special needs? Or does he have mental-health issues? That would make this scenario a whole lot less confusing.

I can't ask that outright, so I say, "Is there anything else I should know?"

Her smile is a little too bright. "I don't think so. He's a very sweet boy. Quiet, but sweet."

Okay, so special needs or mental-health issues might be the answer, and she's afraid to say so, in case I'd jump to ignorant conclusions.

"Got it," I say. "I'll tell the others to keep an eye out for Brodie. Thank you again for the bug intel and the cookies."

I stop myself before asking if there's anything else I can do. That'd be my natural reaction. But while I'd certainly abandon our séances to join a search team, I can't offer.

I say goodbye and head off the other way, as if I'd only planned to walk this far. I have plenty of time. I can take the path along the clifftop, if it isn't too buggy, and then head inside for breakfast.

The walking plan dies before I even reach the house. The sun dips behind clouds and the midges descend. I pick up my pace, and within five steps, I'm testing out the vest's jogging-appropriate claim as I run for the door. I get inside and catch my breath.

There's still no one up except Dr. Cirillo, hard at work. I leave him to it and head into the kitchen to make breakfast while I finish my vest time. I eat in the kitchen, and part of that is about letting Dr. Cirillo work and part of it is about not being in the mood to make conversation. Even without small talk, I'd need to explain about the bugs and Mrs. Kilmer's son.

I'll wait until I can speak to everyone at once. While I eat breakfast, my mind wanders, not really touching down on any topic, just skimming above them, taking note of each.

Mrs. Kilmer's son. The midge invasion. The séance. Last night, hearing Anton's voice. The thumping that I never did investigate properly.

There's a lot to fret about, but I really do soar above all that, acknowledging it while untouched by it, at least for now. Everything that occurred last night—the rattling, the footsteps, my stumble on the stairs—had an explanation, and so the rest will, too.

By the time that's done, everyone's up, and I'm in the mood to be social over coffee and Mrs. Kilmer's excellent cookies.

Everyone agrees the midges are nothing more than inconvenient and annoying. It's bad luck that they arrived right here, right now, but it only means limiting our outdoor time and open-window time. Jin and Dr. Cirillo agree with my assessment of the Brodie Kilmer situation. The young man must have intellectual or mental-health challenges. All we need to do is be on the lookout for him if we go out.

"And . . . not to be paranoid," Jin says, "but if we're at all concerned about his mental health, I'm going to suggest no one goes walking alone."

I try not to squirm, but he sees it.

"I will brave the bug-pocalypse for you," he says. "Anytime you feel squirrelly, we'll walk together."

"What about the cliff?" Shania says.

Jin deadpans, "I will avoid the cliff and the attendant risk of being shoved over it."

Shania rolls her eyes. "I mean this guy. Brodie. What if he fell over? Isn't that a likely scenario, if he disappeared on a night walk?"

We're all silent, until I say, "I think, as someone who lives around here, that would be Mrs. Kilmer's first concern. But it didn't seem to be, so . . ."

"It is strange, isn't it?" Shania says, her voice dropping.

Jin shrugs. "She knows her son, and he's a grown man who probably grew up around here. He's not going to walk off the cliff. Now, what's on the agenda for today, Doc?"

ELEVEN

Nothing is on Cirillo's agenda until this evening. The four of us plan a post-lunch walk down to the water, but five minutes outside sets us retreating.

I've been trying to ignore the bugs. If it'd been raining, I'd have been disappointed but not annoyed. The bugs are different. They get steadily louder until even my noise-canceling headphones can't drown out that incessant buzzing. When I look out any window, the cloud of them seems to envelop the house.

Why here? Why are they right *here*? There's a whole shoreline to invade, and they pick this spot?

I'm irritated, and my irritation is covering the fact that I'm trying hard not to freak out as if it's some sort of bad omen. The migration is a natural event, and if they seem to be hovering near the house, it's something in the trees or the garden, or even the sun-warmed bricks.

When it comes time for cocktail hour, I almost bow out. I'm unsettled and the last thing I want is to sit around drinking and goofing off as if nothing is wrong. But if we're going to do tonight's séance properly, I need to relax. Drinking and goofing off is just what the doctor—Dr. Cirillo, at least—orders.

It's Jin's night, and his booze of choice is gin.

"How could I resist," he says when I groan. "Jin's Gin. It's right there."

That makes Shania laugh. "Good one."

"Which isn't why he picked it," I say. "Gin is trendy right now. God only knows why."

Jin mock-glares at me. "Are you suggesting I'm a trend chaser? Maybe I'm a trend*setter*."

"You keep telling yourself that. Just tell me you brought normal snacks and not some fancy charcuterie board. . . ."

He plunks the board on the table, his look daring me to comment. I sigh. Deeply.

The board is delicious, of course. Even the gin is fine. Yes, it's small-batch locally distilled blah-blah, but at least he puts it into cocktails instead of making us drink it straight. We have French 75s and Grey-hounds, and by the time the doorbell rings, I'm chill, laughing with the others, completely forgetting who would be at the door.

It'll be Mrs. Kilmer with dinner and tomorrow's lunch. And, I hope, news of her son. I tell the others I'll get it, and I'm out the door and about to shut it behind me—on account of the bugs—when Dr. Cirillo catches it and joins me on the porch.

I'm about to inquire after Brodie when Mrs. Kilmer says, "Why don't I take this cooler into the kitchen? I can get everything set up."

Didn't we have this conversation yesterday?

"I'm sorry," I say, hoping I do sound apologetic. "We're still con-ducting our research, and we can't have anyone inside."

"My orders," Cirillo says. "I am the lead researcher, and I must have a clean environment."

"It's . . . actually about my son," she says, stumbling over the words. "He's still missing, and I thought he might be here."

Cirillo's brows furrow. "We'd hardly be inviting him in when we just said we can't have anyone on the premises."

"Not that you've invited him in," she says quickly. "Just that maybe . . . he came in."

"Into the house?" I say.

"The doors have been locked." Cirillo eyes her. "I'm finding this odd, Mrs. Kilmer, so I'm going to be blunt and ask for answers. Your son has been missing since last night, and you think he broke into this house?"

"He isn't missing. He's a grown man who can come and go as he pleases. I don't think he broke in. He does yard work here. He might have forgotten a tool and came to fetch it."

"Why would his tool be in the house?" Cirillo says. "And why would he enter when there are clearly guests? This is making no sense, Mrs. Kilmer."

"Some of the tools are in the basement. He could have slipped in to retrieve them and didn't want to bother anyone. If I can just check the basement . . ."

Cirillo stares at her. "You think he's in the basement? Right now?"

"He might have fallen down the steps."

"The basement door is locked," I say.

Cirillo says, "And it is still locked, as of an hour ago when I mistook it for the bathroom. Are you telling me that your son—as groundskeeper—has a key to the basement and also to the house?"

"Of course not."

"Yet he keeps tools in the locked basement and might have entered—through the locked front door without a key—to retrieve them?"

She straightens, her tone chilling. "I only wanted to check. My son hasn't come home, and I am concerned."

"How would letting you into the house help? Do *you* have a key to the basement?"

"No, but—"

"Do you think we're lying about it being locked? Fine. I will escort you in to check the basement door. That is a violation of research procedures, but I do not want you thinking we might have . . ." Cirillo throws up his hands. "Found the door open and locked it with your son down there?"

"Someone could have closed it behind him," she says. "They saw it ajar and pulled it shut, and now he's trapped down there."

"Unable to call for help?"

"He'd be too embarrassed to do that. He could lose his job. He'd be trying to find another way out."

"Fine. Come in, and check the basement door and we will ask the other two participants whether they touched it."

"Thank you."

The basement door is still locked, and no one has touched it. Of course, we can't go down there to look for Brodie because . . . it's locked. Jin still takes pity on the woman and shouts through the door asking whether Brodie's there, if he needs help.

There's no answer.

"What about a window?" Jin asks. "Maybe we can get in that way?"

"There aren't any as far as I know," I say, "but we can check."

Jin and I do that, braving the bugs to circle the exterior of the house and confirm there are no basement windows.

"Who has the key?" Jin asks Mrs. Kilmer when we come back in.

"The owner," she says.

"We'll contact them and ask—"

She rocks forward, alarm flashing across her face. "Please don't. It's fine."

"Does Brodie have the key?" I ask.

It takes her a moment to answer, which has Jin and me exchanging a puzzled look. She finally says she isn't sure. Then she quickly takes her leave and hurries off.

"Does any of this make sense?" Shania says when Mrs. Kilmer is gone.

"Not to me," I mutter. "She thinks he may have gone into the basement for tools. In the middle of the night? Without a key to the front door? When there are guests here, and she's not even sure he *has* a key to the basement? Either she's desperate and grasping at straws, or there's a big part of this story she's not telling us."

"I'm going for option B," Jin says. "She's not telling us something."

"Agreed," Cirillo says grimly.

I look at that door. "Okay, this is going to sound weird."

"Weirder than 'I think my son is trapped in your basement'?" Jin says.

"I heard noises down here last night."

Jin snaps his fingers. "Right. You mentioned that." He turns to the door. "You think he might *really* be down there?"

"What did you hear?" Shania asks.

"Thumps," I say. "I thought it was a shutter banging, but there aren't any. I tracked the sound to the locked room over there. But what if it was really coming from the basement?"

"That wouldn't explain why the door is still locked," Cirillo says.

"I saw the door last night," Jin says. "It was shut. So any theory that Brodie left it ajar and we accidentally locked him down there is nonsense."

"What about the dumbwaiter shaft?" Shania asks.

We head there, and I open it.

"Too narrow," Jin says. "Even Shania would barely fit in there."

I nod. "If Brodie somehow ended up in the basement, he'd have answered when Jin called. By now, he would have given up on finding another way out."

"Unless what you heard was him falling," Jin says. "What if the key works from both sides? He goes in, shuts and locks it, and then falls down the stairs, where he's knocked unconscious."

"I really want to get that door open," Shania says. "Does anyone know how to pick a lock?"

"The solution is simpler than that," Cirillo says. "We contact the owner and ask for the key."

"Which Mrs. Kilmer didn't want," I say. "Probably because the owner would fire Brodie if they even thought he might sneak in while guests are here."

"I'll handle it," Cirillo says. "I'll tell them we heard noises and fear some animal is trapped down there. I saw the contact number on the fridge."

I considered insisting that I'll contact the owner, but Cirillo is already marching off, and I leave him to it. Jin, Shania, and I grab a board game—Clue—and set up in the breakfast nook.

We're still getting the board ready when Cirillo appears, phone in hand. "The owner is out of town until the weekend, and she is the only one with a key. She has assured me there is no way for an animal to get into the basement. No windows or other access points, as Nicola and Jin confirmed with their walkabout."

"In other words," I say, "she thinks we're jumping at strange noises and, if there is another key, with the cleaner or such, she's not bothering them to come and investigate."

"No, I really do think there's just one key. She said that with the main-floor washer and dryer, there's nothing down there except extra chairs and outdoor equipment for summer, which she brings out as needed."

"No yard tools?"

"Not from what I can tell."

"Curiouser and curiouser," I murmur.

After a moment of silence, Jin waves at the game board. "You in, Doc?"

Cirillo gives a tired smile. "As long as the answer isn't 'the gardener in the basement with pruning shears,' yes."

I want to go outside and watch the sunset. It's even more brilliant than last night's, and as everyone putters about, preparing for the first séance, I'm at the back door, working up the courage to brave the bugs.

They're just bugs.

Harmless insects desperately trying to get laid before their brief life cycle comes to an end.

I should feel sorry for them, maybe even cheer on their buzzing and swarming dances.

You go, bugs. Dance your little hearts out. Catch her attention and win the chance to pass on your genes before you become bird food.

Win the chance to be a daddy.

A chance Anton never got.

Part of me wants to snap "Where did that come from" and get back to my lighthearted rumination on the life cycle of bugs.

But we're all just bugs, aren't we? A life cycle much shorter than we'd like, and only a fraction of it—at least for women—open to baby making. The barest sliver of time in our lives before that ship has sailed.

Anton and I had talked about kids. He'd even gotten tested to be sure he didn't have the CF gene. He didn't, which would have meant any child of ours couldn't have cystic fibrosis. Still, adoption or surrogacy seemed the better option if we wanted to add that to our list.

Did we want to add it? Would it be fair, knowing I almost certainly wouldn't see our child graduate from high school? Would likely not even see them graduate from elementary school?

Had we gone through with it, I would now be raising a child alone when my own health began failing. Our child could very well have been orphaned by the age of ten.

"It wasn't supposed to be you that died, Anton," I say under my breath. "It was never supposed to be you."

A whisper at my ear, and I swear I feel a touch on my shoulder, almost like a squeeze. I turn sharply. No one's there.

My heart hammers, and I struggle to catch my breath. Then the scent of bergamot tickles past. Anton's aftershave.

I wheel, sniffing to catch it. "Anton?"

Nothing.

"Are you there?"

Still nothing, and the smell is gone, and I know it was never there. I was thinking of him, and a random sound became a soundless noise of comfort. I imagined a squeeze on my shoulder, and so, with my mind on him, I smelled his aftershave.

"I just want . . ." I whisper. "I just want . . ."

My throat closes, and I whip around, grab the door handle, and yank. They're bugs. Just harmless annoying bugs, and they will *not* stop me from enjoying this sunset.

I stride out, letting the door shut behind me. As I march forward, the midges drift into my face and fly past my head, but I steel myself against revulsion.

Just bugs. Harmless bugs.

When I smack into a swarm, I divert. The swarm buzzes all around me, bugs in my face, in my hair, crawling on my clothing.

They won't kill me. Just keep going.

I walk three more steps, and the insects engulf me until I need to slit my eyes. One still manages to hit, my left eye stinging enough that I gasp and bugs fly into my mouth and—

I bend over, letting out a near snarl of frustration as everything in me screams to run back to the house.

Just bugs, damn it. Just bugs.

I want to be stronger than this. Goddamn it, why can't I be stronger?

In the end, it isn't the bugs in my eyes or my mouth or my hair that break me. It's the whining buzz of the swarm, setting every nerve on edge after a day of listening to that goddamn buzzing—

I wheel and run back to the house. I get inside, slamming the door, only to really snarl in frustration when I see the small cloud of bugs I brought with me.

I grab a tissue and begin angrily plucking them off the walls. Footsteps approach, and I look up to see Jin hurrying toward me.

"I went outside," I mutter.

"Okay." There's a note in his voice that has me looking up. "Alone?"

I pause. Shit. I forgot that part.

My shoulders fall. "I'm sorry. I just . . . I wanted to see the sunset, and I was focused on braving the bugs. They're just insects, and it's a gorgeous sunset and . . ."

I know how I sound. Ridiculous bordering on unhinged.

"I just wanted to see the sunset," I say as my throat clogs. "We always . . . When Anton was here, we always went out to see the sunset."

Jin's arms go around me in a hug, Then, without a word, he takes a tissue and starts plucking bugs from the wall alongside me.

TWELVE

We're conducting the séance in the living room. The fire is going, despite the fact that we need to keep the windows closed so we don't hear bugs screaming on the screens. We've turned on the air conditioner instead. We want warm and inviting, not a sauna.

Before we start, we try to settle in with a bit of conversation.

"We should tell a ghost story," Shania says. "Get us into the mood. Like last night, when Dr. Cirillo told us about his first big case."

"Uh . . ." Jin says, and his gaze goes to me.

We're here to summon my husband. That's not a ghost story. Not the sort meant for entertainment anyway. But Shania is practically vibrating with anticipation, and if I refuse, gently, she'll realize the idea is inappropriate and feel bad.

"We could do that," I say.

"Do you have one, Nic?" she asks.

I think of Patrice and flinch. Then I take a quick sip of my tea. "No."

"Jin? You're up."

"Me?"

She grins at him, and I can't help but smile. I'd worried she'd be too shy to be comfortable here, especially when Jin and I are good friends, but she started to relax at Jin's cocktail hour—the two of them sharing war stories about working in the medical field.

"Anything," she says. "Any experience that you've had that could be a little scary."

"Well . . ." He slants a look my way. "There was the time Nic offered to cook the turkey for Thanksgiving."

I whip a decorative pillow at him.

He looks at Shania. "I've never actually had a paranormal experience myself, but there was a story my grandmother told me."

"Yes!" she says, looking ten years younger as she pulls her feet up under her. "Grandmother ghost stories are the best."

"Okay. This is my maternal grandmother, who's Chinese. I'm not sure how much you guys know about Chinese ghosts."

"There's one that haunts bathrooms," I say.

He whips the pillow back. "That's Japanese."

"Whoops."

He looks back at Shania and Dr. Cirillo. "There are plenty of ghosts in Chinese culture. Beyond ancestral spirits, though, most of them aren't exactly Casper the Friendly Ghost."

"They are mostly considered malevolent," Dr. Cirillo says. "Which is interesting, because that hasn't been my experience with spirits."

"We grow them different over there," Jin says. "But there's one particular type called the chang. The way my grandmother explained it, a chang is a person who was killed by a tiger. They come back as ghosts doomed to help the tiger forever, by luring in more victims."

"That's not fair," Shania says. "It's punishing the victim."

"Well, I suspect the idea is that you might be pissed off at having been killed by a tiger, and so, being a ghost and not in your right mind, you want others to suffer the same fate. Anyway, that's the myth. Now here's the story."

He sips his tea before beginning. "My grandmother came to Canada when she was seven. They lived in Toronto's Chinatown, which made it easier, with both the language barrier and the culture shock. It was her first summer in Canada, and her parents didn't want her leaving Chinatown. They were very clear on that. But my grandmother made a friend, and one day the two girls decided to break the rules. They went deeper into the city and got lost. Then they argued. My grandmother wanted to try asking for help because it was getting dark. Her friend wanted to find the way back on their own. One of them stormed off, and they were separated."

Jin takes a shortbread piece and tortures us by eating it before continuing. "Night is falling fast, and my grandmother only speaks a few words of English, and she's in a strange city with no idea how to get home. She's wandering around, hoping to see a police officer or a Chinese person, but she's in a residential area, and it's completely quiet. She thinks of going to a door and knocking but . . . Well, the reason her friend didn't want to ask for help is that she'd had some bad experiences. My grandmother is too afraid to knock on doors. She's walking and trying not to cry when she spots a girl playing hopscotch in a driveway. As she's thinking of what to do, the girl sees her and waves, smiling and beckoning her over."

Jin stretches his legs and looks at the fire. "Is it warm in here?"

"Stop that," I say. "You're stalling."

He grins at me. "Fine. Okay, so my grandmother approaches the girl and tries—using sign language and her smattering of English—to explain that she's lost. The girl understands and—with a bit of charades—says that she'll get her parents to help. My grandmother said she could have cried from relief. She starts toward the front door, but the girl motions no, she needs to come in the back way. My grandmother knew that Canadian kids often use the rear door, so this made sense. Once she was back there, though, the girl led her through the yard and climbed the fence, indicating *that* was her house, the one behind."

"Okay, that's weird," Shania murmurs.

"That's what my grandmother thought. Still, she didn't know Canadian customs and maybe the other house didn't have a driveway to play in. So she starts to climb the fence. Then she stops. Or some-thing stops her. She said she felt as if an invisible hand pulled her back. Then her insides went cold, and without even thinking, she turned and ran. She made it two streets and then spotted a police cruiser and flagged it down. She managed to tell the officers she was lost, but she also tried to tell them about the girl. She said she was certain something was wrong and the girl was in danger. Of course, the officers couldn't understand anything except the part about being lost."

Jin nibbles his shortbread, and I try not to glare at him.

He takes far too long eating that teeny bit of shortbread and then, of course, has to wash it down with tea.

Finally, he continues, "So they took my grandmother home, and she told her parents about the girl, but they thought she'd just gotten spooked. The poor English child had been trying to help, and my grandmother misunderstood. Two weeks later, my grandmother is with her mother and a neighbor who's been using the newspaper to teach them both English. There, on the front page, is a picture of the girl my grandmother saw."

Shania sucks in an audible breath.

Jin continues, "She was on the front page because the police had just arrested a serial killer who'd murdered two young girls. The girl in the picture was one of his victims."

"Damn . . ." I say.

"My grandmother was beside herself, thinking she had the chance to save that girl. Then the neighbor, who can read the whole arti-cle, asks whether she's sure the girl she saw was the blond one in the photo, not the brunette. Absolutely sure? She was. The woman stares at my grandmother . . . and then says *that* girl has been missing for a year. And all the police found of her was her bones."

"So she'd been dead . . ." Shania begins. "She was dead before your grandmother saw her."

"A chang," I murmur. "Someone killed by a predator, who then lures other victims to their deaths."

"Yep," Jin says. "My grandmother was convinced that's what she encountered. The spirit of the first victim, who was doomed to lead other little girls to her killer."

Shania shivers. "And if she hadn't gotten a bad feeling, she would have been the next victim."

"That is a fascinating account," Cirillo says, leaning forward. "Might I ask you for details later?"

"You'd need to ask my grandmother."

Cirillo pauses, and Jin lets out a laugh.

"No, I'm not telling you to contact her ghost, Doc. My grandmother is still alive. Ninety-two and sharp as ever. She remembers every bit of that story. Whether she'll tell you is another matter, but I can ask."

Cirillo thanks him and makes a few notes before announcing it's time for the séance.

I'm sitting on the sofa. No one is beside me. That's Anton's spot. It would feel more natural if the others were in the armchairs. Instead, they've brought in kitchen chairs so they can pull right up to the table where Cirillo is working. That leaves me at an awkward remove, feeling half like an observer and half like an experimental subject.

I don't argue. I get what Cirillo is doing. Jin and Shania are here to assist him. Conduits and welcoming faces. I'm the main attraction.

Come sit on the sofa with me, Anton. Curl up by the fire. Just the two of us.

I've been to a lot of séances in the last eight months. I'd rather not say how many. More than five, less than twenty. Most have a very standard routine that calls to mind Victorian spiritualism. Sit in a circle. Hold hands. Light candles. Maybe burn incense. Set out something for the spirit to communicate through, whether it's a Ouija board or an old-fashioned spirit board or a pad of paper and a pen, should the medium be seized by the urge to start "automatic" writing.

Except for the semicircle of three people around a table, this is different. There is only a single candle, which Cirillo explains is to detect drafts in the room. If the room is drafty, that would explain sensations of cold or breezes. There are also mechanical devices to measure everything from room pressure to temperature to motion. Those allow for quantifiable proof of environmental changes. A microphone is set up, too, though it's for amplifying sound rather than recording it.

All this is very rigorous, reminding us that Cirillo is a man of science.

The other items are the ones that remind us that this is a ritual intended to reach beyond science. These are the items I brought. Touchstones to Anton's life.

A row of three small framed photos sits on the table. The first is Anton as a child at Disneyland with his parents. The second is him in his twenties, skiing with friends. The third is us partying after our wedding. Three stages of his life. Three happy memories.

In front of each photo is a memento from that time of his life. A gold medal from a math competition. The key to his first apartment. His wedding band.

And in the middle of the table . . . the wooden box that contains his cremated remains.

I'm supposed to get comfortable on the sofa, which makes me feel even more uncomfortable. I'm dressed in clothing I'd worn the first time I came here with Anton. It'd been early enough in our relationship that I'd forgone the vacation-certified sweatpants and comfy sweaters, instead opting for my clubbing jeans and a cashmere sweater that hugged what few curves I had. Under it I'd worn some of the undergarments I'd rush-bought when it seemed like a good bet that our next dinner date would end in bed. It's not like my drawers had been full of granny panties and shapeless graying bras. Just because I hadn't dated in a while didn't mean I was celibate. But I wanted to go the extra mile for Anton.

Now I'm wearing those jeans and that sweater and even a sexy matching bra and panties. I'm sitting demurely on one end of the sofa with my legs tucked under me, but I still feel as if I'm sprawled here like an offering.

Come get me, big boy. You know you want to.

The others don't notice anything amiss. To them, I'm just curled up in the corner of the sofa, primly waiting for my dead husband to pay a visit.

"Anton Novak," Cirillo says. "We'd like to welcome you to join us this evening. Nicola is here, and she's waiting for you."

Oh, yeah. Come on, big boy. I'm ready and waiting.

I bite my cheek to keep from laughing, but I know Anton would definitely see the humor in this, and if I actually said that, he'd be more likely to respond—with a laugh and a lewd comment—than he would to Cirillo's polite invitation.

So I let myself smile, and I let my thoughts wander into the ridiculousness of this setup, and that's what relaxes me. I imagine Anton really there, flopping onto the sofa and lifting my feet onto his lap.

All this for me? You shouldn't have.

My smile grows, and my shoulders relax as the tension seeps out. I keep picturing Anton there, how he'd look, how he'd react.

Where's the whiskey, Nic? I come all this way, and you aren't even offering me a drink?

The professor guy is very serious, isn't he? I feel like I'm in school. Should I sit up straight? Pay attention?

As Cirillo talks, I conjure Anton until I can feel the solid weight of him under my outstretched legs and the heat of his hand on my calf. I hear his voice, the cadence and the undercurrent of laughter. Yet there is not one second where I think he's actually there. This Anton is fully woven from memories, and in that he is real, but I don't hear a word or see a movement that doesn't come from my head. No whisper at my ear. No squeeze on my shoulder. Nothing.

He is being summoned, and the air around me sits dead and heavy and silent.

It's the same for the others. Neither Shania nor Jin jumps or looks sharply to one side or reports seeing or hearing anything.

When Cirillo touches one of the devices, tapping the screen, I look over.

"Nothing, right?" I say.

"No, actually . . ." He trails off and checks the other devices.

"Dr. Cirillo?" I say.

"This one might not be working." He picks up a device. "It's giving me an unusual reading, while the others aren't moving and I don't sense—"

He stops abruptly, gaze swinging left.

I bite my tongue against an immediate question, not wanting to interrupt, but Shania says, "Doctor?"

He snaps his attention to her, his expression dark enough that she shrinks back.

"I didn't mean—" she starts.

"No, it's fine. I'm just . . ." His gaze goes left again.

"Dr. Cirillo?" I say. "If you want us to be quiet, say so, but you also told us to report anything we sensed."

He taps that one device again, harder now, fingernail click amplified by the microphone, making us all jump. He snaps it off and gets to his feet.

"This isn't working," he says.

"The device?" I say. "Can't we proceed without it?"

"I mean the summoning. It's not working and . . ." His gaze slides sideways again. "I would like to stop."

"Do we have a choice?" I say.

He starts shutting down his devices, each with a firm click or smack on the button.

"Guess that answers my question," I mutter. "Did we do something wrong, Doctor?"

"Davos," he says. "My name is Davos, and I have asked to be called that."

I glance at Jin.

"Maybe, Doc," Jin says, "if you want us to be comfortable calling you by your first name, you should stop reminding us that you're in charge of this experiment by shutting it down without explanation, when you have clearly seen or heard something that you don't want to explain, despite chiding Nicola to share her experiences."

"Nicola is the reason we are here. She ostensibly wants to contact her husband."

"Ostensibly?" I push to my feet. "If we make contact with Anton, *Davos,* I will fall on my knees crying. I will write every glowing recommendation you want, no matter how it makes me look, out of sheer gratitude for you giving me what I desperately want."

"No matter how it makes you look," he repeats. "Your attitude toward this speaks volumes, *Ms. Laughton.* You are blocking this summoning, and to me, that means you don't really want it."

"Doctor . . ." Jin warns, rising.

"Blocking?" I throw up my hands. "How am I blocking? I was sitting there thinking of Anton, imagining him with me. If that interferes, then okay, I was blocking, but not intentionally."

"*Would* that interfere?" Jin says.

Cirillo runs his hands through his hair and exhales. "No. It's the best thing you can do."

I glare at him. "So I'm *not* blocking you?"

"Maybe not."

"'Maybe'?"

"I've been doing this for nearly twenty years. I can tell when something is blocking. I sensed something that told me to shut this down."

Shania says carefully, "Whatever spirit you sensed told you to stop?"

"I worded that poorly. Whatever I sensed, which was likely *not* a spirit, made me decide to shut it down. What I sensed was wrong. I can't explain better than that." He looks at the photos and mementos and waves a hand across them. "Is there a chance that isn't his medal? Or that's not his old key?"

"As far as I know, they're legit. The ring obviously is. It matches mine, and it's inscribed. If you're concerned, we can remove the medal and key and try again."

"Tomorrow," he says. "This session has been disrupted."

Gotta love the use of the passive tense there. *This session has been disrupted.* Not that he disrupted it.

Did he really sense something? Or did the malfunctioning device unsettle him and he mistakenly thought that sensation came from outside himself?

All I know is that I'm pissed off, and I want to tell Cirillo he was out of line, but I can't afford to send our medium stomping off in a snit. We can't do this without him.

"I'm going to read in the other room," I say. "I'll see everyone in the morning."

Jin's questioning glance asks whether I want company. I shake my head with a look I trust he'll interpret correctly. I'm in a mood, and it's best to leave me alone.

I take my leave of the others, grab my book from the end table, and walk away before I say anything I'll regret.

THIRTEEN

Yep, I'm sitting in the room that I mocked for being a terrible place to sit. But it's quiet and it's small, and instead of being claustrophobic, that's comforting. It's me in my little cocoon with a blanket and a book. Even the glassy-eyed dolls seem more like what they were intended to be, friends for a child, keeping them company.

I lose myself in that book, a sweeping family saga filled with death and disillusionment. Maybe that seems the worst possible choice for a grief-stricken widow, but it too is oddly comforting, reminding me that this is the way of the world, and it always has been. Parents lose children, children lose parents, spouses lose partners. And they persevere. They stitch together the tatters of their lives and move on.

The problem is that their situation isn't mine. They move on to the rest of their lives, refusing to give in to grief when they have so much ahead of them.

How much do I have ahead of me?

How much good health? How much time?

I'll be waiting.

Those were Anton's last words, and some days, I find comfort in them, but other days I want to scream that I don't want him waiting over there. I want him waiting *here*.

When we made the vows "till death do us part," we'd really meant until *my* death did us part. Not his. Never his.

When a board creaks in the hall, I grumble and glare at the door as I set my book aside, as if I hadn't already surfaced from its spell.

A hand on the knob, the barest click of the plunger, as if they're hesitating there, uncertain whether to enter.

I sigh. "Come in."

It won't be Jin. He knows that I'm not the sort to say I don't want company when I secretly do. I could hope it's Cirillo coming to apologize, but the approach seems too soft and tentative for him. Shania then, which means I need to put on my best face because she deserves none of my snippy bullshit. Before I stomped from the séance, I should have spoken to her, to make sure *she* was okay.

Yep, I suck at this big-sister stuff. I was clearly made to be the bratty younger sibling.

When the door doesn't open, I call again. No answer.

With a stifled groan, I get up, go to the door, and swing it open.

No one's there.

I squint down the semi-dark hall. Shania's gone.

Damn it, I clearly zoned out for longer than I thought. These days, my distraction sucks up time like an industrial-strength vacuum.

I consider going after her. I'm not in the right mood, though, and I don't want to seem as if I only grudgingly checked on her. Give me a couple of minutes.

I thump back onto the recliner and pick up my—

Laura has moved.

Laura the red-haired pioneer doll. When I came in, she was on the shelf opposite me. She's still there. But she'd been facing sideways, her glassy gaze on the door. Now it's on me.

I vault out of the recliner, and as I do, something brushes my arm, which sets me scrambling all the more, nearly falling backward over the recliner footrest.

"Sorry."

The whisper comes at my ear, so soft it's almost a sigh. I spin again, and there's another sound, like an apologetic curse.

No one's there. No one *can* be there. There's one way in and out of this room, and I didn't step far enough through that doorway to let anyone enter behind me.

I look at the doll and remember who had moved it around the last time we were here, turning her head like that to make me jump and curse *him* out.

"Anton?" I whisper.

No answer.

"Anton, if that's you, can you say something?"

Silence.

"Can you do something? Anything?"

Nothing in the room moves. Tears fill my eyes.

Am I sure the doll wasn't already facing me? Am I sure I heard anything?

If you're there, give me a sign.

I don't say the words. They're too hokey.

Does that matter? Anton wouldn't judge me for hokey.

A rap at the door has me jumping again. Then it opens, and Jin pokes his head in. Seeing me on my feet, he frowns.

"Everything okay?"

I nod.

"I'm heading to bed to watch something on my laptop. Unless you want to watch something together. . . ."

"Not tonight." I pick up my book. "But I'll probably turn in early, too."

I follow him out. Before I go, I give one last look around the room. Then I turn off the light and shut the door behind me.

I'm lying awake in bed when a rap comes at the door, and I could almost laugh. I might even give a half snort into my pillow.

"Nic?" Shania whispers. "Are you still up?"

I roll out of bed and get to the door before she can leave. I open it to find her dressed in a T-shirt and sleep shorts with an eye mask propped on her forehead.

"Hey," I say. "I'm sorry about earlier. I didn't get to the door in time. I wasn't ignoring you."

"Earlier?"

"Downstairs?"

Her frown says she has no idea what I'm talking about, but she doesn't pursue it. The distant look in her eyes says she barely hears me.

"You okay?" I say.

She shakes her head, eyes brimming with sudden tears. I reach out to tug her inside.

"I . . ." she begins. Then she wraps her arms around herself and shivers. "Something . . ."

"Something happened? Come in. Talk to me."

I back up onto the bed and wave her toward the chair beside it.

She takes the chair but says nothing.

"What happened?" I prod.

"I . . ." She inhales deeply. "Can I not talk about it? Please? I know we're supposed to, but I also know it was just . . ." She taps her temple. "I was dreaming about Dr. Cirillo saying he was being blocked, and in the dream, there was . . ." She swallows and shakes almost convulsively. "It was a dream."

"It might help to talk about it."

She hesitates and then blurts, "I thought I woke up, and there was someone in the room and he had his hands around my throat. But then I woke up for real, so I know it was a dream." She touches her throat. "I'm still freaked out."

I turn the light on to get a look at her throat.

"There's a red mark," she says. "But it's from me rubbing it."

"It's the stuff about Brodie Kilmer, isn't it? You thought he was in your room."

"No, it was someone older, with dark hair and—" She glances away. "Yes, I think it was supposed to be Brodie."

"Any time you want to go home, Shania, you only have to say the word. I'll drive you back to Toronto right now if you like."

She shakes her head vehemently. "It was just a nightmare, and I feel like a baby even coming in here."

"No," I say firmly. "This is a séance, and nightmares are going to happen." I consider telling her about my hypnagogic hallucination, hearing footsteps in the attic after Cirillo's story, but it might just give her more nightmare fodder.

I continue, "It's also going to conjure up grief over your sister. I never forget that you're mourning, too. If it seems I do, please say so."

Another firm headshake. "I don't want to make this about my sister. If anything, I'd rather not tell Dr. Cirillo that I lost someone."

"Absolutely. If you aren't comfortable with that—"

"I mean I don't want to make this about me. It feels like talking about something horrible that happened, and a friend pipes up with an experience that pales in comparison. Like when I say I lost my sister and someone says their dog just died."

"If you mean that the loss of my husband is bigger than the loss of your sister, that's not true at all. I only had Anton for three years."

"But he was your husband. The love of your life. When you talk about him . . ." Her eyes mist again. "All I can think is that I want that. I want to find someone I can talk about like that."

I soften my voice. "And I want you to find someone who talks about you like that."

"You loved him so much, and I just hope he was worthy." At my frown, she blinks. "Oh, that sounded awful. I mean I hope he knew how you felt."

"He did," I say. "And I hope your sister knew how you felt." I settle in. "Can you tell me about her? You can say no, and I suspect, since you don't talk much in group, that you'd rather keep those memories to yourself. Or share with people who knew her."

"No one knew her," she says, and there's a sad twist of bitterness in her voice. "Not even me, really. She was good to me, really good, and I loved her, but I didn't *know* her. After she died, I was going through stuff and found her high-school journals, and I got to know her. It sounds awful, but that's when she became a real person. After she was gone, and that's just . . . It hurts."

I reach out tentatively, and Shania falls into my arms.

Shania continues, "In her journals, she fretted over boys and hung out with her best friends. There were teachers she hated and classes she loved. It was such ordinary teen girl stuff that I keep thinking how much I'd have liked getting to know her better. But she was already gone."

Shania's sister died of an infection. I know that much. One of those mundane things that's maybe even worse than a car accident, because it seems like it should be easily fixable.

People aren't supposed to die driving home, but they're *really* not supposed to die from a cut that doesn't even require stitches.

"Can you tell me something else about her?" I ask.

She smiles and wipes her eyes. "I can."

Shania and I talk for an hour about her sister, which gives her a chance to relive those memories and me a chance to get to know her better. Get to know Shania, I mean. Her sister sounds lovely, but the person I'm interested in is Shania and that conversation gives me a little more insight into the young woman I've befriended.

Shania's first memory is of her sister. It'd been Canada Day weekend, and the fireworks scared three-year-old Shania, so her sister distracted her by looking at the stars instead, as she held her hands over Shania's ears. Shania never forgot that, and while she still hated fireworks, she always went along with family or friends, to lie on a blanket, with her headphones on while she looked at the stars.

Years later, when Shania was a teen, her sister had been in the hospital for an illness on Canada Day. Shania stayed with her, and they'd snuck onto the roof to watch the stars and distant fireworks. They'd been caught by one of the nurses, and her sister had an excuse, but Shania had blurted the truth, unable to face lying. The nurse let them stay on the roof and, afterward, made a point of talking to Shania, which had started her on the road to becoming a nurse herself.

By the time Shania leaves, I'm ready to sleep and I drift off easily. What I drift off into, though, isn't dreams. It's memory.

FOURTEEN

It's the night of the séance with Patrice and Heather. We're holding it in the forest, because that's what teen girls did in the nineties. They were too old for huddling in a bedroom, giggling over a Ouija board. Movies and books had shown them how this was done, and if you couldn't get into some creepy old house that'd once hosted black-mass orgies, you had to go into the forest.

Patrice was in the lead. She might have started off letting Heather take charge, but she'd found her footing fast enough.

"How far are we going?" I say. "I've already lost my shoe once in this bog."

"It's not a bog," Patrice says. "It's just muddy, and you lost your shoe for two seconds, Nic. Stop whining."

"But how far—"

"Are we there yet?" Patrice cuts in with a whiny-little-kid voice.

I bop her in the back for that. "Legit question. I'm the only one who brought a decent flashlight, and I can still barely see. Weren't we supposed to do this on a full moon or something?"

"Full *dark,*" Heather says. "That's how real séances are done. As for where we're going . . . You tell her, Pat."

"We're going to the site of a murder. A *double* murder."

"Uh . . ." Heather says. "Not to be pedantic, but it was a murder-suicide."

"Are you sure?" Patrice turns, her weak penlight under her chin, as she intones, "Are you *really* sure?"

Heather rolls her eyes and catches up beside me. "Two teenagers died out here about twenty years ago. A guy and a girl. There was a big bonfire, and they took off to get laid. Only they never came back. The next day, a search party found them."

"God, Heather," Patrice says, "how do you make a double murder sound boring? Can you *try* adding a little imagination?"

That wasn't just mean. It was downright cruel, and when Heather falters, I want to snap back with the worst thing I can think of. Maybe address the rumor that Patrice gave Cody a blow job behind the school last year.

I wouldn't do that, though. I swallow my anger and say to Heather, "So the next day, a search party found them . . ."

"Let *me* tell the story," Patrice says with a dramatic wave of her arms. "From the top."

"No need," I snap. "I got the gist—"

"It's fall," Patrice says. "The week before Halloween. There's a chill in the air, and the night is pitch black, no moon. Just like tonight."

I bite my tongue. I don't actually want this story. I just want to get where we're going and finish this bullshit séance.

Patrice continues, "There's a bonfire with kids from our school. My aunt Lori is one of them." She glances at me. "She's told me the *whole* story, including the parts the news refused to cover." She pauses for effect. "Like how some of those kids weren't just drinking and partying. They were summoning dark spirits."

"Uh-huh."

"They were doing that, when all of a sudden, this guy, Roddy, gets up and walks into the forest. He doesn't say a word. He just stands up and walks into the darkness. Roddy was dating my aunt's friend, Samantha, who went after him. My aunt tried to, but Sam told her to stay, that they'd be right back. My aunt always said Sam saved her life there."

Patrice pauses, and I'm hoping that's the end of the story. I can deduce the rest. Sam follows Roddy, they get into a fight, Sam dies, Roddy kills himself. But Patrice is only pausing to check our location, and after she points down a side path, she resumes the story.

"When they didn't come back, my aunt figured Roddy stormed off to his truck and they left together. That meant she'd lost her ride home. So she had to stay until the end of the bonfire, waiting for other friends to give her a lift. When she reached the parking lot, though, Roddy's truck was still there. My aunt was worried—she wanted to go look for them. The other kids said Roddy and Sam took off to screw around in the forest and probably fell asleep afterward. If Aunt Lori wanted to go look for them, she was doing it alone. She decided they were right—and didn't want to be left by herself—so she took the ride. When she got home, she thought of calling Sam's place, but it was two in the morning."

Patrice pauses again, lifting her weak flashlight. "Just over here. See that big tree with the black marks? That's the spot."

I lift my own light and spot a massive maple with what looks like lightning damage. Once we reach it, though, the black marks seem to be . . .

"Fungus?" I say, peering at the trunk. "No, it's missing pieces of bark, and the wood's all black below. Some kind of disease?"

Patrice smiles smugly. "That's where they found her."

"Sam?"

Patrice takes out a blanket. Heather, who has been silent since the insult, catches the other end to help spread it.

I'm ready to prod again when I stop. I don't want this story, right? Except now, seeing that tree, I kinda do. Damn it.

I take candles from my backpack. Bringing them was my responsibility. Plain black candles, which seemed easy enough, until I realized they weren't the sort of thing you could grab in Kmart or Zellers, not in May. Apparently, black candles are for Halloween, and if you want them any other time . . . Are you one of those goth kids? Doing some dark ritual?

No . . . and yes. But not being goth, I didn't know where to buy black candles out of season. So I had to make my own stubby, lumpy ones.

The others brought the rest of the supplies—bowls and chalices and, of course, the mushrooms. I light the candles—they work!—while Patrice pours red wine she swiped from home.

When Heather sprinkles the mushrooms in two glasses of wine, I watch carefully to be sure none gets in mine. But Heather isn't Patrice. While Patrice might think it was funny to "accidentally" drop some in my wine, Heather wants me clearheaded in case anything goes wrong.

Heather puts some stuff into the bowl. I don't know what it is, only that it comes from multiple little baggies, and she tops the mixture off with a sprinkle of the mushrooms.

We all take our places, wineglasses in hand. They sip theirs, and I do the same. I have no idea if it's good wine or "plonk" as Mom would say, but it tastes foul.

"They found her in the tree," Patrice says, startling me.

I frown. "They found Sam in the tree?"

Her eyes glitter, and I realized I might really *not* want the rest of this story.

"The search team came out the next day. Roddy's dad was a cop, so they didn't wait twenty-four hours."

Which they wouldn't if two teens disappeared in a forest, but I don't correct her.

"They had dogs and everything," she says. "The dogs brought the searchers to the foot of this tree. My aunt was with them— she'd admitted to being at the bonfire and showed the search party where to go. She said as soon as they got close to the tree, they spotted Roddy. He was sitting at the base, like he was asleep, with his head tilted to one side. Except his head was *really* to one side, almost flat against his shoulder. The others didn't notice, and his dad marched forward to shake Roddy's shoulder . . . and his head almost fell clean off."

"Oh!" Heather says, her hand flying to her mouth. "I never heard that part."

"Because it wasn't in the papers."

Heather frowns. "So he *didn't* kill himself?"

"He did. He was still holding the knife. He cut his throat so deep, he nearly decapitated himself."

"Is that . . . possible?" Heather asks.

Patrice's eyes glint in the candlelight. "That's the question, isn't it? The coroner ruled it a suicide, but can someone really do that to themselves? My aunt said that no one who saw Roddy that night believed he killed himself. And then there was Sam."

She pauses to be sure she has our full attention. "When they realized Roddy was dead, his father went apeshit. Starts ranting about 'that little bitch' killing him. This guy—another cop—is trying to calm him down and wipes his own forehead, like he's sweating. Only it's blood. Blood dripping from the tree. He looks up . . . and there's something up there."

"Sam," Heather breathes. "I heard she was found in the trees. I thought that just meant she was in the forest."

Patrice smirks. "That was how they worded it. She was in an actual tree. This one. When Aunt Lori looked up, she thought it was some kind of animal. All she could see was blood and guts. Literally guts, intestines hanging down. It was my aunt who saw Sam's face first. Sam was lying over the branches with her stomach ripped open. My aunt looked up . . . and Sam's eyes opened."

Heather lets out a strangled yelp.

"She was still alive?" I say. "After spending the night in a tree with her stomach ripped apart?"

Patrice's mouth sets in a firm line. "It can happen. Stomach injuries take a long time to kill you."

"Yes, but—"

Her glare silences me. I glance at Heather, and I'm prepared to stop Patrice if she's genuinely disturbing Heather, but I recognize the look in Heather's eyes. It's the look of anyone listening to spooky stories in the dark. Scared shitless . . . and loving it.

"Her eyes open," Patrice says. "Her lips part. And she says one thing. One last thing before she dies."

"What?" Heather whispers.

"*It did this.*" She looks from Heather to me. "Not *he* did this. Not *Roddy* did this. *It* did this. My aunt went to her grave believing the other kids had summoned something dark, something evil, and it killed her friend." Patrice shifts. "After what Aunt Lori saw, she was never right again. I said that she told me this story. But I didn't say where she told it from."

Patrice looks between us again. "A mental hospital. Aunt Lori never recovered from what she saw right here, in this clearing."

Patrice points at the old maple. "That tree never recovered either. Those marks were there when the search team found Roddy. And they're still there."

Patrice reaches for her wineglass and takes a bigger swig. "That's not the first thing that happened in this forest either. People have disappeared. People have died. Every now and then, someone buys the land for a housing development. Then they hear the stories, and they realize no one would ever want to live here."

Patrice sets down her glass. "My aunt said it all started when settlers first arrived in Alberta. They weren't prepared for Canadian winters, and things got bad, and when spring came, there were a lot fewer people in their little village. They claimed they'd buried all the dead. Somehow buried them in frozen ground. Everyone knew what happened, but they all pretended to believe the story. But here's the real question . . ."

She leans forward, eyes nearly red behind the flames. "Is this place cursed because of what those pioneers did? Or were they driven to do it because this place is cursed?"

I know this story is ninety percent bullshit. Yes, I'm sure Sam and Roddy died. He killed her, maybe stabbing her in the stomach, and then he slit his own throat. But the embellishments belong to Patrice—or her mentally disturbed aunt.

The story is intended to prepare us for the séance. We did that at the middle-school ones, too. Tell a spooky story to get everyone in the mood, ready to jump at a whisper or a breeze through the window. It's just different hearing them in the security of someone's bedroom . . . versus hearing them in a dark and empty forest where two teens actually did die.

I want to stop this. I want to get up and walk away, and if Patrice and Heather stay behind, then that's their choice.

But if I back out now, they'll never let me live it down. I'm the logical one, the reasonable one. If I get spooked and quit, then every time I try to play it cool, they'll remind me of the time I ran away from a séance.

Other kids will hear about it, too. Patrice won't keep her mouth shut. She'll tell someone, who'll tell someone, and if I complain, she'll mock me for "whining."

So remind me why I'm friends with Patrice? She can be mean and downright cruel. She has no sense of loyalty. In fact, most times, her friends are the target of her cruelty.

I'm being grumbly. I know that. I'm unsettled and taking it out on Patrice.

In the end, I stay because of what's floating in those damn chalices. Because I promised Heather I'd stand watch while she took the mushrooms and she's already drunk that wine.

"Shall we begin?" Patrice says in a singsong voice.

I mutter under my breath, but I don't say anything aloud. When someone needs to contribute a drop of blood to the bowl, it's Patrice, so I must give her credit for that. She volunteered, and she sticks out her hand and Heather picks up the knife.

At the last second, I realize I'm letting a girl who just drank mushroom-infused wine wield a knife. But before I can stop them, it's done. One small cut to the tip of Patrice's finger. Patrice barely flinches. Heather massages out three drops of blood, and I watch them fall into the bowl, on top of the mixture within.

Then Patrice begins the incantation. It's the one Heather got from the cousins in Cuba, but Patrice had added stuff from a book.

What book?

I hadn't asked.

Where did it come from?

I hadn't asked.

Should I have asked?

I pick up my wineglass, mostly to feign taking another sip. I double-check the contents. Clear red wine, no bits of dried mushroom. I saw Patrice open the bottle, so it can't be dosed. And I've only had a sip.

I'm spooked. That's what it comes down to. I'm spooked by that damn story and these damn woods and that damn tree. And Patrice's damn incantation isn't helping.

As she speaks, dread settles in my gut. I want to stop up my ears against the words, and then I'm shamed by the impulse. It's silly words in a silly ritual.

Something moves in the darkness, a shadow against the black night. I turn sharply, but nothing's there, and Patrice is still talking.

Now I'm really spooked. I'm—

"Sam . . ." The voice comes from the trees, and it's Heather who jumps first, yelping.

"Samantha . . ." That comes from the other side, and I twist, tracking the sound.

A footstep sounds, slow and deliberate. My gaze shoots that way, my heart racing. Another footstep . . . from the other direction. A twig cracks underfoot, and I jump.

Then another twig, this one behind Heather.

As I stare into the forest, a whisper floats out. "Where are you going, Sam?"

Another whisper from the opposite direction. "There's no point in running."

"You hear that, right?" Heather says to me, her eyes huge.

I nod. We both stare into the forest, where we can still hear footsteps, at first to my left and then behind Heather.

It's only then that I realize Patrice hasn't said a word. She's sitting where she had been while she recited the incantation. Her eyes are open and unfocused and staring.

"Patrice?" I whisper. "Are you hearing—"

She pushes to her feet, still staring straight ahead.

"Nic?" Heather whispers. "What's wrong with—"

Patrice turns on her heel, sharp enough to startle us both. Then, without a word, she marches into the forest.

FIFTEEN

I wake up, gasping and shaking. My hands immediately fly to the nightstand for my inhaler and then stop as I realize it's not my lungs causing the problem. I catch my breath while I sit up, head dropped into my hands, my heart pounding as if I'm back in that clearing, watching Patrice walk out, hearing her words from earlier that evening.

Roddy gets up and walks into the forest. He doesn't say a word. He just stands up and walks into the darkness.

Heather and I had gone after Patrice that night. It'd seemed simple enough to catch up, but in our haste, we hadn't grabbed our flashlights, so we were staggering through pitch-dark forest. The obvious answer would have been to return for a light. At the very least, we should have stopped to listen for her. We were too panicked for that, too certain she had to be *right there*.

While it probably only took ten minutes to find Patrice, it felt like hours, stumbling and smacking into trees and calling her name. Then there'd been a whistle, and we'd run toward it and found Patrice still marching through the forest.

When we caught up with her and shook her, she . . .

I can't say she snapped out of it. That would imply she woke abruptly. Instead, she half surfaced from whatever world she'd been in, just enough to acknowledge us.

Confused and docile, she'd wordlessly followed us to the car. We all had our licenses—you could get them at fifteen in Alberta—but only Heather really drove. She dropped me off at my place first.

I should have insisted on helping her take Patrice home. But I'd only been relieved that I didn't need to explain anything to Patrice's parents.

I was racked by guilt for letting Patrice take those mushrooms. I'd been sure the drugs had put her in that state. All those antidrug lessons left me with one message: Drugs bad. Drugs could mess you up permanently. Just one dose, and if things went wrong, you'd never come back from that trip.

I know better now, but at the time, I'd been convinced the mushrooms did that to Patrice. As for those voices and footfalls in the forest? No one was talking about that.

It was a week before I saw Patrice again. A week where she'd been kept home from school, and we weren't allowed to visit, and I overheard my parents whispering about "psychiatric issues," but when I asked, they only said Patrice was unwell and I could see her as soon as her parents allowed it.

Then she appeared at school, standing on the edge of those damn woods.

At first, I thought I was imagining her or, worse, seeing her ghost.

She certainly looked like a ghost, pale and dressed in oversized sweats. I grabbed Heather, and we hurried over to see her. The closer we drew, the worse Patrice looked, her white skin nearly translucent, her eyes fever bright, the brown nearly black.

"We need to go back," she says, her voice a croak.

"Hey," I say. "Are you okay? We've been worried—"

She grabs my arm, ragged fingernails digging in and making me wince. "We need to go back. Undo it."

"Undo what?"

"It . . . got into me." She claws at her throat. "Need to get it out. Send it back."

"Send it back?"

At the time, I'd felt weirdly calm, as if this were a normal conversation. Now, looking back after twenty-two years, I don't see a calm and collected teenage Janica. I see a girl in shock, fixated on how sick her friend looks, unable to comprehend what she's saying.

In that moment, I would have done anything to help. Whatever happened in that forest was my fault. I didn't stop my friends from taking the drugs, and now something had happened to Patrice.

"Please," she says, tears spilling over her cheeks. "Help me get rid of it."

Get rid of what? That was the obvious question, and I've always wondered why I never asked. Now I realize I didn't want to ask because I suspected the answer. Patrice thought we'd raised something in that forest. Like the kids at that bonfire twenty years before us. We'd raised whatever had possessed Roddy to murder his girlfriend.

I knew Patrice was wrong. The only thing that got into her was those drugs. Drugs and the power of suggestion, and if we'd heard something that night, something that sounded like Roddy calling Samantha, it was a shared hallucination.

A shared auditory hallucination.

"What do you need us to do?" I ask.

"Come back to the forest with me. Tonight. Help me get rid of it."

I look at Heather, silent until now. She nods mutely, her eyes dark with worry.

I don't want to go back into that forest. Forget the fact that I had neatly explained away what happened. My brain might say Patrice was suffering the aftereffects of a bad trip, but my gut told me never to step in there again.

I didn't have a choice, though. Not if I wanted to help Patrice.

"Okay," I say. "We'll do it."

Later, I wake again, this time to a creaking noise. Not a creaking floorboard or door, but what sounds like a pulley in need of greasing.

The sound of a dumbwaiter, creaking up on its rope.

I groan and bury my head in my pillow. Isn't that exactly what Jin joked about? The ghostly dumbwaiter creaking upward in the night?

I pull the pillow away. Silence. There. See? I roll my eyes at myself and flip onto my back.

Creak. Creak.

With another groan, I lift my head. What is it with nights in this house, my imagination going into overdrive?

Because I'm not well. Mentally not well.

I grit my teeth. No, I'm emotionally and psychologically not well. I lost my husband, not my mind.

Creak. Creak.

"Oh, for fuck's sake," I mutter, and roll out of bed.

I know I'm imagining this because there is no dumbwaiter in that damn shaft, but apparently, I'm going to need to prove that to myself before I can sleep.

"Feels a lot like déjà vu," I mutter as I cinch my wrapper and stomp into the hall.

Where does that dumbwaiter come out up here? I heard the sound somewhere behind my headboard and . . .

And that's where I see the panel inset in the wall.

Which proves nothing because I've passed it dozens of times and subconsciously registered that it was there, putting the shaft right behind my headboard.

I march over and peer at the panel. The one on the main level opens easily, but with this one it takes me a moment to find the latch. Finally, I do, and I swing the hatch open . . . to see a pitch-black shaft.

Damn it, I'm going to need my phone's light.

Stomp back into my room, heading for the nightstand where I plugged it . . .

My phone isn't there. For a split second, paranoia washes through me. Someone took—

No, I don't remember plugging it in last night. So where did I leave it?

Forget that. There's a penlight in the drawer for power outages. I snatch it out, check that it works, and stride back into the hall.

At the dumbwaiter, I need to duck my head in to get a look upward. I expect the shaft to stop right above this spot, but it continues up to the attic, and I can see the pulley is there, but there's very clearly nothing attached to it—not a dumbwaiter and not even a rope for the pulley.

With a growl at my treacherous imagination, I start back out. As I do, the weak penlight shines down and . . .

There's something down there. Way down there, past the main floor. Something pale.

Thoughts of Brodie Kilmer flash, and my heart jams into my throat. We'd said the shaft was too small for him to climb, but what if he tried? What if he got wedged in there?

I shine the light straight down, and what I see isn't a person.

It's a piece of paper. No, it's a newspaper, an old one, seeming to float in the shaft. The front page of a newspaper with two photos on it. Photos of girls. One blond and one brunette.

Jin's ghost story bubbles up in my brain. The photograph of the two victims. I stretch my arm down for a better look and—

My breath catches, and my heart seems to stop.

It's not the newspaper article from Jin's story. It's the one from mine. School photos of Patrice and Heather smile up at me, under a headline half lost in the shadows, the remaining words seeming to leap from the page.

Teen Girls
Satanic Ritual
Horrific Murder

I yank back, heart racing. I squeeze my eyes shut. I'm imagining this. I must be.

Plink. Plink.

The sound of drips hitting distant paper. I brace myself and lean into the shaft again. Spots of red bleed into the newspaper below. Crimson red.

Blood splashed through a forest clearing.

I start to back out, but a drop from above hits me and I drop the penlight and stumble backward into the opposite wall. My hand flies to my face and finds a damp spot, but when I pull back my fingers, nothing's there.

I run my hands over my face, as if I've missed the spot, and then I stare down at them.

Nothing.

I run into my room and into the bathroom, flicking on the light. Then I stare at my face in the mirror. There's a damp spot on my cheek, but it's clear, like water, with no trace of red. All I see is my own wild-eyed face, drooping and drawn with exhaustion, giving me a preview of what I'll look like in five years.

The haggardness reminds me of Keith . . . and I remember where I left my phone. Downstairs after texting him.

I turn around and—

My foot flies out, the bathroom rug yanked from under it, and I crack down to one knee, my hand braced on porcelain.

I grit my teeth, pain blocking everything for a second. Then I look to see my hand on the freestanding tub and realize if I hadn't caught the edge, I'd have smashed my head on it.

Bathroom falls. One of the leading causes of accidental death at home. The other one being falls down the stairs . . . which I'd almost done last night.

I shake my head. I need to be more careful. Obviously, in my haste, I'd slipped on . . .

I see the bathroom mat, wrinkled and lying against the wall. Then I remember what I felt. One foot touching down, the other rising, the mat yanked sideways. And that's where it lies—to the side, not behind me, where it would have gone if I slipped. To the side, as if yanked from under me.

I stay on one knee, catching my breath as paranoia seizes my brain in icy claws. I thought someone grabbed my shirt on the stairs last night. I just felt the rug yanked from under my feet.

And the dumbwaiter. That old newspaper article in the dumbwaiter shaft.

I need a photo of it. I have to prove it's there.

Who am I going to show it to? Jin, Shania, Cirillo . . . three people who know nothing of my past?

I'm going to show it to myself. Just prove I saw it . . . and then figure out who the hell put it there. Because no one in this house is supposed to know my past, but someone obviously does.

SIXTEEN

I left my phone in the kitchen. I'd been texting with Keith right before the séance and set it down when the others called me in. I retrieve it and stride to the dumbwaiter shaft. It opens easily, and I lean in, shining the light down. . . .

Nothing.

The shaft drops into the darkness of the basement. Clearly there isn't any newspaper hanging there or lying on the floor below.

I twist to look up, shining my cell phone light, until I can see clear up to the pulley. Nothing's there.

I back up, and I'm standing in the hall, biting my lip as I think, when I catch a voice, barely above a whisper.

The hairs on my neck rise. A male voice drifts from somewhere in the house.

Anton?

It's male, but too soft for me to tell anything more.

The voice continues in that whispering undercurrent, just distinct enough that I can follow it. When I reach the basement door, I stop, pivot slowly, and then twist the handle.

Locked.

The voice comes again. It's farther down, near the back of the house.

I keep following it until I'm approaching the breakfast nook.

There's a light on in there. A wavering light.

The voice has stopped, but it soon starts again, something between a whisper and a rumble. Undoubtedly male. Undoubtedly not Anton.

Brodie Kilmer?

What if he's been in our basement this whole time, with a key to sneak up at night.

No, if any of us thought there was an actual chance Brodie Kilmer was still in the house, we'd have taken the door off its hinges to check.

Maybe we should have done that anyway.

I take one careful step toward the breakfast nook and then stop as I see the figure seated at the table. It's Cirillo, still dressed in his golf shirt, but with his hair messy enough that he looks as if he rolled out of bed. He has glasses on, suggesting he usually wears contacts.

He's at the table, with all of his equipment. With the photos and mementos.

With my husband's ashes.

For a moment, even though he's facing my way, he doesn't see me. He's too engrossed in what he's doing.

Somebody staged that newspaper in the dumbwaiter and lured me in with the creaking of the pulley. Somebody who'd dug deep enough into my background to uncover my past.

Who would be looking into me like that?

The guy I'd hired to contact my dead husband. The researcher who had to be sure I wasn't some crank out to embarrass him.

So . . . after setting up that newspaper, he'd now be openly sitting in the breakfast nook talking aloud, where I can find him and wonder why he's awake?

I can understand Cirillo researching me, but what would be the point of staging that newspaper?

What would be the point of *anyone* staging it?

I think back to what I experienced.

A newspaper article . . . just like in Jin's story about his grandmother.

Dripping blood . . . just like in that story about Roddy and Sam.

I heard a rope in the pulley . . . but there isn't a rope on it.

I saw blood dropping and felt it hit my cheek . . . but my cheek is clean.

I'm losing it.

I roll my shoulders. No, I'm not. I'm on edge after the séance, and I imagined the article on Patrice and Heather and the dripping blood, because I just dreamed of *that* séance.

I'd been half asleep, and my imagination took advantage of that susceptible state.

I should talk to Cirillo about it. I know last night's footsteps in the attic were a hypnagogic hallucination. I should tell him about that and also get his opinion on what just happened with the dumbwaiter. He's the expert, after all.

I bite my lip again.

I don't want to tell him.

I don't trust him.

Part of me scoffs at the thought . . . but then I look at him, sitting in the dark, with my husband's ashes, and he might not have had anything to do with the dumbwaiter, but he's up to something.

I step forward.

He notices me and gives a start. "Nicola."

"Davos."

He follows my gaze to the items on the table. "I . . ."

"Can explain? I'm guessing those are your next words."

He pushes back his chair. "I wanted to continue the séance."

"Alone? After telling us it was over? Practically sending us all to bed?"

"It wasn't like that. I did go to bed, even before you did. I came down about an hour ago."

"In the middle of the night?" I ease back, trying to look casual. "Did you hear something?"

He seems genuinely confused. "No." He searches my face. "Is that why you came down?"

"I heard someone talking down here. Seemed to be conducting a séance without me."

He rubs his mouth. "Sorry. I thought I was being quiet, but Jin did say you have good hearing."

He tries for a smile. When I don't return it, he clears his throat. "I came down because I couldn't sleep. What happened this evening bothered me, and I wanted to try understanding it without the pressure of an audience."

When I don't speak, he says, "I don't know what happened earlier. Nor was I prepared to deal with it."

He runs a hand through his hair and waves to the chair opposite. I hesitate, not sure I want to move to conversational quite so quickly, but my brain is still spinning from that newspaper—and the realization I'd imagined it. I'm suddenly exhausted.

When I sink into the chair, he continues, "I hate admitting that I don't understand something I'm supposed to be an expert in. I'm a scientist. To start talking about feeling blocked and sensing something wrong? That's for the kind of mediums you've been dealing with. It's woo-woo, and I don't do woo-woo."

"Okay."

He holds my gaze, as if searching for something. Then his shoulders slump. "I was an ass earlier, wasn't I?" When I don't answer, his lips quirk. "Let me rephrase that as a statement, not a question. I was an ass earlier."

"Yep."

He blows out a breath. "I'm not usually . . ." An inhale. "I was going to say I'm not usually like that, but that'd be a lie. I'm not like that at *séances*. I'm a professional, and I behave professionally. But this . . ." He waves around the room. "This is different. I'm excited about it, but I've never done this before. I don't live in a house with my subjects."

"You're the one who suggested this arrangement."

"I wanted to see how spending time in the environment and getting to know the other participants affected the outcome. What I meant is that this isn't a side of me that clients see. My grad students, though? That might be another story."

He passes me a quarter smile. "When I first became a thesis advisor, I'd sometimes have one student leaving while the other came in, and there'd be this weird exchange. Not hello or goodbye, but H or J."

I arch my brows.

"The letter H or J," he says. "That's what the one leaving would say to the one coming in. Finally, someone told me what it meant. An ode to Robert Louis Stevenson."

I think for a moment. Then I say, "Hyde or Jekyll."

He nods. "They were passing on information about my mood, warning the next student who had to work with me. Ninety percent of the time, the answer was J. But if I'm in a mood, frustrated or irritable, it's enough of a personality shift to be noticeable. It bothered me that they had to warn each other, even if it was jokingly."

He locks his hands on the table. "Which is to say that I know I can be an ass. I apologize, and I will try to do better."

"I wasn't responsible for what happened earlier."

He sighs, slumping. "I know, and I snapped at you, which is inexcusable, particularly under these circumstances. I might be excited about the research possibilities, but you are still the client."

"So I'm in charge?"

He tilts his head with a mock-thoughtful frown. "I wouldn't quite go that far."

I give him a hard look. Then I say, "Do you want me to leave you alone while you figure this out?"

He shakes his head. "Whatever I felt earlier is gone."

"Would it help to continue the séance with me?"

He hesitates. "That would be unethical. Shania and Jin are here to act as observers, which is also for your benefit."

"Right. But if I waived that . . . ?"

He's quiet for a moment and then gives a decisive shake of his head. "No. I would regret it later. I want you to have others present."

"Okay." I glance at the doorway, ready to go. Instead, I blurt, "I've been having experiences."

Shit! No. Don't go down that road.

I change direction fast. "Good experiences. I suspect they're just wishful thinking."

I tell him about being at the back door, hearing a voice and feeling a hand on my shoulder. Then I tell him about the sitting room tonight—the creaking board, the click of the knob, the moving doll—

"Hold on," he says, leaning forward, eyes glinting behind his glasses. "May I tape this?"

I frown. "I thought we agreed to a written transcript only?"

"This would just be for my records. I will destroy any recording if you ask me to. As for your experience at the back door, it was . . . typical."

"For someone desperate to make contact with a loved one?"

"Yes. Which isn't to say that it wasn't real, but the experience in the sitting room is different. May I tape you retelling it?"

"Sure, but I'd like you to remind me that you have the recording, in case I forget. I will probably want it destroyed."

"I'll compile a list of any recordings I make—all of which I will receive your consent for—and send them to you later."

He sets the recorder on the table, moving aside a photo of Anton to do it.

"Can we do this in another room?" I ask. "Or move all this?"

"Certainly." He makes a move to stand.

"Also, may I ask that you don't touch his ashes again, please? I know I should have taken them upstairs last night, but please ask me when they need to be moved."

Color rises on his cheeks. "Yes, of course. I'm sorry. I wasn't thinking."

"It's fine. I know I'm making it weird."

"You're not. It's perfectly understandable." He looks at the box. "Cremains mean something different to everyone. My grandfather kept my grandmother's remains in his closet inside a cookie tin. I was horrified."

"Did you accidentally open it and take a bite?"

He chokes on a burst of laughter. "Thank God, no, though I did read a story once about a teenager who found a relative's cremains and thought it was cocaine."

Now I'm the one trying not to laugh. Then I look at the box. "I don't think of that *as* Anton. His wedding ring means more to me. His ugly class ring means more. The closet of clothing I haven't cleared means more. This is . . ." I finger the box. "A responsibility. I haven't decided what I'm doing with them yet, but it feels like the one last thing I can do for him. Find the right place for his remains."

"I hear good things about closets. He liked shortbread, right? They make some lovely shortbread tins."

"You laugh, but Anton would approve. He'd probably also make some really juvenile joke about storing his remains in my panty drawer."

"Seems reasonable to me."

I stand with the box. "We're both tired and a little giddy. Let's get this recording done before we wake the others." I glance through the doorway. "The sitting room would be appropriate, if that works."

"It does."

I put the cremains box on a bookshelf in the sitting room and ask Cirillo to remind me it's there. That's what I think of it as. "The box" or "the cremains box." I'm not putting Anton on a shelf. I'm certainly not putting the last mortal remains of my husband on a shelf.

I explain what happened here. First I tell the story. Then I reenact it—getting up and standing in the doorway, proving no one could have slipped in behind me. I show exactly how the doll had been sitting when I was reading and how her head was turned when I sat down.

"And that was a thing Anton did?" Cirillo prods. "Moving around the dolls?"

"We both did it. Just being funny. He did more of it, though, and this doll was his favorite because of the red hair."

I add for the recording, "I also have red hair. He named the doll Laura Ingalls, because of the pioneer outfit and pigtails. Also the hair, but I pointed out that the character had brown hair and he was probably confusing her with Anne of Green Gables. We kept it as Laura, though."

"But seeing her head turned last night, you were understandably startled. You interpreted the apology as being for that. Because you leaped up and tripped."

"Yes."

"But the apology startled you again, and you heard what seemed like a curse. Also indicating apology, you believed."

"Yes."

"In life, how would Anton have reacted if he accidentally spooked you into tripping?"

"Exactly like that. Our sense of humor didn't extend to people getting hurt in pratfalls."

He asks a few more questions. Then he says, "Is there anything else?"

I motion to the recorder. He hesitates, but then hits the Pause button.

"There is more then?" he asks.

I think of the footsteps in the attic. The newspaper in the dumb-waiter. No, I've explained those away, and if I pile too much on, it'll dilute the rest.

Instead, I tell him what happened on the stairs and in the bath-room. He listens, and by the end he is sitting perfectly still.

"Two near accidents," he says slowly. "Potentially serious accidents. Both times, your initial sense was that they felt intentional."

I make a face. "Not like that. Someone didn't shove me down the stairs. They plucked at my shirt, and I tripped."

"Which could have been an affectionate prank gone wrong, like startling you with the doll. But the bathroom rug? That's not a prank."

"There was definitely no one in the bathroom. But ghosts don't pull rugs from under people, right? That's why I'm telling you. Your job now is to say to me that I'm distracted and need to be more care-ful in an unfamiliar house."

He leans back, a finger rising to his lips. At first I think he's shush-ing me because he heard something. Then I realize he's just thinking.

"Dr. Cirillo?"

No answer. He sits there, looking at me but not looking at me, finger still resting there.

"Davos?"

That snaps him out of it. He rocks forward, finger falling from his lips. "I don't know what happened to you, Nicola. After hearing about Anton's prank here in the sitting room, I would guess that the stair incident was also him."

My reaction must show, because he says, "You disagree. That doesn't sound like something he'd do?"

"It doesn't. But I'm also struggling to accept that what happened in here was Anton. I would be more comfortable qualifying it, saying that the doll prank *could* have been Anton."

His soft sigh says I'm splitting hairs. Maybe I am.

"Do you think it was someone other than Anton?" Cirillo asks. "A different ghost?"

"What? No."

"So it's an if-then statement." He smiles, pleased at himself for making a coding reference. "*If* it was a ghost, *then* it was Anton."

"Yes."

"But on the stairs . . . ?"

"My mom had a friend who fell down the stairs and broke her neck. I never goof around on the stairs, and Anton knew that. He'd taken a tumble once himself as a child. Lost a tooth. He would not have tried to spook me on the stairs."

"If not Anton, then . . ."

I lean back. "If not Anton, then I just tripped. Or my shirt caught on that splinter."

"So again, *if ghost, then Anton*. But the bathroom rug?"

I tug over a throw pillow and hold it on my lap. "Absolutely not Anton."

"So a second ghost, which defies the last equation. If there are two ghosts, then neither incident was necessarily Anton."

"*Could* there be a second ghost?" I say. "Is that what's blocking you?"

He's quiet. Then he says, softly, "Whatever I sensed didn't feel like an ordinary ghost. Something . . ." He sits back abruptly. "I don't know what it was. You said the house has no history of hauntings?"

"Nothing."

He nods slowly. "I didn't sense anything when I arrived either."

"But that changed last night?"

He doesn't reply.

"What do we do?" I say. "Leave?"

"No." The word comes quick and harsh, and after it, he stops and rubs his mouth. "Yes, of course we would stop if you felt unsafe. You're the one who narrowly avoided two dangerous falls."

I lean forward, the throw pillow clutched against my stomach. "Is it significant that no one else has experienced anything?"

He says nothing. It *is* significant. My gut says so.

"Jin thought he heard Anton's laugh," I say. "You sensed some unknown whatever blocking you. But I'm the only one with real experiences, and definitely the only one with dangerous experiences."

Anton wouldn't pull out a rug from under me in the bathroom.

Did Cirillo sense some dark force that's only targeting me? Except the experiences that seem to be Anton also almost exclusively target me.

What if that dark force *is* Anton?

Jekyll and Hyde.

No, that's ridiculous.

Is it?

Remember what happened in high school. You've never been completely sure—

Of course I was sure Anton wasn't involved. I'd never have married him otherwise.

Jekyll and Hyde.

A whisper rises from my memory, from being in this room, hearing Anton's voice.

The apology.

What if he wasn't apologizing for frightening me? What if he was apologizing for whatever compelled him to do it?

No.

I know Anton. I never caught a glimpse of anything darker.

I turn to Cirillo. "Is it safe to stay? Finish the séances."

"Definitely," he says, a little too quickly. "But you must tell me everything you experience, however much your mind is insisting there's a rational explanation."

I force myself not to hesitate. I don't agree, either, just make a noise he can interpret as that.

What if the danger is Anton?

Then I need to know that. Maybe someone else would march out of this house the moment they felt the first twinge of doubt. They'd want to hold their loved one's memory sacred and polished and block anything that could tarnish it.

Nope, sorry, I can't hear you. La-la-la.

I want to know, and maybe that doubt already tarnishes his memory.

If it does, then I'm sorry, Anton. I don't honestly believe you tried to hurt me, but it would be worse to leave with those doubts festering, always wondering "what if." I need to set those fears to rest and be confident—absolutely confident—that you were the man I remember.

SEVENTEEN

We go back to bed after that. Cirillo makes me promise to be careful. He even asks, for tomorrow night, whether I'd be okay switching to the room with two twin beds and sharing with Jin or Shania. I say I will, on the condition we don't tell Jin about my near falls. If Jin knows, he'll worry, and he'll also be compelled to tell Keith, who will drag my ass home.

I *will* be more careful. That was the real danger both times. Carelessness. On the stairs, I'd been distracted by hearing noises downstairs. In the bathroom, I'd been distracted by the dumbwaiter.

Walk with care. Hold railings. Pay attention.

I crawl into bed but it's soon obvious that I'm not going back to sleep. It's after five, and I'm far too unsettled. Maybe I'll go for a walk to clear my head.

I roll out of bed and open the blind. It's still dark, but the bugs are definitely there, their buzzing audible even through the windows.

I yank the blind down hard enough that it flips back up when I let go. I ignore it, dress, and head downstairs. If I can't walk today, I'll wear my vest while emptying the dishwasher, tidying the kitchen, all the little things in a house where everyone feels like a guest and waits for the nonexistent host to clean up.

At least everyone's been putting their dishes in the dishwasher, although I have doubts about whether they were rinsed. Rentals don't usually have new or high-powered dishwashers. Maybe I should wash dishes by hand. It's been a long time since I did that, and I don't mind—it was my chore as a teen. Put in my earbuds, hit a podcast, and off I go.

I get downstairs, and that bubble of purpose pops. Suddenly, the couch and a coffee and my book seem like a far more tempting combo. I brew a pot and take my book onto the sofa. No sitting room for me just yet. That's a little too isolated in a predawn house where everyone else is sound asleep.

I'm halfway through my coffee when a sound comes from the hallway. The click of a door latch. Someone must be up early. I'll tell them there's a pot of coffee ready.

I head into the hall. It's empty. The door I figured I'd heard click shut is the one to the bathroom. It's wide open, and the light is off. So what did I . . . ?

The basement door is open.

I blink. I must be seeing wrong. It seems to be just barely ajar, as if someone pulled it shut but it didn't latch.

I walk over.

The door is definitely ajar. The knob turns easily in my hand.

It was locked last night.

No, it was locked an hour ago when I checked it.

It's open now, though.

Was Brodie in the basement and now he's up here?

I shake my head sharply. I've read too many weird news stories where someone moves into a new house and discovers a stranger living in the attic. The attic would make sense—there's probably a window to climb in and out. But a windowless basement, where they could only come and go through the house?

Also, if Brodie wanted to flee, he'd have come up in the middle of the night. Same if he wanted to murder us all in our sleep.

Yeah, I've definitely read too many stories.

We aren't dealing with a killer in the basement. If it were even remotely possible that Brodie had been down there, it was because he was looking for a place to sleep. Maybe he had a fight with his mother and snuck into the basement to sleep . . . only to realize too late that the house was occupied and he didn't dare come upstairs again.

But there are cars in the drive. Two of them. He'd have *known* the house was occupied.

As I'm working this through, I'm on the move. I check the front door. It's locked.

I circle through the main level. Empty. The rear entrance is also locked.

I end up back at the basement door. There's no one in the house, and no sign that anyone left. I haven't heard a footstep or a creaking board. Just the click of this door opening, as if from a change in air pressure.

As if it hadn't been locked.

But it was just an hour ago.

Am I sure? Apparently, I hallucinated an old newspaper and dripping blood around the same time.

I rub my temples. Then I open the door wide. Making sure I have my cell phone in my pocket, I turn on the light, and I head down, one step at a time with my hand firmly on the railing.

At the bottom, I glance over my shoulder. The door atop the stairs is still open. I check my phone. I have three bars. All good.

No, all is not good. You are in a basement that has been locked *since you arrived.*

"Hello?" I call.

Yes, because clearly the serial killer hiding down here will answer you.

That's ridiculous. There can't possibly be a serial killer down here. The probability of both a killer and a ghost being in the same house is infinitesimal.

I snort a laugh under my breath.

Maybe it's a serial-killing ghost. Or the ghost of a serial killer. Dad always said I was an overachiever. A mere ghost or mere killer wouldn't be enough for me.

I peer around the basement, which is well lit, the bulbs overhead not even wavering. As spooky basements go, it's kind of disappointing. Oh, the floor and outside walls are concrete, the inner ones drywall and tape. Those bulbs don't have any fixtures attached. But it's the cleanest—and emptiest—unfinished basement one could hope to find.

This first room is the one where they'd kept the washer and dryer. And there's still a washer and dryer there, probably so the cleaners can whip through the bedding and towels faster by using both sets.

There's a shelf with detergent, bleach, dryer sheets, and empty laundry baskets perfectly stacked. Otherwise, this room is empty.

I'm turning when I catch sight of a panel in the wall. A panel that looks a lot like the one on the dumbwaiter shaft. Because that's what it is. The dumbwaiter would have been used for moving things from one floor to another, and one of the main things it would be moving is laundry.

I open the panel. It's empty, of course. What did I expect? The front page of a twenty-two-year-old newspaper? Drops of blood?

I'm about to shut it when I remember something else that should be in there. The penlight I dropped. I use my cell phone to examine every shadowy corner of that space, and there is no sign—

Nope, there it is.

I didn't imagine looking into the dumbwaiter shaft then. Just the part about seeing the newspaper and feeling blood drops.

I dwell on that for a moment before I scoop up the penlight, shake off my thoughts, and refocus on the basement. Doors lead to other areas on either side. When I'd been here with Anton, both had been locked, which made sense when the basement was only open for laundry access.

One of those doors is still shut. The other is cracked open.

As I pass the stairs again, I look up. Yep, the door at the top hasn't mysteriously swung shut. I approach the partly open door down here with care, listening intently. Once I reach it, I knee it open and jump back. Nothing leaps out at me—or scurries away—so I reach in and flick on the light. Then I stay in the doorway and look around.

It's exactly what the owner had said earlier. Extra storage. Outdoor furniture, folding chairs and folding tables, boxes labeled WINE-GLASSES and LINENS. The house is available for events—dinners and small weddings—and here's where they store the supplies. The door was open because, with the upstairs one now locked, there's no need to secure this one.

I back out and shut the door behind me. Again, I check upstairs to be sure the main-level door is open. Then I continue to the closed basement one. I reach for the knob and turn, expecting it to stop, but it continues turning, unhindered by a lock.

I repeat my ridiculous "safe entry" routine. Knee it open. Jump back. Wait for noises. Turn on the light. Push the door wider open and survey from the doorway.

It's the furnace room, which contains . . . Wait for it. The furnace. And holy shit, Anton was right—the thing is massive, taking up half the room. In fact, it seems to be two furnaces, one smaller and more modern and the other the ancient behemoth Anton remembered, complete with a door for shoveling in wood. There's also a hot-water heater. Otherwise the room is empty.

Well, that's underwhelming. Maybe there's another door? The basement seems smaller than it should be.

Are you really looking for a secret room?

Not really.

Okay, kind of?

I return to the storage room, and I can see all four walls. Same as I can see the fourth wall in the laundry room—the other three holding the stairs and two doors. When I map it out, I must admit there isn't a chunk missing. The basement seems small because the entire area hadn't been excavated. It's a perfect rectangle, comprising those three rooms.

Disappointing, indeed.

The only wall I can't quite see is behind that monster of a furnace. I'm walking toward it when a scratching sound halts me. The sound stops, too. When I move forward again, I listen, but it doesn't come.

I'm lifting my foot when I feel something under it. I lean against the furnace and raise my stockinged foot to find a piece of concrete from where the floors are crumbling. That must be what made the sound—the stone-sized piece scraping against the concrete floor.

Did it sound like that?

No, it sounded more like . . .

I'm not even sure, but I don't hear it again, so I chalk it up to the pebble. Then I catch another sound. This one soft but distinct.

A drip.

The very clear sound of a droplet plinking onto metal. I turn slowly, trying to track it . . . and my gaze lands on the hot-water heater.

Yep, the sound of water dripping in a room with a water heater. Shocking.

It didn't seem to come from there, though. It came from closer to the furnace.

I look up to see pipes snaking everywhere. Including pipes from . . . the water heater.

Really? Are you that spooked, Nic? Freaking out at drips and scrapes in a furnace room? It's a wonder the whole furnace isn't groaning.

Well, no, it's not a wonder because the active furnace is new, as is the water heater. The monstrous old one probably hasn't been used in decades. It's just still here because the house was built around it, and it's not going anywhere.

I nearly turn and walk away before I remember what I'd been doing. Not investigating strange noises but looking at the other side of the furnace.

Right, looking for your secret room.

Hey, I'm going to be thorough, because I know how this goes. If that door upstairs doesn't slam shut, locking me in, then once I leave, it'll relock before I can fetch the others. I am checking all possibilities while I'm down here.

I take another step, and when my foot slides, it's only the barest of slips, but my brain goes wild, proving I'm not nearly as calm as I'm acting. Both hands fly out to catch myself, one slapping the side of the new furnace.

As I catch my breath, I chastise myself for overreacting. I hadn't nearly fallen. My toe had just slipped a little on something.

Slipped on what?

I go very still and slowly glance down. I catch sight of plaid fabric under my foot and I dance back with a yelp, remembering what Mrs. Kilmer said about Brodie wearing a plaid jacket. In my mind, I'm stepping on a dead body. In reality, I've stepped on the slippery edge of a plaid sleeping bag.

An *empty* sleeping bag.

I catch my breath again as I brace against the furnace. The sleeping bag is tucked into a gap between the old furnace and the new one. If I hadn't walked over here, I'd never have seen it, which seems to be the point. A hiding spot with a sleeping bag and a rucksack. Empty pop cans and chip bags spill from a grocery-store polyester bag clearly being used for trash.

It looks like a teenager's hidey-hole. The place he goes to escape parents who are just too annoying to handle for a moment longer. Brodie might not be a teen, but if he's troubled or developmentally delayed, this could still be where he comes to escape an overprotective mother.

It's clear he's not here, though. The sleeping bag is empty, and that wall I came to check has no secret doors or windows. I bend to touch the bag. Cold. I'm pulling away when something pricks my hand and, again, I overreact, stumbling back and falling flat on my ass.

I lift my hand to see a tiny scrape, not even deep enough to draw blood. I crouch by the sleeping bag and pull back a fold where my hand touched down. A needle rolls out, the plunger depressed.

I pull up the sleeping bag. There's another needle underneath, and when I check the bag used for garbage, there are more in it.

The explanation for this could be that Brodie is a diabetic. I know more about the condition than most, because nearly half of CF patients eventually contract it when our disease affects our pancreas to the point where it no longer produces insulin.

But that needle isn't for insulin taken before Brodie consumes the snacks. I don't just find syringes. I find a rubber hose, a spoon, and a lighter.

Seeing that, I sink onto my haunches, overcome by a wave of sympathy for Mrs. Kilmer. We'd been trying so hard to figure out what "issue" Brodie might have. Why would she think her adult son might be in our basement?

Because he was shooting up. The owner said no one else had keys, but Brodie obviously found or made a set, using his position as a part-time groundskeeper. While the house would often be empty at this time of year, he still wasn't taking the chance of shooting up in the living room. He had his hiding spot down here, with snacks and a lantern, in a windowless space where even the glow of his lantern wouldn't be seen. A sheltered and warm spot near the furnace where he could do what he obviously couldn't do at home.

His mother knew he was an addict and, apparently, knew where he liked to shoot up, and she was handling it in her own way. Better to keep him at home and work on his addiction than give ultimatums that sent him into the streets, beyond her reach.

I understand her desperation now. Brodie came here to shoot up and maybe to sleep it off, and if he hadn't snuck back the next morning, that could mean her worst nightmare come true. Her son had overdosed. Overdosed in a place where she couldn't get to him, and she was obviously too afraid—of censure, of judgment, of losing her job—to tell the truth.

Had I known what she feared, I would have broken down the door. I'm horrified and heartbroken thinking of how panicked she must be, at how cruel we'd unknowingly been, brushing her off like that.

If Brodie had been here, he's gone now. Either he's been slipping in and out or he'd been on a bender for the past two days and snuck out this morning, forgetting to close and lock the basement door behind him.

I suspect he's already home, with an excuse at the ready for when his mother wakes. Still, I'll head to her house after breakfast. I won't shame Mrs. Kilmer by admitting I know the truth. I'll say I'm concerned and want to know whether he's come home, and she'll say he has, and that will be the end of it.

One mystery solved. Maybe I should be relieved, but I'm not. What happened to Anton was a tragedy made all the worse by the mundaneness of it. My life was ripped apart that night. On that same night, five people died in car accidents across Canada. Five other families experienced life-exploding pain that day and then five more the next day and five more the day after that. The same goes for this family tragedy. It is all too commonplace—a child caught in the grip of addiction, a parent desperately praying the next needle isn't their last.

These things happen. It's a breathtakingly cold fact, and it leaves me sitting beside that sleeping bag, crying for Anton and crying for Mrs. Kilmer and crying for a young man I don't know, until I hear Jin and Cirillo talking as they make coffee upstairs. Then I wipe away the tears and head up to tell them what I found.

EIGHTEEN

An hour later, everyone has seen the nest behind the furnace. Everyone has come to the same undeniable conclusion. We are dealing with the family tragedy of addiction.

Still, we're cautious. Jin grabs a spade he spotted in the garden and brings it down, apparently as a potential weapon. Then we all search the basement, just to be absolutely certain there's no chance Brodie crawled behind a stack of chairs and died of an overdose. He didn't. He was here, and now he's gone.

"I'm very sympathetic to Mrs. Kilmer's situation," Cirillo says as we head back upstairs. "But her son has a key to this house, and that's very troubling. I had a younger brother who suffered from addiction. Thankfully, he pulled through, but there was a time when we couldn't leave him alone in the house, and not just because we feared an overdose. He stole everything he could get his hands on."

"And we're leaving laptops just lying about," I say.

"Not only that but . . . We don't know this young man and how desperate he is. We could be in danger of losing more than valuable but replaceable tech."

"Are you saying we should leave?" Shania sneaks a look my way.

"Obviously, it's up to Nicola, but I'm willing to take whatever precautions are necessary."

"Precautions should be enough," Cirillo says. "We'll speak to Mrs. Kilmer and be compassionate but firm. We'll lock the doors and put something behind them to alert us to entry. We'll check all the windows to be sure they are closed and locked. Nicola and Shania should share a room, if that's all right with them."

I glance at Shania, who nods. She's obviously eager to stay. We're close to getting proof of an afterlife, and that's what she's here for.

"Can anyone think of other steps we can take?" Cirillo asks.

"I'll think on it," Jin says. "I'm really hoping, though, that a talk with Mrs. Kilmer will do the trick."

"It should."

After my nebulizer therapy, Jin and I head out to speak to Mrs. Kilmer. We'd debated driving, but the bugs seem better today, and I really could use a walk. I wear my vest to get that over with.

As we quick-march down the road, I swat at bugs and growl under my breath. "I thought they were better."

"They are," Jin says. "Doesn't mean the stragglers are any less annoying."

I pull up the hood on my sweater and cinch it tight as the bugs drift around us. Individually, they don't make any audible noise. They just fly into us and drift around us.

"I'm not sure what I'm more annoyed with," I say. "The bugs themselves? Or the fact that I'm letting something so harmless get on my nerves."

"And there, Nic, you have a metaphor for life." Jin swats at insects. "Or maybe it's a simile? A symbol? I'm a science guy. The point is that it's easy to let the little things bother us, even when they're harmless. One or two minor annoyances pass with barely a ripple, but when they're nonstop, like these damn bugs, it's a constant irritation that doesn't let us relax. Then we get annoyed with ourselves for not toughing it out. Like we get annoyed with ourselves for being conned into hiring spiritualists to contact our dead husbands."

"That was the worst segue ever."

He shrugs. "I take them where I can get them. You're angry with yourself for not toughing out the bugs. You're angry with yourself for not moving faster through the stages of grief. You're angry with yourself for being conned by charlatans who take advantage of that grief. Stop being so hard on yourself. The bugs annoy you. Accept it. Accept that you'll experience grief your own way, and that the ones to blame for preying on that are the predators."

"I don't like being prey," I mutter.

He puts an arm around my shoulders in a quick squeeze. "I know."

We walk past a row of maples, and Mrs. Kilmer's little house appears ahead.

"Do you think Dr. Cirillo is preying on me?" I ask.

Jin shakes his head. "No. I don't consider his field hard science, but he isn't a quack running home experiments. He's the closest thing to legitimate you can get. Or, at least, that was my impression when we hired him."

"And now?"

"Now?" He shrugs. "I'm still not ready to believe anyone can speak to the dead but . . I heard Anton's laugh the other night, Nic. I can tell you've had more happen, including things you aren't ready to discuss with me. We're on the cusp of something here. A breakthrough. An answer. If that answer is ultimately silence, then that *is* an answer. If Dr. Cirillo can't summon Anton, then I don't think Anton can be summoned."

Jin looks over at me. "How are *you* feeling about it?"

I lean my head to touch briefly on his shoulder. "Same. I'm not ready to accept what I'm experiencing as proof, but I feel that either we're going to get that proof or the lack of it will answer my question.

That doesn't mean Anton isn't somewhere, just that he can't communicate with me."

The Kilmer house is tiny compared to Eventide Manor. I'd peg it at mid-twentieth century, a little brick bungalow with a fence surrounding a yard that would be massive in the city. The gardens are immaculate and already bursting with flowering annuals. More flowers hang from baskets. In the middle of the front yard, there's a chair under a tree, with a little table that begs for a book and a glass of lemonade.

The driveway is empty, but there's a garage that I'm hoping holds Mrs. Kilmer's vehicle, meaning she's at home. As we head up the drive, I realize that I don't know whether there's a Mr. Kilmer. I get the impression there isn't and hasn't been in a very long time. Widowhood? Divorce? Or just never a "Mr." Kilmer in the picture?

Until she mentioned a son, I would have guessed she lived alone. I'd had multiple conversations with the woman when Anton and I were here last time, and yet all I knew for sure was that she was an excellent cook.

The front door is teal blue, like the garage door. A burst of cheerful color against the gray brick, bolder than I could have expected from the woman I've met. There's an antique door knocker, polished bright.

I use the knocker, and I swear I'm still lowering it when Mrs. Kilmer throws open the door.

"Mrs. Laughton." Her face lights up with such a glow that my heart sinks. I tell myself I'm wrong. She's just happy because her son has come home.

"Hey," I say. "I've been thinking about your son, and I wanted to see whether you've heard from him."

She deflates, and I know she opened this door hoping we'd brought news . . . because she doesn't have any.

She doesn't answer. Just shakes her head.

I glance at Jin, seeing my own disappointment reflected back.

"I'm sorry to hear that," I say. "I really hoped he'd returned. We managed to get into the basement, though."

She goes still, and that look on her face now makes me feel cruel, as if I'm intentionally inflicting this pain on her.

"He's not down there," I say quickly. "All four of us searched the basement thoroughly because . . ."

Yep, I need to rip off this bandage. It's the only way to set her mind at ease on this one score—that her son isn't dead of an overdose in a hidden corner, our "thorough" search being the half-assed check of people who don't understand the situation.

"There's a sleeping bag down there," I say. "And . . . used needles."

Her entire body sags. When she speaks she seems to be forcing the words out. "I was afraid of that. I knew he was going somewhere to . . . do it, and he swore he didn't have keys to the house, but I found oil on his shirt once, like from that old furnace."

"He isn't down there," I say. "And we didn't break the door open. It was ajar this morning. If he was down there, he left."

Her eyes fill. "I am so sorry. He was—he was such a good boy. He still is, deep down. But when he moved out, he fell in with new friends. I'm trying to get him into a program, but there's a waiting list."

"You don't need to explain," Jin says softly. "We're just glad he seems to be okay."

"If you want to come up and look around the basement," I say, "please do. I understand why you didn't explain the situation, but now that we know, we want you to be sure he's not in the house, and we would strongly suggest you call the police."

She nods. "May I come over now?"

"Absolutely."

We walk back with Mrs. Kilmer, and now I do wish I'd driven, because that's one hell of an awkward walk. Do we talk around her addicted son and his disappearance? Discuss the weather instead? Thankfully, Jin takes over the conversation by steering it toward help for her son. Working in a hospital, he has a better understanding of what's available, and Libby will know even more from her perspective as a therapist.

There are many wonderful things about living in a country with a national health-care system. It allows someone like Mrs. Kilmer to get help she likely couldn't otherwise afford. However, just because help is free doesn't mean it's freely—*readily*—available for mental-health issues and addiction.

If you can pay, there are private clinics and rehab. The free version has a wait list, and the system isn't always easy to navigate. Jin offers help with that. He can put Mrs. Kilmer in contact with the right people so Brodie gets the help he needs sooner than he might get it going through the usual channels.

It's wrong that she needs this kind of networking to get help for her son, but our health-care system isn't perfect. As someone with a chronic illness, I know very well, though I always hesitate to bring it up in front of Americans, knowing some will leap on "it's not perfect" as proof that a national health-care system doesn't work.

Back at the house, I warn Cirillo that Mrs. Kilmer is coming in. I expect he'll balk, but the guy isn't a monster. He understands that as much as he might like to keep our "lab" pristine, finding Mrs. Kilmer's living son is more important than contacting my dead husband.

We take Mrs. Kilmer downstairs. She tries very hard to ignore the sleeping-bag nest, her cheeks coloring each time she glances that way. A symbol of a shame—and maybe a guilt—that she takes very personally.

We let her search the basement to her heart's content although, again, there's not much to search. In the end, she must admit that the scenario seems to be what I first imagined. Brodie was in the basement, and then he snuck out last night. The only difference between my theory and the apparent reality is that he didn't go home.

She apologizes profusely for what he did, but she doesn't ask us to keep it a secret, and I appreciate that. I don't want Brodie losing his job over this. I certainly don't want Mrs. Kilmer losing hers. But if it comes to a missing-person search where the police need to know he was in the house? Then that's in his best interests, whatever the fallout.

For now, we're letting her handle this. She has promised to go to the police. What she tells them will be up to her, for now.

This settles the mystery of the noises I heard the first night and the locked door that was suddenly open. No supernatural explanation needed for either. I can put that aside and get back to the reason we're here.

We eat lunch together, and then Shania has an online meeting and Cirillo wants to take some readings in the basement, now that it's open. Jin and I retire to the sitting room. I can't help it. I'm drawn there, pretending I just find it unexpectedly cozy when I'm really hoping to hear from Anton.

Would I rather be alone? On the one hand, if Anton's here, I want him to be entirely comfortable reaching out. On the other hand, if anything happens again, I'd like a witness. So when Jin offers to keep me company, I don't argue.

We both work on our laptops. I'm mostly doing correspondence. Part of me would love to get wrapped up in coding, but I just can't find that degree of focus. Better to get the less enjoyable tasks out of the way.

Yes, I find coding enjoyable. It's problem solving, and I can get as immersed in it as Anton would get in his mathematical equations. We were both in the rare and enviable position of having jobs we genuinely enjoyed. That was one of many things that drew me to him. I'd been with guys who complained nonstop about their work, or who made me feel guilty for liking mine, as if I were giving in to "the man." I wanted a healthy work-life balance, but I also didn't want to be mocked for enjoying my job.

Within an hour, I achieve inbox zero. That sounds impressive until I admit that I have a very organized email system that snoozes anything I don't need to handle right away. Once all the important emails are answered, I move on to project management, double-checking my schedule and moving things around my task list.

I'm in the midst of switching the order of two projects when I hear my name.

"Nic . . ."

I glance at Jin, even as I know that's not his voice. It's Anton's.

Jin doesn't notice my pause. He's typing something, his keystrokes far softer than mine, but his attention even more riveted on his task.

"Everything's okay," Anton whispers.

Jin's head whips up, and he looks from side to side before his gaze shoots to me.

"Did you hear . . . ?" he says.

"Yes," I whisper, barely able to get the word out. My heart hammers so hard I have to struggle to breathe.

When Anton's voice comes again, it slides from another corner of the room.

"I love you," he says, barely louder than a sigh. "I'm waiting."

"Holy shit," Jin breathes, his eyes wide.

"You . . . heard that?"

"Anton's voice? Saying he loves you, that he's waiting?"

I nod, my entire body drum-tight, my teeth aching from clenching.

Don't get too excited. You've been fooled before.

As if reading my mind, Jin glances toward the door and whispers, "We need to be sure, right? That Dr. Cirillo isn't doing it? With speakers or something?"

Another wordless nod. Jin slides silently to his feet and eases the door shut. Then he comes back to me.

"Anton?" Jin says, looking around.

No response.

"If you're there, can you give us a sign?" Jin says, and then whispers to me, "Is that how it's done?"

I'm going to say something sarcastic when I see the earnestness in his eyes, and I say, neutrally, "That's classic séance-speak."

"Which means it's probably Hollywood bullshit."

"Classic spiritualism, I should say, which predates Hollywood."

Jin looks around. "Anton?"

Nothing.

"You try," Jin says. "If he's come back, it's for you."

There's something in those words that sets the hairs rising on my neck. Jin says it with that same earnest calm, but what I hear is almost a threat.

He's come back for you.

I'm waiting.

This is Anton, and that's not how he'd mean it.

I entreat him to speak to me, but there's no response.

"Where did you hear his voice coming from?" I ask Jin.

"I think—" Jin stops. "No, we should approach it scientifically. Close your eyes. I'm going to mark the directions I thought the voice came from. Then you'll tell me where you heard it."

I give him a look.

"Do you have a better idea?" he says.

I shake my head and shut my eyes.

A moment later, Jin tells me to open them and says, "So where did you hear the voice from?"

"Two directions." I point. "There, near the door, and there." Another gesture. "From that bookcase."

He walks to the love seat near the door and takes a piece of paper he'd placed behind it. Then he takes another from the bookcase I indicated.

"What exactly did you hear?" he says. "I only clearly caught the last lines, which I wrote here." He lifts the paper from the shelf. "For the other one, I wrote what I thought I heard."

His second note exactly matches my recollection—"I love you. I'm waiting." For the first, Jin thought he heard "It's okay" instead of "Everything's okay."

"Can we agree that's close enough?" he asks.

"It is."

"So now we search for speakers."

We take everything off the bookshelf and examine each item. Look behind the bookcase. Look under the bookshelves. Look behind and under the love seat. Take out the cushions of the love seat. We even check for holes in the fabric where a speaker could have been stuffed inside.

"Nothing?" he says.

"Nothing," I say.

A slow grin spreads across his face. "So we heard him, right? We really heard him."

I nod, not daring to speak. Jin catches me up in a hug and then says, "Let's go tell Dr. Cirillo."

NINETEEN

Cirillo insists on conducting his own search. He refrains from stating the obvious—that he needs to be sure *we* didn't plant equipment. I don't care. I want as many eyes on this as I can get.

After he searches, Cirillo wants to use his equipment to conduct some experiments in the space. I beg off in favor of a nap. I've had two rough nights. My CF means I'm susceptible to infections, so I try to keep well rested. Or that's a fine excuse. The truth is that I want to get away from everyone else in hopes Anton will reach out.

Before, I'd wanted him to make contact in front of others, for independent confirmation. Now that he's done that, I want him all to myself, in hopes he'll do more than whisper reassurances.

I head up to my room, pull the blinds, turn off the lights, and crawl into bed.

"I'm here," I whisper. "If you want to talk to me, I'm listening."

There's no answer.

"I'm getting a little tired of these one-sided chats, Anton. How about you stop whispering in my ear and have an actual conversation?"

No response. My words settle, and I squirm under them. I might have been teasing, but there's truth there, too. He hasn't tried to talk to me. He's talked *at* me. Maybe that's how it works. I can hear him, but he can't hear me.

If Anton is passing along messages, rather than trying to communicate, what is he saying? Warning me? Or reassuring me? The ones from today are exactly what I'm hoping to hear, which makes me all the happier that those are the ones Jin also overheard.

So why does another, darker, possibility keep nudging at me?

I'll be waiting.

Kneeling in the snow beside his dying body, I'd heard nothing but reassurance in those words. *I'll be on the other side, and I'll be waiting for you.*

But today, especially when Jin said them—*he said he loves you, that he's waiting*—I heard something vaguely sinister.

I love you.

I'm waiting.

A reassurance? Or a threat?

I shake it off. That's not Anton. It was never Anton.

Remember what he confessed to? Not at the end, but before? What he'd done?

A stupid teenage mistake, for which he'd suffered so much guilt. He couldn't have foreseen the consequences, which really did have nothing to do with him.

Am I sure?

I'm struggling to make sense of the messages, half reassurances, half warnings. What if they're all warnings?

How can "Everything's okay" be a warning?

Even as I think that, I know the answer. They could be false reassurances.

Relax. Everything is okay. Stop worrying. Stop questioning. Stop protesting. Stop fighting.

Words parents use to control children who are refusing to do something. But they're also words that can be used by anyone in a position of control.

Words from a man to a woman.

Words from a husband to a wife.

I squeeze my eyes shut. Stop this. I'm rewriting history. I have known controlling guys, and I ran the other way even if I suspected they didn't *realize* they were being controlling.

Anton never tried to control any part of my life. If I wanted advice, he was there, but otherwise, it was my business, my finances, my inheritance. Before we married, I told him about my parents' trust fund, how anything left at my death reverted to Keith.

"As it should." That's what he said.

When I pressed, he'd only smiled, that crooked smile, a little self-conscious as he said, "I'm not exactly hard up for money, Nic. I might be a mathematician, but I have a sweet side gig."

Stock-market analysis. He'd made a lot in the technology boom, taken his money out at exactly the right time, and invested it wisely.

"I'll sign a prenup," he says. "Just so it's clear."

"No, no."

He pulls me to him in a kiss. "I'm making the call tomorrow."

He'd insisted on a prenup, which said he would make no claim on the trust fund or any of my premarital assets. After the marriage, I quietly changed my will, giving half of my personal assets to him, the remainder to be split between my niece and nephew.

Insisting on a prenup in my favor was *not* the behavior of a controlling man. It was not the behavior of a charming con artist who married a financially comfortable and chronically ill woman. Of course, I'd had to worry about that. But when Anton died, his entire estate went to me, because he'd written a new will, too, and I discovered how right he'd been about his personal finances. He absolutely had not needed my trust fund.

That's one thing about losing a spouse. If they were hiding anything, it's going to come to light, no matter how independently you lived. Local hotel charges on their personal credit card? Abusive porn on their computer? Creditors suddenly banging on the door? Baby mamas showing up with DNA tests? With Anton, there'd been none of that.

He'd been even more organized than me, and I'd found passwords and authorizations to everything tucked in with his will. The most scandalous thing I discovered? An ex sending him nudes until he blocked her. The biggest secret I uncovered? He'd secretly paid college tuition for the two kids Cody had abandoned after leaving his wife for the babysitter, which might be the most on-brand thing Cody ever did.

Anton wasn't a saint. I found a letter from a college girlfriend he'd dumped and hurt. And I found emails from his mother, wanting more contact. He made mistakes. He owned them. He'd kept that letter rather than throw it into the trash. He'd always meant to call his mother more and felt bad when he realized how long it'd been.

Anton was human. But he wasn't controlling, and he wasn't a con artist.

Whatever I'm interpreting from those ghostly messages, that's on me. When he lay dying on that roadside, saying he'd be waiting, I did not for one second hear anything but love in it.

I went upstairs with the excuse that I was tired, and it wasn't purely an excuse. Once I force myself to focus on good memories, I drift off. And I drift off into memory.

I'd been thinking of the past, of Anton's confession, and that is where my sleeping mind goes.

To his confession.

It's three years ago. I'm in a funky little indie coffee shop, where I've taken a table under a display of local artists' work, all of it with yellowing price tags that make me want to buy something. Anton sits across from me. This is our third post-reunion meetup, and I'm giddy with the promise of it. But today Anton isn't his usual cheerful self. He's been quiet and restrained.

A nton leans over the table. "I want to ask you out."
I look around. "You already did."
"No, I mean ask you out on a date."
Is he nervous? He doesn't seem nervous. He seems as if he's already resigned himself to rejection, which makes no sense, because he couldn't have missed the way I waltzed in here, wearing a skirt and heels for a coffee date, my face lighting up when I saw him.
"Go ahead," I say. "I like your odds."
I'm smiling, but his expression doesn't change. He's somber, even dour.
Anton reaches for my hand. "Before I do that, I need to confess something. It's going to change those odds, Nic. And not for the better."
My heart stops. I knew this was too good to be true. *He's* too good to be true.
He's going to tell me that he's moving back out west. Or, worse, that he's married, with some excuse like separation or an open marriage, and no matter how he explains that away, it will be a deal-breaker, as would having him move back across the country. I don't do long-distance relationships, and I sure as hell don't do extramarital affairs.
"We were at your séance," he blurts.
I think I've heard wrong. I must have. These words make no sense. "What?"
"Your séance, with Patrice and Heather. We were there. Me and Cody and Mike." The words come in a rush. "Cody and Mike overheard you guys planning it, and they wanted to stage a haunting for you. I argued but . . ."
He inhales sharply. "They were going to do it anyway, and I went along to keep them in line."

"You . . . were there?"

He nods mournfully, his gaze not meeting mine.

I work it through, remembering and putting the pieces together.

"You heard the story about Samantha and Roddy," I say. "You pretended to be Roddy stalking Sam—"

"Not me. Cody and Mike." He rubs his mouth. "Which is an excuse. I was there, and I didn't stop them."

"Okay." I continue processing his words. I remember we'd heard whispers and footsteps coming from two directions. Cody and Mike.

"And then when Patrice walked off?" I say.

"I didn't realize what was going on at first. We heard you guys calling her, and I thought she freaked out and ran into the forest. I made the guys stop, and I went after her. When I saw her, I whistled, so you'd find her."

His head drops further. "Fuck. I should have done more than whistle. I should have helped you with Patrice. I was a coward, Nic. Too chickenshit to stop my friends. Too chickenshit to warn you when I couldn't stop them. Too chickenshit to step up, let you see it was me and help with Patrice. I look back now, and I'm so fucking ashamed of myself."

I say nothing.

After a moment, he continues, his voice hoarse. "After . . . what happened. The second time. I had to come clean. I told my parents what we did the first time. I wanted to go to the police, but my parents said it wouldn't help. I wasn't there the night *it* happened. Cody and Mike weren't either—we'd all gone to a movie. What we did that first time was wrong, but we had nothing to do with what happened later, and my parents said if we went to the police, they might turn it around and find a way to blame us for the rest."

I nod, silently, still working it through.

His gaze rises, finally meeting mine. "I still should have gone to the police. Yes, we weren't there the night . . ." He swallows. "The night you went back. I wish I had been. I wish to God I had been. But my parents were wrong that we had nothing to do with it. If we hadn't played that stupid prank, Patrice might never have gotten it into her head that she was possessed, that Roddy or whatever got into her. We set into motion the chain of events that led to what happened, and I have never forgiven myself for that."

When I look into his eyes, I know he believes what he's saying. To him, the answer is obvious—they caused what happened to Patrice. But it's not that simple. I remember that night, the noises and voices Heather and I heard, how we'd looked over at Patrice, and she hadn't seemed to even hear them.

Yes, Anton should have warned us that his friends planned to fake a haunting. But teens are notorious for poor choices. Anton decided the best course of action was to accompany Cody and Mike to monitor them. Wasn't that the same reason I went? To monitor my friends while they did something stupid because I didn't know how to stop them from doing it?

His whistle had brought us to Patrice. I can wish he'd done more, but we'd been able to handle it after that. He'd stayed in the shadows out of fear. To him, their fake haunting had sent Patrice running into the woods, and he didn't dare admit he was there.

In that coffee shop, I saw the anguish he still felt after nearly two decades. That told me the sort of person he was, and that's when I decided I didn't want a date with him . . . I wanted more.

Yes, Anton had picked shitty friends, but we'd both been at that age where we needed friends and we could make bad choices.

His parents stopped him from confessing, and now he can look back and say he should have gone to the police, but what sixteen-year-old would do that? His parents convinced him that their prank hadn't caused the rest, and he desperately wanted to believe that.

If their prank *did* influence what came later, it was an unforeseeable consequence. Anton wasn't there the second time we went into the forest. He had nothing to do with that.

Now, sitting on the bed, picturing him in that booth, I remember how I'd been struck by his guilt and remorse. . . .

I'd been struck by the depth of it. Such regret for a mistake his friends would have long forgotten. I'd taken it as a sign he was a good man, empathetic and compassionate.

But what if there was a reason his guilt outweighed his crime?

The night he died, lying on the roadside, when he said he had something to confess, my gut had seized, not wanting to hear it, afraid . . .

Afraid there was more to the story than what he told me in that coffee shop.

On that roadside, had he seemed to hesitate? To pause and then confess to something sweet, admitting he hadn't hired me by accident?

What if he'd been about to say something else? Something about that night, and then he stopped himself and changed direction?

What had he really been about to say?

I take a shower after that. With everything that happened this morning, I'd skipped mine, and now I really need it. A hot shower and plenty of soap, enough to scrub any traitorous thoughts from my brain.

I'm in the shower long enough for the water to run cold. Then I grab a towel, about to step out when I stop myself. The shower has handrails for people with mobility issues, and I use those and then I dry myself off completely. I don't step on the bath mat. I don't walk with wet feet. I am taking no chances.

I dress quickly and head for the bedroom door, suddenly eager for company. I throw it open, step out, and . . .

I don't slip, per se. It's like before, when I stepped on the rug and overcorrected. But there's something under my stockinged foot that slides, and I grab the doorway as if I stepped on a banana peel.

I look down to see . . .

There are ashes on the floor. A scattering of ashes right outside my door.

My brain short-circuits, and my breath stops. All I can see is me carrying the box with Anton's ashes, being careless with it, the lid somehow opening and cremains falling.

Except the cremains are downstairs. I forgot to bring them up again.

Did someone else touch them? Was someone careless with my husband's remains?

Braced against the wall, I gently remove the sock that slipped as I try not to think of what I stepped on, the horror of that almost as terrible as the horror of my thoughts twenty minutes ago, wondering whether Anton had anything to do with the tragedy from our past.

As I bend, though, a smell hits me. I have no idea what cremains smell like and no interest in finding out, but what I do smell is familiar. It's a smell I never thought I'd recognize, and yet I do.

It's the mushrooms. Those damn mushrooms Heather said she'd brought back from Cuba.

I bend closer, holding my breath so I don't inhale, which makes it hard to get a sniff. I don't need that sniff. My brain tells me what it is even when I try to argue that my senses are affected by the dream.

I dreamed of the séance with the mushrooms. Now I think I smell them.

It's definitely not cremains, though. These are flakes and bits of plant matter, not ashes.

"Nic?"

I look up as Shania crests the stairs.

"Are you okay?" she says as she rushes forward. Then she must realize I'm only crouched, not sprawled on the floor, and she slows. Her gaze goes to the hardwood.

"What's that?" she says, flicking on a light. Before I can answer, she says, "Oh."

I open my mouth to say it's not cremains, but she lowers her voice and whispers, "Dr. Cirillo doesn't take off his shoes."

I frown, trying to make the connection.

She gives a half smile. "Americans, right? I've already cleaned up mud in the kitchen that he tracked in. He must have been wandering around the gardens."

I look down at the flakes and bits. Shania thinks it's detritus Cirillo brought in on his shoes. Except it's all in front of my bedroom door. To leave a mess right here, he'd need to stand outside my closed door.

But it *does* make sense that it's organic matter from outdoors, tracked in on shoes. I take a closer look. Flakes and lumps that suggest a decayed spring garden.

But that smell?

Mushrooms are dried plant matter, just like this. That's what I must be smelling.

"Nic?"

I look up.

"Is everything okay?" Shania asks.

No, everything is not okay. I'm dreaming of a past séance. I'm questioning my husband's role in it and questioning the communications I might be receiving from him now.

I smile and tug my sock back on. "Everything's fine. That nap was just what the doctor ordered, but now I'm in need of coffee and sugar. Are there any of your Nanaimo bars left?"

She perks up. "There are. I think Jin and Dr. Castillo find them too sweet."

"Not possible. Let's go get some caffeine and sugar."

TWENTY

Shania and I eat our snack in the kitchen, leaning against the counter and talking. Jin hears conversation and joins us in the coffee, but takes an apple instead of the sweet bars. At some point, Shania slips off to take a call from work, and Jin and I keep talking. Then Keith calls Jin, and I get out of there fast.

I'd phoned Keith earlier, but he'd clearly wanted more details than I gave, and I'm not sticking around to be pulled into that. I'm trying to forget what happened upstairs—with the dream and flakes on the floor—and talking to my brother is guaranteed to yank that back.

Jin is the kind of person who brightens any room he's in, which makes him an excellent partner for my brother. Keith has a gravitas that always makes me painfully aware of anything I'm trying hard to ignore. Like when, as a kid, I'd do something wrong, and just having Keith in the room somehow drove me to confess. It was like having our own resident black-frocked priest.

As Jin talks to Keith, I catch snatches of their conversation, Jin's voice light and teasing, and then dropping as he tells Keith he misses him. I move away, partly to give them privacy, but also partly because, while I'm thrilled that my brother has found someone, it hurts listening to them. All I can think of are my phone calls with Anton, when he'd been away at conferences, how I'd long to hear his voice and then chastise myself for acting like a schoolgirl getting a call from her crush. After all, he'd only be gone for a few days.

And then he'd be back.

I grab two fresh cups of coffee and go in search of Cirillo. I'd heard him in the hall, but he'd veered off, as if not wanting to disturb my conversation with Jin. Now I wonder whether he'd been coming to grab his own afternoon caffeine, and I feel bad if we'd kept him from that.

I think he'll be in the breakfast nook, which he seems to have commandeered as his office. When I don't find him there, I check the sitting room. He's not there or in the living room, which I passed through, along with the dining room.

I'm circling back to the kitchen when I spot him in the back gardens. Taking advantage of the bug diminishment. I should do the same. I've been mentally snarling like a caged lion, and now that it's nearly bug-free and a sunny twenty degrees, I should be outside, basking like a lizard in the sunshine.

I return to the kitchen to grab a couple of apples and a small tray. At the door, I remove my socks.

I slip out the breakfast-nook door into the gardens. I literally get one step outside before a midge smacks into my face. Hey, I did say *nearly* bug-free. I blow the bug from my face, take another step and—

"—really have something here," Cirillo is saying.

I perk up, thinking he's talking to me. Then I see the back of his head and the phone against his ear.

"I'm serious," he says. "We not only seem to have made contact with her husband, but there's something else here, too. I can't describe it."

My eyes narrow. This is supposed to be a private and confidential séance.

I slip back into the shadows and keep listening.

"No, actually, I *can* describe it," Cirillo says. "I just don't like to because it makes me sound like a carnival clairvoyant. There's something dark here, a negative force. Oppressing. A dark force watching and waiting, like a vulture waiting for its prey to die." He gives a short laugh. "God, did I really just say that?"

He pauses, as if listening.

"Dangerous? No. Spirits are never dangerous. This one reminds me of the Moorehouse case."

I lift my phone and silently tap in "Moorehouse case ghost" but nothing comes up.

Cirillo continues, "I've never forgotten what that boy's spirit felt like. Malevolent. Accidental shooting, my ass. Someone put that kid down like a rabid dog."

I add more search terms. Still nothing.

"That's what I felt here," Cirillo continues. "A malevolent spirit. But the guy we're summoning is just a regular joe, volunteered with disadvantaged youth on the weekends, for Christ's sake."

Pause.

"Yes, I know that could have been a cover, but my point is that *something* is here. The wife and her brother-in-law are having experiences, and both are definitely skeptics. No one's hearing pipes creak and calling it spectral footsteps."

He listens for a few minutes. Then he says, "I should go. I think I hear voices. Someone might be coming out."

He hangs up. I move from the shadows, quietly set down the tray, and wait. Cirillo turns, pocketing his phone. He sees me, standing with my arms crossed, and gives a start.

"Done with your call?" I say.

Guilt creeps into his gaze before he straightens with the air of a man who refuses to feel guilty for such things. I'm still struggling to get a read on Davos Cirillo. He comes off as pleasant, mild-mannered, and passionate about his work. Every now and then, though, there's steel in Cirillo's gaze and in his words, and I get the sense that if I mistake him for a mild-mannered professor, I've fallen into a trap that is to his benefit.

Maybe he really is pleasant and mostly mild-mannered, but it also serves his purpose, making us snap to attention when his voice and manner firm. It leaves me feeling like we're his grad students—he's fine with letting us do our thing until we forget who's in charge.

"Yes, I was eavesdropping," I say as I take my coffee and apple from the tray. "I would have walked away, except that the first words I heard were you excitedly telling someone that we've made contact, when you assured me this was a private session with all data to be used anonymously."

I meet his gaze. "When did that change? When you realized my dead husband might actually be here?"

"Ouch." He tries for a smile. "You don't pull your punches, do you?"

"Oh, I haven't even started. I have all our correspondence, in writing, with your assurance of anonymity. This is scientific data only. I don't know whether you're trying to change that, Davos, but if you do, you'll see how well I can throw my punches."

He lifts his hands. "I yield. Nothing has changed. You didn't hear me use names, right? It's all still anonymous."

"So why were you excitedly calling someone about our sessions?"

He makes a face and settles into a patio chair. "Because of the boring side of research. Funding." He looks up. "Your husband was a mathematician. A university professor? I don't know much about math, so maybe grants aren't a thing there."

"Grants are always a thing in academia."

A faint smile. "Then you might understand what it means when I say I'm in danger of losing my funding. My expenses are low, but they exist, and since I'm hardly discovering a cure for CF, it's difficult for me to get funding, and rightfully so."

"Okay."

"If I'm excited about what I have here, it's because success would help me secure funding."

"You should have told me that."

"It will still be anonymous data, Nicola. The person you heard me talking to is the department head, who is also a friend and supporter. He knows nothing specific about you or your husband."

"I mean that if you need funding, and success here would help you secure it, then you aren't as unbiased as I needed you to be."

"I am." He meets my gaze. "Because I'm a scientist and, yes, there is always a bias toward proving what we set out to prove, but in a field like mine, the worst thing I could do is inflate the data. There are professors in my own department looking for an excuse to discredit me. They consider me an embarrassment to the college. I'm excited because the most I expected was possible signs of contact, and I have much more."

"A malevolent spirit."

He stops short, as if just realizing I'd heard that.

I continue, "You said it wasn't a second ghost."

"I said it wasn't an ordinary ghost, meaning we didn't accidentally summon some ancestor of Anton's who died in this house and wants us to pass on a message. When you think of contacting someone like Anton, that is a ghost. When you think of a haunting, that is what I call a spirit. The difference is twofold. One, the intent— whether to communicate or to frighten. Two, whether it has been summoned . . . or comes of its own accord."

"So you think Anton is here as a ghost, but there's a malevolent spirit, too, which your department head suggested could also be Anton."

He makes a face and gives a dismissive wave. "It's not."

I want to pursue that, but I don't dare speak the words. They're a betrayal of my husband. Whatever "dark spirit" is here, it's not Anton. It can't be.

Can't it?

"Tell me about the Moorehouse case," I say.

He sighs.

"Since you used a name, I presume *they* didn't require anonymity," I add.

I get a sour look for that, but he says, "No, they did not. Still, the family never went public, so there's a limit to how much I'm willing to say, particularly now that you have their surname."

I grudgingly respect that. He's protecting his source even if they didn't demand anonymity.

I take a seat and pass him his coffee and apple.

"Oh, so I've earned these now?" he says.

"Nah, it's a bribe for the basics of the Moorehouse case. Also, the coffee is probably cold by now."

"Well, so is this case." He glances at me and sighs. "Fine, my sense of humor needs work."

"Never said it, Doc."

He opens his mouth as if to say something, and then sips his coffee instead. He takes a bigger swig before putting it on the table. "The Moorehouse case was a sad one. The family lost their fifteen-year-old son in a shooting."

Accidental shooting, my ass. Someone put that kid down like a rabid dog.

Cirillo continues, "The family became convinced that their son's ghost was haunting them. They thought he was tormented because his killer hadn't been caught, and so his ghost was acting out in desperation."

"And . . ."

"And I encountered the very malevolent spirit of their son, who was not the sweet and gentle soul they'd made him out to be. I later discovered that the boy had a police record for torturing cats, and two young women had taken out restraining orders against him. He was charged with the assault of a third young woman, which was still before the courts when he died."

"Huh."

"Yes, so this was not a poor soul seeking justice. It was the angry spirit of a disturbed and dangerous young man. Except, in death, his target became his family."

"What did he do?"

Cirillo settles into his seat. "Typical haunting manifestations. Mostly frightening his family with noises. There was one incident of a push on a staircase, but it was a light shove, barely causing a stumble."

"Like what I experienced. As if the spirit managed to make physical contact, but not enough to cause serious harm."

"Yes. The family was never in any real danger, which is why I haven't insisted we leave. You are, of course, welcome to do so if this new information changes that, though I hope it won't."

Yeah, you hope that because your funding is on the line.

Cirillo is not an unbiased observer.

Am I?

No. I am not.

I can't even truly say he was unbiased before I found out about the funding concerns. Science is about proving a theory. Evidence that disproves a theory is valuable, but it's never going to be the result the researchers hope for.

So what do I do? Tell Shania, who will follow my lead? Tell Jin, who'd be trapped between me and my brother if I decided to stay? Tell Keith, who would come and drag me out of here if I even hinted that a ghost made me stumble on the stairs?

"So far, no one else has had a negative experience. If they do, we'll leave. I can accept risk for myself. I won't accept it on behalf of Shania or Jin."

"Fair enough," he says.

I see the relief on his face, and I know that should worry me.

He's not impartial. He doesn't have my best interests in mind.

I shake it off. He's a professional, and I need to trust him.

TWENTY-ONE

I'm back in the sitting room, lost in my thoughts. Have I made the right choice? Am I endangering others?

"Any thoughts, Anton?" I whisper. "Knock twice if I'm making a mistake."

Silence.

"Knock once if I'm not?" I say.

Silence.

"Okay, do nothing if you just don't give a shit."

Silence.

I shoot a thumbs-up to the empty room. "Got it."

I settle in, letting my eyes half close. I'm drifting into my thoughts when I catch sight of one of the dolls. It hasn't moved—thankfully. It just snags my free-floating mind, lost somewhere between past and present. It's a plain-looking doll, with straight brown hair and a dress that seems as if it belongs to another, fancier doll. It reminds me of Heather, her brown hair always parted down the middle, her outfits trying for an artistic flair that—I hate to admit this—always made it seem as if she'd raided an artsy sibling's closet.

I'm staring at that doll, and my mind drifts again. The doll becomes

Heather, trudging into the forest for a second séance, casting anxious glances back at me.

Once again, I don't know what to do, and I hate that. I feel as if I made a mistake the first time by agreeing to the séance, and yet if I hadn't, they'd have done it without me, to the same result, only without me to help get Patrice out of the forest.

Now I'm back in the same position, and part of me is screaming that I'm making the same mistake, and part is screaming back that I'm still not sure I *did* make a mistake.

No, I did. I made the mistake of not telling my parents what happened. I'd been afraid. Not of what they'd do—my mom and dad were great. But when you have parents you actually respect, you're afraid of disappointing them.

And what *had* I done, really? Supervised my friends with a relatively mild bit of drug experimentation? My parents wouldn't be concerned about the séance part. Kids will be kids, and my parents were rational people who recognized things like "dark entities" as irrational. Their entire focus would be on the drugs.

I should have confessed *because* of the drugs. Because something is wrong with Patrice, and I'm withholding vital information from her doctor.

I'll fix that. I swear I will. I'll tell my parents, who will tell Patrice's family. I can even swipe a sample of the mushrooms tonight.

There. That's a reason for coming, right? To get that sample?

"What do you think is going on?" Heather whispers as we walk.

I want to glare at her. After we promised Patrice we'd do this, I'd tried to talk to Heather. We had time then, without Patrice around to hear. Heather didn't want to talk about it, just like she's refused to discuss any of it for the past fucking week.

We're trudging through a dark forest, five feet behind Patrice, and *now* Heather wants to talk?

"Nic?" Heather whispers.

I can't answer. Patrice is too close. I slow my steps, thinking Patrice will notice, but she's marching on like she did that night, as if we aren't even there.

Finally I deem her far enough away.

"I don't know," I whisper to Heather. "I think it's a bad trip."

"Lasting this long?"

I say nothing.

Heather whispers, "What about the voices? The footsteps? Roddy's ghost was there."

Was it? At the time, it seemed obvious that we'd conjured the ghost of Roddy, come searching for his Sam. But since then, doubt has crept in.

Did we really hear anything? And if we did, are we sure it was a ghost? The longer I thought about it, the more it felt like a prank.

The adult me rouses from the memory then. Had I really thought this at the time? Or was that my current knowledge rewriting history?

No, I *had* thought it. At that moment, in that forest, my gut had told me the truth. That "Roddy" had been fake.

I hesitate, torn between mulling over that and returning to the memory, so vivid it's like I'm watching a reenactment.

Go back. There are answers there. Go back.

If you dare.

That last part does it, as if my inner voice is my child self, knowing exactly which button to press.

I sink back into the memory.

Heather has just mentioned the voices and footsteps from the first séance, and I shrug and mutter, "I don't know."

"Something happened to Patrice," she hisses. "You know it did."

"Then I'm hoping this will help. The drugs made her hallucinate that something got into her—Roddy's ghost or whatever—and she believes this ceremony will send it back. That's the power of sug-gestion. She thinks it happened, so this time, we convince her it un-happens."

Heather doesn't answer, but I'm on a roll, so certain I have all the answers.

"If it fails," I say, "then it's the drugs, and we tell her parents. We need to do that. For her own sake."

"It's not drugs," she whispers.

"You don't know what caused—"

"The mushrooms aren't drugs."

I sigh. "Fine. They're 'organic' or whatever. Still—"

"They're not drugs," she hisses. "They're just regular store-bought mushrooms. Dried ones for cooking."

"What?"

My voice goes high enough that her eyes round in alarm, but up ahead, Patrice doesn't seem to notice. It's as if we could stop walking, and she'd just keep marching through the forest.

"I made it up," Heather whispers. "Not the séance stuff in Cuba, but the woman giving us mushrooms and me bringing them back."

"You what?"

"The cousins said they had used mushrooms once, and it helped with a séance. I knew Patrice really wanted to try something, and mushrooms are natural, so I figured that was safe enough. I planned to buy some from Freddie, but when I asked, he laughed at me. So I had to improvise."

"With store-bought dried mushrooms?" I would have laughed if my brain weren't spinning. If Patrice didn't take any drugs . . .

"It's not a bad trip," Heather says, "and she didn't drink enough wine to be drunk. I *know* we heard Roddy. You know it, too. It's because we did the séance where they died, and because you let Patrice change the wording of the summoning."

"I *let* her change it?"

"I said it wasn't a good idea, and you never backed me up. She actually summoned Roddy, Nic, and now she's possessed, and we're alone in the forest with her, while she's possessed by the spirit of a crazed killer."

I bite my tongue not to laugh at how ridiculous she sounds.

"I really don't think it was actually Roddy," I whisper.

"Well, she's possessed by *something*. Have you seen her eyes? Have you seen the way she shakes? Everyone thinks she's sick. Only she's not sick in her body. It's in her head. Just like her aunt."

My jaw sets. There's a twist in Heather's voice, as if Patrice's aunt Lori were a raging lunatic locked in a padded room instead of a woman dealing with the horror of seeing a violent tragedy. I have relatives with mental illness, and we don't talk about them that way.

"What are you two whispering about back there?" Patrice says, startling us.

She's standing ten feet away, lit only by my flashlight beam.

"Just talking," Heather calls back in an unsteady voice.

"Well, stop. Especially if you're talking about me. This was your idea, Heather, doing that séance and bringing those mushrooms. I've been trying not to blame you for what's happening."

"What *is* happening?" I say. "Can you talk about it? So we understand?"

Patrice just wheels and marches onward. Heather leans in, as if to keep whispering, but I break into a jog to catch up to Patrice. She must hear my footfalls—and see my wildly bouncing flashlight beam—but she just keeps moving at the same pace.

"Patrice?" I say, my voice lower. "If we had some idea what was going on, we could help."

"You *are* helping. By sending it back."

"Sending what back?"

She doesn't answer, just moves faster as if she can lose me that way. I pick up speed.

"Patrice?" I say. "Please. You're going through something, and I want to know what it is."

No answer.

"Patrice? If I've done something—"

She spins so fast I jump.

Fever-bright eyes fix on mine. "I don't know. *Have* you done something?"

"If I did, I'm sorry."

"It wasn't you. I know who it was." She looks over my shoulder. "Traitor."

"What?" I say.

Patrice resumes walking. I fall back to Heather and lower my voice. "Does she know about the mushrooms?"

"I think you're right, Nic," Heather says, voice hardening. "This is all bullshit. An act."

"Are you going to pretend you don't know what I'm talking about?" Patrice says. "He's the one who started it, but you're blaming me. Your guy messes around with me, and I'm the one you cut loose while he gets off scot-free."

Heather's face scrunches up. "What the hell are you talking about?"

"Has everyone lost their fucking minds?" I look between them as my mind races. "Is this about Cody? Heather, did you and Cody have a thing before—"

Her look of disgust answers before she says, "Absolutely not. I seriously have no idea what she's talking about."

Something cracks in the forest. Heather wheels toward it.

"Did you hear that?" she says.

"Roddy," Patrice whispers.

"It isn't Roddy," I snap. "We're in the forest, and that's a goddamn forest animal. I want to know what the hell you are going on about, Patrice."

Patrice ignores me and resumes walking.

I seethe and turn to Heather. "What is this bullshit?"

She flails a wild shrug. I want to storm out of this forest. Say to hell with both of them and their drama because, seriously? Something is very wrong with Patrice, and they're sniping about *boys*?

Unless Heather is right. Unless nothing is wrong with Patrice. Unless this is part of the drama. Patrice likes a boy—presumably

Cody, though the thought makes my skin crawl. She thinks Heather has been messing around with him, so she's pulling some weird séance shit to scare us.

If that's it, I'm done. I don't have time for this bullshit.

But am I leaving right now? No. Keith is the uber-responsible one, but whatever he was taught, I was taught too. I might rebel, but at heart, I know the right thing and I do it.

My gut says that the right thing is to see this through. Play referee. Make sure it doesn't get out of hand. If these two are at each other's throats—even over a boy—I need to stick around.

We reach the spot. Heather yanks out the blanket and slaps it down, along with the chalices. She sloshes in wine and then—as she sprinkles harmless mushroom powder on hers and Patrice's—she looks at me, her jaw set.

What the hell is that look for? Defying me to say the mushrooms are just regular fungi? I don't give a shit. In fact, if anything *is* wrong with Patrice, it's in everyone's best interests for Patrice to think the drugs are real. The power of suggestion. We are repeating the ritual exactly, and that will "fix" her.

I am so done with this fucking bullshit.

I drop to the ground hard, and if I'm scowling like a toddler, I don't care. So is Heather. Patrice just keeps glaring at her, and Heather glares back, and fuck my life. Really? Keith should be here to see this, get a laugh out of his little sister needing to be the mature one for once.

"Well, go on," Heather says to Patrice. "Summon the ghosts or whatever. If you're not too *possessed* to do that."

Patrice only looks at her, and it's less glare than stare now. A stare so cold it curdles my anger and has me rubbing down goose bumps.

She starts her incantation, but this time, I can't make out what she's saying. I struggle to concentrate on words so garbled, it's like she's talking through a mouthful of marshmallow.

Something isn't right. It's not right at all.

She's faking it.

Drama club kid.

Drama queen.

We're all kneeling when Heather yelps and falls back, braced on one arm. I twist to see her staring into the forest, her eyes wide.

"D-did you see that?"

She's looking over my shoulder, so no, I didn't see it, and my righteous anger licks back. Heather is playing Patrice's game, except Patrice isn't paying any attention, meaning I'm the one she's spooking, and I'm not having it.

Except . . .

Except Heather's not this good an actor. She's staring over my shoulder in what looks like genuine fear.

When I don't respond, she yanks her attention back and rolls her shoulders. "Never mind," she says, snapping off the words. "I was kidding. I didn't see anything."

Patrice is still reciting her incantation. She never stopped. Never even faltered. Her gaze is straight ahead, face blank, those garbled words—

Heather yelps again, and this time, I see it. A dark shape darts through the forest. I grab my flashlight and shine it into the woods.

"You saw that, right?" Heather whispers.

I nod grimly. "Some asshole is out there."

"But I don't hear anything. They're not making any noise, Nic. They should make some noise. Footsteps or twigs cracking."

Her voice rises as she speaks, and I resist the urge to snap at her. Instead, I turn on Patrice.

"Shut up so we can hear—" I begin.

Patrice isn't there. She's on her feet, still reciting that indecipherable incantation, her notes left by her chalice as she walks into the forest.

"Not this shit again," I say, scrambling up, flashlight in hand. "I'll get her."

I stride after Patrice. She's ten feet away, stepping into the forest. I can see her in my flashlight beam. Just march over, grab her by the arm, and haul her ass back into the clearing.

But the moment she steps into the forest, shadows swallow her, and I falter, blinking. Then I give my head an angry shake. She walked behind some bushes. That's all.

I pick up my pace, and when I step into the clearing, I spot bushes. See? Everything is fine. I'm just letting myself get spooked by their bullshit.

I'm done. Really am. Finishing this and getting out.

That's my mantra as I march into the pitch-black forest, flashlight outstretched before me.

Done, done, done.

Instead of stopping to question why I can't see Patrice, I take it as further proof that this is all teenage drama. Fake séance. Fake bad trip after taking fake drugs. The point is that it's all fake, and once I haul her ass back, I'm done, and—

A hand slams between my shoulders. It's so sudden and unexpected that I sail off my feet, and the flashlight flies from my hand. It hits the ground, and the forest falls into darkness.

TWENTY-TWO

I scramble up. My lungs scream from that blow, and my CF-trained brain interprets it as difficulty breathing, panics, and holds my muscles hostage. *Stay still. Catch your breath. Nothing is ever as important as breathing.* The other part screams that someone just hit me, and I sure as hell can't stand there catching my breath.

By the time I wheel, my attacker could have taken me down, and I'm very aware of that, my brain shrieking at me.

I need to be better than this. I can't let anything slow me down, freak me out. Once I start allowing that, I will never stop. I can't think of how long I have to live, can't listen to speculation about my life span, can't imagine what it would be like to die because I can no longer breathe, because my body has betrayed me, because it has been betraying me since I was born.

My body is not the enemy. It did not betray me. My body and I are enduring this disease together, and that body does so much for me. In that moment, I need to focus on what it *can* do.

What it can do is spin, fists ready, self-defense lessons flying back.

But there's no one to hit. Nothing to fight. It's so dark that some-one could be right there, laughing at me—

No, I see dim shapes. Trees and bushes, enough to know nobody is there.

I stop breathing and listen. The forest has gone silent, and I can't hear anyone moving. No one is—

There! Off to my left. A twig crack, a rustle, someone on the move, but not near me. Heading back to the clearing.

I run to where I think the flashlight fell, but the thick undergrowth hides it. I smack around, hoping to touch down on plastic, but when I don't, all I can think about is that someone is walking toward the clearing where Heather waits.

The irrational part of me panics with thoughts of Heather, alone and frightened while there is someone in this forest, someone who hit me, and I need to get back to Heather before she's hurt.

The rational part insists that the sounds are Patrice heading back to the clearing after smacking me, and that my real concern should be that they'll argue and Heather will stomp off and drive home, leaving me behind.

Either way, I take two more seconds to find the flashlight, and when I don't, I head for the clearing, waving my arms in front of me so I don't smack into a tree.

"Samantha!"

I stop, stumbling over my feet. The voice came from my left, in the direction of those footsteps. It's not the male voice from last week. It sounds like Patrice, but it's so raw and hoarse I can barely make out words.

"I know you're out here!" she shouts. "Don't think I won't find you! I can smell you, bitch."

I stand there, frozen. Then I take a slow step backward. When I strike a tree trunk, I clap both hands over my mouth before I yelp.

"You are never getting out of here," she yells. "I will cut you open, and I will gut you."

Hands still over my mouth, I force my feet to move, slowly, not daring to crunch down on anything.

Get to Heather. Get her out of here. Call the police. Send them back for Patrice.

But what if this is all part of Patrice's prank?

I don't give a shit. I don't care if it's a prank and Patrice tells everyone I called the cops, and they all think I'm a very silly girl. Fuck them.

I keep moving, step by careful—

"N–no," Heather's voice sounds, sharp with alarm. "It's me. It's just me. I—"

She screams, and it is a sound I will never forget, an animal cry of terror and pain.

I break into a run. I'm charging toward the sound of Heather's voice, and she is screaming, and I am running blindly through the forest when I smack headlong into a tree so hard it knocks me back.

I stagger and keep upright, but I'm woozy, confused. Blood pours from my nose, into my open mouth, and I spit, doubling over. Blood spatters the bushes, and for a moment, I stare, transfixed.

Then I remember why I was running.

I stagger forward, my wispy thoughts refusing to stitch into coherence. When I catch movement, relief floods me.

"Heather," I breathe.

Only it's not Heather. It's just a shadow, darting through the trees. I start to follow it.

No, remember Heather. You heard her scream.

Only she's not screaming now.

When I pause, a whimper cuts through the quiet.

Heather.

I stumble toward her, and then my thoughts mend and my feet find their footing, and I break into a jog.

I follow the whimpers, and as I do, I'm not even sure I'm hearing a person, much less Heather. It's such a soft sound, like some woodland baby critter abandoned by its mother, trying hard to keep silent but unable to suppress those little sounds.

I keep going.

When I reach the clearing, I come out of the trees so fast, I nearly topple again. One minute my hands are moving from tree to tree, and then there's nothing.

I catch my balance and squint. It's so damn dark. There must be a moon somewhere, but it's covered along with the stars, and I can't see—

A soft sound, like the exhale of breath.

I blink hard, and then I see a figure in a pink hoodie on the ground.

"Heather," I whisper.

I run forward and drop beside her, only to realize I'm at her back. She's on her side, fetal position, arms and legs drawn in, and she's whimpering, ever so softly. Whimpering and shaking.

"Heather?" I touch her shoulder, and she jerks and lets out a mewling sound.

"It's me," I whisper. "Nic. You're okay. I'm here."

I'm crawling up near her head when she says something I don't catch.

I stop and lean toward her as I listen.

"Don't understand," she whispers. "I don't understand. I . . ."

She trails off in a long, slow exhalation. And then she stops shaking.

I scramble around to the front of her. I can just make out her face, pulled down toward her chest. Both arms are drawn in protectively, her knees up.

"Heather?" I whisper.

No answer. She's passed out. Did she get hit in the head? I don't see any other sign of injury, but it's so damn dark I can barely make out anything.

Then the smell hits.

I know that smell, even if I'm too flustered to identify it immediately. It reminds me of babysitting the neighbors' baby at our old house and—

The smell of soiled diapers. Of piss and shit.

And something else. Something less familiar. Coppery and—

Blood.

I smell piss and shit and blood.

I grab one of Heather's hands and pull it away from her chest, and it's red. Soaked so red that my brain refuses to believe it's blood. It's a prank, someone squeezing out a whole bottle of ketchup.

Then I see what she's been covering, and I fall back, retching. I squeeze my eyes shut, but that only sears the image against my eyelids.

Blood and muscle and . . . and more.

Intestines. I'd seen her intestines.

I will cut you open, and I will gut you.

No. I'm hallucinating. The mushrooms—

I didn't take the mushrooms.

Heather must have given them to me, and I didn't notice.

But the mushrooms weren't actual drugs.

They must have been. Goddamn it, this is not real. It cannot be real. Heather is lying here, holding in her own—

I retch and fall onto all fours, puking everything I have into the grass.

I hit my head, right? On that tree? Or when someone struck me from behind. They must have hit me in the head, too, and I forgot it because I'm unconscious. Unconscious and having a nightmare.

A twig cracks.

My head shoots up.

Patrice.

Where the fuck is Patrice?

I crawl back to Heather and put my hands to her neck, checking for a pulse.

Seriously? You think she's still alive?

But she had been, when I arrived.

I remember her last words. *I don't understand.*

Oh, God, Heather, neither do I, and I really hope I'm dreaming or hallucinating or *something*.

A whisper, and it's only the wind, but it makes my head jerk up, my heart pounding, reminding me that whoever did this to Heather is still out there.

Whoever did this?

Patrice did this. You heard her screaming that she was going to find and gut Heather.

I push to my feet and wobble before I grit my teeth. I need to get it together.

No, I need to get it together *and* get the hell out of here. If this is real—*you know it's real*—then I need to get out of here before Heather's killer—*you know it's Patrice*—finds me.

Again, movement catches my eye. I spin. Was that a shadow?

Run, Nic. Run now.

I stifle the urge. Run, and I will smash into another tree. Run, and I won't hear anyone coming after me.

I pause to orient myself. We came into the woods from that direction. The school is over there.

I take a second to listen, but everything has gone silent again. I start walking, quiet and careful until I reach the path. Then I pick up speed, my ears trained for the slightest sound.

I want to run. God, I want to run like I have never run in my life.

Walk. Breathe. Listen.

I keep going, blood pounding in my ears.

Blood on my hands. Heather's blood on—

Stop that.

I will cut you open, and I will gut you.

That's what Patrice did. Exactly what she did. Cut Heather open and gutted her.

I don't understand.

Tears prick my eyes, which fill until I can't see and I have to blink to clear them. Blood and tears and snot run down my face.

None of that. Break down later. I need all my senses and all my *sense* to get out of this forest.

Just keep—

I stumble over something on the path. I've been so hyperaware of what's ahead—as much as I can see it in this goddamn darkness— that I haven't looked down, and I've tripped over a root or a branch or . . .

An arm. I've tripped over an outstretched arm. An arm with a worn friendship bracelet around the wrist.

Patrice's arm. The bracelet Heather gave her years ago.

That's when I see blood. It covers the hand, and I follow it up her arm to see her lying on her stomach, limbs splayed.

"Patrice?"

What the fuck are you doing? Run!

I step over her hand and then turn around to walk backward, continuing along the path as I keep my gaze on her. There's more blood spattering the undergrowth and on her light shirt and a cut on her collar, dripping blood.

She's hurt.

She didn't kill Heather. She's another victim of whoever did.

Patrice groans, and I move forward. I'm about to drop to my knees beside her when I see her other hand, the right one stretched out with something lying right beside it.

A *knife* lying right beside it. A hunting knife with its blade coated in blood.

"Nic?" Patrice mumbles.

Her head rises. "Nic? Is that you?"

I don't answer. I just take a slow step back.

"Please," she whispers. "I'm hurt. Help me."

Trap!

My brain screams the word so loud I expect her to hear it.

"Nic? Please?"

Her gaze locks with mine as her fingers inch toward the knife handle.

"Nic? Help me."

Her fingertips graze the knife. I wheel and run.

TWENTY-THREE

I jolt from the memory, gasping, my heart pounding as if I'm six-teen again and running through that forest like the demons of hell are on my tail.

Not demons.

Just my best friend.

One of them, at least. The other lay dead in a clearing.

I rub my hands over my face.

There was no near-death conclusion to that tale, where I reached safety just as Patrice grabbed for me. She never caught up with me that night. I'm not even sure how hard she tried, because after I glanced over my shoulder once, I never looked back again.

The police found her wandering through the forest, raving about Sam and Roddy. Her injuries seemed self-inflicted, including the cut on her collarbone, as if she'd tried to emulate Roddy's suicide.

I don't remember a lot of what happened afterward, only that I was interviewed over and over by the police.

Was I ever tempted to fudge the truth and be absolutely clear that Patrice killed Heather so she didn't escape justice? Yes, but I told the truth.

I repeated what I heard shouted in the woods. I also told them that the voice had been hoarse, and so I couldn't say with absolute certainty it was Patrice. I told them what I heard Heather say.

"N-no. It's me. It's just me. I—"

She did not indicate who she was speaking to. I did not see Patrice in that clearing with Heather. Before her death, Heather never spoke Patrice's name. She only said those three words.

I don't understand.

Twice I heard someone in the woods, but I saw only a shadow. When I ran for help, I stumbled over Patrice. The knife was lying beside her. She reached for it, and I ran. I heard her rise. I looked back and saw her, and I didn't look back again. I just ran.

In the end, all the séance stuff was ignored. Three girls playing a slumber-party game, that was all. If we heard voices, it was other kids goofing around. There was no "bad trip"—an analysis of the mushrooms proved they were just regular grocery-store fare.

Three teenage girls who'd clearly watched *The Craft* too many times. Three teenage girls who'd been raised during the Satanic Panic. All that nonsense burrowed into Patrice's brain and made her think she'd been possessed, and she'd murdered her friend just like Roddy Silva once murdered his girlfriend.

Susceptible teen girls. Hysterical teen girls. Blame hormones. Blame movie nonsense. Blame Patrice's family history of mental illness. Her mind snapped and, really, people whispered, it was better if it stayed snapped so she never truly realized what she'd done to Heather.

For the next two months, I stayed home, rarely leaving my room. No one expected me to finish the last few weeks of school—they just gave me whatever grades I had and let me skip exams. Then it was off to Toronto. Dad "just happened" to get a job transfer . . . which I suspect he applied for. My parents let me change my name and whisked me across the country in hopes it would help me get past the tragedy and the horror of what happened.

And Patrice? Well, she was never getting past it. A court found her not guilty because of her mental condition and remanded her to a high-security psychiatric institution.

After that night in the forest, I didn't see Patrice again. My parents made sure of that. I had to return to Edmonton to testify, but she wasn't in court. She wasn't in any shape to be in court.

What happened that night?

Twenty-two years later, I still don't know for sure. Most days, I'm convinced it was exactly what everyone said—Patrice suffered a mental breakdown brought on by the first séance and her subsequent belief she was possessed. After Anton told me that he and his friends were responsible for the "haunting" that first night, it seems even more obvious that everything else could be explained by a psychotic break.

Then there are the nights when I remember something—Patrice's eyes, her expression, her voice, those shadows in the woods, that *feeling* of something wrong—and I wake up, wondering how the hell I bought the "she just snapped" explanation.

Snapped and gutted her best friend?

There'd been more to it. I have always felt that, as hard as I've tried to believe otherwise. That's why I let myself fall into this bull-shit of trying to contact Anton. Because after what happened in that forest, I cannot shake the conviction that there is life after death.

So what do I believe? That the deranged spirit of Roddy Silva possessed Patrice and reenacted what he'd done twenty years before?

Am I even sure it was Patrice who killed Heather? Her hand that wielded the knife?

Of course it was. It had to be.

Shadows in the forest. The crack of twigs. The rustle of dead leaves.

This is why I refused to give the police more than the facts, forcing them to make all the interpretations.

Because I had doubts?

I pull back the memories I just relived. In that moment, kneeling beside Heather's body, even as reason told me Patrice killed her, I hadn't been ready to commit to that absolute certainty.

Shadows in the forest. The crack of twigs. The rustle of dead leaves.

I need to tell you something. A secret.

Hairs rise on my arms, but I rub them hard, bristling with annoyance. What the hell am I thinking? That Anton murdered Heather? That Patrice's injuries weren't self-inflicted? That she'd been attacked and posed with that knife?

But I'd seen her grab it.

No, I just saw her touch it. What if she was only reaching out, getting her bearings, trying to rise, and her hand brushed the staged knife?

I never saw her *holding* it.

I close my eyes and resurrect the memories. Patrice lifting her head, gaze locking with mine. Her hand reaching toward the knife. Her fingers grazing the handle.

I'd run then.

What if I got it wrong?

It doesn't matter, because it wasn't up to me to interpret. I gave the facts. That's all.

I can hear the prosecutor asking whether it was Patrice who'd shouted that she'd gut "Samantha."

"I thought so at the time."

"You thought so, Janica? You aren't sure?"

I hesitate, panic rising. Am I supposed to say I'm sure? Is that what he wants?

I should say it was Patrice. I was sure at the time.

Was I?

I tell the truth. "The voice was raw, hoarse. At the time, I thought it was Patrice. But if you're asking whether it couldn't possibly have been anyone else, I can't say that."

He'd been disappointed. I'd seen that. But afterward, when I fretted, Mom said I'd done the right thing. Dad agreed.

Tell the truth. Let the police and prosecution make a case. That wasn't my job.

I wish I'd thanked my parents for that advice. I realize now why they'd been so adamant that I only tell the truth, no matter how hard anyone pushed for more. I should not make any assumptions or feel any pressure to say anything I wasn't sure of. Because if I did, and I ever doubted Patrice's guilt, my words would come back to haunt me.

I leave the sitting room. When I reach the living room, the clock strikes five, and I flinch. Cocktail hour. Shit, I really don't want that today.

I glance around, but no one's in sight. Maybe they've forgotten it, too. Good. I swing through the living room, where I left my laptop, and take it outside to a small wooden table and chair in the gardens, close enough to still pick up the house's Wi-Fi signal.

I sit facing the house, so I can see anyone coming out. It'll be dinnertime soon. Jin was grabbing takeout, relieving Mrs. Kilmer of her catering tasks while she searched for her son. I'll keep an ear out for the sound of his car.

I launch my browser. I'm about to start searching for the case when a little voice whispers to open a VPN and put the browser into incognito mode.

Incognito mode? I'm not researching how to make a bomb. I'm looking at a twenty-two-year-old murder case to refresh my memory and see whether I could have missed anything.

A murder case that hit national news. A murder case that involved me under another name.

A murder case that also involved my dead husband, even if the rest of the world never knew that.

I want to dig deep, and I'm not going to feel comfortable doing that if I'm worried about cyber traces showing that Nicola Laughton was researching someone named Janica Laughton, witness to a horrific murder. Nor will I be comfortable typing Anton's name in association with that case.

Am I ashamed of doubting my husband? Yes.

I am further shamed by the little voice that whispers I'd only truly known Anton for the past three years, and even then, how well does anyone know anyone? That voice feels like a cop-out and a betrayal. But the only voice I need to ignore is the more shameful one that whines that all this does no good because even if I found out Anton played some role, he's dead and can't be prosecuted, so I should just let it lie. Keep my good memories intact. Except I can't, can I? Those memories are tainted until I have answers.

"I'm sorry, Anton," I whisper . . . and then I start typing.

I don't know what became of Patrice. Oh, I know she was remanded to a psychiatric institution. I know that my parents promised to keep an eye on her case and warn me if she was ever released, so we could be prepared.

Prepared for what?

I don't think any of us knew. Would she blame me for testifying? Or would she be the old Patrice, her mind clear, horrified by what she'd done? I couldn't have handled that any better than I'd have handled angry Patrice. I have spent too many sleepless nights putting myself in Patrice's place.

What if I had a psychotic break and murdered a friend?

What if I were possessed by a killer and murdered a friend?

Am I a coward for not wanting to see her again? Maybe. But sometimes, as much as we want to help others, we need to protect our own mental health.

I may have outwardly buried sixteen-year-old Janica, but I spent years in therapy dealing with what happened, the trauma of what I went through and the survivor's guilt of needing therapy when I was the one who escaped.

After my parents died, maybe I should have kept tabs on Patrice myself, but honestly, I never thought of it. It's been over twenty years, and I'm long past the old nightmares where she shows up in my bedroom with a knife. Or where she shows up sobbing that I'd betrayed her.

After Anton confessed to the pranking, we didn't really talk about the rest. He was sorry he'd never gotten in touch afterward, at least to tell me he was thinking of me and what I'd gone through. But sixteen-year-old boys don't do that. Hell, *no one* reached out to me after Heather died. I disappeared into my bedroom, and not a single classmate tried to see how I was doing.

Anton and I never discussed that second séance. I certainly didn't ask him what happened to Patrice after I left Edmonton.

Now I need to know, even if it has nothing to do with my questions about Anton. I need to know what happened to a girl who'd been my friend.

I find an article from when she turned eighteen and was transferred to an adult facility. There's another from ten years ago, when her parents tried to appeal her sentence and ask for her to be transferred to a private hospital.

According to those articles, Patrice never recovered. In the early days, she'd vacillated between catatonia and psychotic outbursts. Eventually, the catatonia took over, which is why her family had lobbied for a transfer, since she posed no threat in that state. Their request was denied and the trail ends there, leaving her in that secured facility.

As I stare at that decade-old article, I realize it wasn't just one friend who died that day in the forest. It was two. The Patrice I knew never came back, and now, in a secure psychiatric ward somewhere, there is a middle-aged woman living out her days, the girl she'd been long gone.

I will mourn for Patrice later. I might even commit to getting in touch with her parents and saying . . . I don't know. Giving whatever solace I can offer with twenty years of maturity and distance.

Now I need to dive into the case itself and see what I missed. It happened at the end of the nineties, the era of AOL, when I certainly could have found news on the case, but it wasn't in my face, all the time, as a sensational case would be these days.

I spend the next half hour reading articles from that time and growing increasingly frustrated. They all rehash the same facts and, sometimes, the same rumors and theories that I'd thought were only local gossip. Rumors about Heather bringing back "voodoo" from Cuba. Rumors about Patrice practicing witchcraft. And one rumor I'd never heard, thanks to my parents—that a source claimed I missed a lot of time at my old school because I'd been the victim of a satanic cult. Not that I have CF, which is easily discovered information. Why blame a chronic illness when you can blame the devil?

I can see now why my parents didn't hesitate to let me change my name. According to this so-called source, I'm a satanic-cult survivor who mysteriously—suspiciously?—also survived the bloodbath that erupted when my new friends mysteriously—suspiciously?—got into witchcraft less than a year after meeting me.

Respectable papers leave my name out of it. I was a minor, after all. But of course everyone in the region knew who I was, and it takes little effort to find "Janica Laughton" named as the survivor.

As for what happened to Janica? To my relief, no one seems to have cared. There are no "what ever happened to" blog posts from later years. None on Patrice either. We were huge news at the time, but our story had a definitive and tidy ending. A teen girl experienced a psychotic break and murdered one friend. Her other friend escaped. The killer was immediately apprehended, tried, and convicted. End of story.

I'd hoped to discover that there was more to the case, that the police had evidence I didn't know about. Or that Patrice "woke" and confessed. That didn't happen. The evidence that convicted Patrice was exactly what I remembered. She was found with the knife that killed Heather. It had her prints on it. Heather's blood was on Patrice. Then there was my story.

Reading those articles, I see how much weight my story was given. According to some reports, I definitely identified Patrice as Heather's killer. One even had me finding Patrice stabbing Heather. That's all embellishment. When I read the trial transcripts, I can see that I said exactly what I remember.

What matters here is that I don't find evidence that proves—beyond any doubt—that Patrice murdered Heather. All the killer had to do was knock Patrice out, wipe Heather's blood onto Patrice's clothing, and put the knife beside her hand.

Those transcripts confirm that Patrice was never able to speak in her own defense. She didn't regain that ability for even a taped interview.

Had it been up to me to defend her? To say I couldn't imagine my friend doing something so horrific?

At the time, I'd been so certain Patrice did it. She'd been in the grip of madness and maybe, just maybe, it was our fault. Our fault for holding a séance that left her convinced we'd released some evil entity. Or our fault for releasing some evil entity, whatever had once possessed Roddy Silva to murder his girlfriend in the same way.

If the court found Patrice not guilty because of her mental condition, that meant she did it . . . she just hadn't been in her right mind.

I pause, fingers over the keyboard. Then I look at the house. I can hear voices, muffled. Just ordinary conversation.

I take a deep breath and type in the words I've been dreading.

Patrice Jones. Heather Mueller. Anton Novak. Murder.

I get back a string of results with "Anton Novak" crossed off the search terms. Seeing that, I exhale. What did I expect? That he'd been questioned and I never realized it?

My gaze skims over the list of search results. Then it stops on one with Anton removed . . . but not Novak.

I stare at the preview of that result. It's from a *Haunted Alberta* blog. When I see that, a shiver runs up my spine, but I push it down. Yes, I'm sure Patrice gets mentioned in local ghost tours, not by name, but as the story of a girl who murdered her friend after conducting a séance.

The post begins by regurgitating the story of Heather's murder. The focus, given the blog title, is on the séance and my testimony that Patrice thought we'd contacted the spirit of Roddy Silva.

The post then switches to telling the story of Roddy Silva, and here I slow down to read. Back when Patrice first told this story, I hadn't been sure it was even true. After it became part of Patrice's murder trial, I'd heard enough to know it was very real.

Before slitting his own throat, Roddy Silva had killed his girlfriend in the same way that Heather had been killed. Samantha had indeed been found in a tree. Patrice's aunt Lori had been with the search party that found her, and Lori had never recovered, being committed to an institution, much as her niece would be two decades later.

The blog takes extra care drawing those parallels. It also dug deeper into the Roddy Silva story. That began as Patrice said, with kids having a bonfire, some of them goofing around with a séance, and then Roddy walked into the forest, with Samantha following.

It is only then that I see why my search picked it up.

> Surprisingly, the Silva family continued to live in Edmonton afterward. For this story, we tracked down his younger sister, Mary Novak (née Silva), who refused to give a statement regarding her brother's crime.

I stare at that name. Mary Silva. Mary Novak.

Anton's mother's name is Mary.

I shake it off. Mary is a common name, and Novak isn't *uncom-*

more guilty than he had any reason to be, and I thought that was just Anton being sweet, but now I'm worried . . ."

She looks at me and waits. I think the answer is obvious, but when I don't say it, she prompts, "Worried about what, Nic? That he was there? That he saw what happened and couldn't save your friend?"

I shake my head. "I'm afraid . . . he was there, yes, but not just that he didn't save her. That maybe he . . ."

She continues to stare in obvious confusion. Then she says, "You don't think he killed her, do you?"

I nod, and she gives an exhale of a laugh, as if she'd been holding her breath. Then she rubs it away. "Sorry, I shouldn't laugh. I can see you're serious, and I understand how this . . ." She waves toward the house. ". . . could all be a bit much. The excitement of actually making contact, and then that nonsense Dr. Cirillo gave about dark forces. He shouldn't have said that. It's obvious that Anton is here, and he's reached out to you in the way he can, and maybe he'll do more tonight."

My cheeks heat. "So I'm being silly."

"No, no." She squeezes my arm as if I'm the much-younger friend. "There's a lot going on, and resurrecting those old memories is naturally going to cause confusion between the two, like you said. The link is Anton, so your exhausted brain is leaping on that and thinking it's a bigger connection than it is."

"Okay."

She peers at me. "Do you honestly believe Anton could have done that?"

"I . . . I should say no. He was wonderful. Sweet and gentle. But Dr. Cirillo mentioned a case of a boy who seemed sweet and turned out to be a sociopath."

"You know what I think? That Dr. Davos Cirillo needs to keep his damn mouth shut more often."

I bite my lip to keep from smiling. She looks so stern, even that mild profanity ringing false, like a child trying it on for size. That relaxes me a little.

"He didn't say it in connection with Anton," I say. "It was an unrelated conversation that preyed on my mind. There's something else, too. My friends and I conducted our séances at a spot where someone had died, and we thought we'd conjured the killer. That killer turns out to be related to Anton."

She frowns. "So you may have summoned the spirit of Anton's murderous relative?"

"I . . . I don't know about summoning but . . ."

"You think this relative possessed Anton? Made him murder this girl?"

That wasn't what I was thinking. More like that sociopathy might run in his family. But now that she says this . . .

"Maybe?" I say. "I just can't get the idea out of my head."

"Then you need to ask him."

"Ask . . . ?"

"Anton. Tonight. At the summoning. Bring up the killer's name. Ask him about it."

"Ask whether he murdered my friend while possessed by the spirit of a psychopath relative?"

She gives me a look. "Of course not. Unless you want to tell Dr. Cirillo and Jin what's going on."

"*No,*" I say emphatically.

"So just mention his relative's name. Mediums always give you the chance to ask the dead any questions. Ask Anton about his cousin Esther or whatever. Just like that. For Dr. Cirillo and Jin's sake, pretend you're doing it to confirm his identity."

"'If you really are Anton, tell me about your cousin Esther'?"

"Sure, something like that. See how he reacts. What he says." She squeezes my arm again. "I don't think Anton did this. I never met him, but I know you and now I know Jin, and you both think Anton mon. Still, I scroll through the rest of the article, looking for more, for proof that this is a coincidence. A photo appears. A high-school photo of Roddy Silva, and I find myself staring into his eyes.

Into Anton's eyes.

"Nicola?"

I jump so high I nearly topple the deck chair. Shania stands in front of me, frowning. I slap the laptop shut.

"Yes?" I say, a little sharply.

"Jin's back with dinner," she says. Then she eyes me uncertainly. "Is everything okay?"

When I give a curt nod, her eyes shutter.

"Sorry," I say. "I was just . . ." I rub my temples. "There's a lot going on, and I'm not handling it well."

"Not handling what well?" She frowns. "You're doing awesome. There's been some weird stuff, but Anton really seems to be trying to make contact and . . . Nic?"

"Hmm?"

"What's wrong?"

"Wrong?"

She peers at me. "I mentioned Anton, and you flinched." She pauses, as if working it through. "Do you think the ghost isn't him?"

"No, it's just . . . something else."

Her jaw moves, as if she's chewing the inside of her cheek. "I'm not going to pry, Nic, but you know I'm here, right? For anything you need to discuss?" She eases back, looking self-conscious. "I'm here. That's all I'm saying."

I rise and squeeze her shoulder. "I know, and I appreciate it. Now let's get dinner."

Over dinner, I decide to confide in Shania. She really is the right choice. Jin is too close to this and to me, and I'm not eager to tell him what happened twenty-two years ago, especially if he might consider it a secret Keith didn't trust him enough to share. I'd rather keep the details to a bare minimum, and that's awkward with a good friend. I'm sure as hell not talking to Cirillo. I'm already nervous that he'll dig up my past. More fodder for his funding.

After dinner, there's a break before the next séance. Cirillo slips off to prepare for that, and I ask Shania if she'll walk with me. Jin takes the hint and offers to do the dishes, which doesn't quite seem fair when he picked up dinner, but when I say so, he's quick to reassure me.

"There's a reason I offered to get dinner," he says. "I am seriously low on my espresso quota so I hit a coffee shop for a double shot. Now I need to work off the caffeine."

I smile. "Okay, but tomorrow, you're chilling."

"Er, actually, that's another reason I'm being so helpful. I need to head back to Toronto tomorrow for an emergency meeting I can't do over video chat. Is it okay if I take your car?"

"Sure," I say. "Do you want to just stay and come back Friday with Keith and the kids? Tomorrow is our last full day here."

"It's also our last séance," he says. "I want to be here for that. I should be back by dinner, but if I'm not, I need you to promise you won't start without me."

"Keith's rule?"

Jin shrugs. "Keith's request, and my agreement. Shania is a good kid, but she's a believer. You need someone to join you in playing skeptic."

"Fair enough. Okay then. Enjoy the dishes, and I'll see you in an hour or so."

TWENTY-FOUR

Shania and I stand near the cliff edge. I'm not as close as I was the other day—not after what happened on the stairs and in the bathroom. As we gaze out, I squint at what looks like a funnel cloud.

"Tell me those aren't bugs," I say.

Shania swats a stray one from her face. "These definitely are." Then she sees where I'm pointing and groans. "I thought they were almost gone."

"Hopefully they'll make landfall someplace else."

"I never knew bugs could, well, *bug* me so much."

I laugh. "It's right there in the name. But yes, I keep wondering why I can't just ignore them when they aren't biting."

I look out over the water. "Once I get an idea in my head, it's just like these damn midges. I can't ignore it, even when I want to. What we're doing—the séances—they're triggering something from my past, and the more I think about it, the more the two events start to overlap and merge."

"That can happen."

"There's a commonality, too." I cross my arms and gaze out at that cloud of midges. "When I was in high school, some friends and I held a séance. Things went wrong, and a girl died."

"Oh my God."

I pass her a wan smile. "Yep. I don't talk about it. Even Jin doesn't know."

"Did Anton?"

"That's . . . the problem. Remember I said we were classmates briefly? In high school?"

"Oh!" Her eyes round. "He was there? He went to the same school, I mean?"

I consider how to word this, being honest while not divulging too many details. "My friends and I held two séances. At the first one, we heard voices that seemed to mean we'd contacted the dead. Apparently, it was Anton and his friends."

"Ah. They pranked you."

"Yep, though I didn't know it until a few years ago. But it was the second séance where my friend died."

"Was Anton there?"

I shake my head. "He was at a movie with his friends."

"Your friend had a scare, though? A heart attack or something?"

I almost say yes. This is an easy answer. Pretend Heather was scared to death and that I'm worried that Anton and his friends might have spooked her the first time and that carried over to the second séance. But that doesn't get to the core of my fears. If that had happened, then it would be a tragedy, but not the boys' fault in the way it would be if one of them actually murdered her.

I shake my head. "There was some confusion. We all separated, and she was murdered. Someone was arrested and convicted."

Her hands fly to her mouth. "Oh my God. I am so sorry, Nic. That must have been terrible. I can see how this week would trigger the trauma. Two séances, both involving Anton in a way."

"It's not just that. I . . . ." I take a deep breath. "Before Anton died, he said he had a secret, and then he told me something that wasn't really a secret. Also, when he confessed to pranking us, he felt far more guilty than he had any reason to be, and I thought that was just Anton being sweet, but now I'm worried . . ."

She looks at me and waits. I think the answer is obvious, but when I don't say it, she prompts, "Worried about what, Nic? That he was there? That he saw what happened and couldn't save your friend?"

I shake my head. "I'm afraid . . . he was there, yes, but not just that he didn't save her. That maybe he . . ."

She continues to stare in obvious confusion. Then she says, "You don't think he killed her, do you?"

I nod, and she gives an exhale of a laugh, as if she'd been holding her breath. Then she rubs it away. "Sorry, I shouldn't laugh. I can see you're serious, and I understand how this . . ." She waves toward the house. ". . . could all be a bit much. The excitement of actually making contact, and then that nonsense Dr. Cirillo gave about dark forces. He shouldn't have said that. It's obvious that Anton is here, and he's reached out to you in the way he can, and maybe he'll do more tonight."

My cheeks heat. "So I'm being silly."

"No, no." She squeezes my arm as if I'm the much-younger friend. "There's a lot going on, and resurrecting those old memories is naturally going to cause confusion between the two, like you said. The link is Anton, so your exhausted brain is leaping on that and thinking it's a bigger connection than it is."

"Okay."

She peers at me. "Do you honestly believe Anton could have done that?"

"I . . . I should say no. He was wonderful. Sweet and gentle. But Dr. Cirillo mentioned a case of a boy who seemed sweet and turned out to be a sociopath."

"You know what I think? That Dr. Davos Cirillo needs to keep his damn mouth shut more often."

I bite my lip to keep from smiling. She looks so stern, even that mild profanity ringing false, like a child trying it on for size. That relaxes me a little.

"He didn't say it in connection with Anton," I say. "It was an unrelated conversation that preyed on my mind. There's something else, too. My friends and I conducted our séances at a spot where someone had died, and we thought we'd conjured the killer. That killer turns out to be related to Anton."

She frowns. "So you may have summoned the spirit of Anton's murderous relative?"

"I . . . I don't know about summoning but . . ."

"You think this relative possessed Anton? Made him murder this girl?"

That wasn't what I was thinking. More like that sociopathy might run in his family. But now that she says this . . .

"Maybe?" I say. "I just can't get the idea out of my head."

"Then you need to ask him."

"Ask . . . ?"

"Anton. Tonight. At the summoning. Bring up the killer's name. Ask him about it."

"Ask whether he murdered my friend while possessed by the spirit of a psychopath relative?"

She gives me a look. "Of course not. Unless you want to tell Dr. Cirillo and Jin what's going on."

"*No*," I say emphatically.

"So just mention his relative's name. Mediums always give you the chance to ask the dead any questions. Ask Anton about his cousin Esther or whatever. Just like that. For Dr. Cirillo and Jin's sake, pretend you're doing it to confirm his identity."

"'If you really are Anton, tell me about your cousin Esther'?"

"Sure, something like that. See how he reacts. What he says." She squeezes my arm again. "I don't think Anton did this. I never met him, but I know you and now I know Jin, and you both think Anton was a great guy. That tells me he was. But you need to ask the question and get it answered and out of your head. Right?"

I hesitate. Then I nod.

I don't want this séance. I don't want to ask Anton anything about Roddy Silva. I want these last few days to have been a bad dream, and I'll wake from it and realize all this séance nonsense has been exactly that: nonsense. I'm grieving and lost and maybe a little bit—okay, a lot—broken.

I've told myself I'm looking for answers, but that's bullshit. The only question I want answered is "Why?" and that's not even a question as much as a primal scream to the universe.

Why did you take him?

I found someone I wanted to spend the rest of my life with, and we had so many plans, and when "till death do us part" came, it was supposed to be me.

It was supposed to be me gone and him left behind. What the fuck do I do now? Sit and wait to die?

I'm angry at the universe, and I decided contacting Anton would somehow fix it, and the universe laughed in my face and made it worse.

I want to wake up now. Take this nightmare as a cautionary tale, and move on with my life.

"Move on with my life" is the real answer to my question. What do I do now? Keep going. Hold fast to those amazing memories of Anton and move forward. In questioning those memories, though, I've tarnished them.

The universe didn't steal Anton from me. It gave me a gift—a few years of incredible happiness with an incredible man. Now I'm questioning that.

What's the saying about looking a gift horse in the mouth? I've pried those jaws open, and I'm peering into a future hell where the man I loved was actually a killer.

The four of us meet in the breakfast nook. That's where Cirillo has set up tonight's séance. I'm the last one to join, dragging my sorry ass in, clutching the box of Anton's cremains. I put it in its place of honor and then take my seat.

"Nicola?" Cirillo says.

I glance his way.

"Are you all right? I sense you don't want to be here tonight."

"I'm just tired," I mumble.

Shania shoots me an anxious look. Now that she knows I have concerns, I can't make an excuse to skip this.

"I'm fine," I say, straightening.

Jin frowns over at me. "We don't need to do this, Nic."

Cirillo clears his throat. "Jin is correct. However, if we don't, we run the risk of losing Anton."

Asshole.

Ooh, I really *am* in a mood, aren't I? Still, Cirillo is not my ally here. He has an agenda, and I'm angry about that because we picked him specifically for not having an agenda. He's a scientist, and he promised anonymity and impartiality.

Knowing he's hoping to use my story for grant money feels like trusting a doctor to give an unbiased opinion and then discovering he's getting kickbacks for the medication he put you on. I cannot rely on Cirillo having my best interests in mind.

Jin lowers his voice, as if only I can hear him. "I'm happy to cancel if you want, Nic, but maybe . . ." He shrugs, looking sheepish. "I think Dr. Cirillo is right. Anton *is* here."

"I wasn't going to cancel," I say. "I'm just not sure I'm fully committed to it tonight."

"Well, you need to be," Cirillo says, with a laser stare that tells me I'd better not fuck up his séance.

My séance, asshole.

"I'll do my best," I say, saccharine sweet, "but if we don't make contact, then I understand it's entirely my fault, and I accept responsibility for my own disappointment."

His lips tighten a fraction, not enough for the other two to notice.

Too bad, asshole. My trauma isn't your fucking meal ticket.

"We should have a ghost story," Shania blurts.

Jin obviously struggles to hide a wince. "I'm not sure that—"

"No, it's fine," I say. Anything to distract me. "So, whose turn is it?"

Cirillo looks my way. "Nicola? I have a feeling you might have an old story for us."

I go still. Very still. My gaze slowly pivots his way, but he's just sitting there, watching me.

Does he know about Patrice?

"I have one," Shania cuts in. "Let's save Nic for tomorrow and the last séance. This one's mine."

Cirillo clears his throat. "Actually, I think we'll skip tonight's ghost story. Can we get yours tomorrow, Shania?"

Her look of disappointment has me opening my mouth to say no, let her tell her story. But everyone—Shania included—quickly gets into place, and Cirillo is beginning before I can object.

After a few words, I tune out Cirillo's invocation and force myself to relax. If I self-sabotage, I'll blame myself for it later. I'm really good at that.

Anton? If you're out there, we need to talk.

Yes, I'm using that voice, the one you always said reminded you of when your parents said they needed to talk to you and you knew you'd done something.

But even when you knew it wasn't going to be a happy conversation, you always talked to me. You never blew me off or made excuses.

Please. I'm sorry if anything I say upsets you, but understand that I need to know, and if the situation were reversed and you had questions, I would absolutely want you to ask.

I'm beating around the bush, and I hate that. Shania said to reach out and just ask, and Anton and I had the kind of relationship where I could do that. But imagine wanting to ask your spouse a vital and personal question and needing to do it before an audience.

Anton, I'm sorry. I just need to talk to you.

A sigh ripples past, and my eyes fly open. I look around. Everyone else seems to have their eyes shut, but Jin must be peeking because he glances over, frowning. My headshake tells him to ignore me.

When he shuts his eyes, I whisper as softly as I can, "Anton? We need to talk. Please."

That sigh again, and in it, I feel a frisson of something like frustration. I open my eyes with my face turned away from Jin.

"Are you there?" I whisper.

That bristle-static sense of frustration increases. Then it vanishes, and everything goes silent, preternaturally silent, as if I've fallen into a vacuum. I'm straining so hard that when I hear something, I jump, and the table jumps with me.

"Nicola?" Cirillo says. "Did you experience something?"

I shake my head, and Cirillo's voice firms, as if I'm a stubborn child.

"Nicola? If you're experiencing anything—"

"I will tell you," I snap. "Something startled me. Now I'd like to focus on figuring out what it is."

He holds my gaze, every bit the professor with an uppity grad student. I only meet his stare. If he wants a battle of wills, I can give him one.

"All right," he says. "I trust you will let us know when you hear something."

"I will."

Everyone goes quiet again. I'm not even sure what I *had* heard—it really happened so fast that my body jumped before my brain could process. Then the sound comes again. Someone breathing.

I peek and look around the table. Everyone's mouth is closed. Whatever I'm hearing, it isn't from them.

I shut my eyes.

"Anton?" I whisper.

The breathing draws closer. I grip the edge of the table to keep from jumping. The sound is a rhythmic in and out, in and out, closer, closer, right at my ear, so close I expect to feel breath on my skin. Then it stops. I tense, every muscle held tight like I'm bracing for the jump scare.

"Janica . . ."

I stop breathing, and I hang there, tight enough that the slightest touch would send me flailing. But no touch comes.

"Anton?" I whisper.

A footfall answers. Then another. Footsteps walking away.

A board creaks.

"Did you hear that?" Shania says.

We all look, and she covers her mouth.

"Sorry," she whispers. "Should I not say anything?"

"What did you hear?" Cirillo asks.

"A board creaked." She points.

"I heard it," I say. "I thought I heard footsteps, and then came the creak."

"Let's all listen," Cirillo says.

We go quiet, and I still hear footsteps, slow and methodical. Another board creaks, and Shania lets out a yelp, along with Jin saying, "I heard that," and Cirillo adding a murmur that he does as well.

"Anton Novak," Cirillo says. "You seem to be with us. Can you confirm that? Nicola hears footsteps. If you can hear me, stop walking."

The footsteps continue. Cirillo glances my way, but I shake my head.

"Anton?" Cirillo says. "Can you make yourself known by extinguishing a candle?"

The footsteps grow closer to me. Then they pass.

"Nicola?" Cirillo says. "Would you try, please?"

Here's my chance. Ask about Roddy.

Only I can't say it right away. I need to lead up to the question.

"Anton?" I say. "If you can hear me, will you stop walking, please?"

The footsteps continue, as if he's slowly circling the table.

Circling. Considering. Stalking.

Stop that.

"Anton?" I say. "I think you were trying to speak to me. Please try again."

That frisson of electricity, making me gasp.

"Did he?" Shania says.

Cirillo's look silences her, and I swallow and shake my head.

"I think I'm spooking myself," I say. "The footsteps just keep circling the table."

Stalking.

"Anton?" I say. "Please. If you're here—"

A whisper sounds, and I jump. We all do. Jin is on his feet first, staring toward the door.

"Did everyone else hear that?" he asks.

"I heard something," Shania says.

An indecipherable whisper comes from the next room. Then the voice becomes Anton's.

"Nic," he says, then another word I can't catch and . . . "Love you."

"Did you guys hear that?" Shania says.

"Holy shit, yes." Jin heads for the door. "It came from in here."

He takes off at a jog, and then Shania is on her feet, following. Cirillo grumbles, but he goes after them.

That's when I realize the breakfast nook is empty. I can say whatever I want.

"Anton?" I whisper. "It seems we're alone now." My voice cracks on a half laugh. "If you lured them out, thank you. Better make this quick."

I take a deep breath. "I have questions about what happened with Patrice. I'm sorry. I know that you're Roddy Silva's nephew and—"

My chair flies back. One second I'm sitting there, trying to speak calmly, and then my chair flies backward and I hit the floor, my head smacking into the hardwood, the world going gray as I let out a startled cry of pain.

I don't have time to process what happened before Jin is at my side, helping me up.

"What happened?" Shania says.

I hesitate only a split second. Then I see Jin's expression, and I know if I admit my chair was yanked over backward, he'll haul my ass out of this house.

"I fell," I say, making a face as I rub the back of my head. "I was getting up to join you guys when my leg caught the chair and I went over backward."

I don't pause to see their expressions. I just make a show out of rubbing my head and grimace as I roll my eyes.

"Sorry, guys," I say. "I messed up your séance, being a klutz."

"It's your séance," Shania says, "and you didn't mess up anything. We heard Anton, Nic. We really did." She looks around. "Right? What did you guys hear?"

Jin glances at me, obviously not ready to ignore the fact that I just fell flat on my back.

"What did you hear?" I ask.

"He said your name," Jin says, after a moment of obvious reluctance to change the subject. "Then that he loved you. When I got in there, I heard 'Everything's okay,' and something I couldn't catch."

"He said 'I'm fine.'" Shania's voice was thrumming with excitement. "He said 'Nic, I love you, everything's okay, and I'm fine.'"

"I didn't catch all of that," Cirillo says, "but I heard enough to confirm that it was an audible male voice, and I heard at least a third of those same words."

Shania turns to me, her face glowing. "Anton was here. He was really here, Nic."

I nod, unable to speak, struggling to make my expression as close to happy as I can. It must work, because she throws her arms around my neck.

"See?" she whispers. "He's fine. Everything's okay."

Everything is not okay.

Not by a long shot.

TWENTY-FIVE

J in hovers over me after that. He insists I sit down, and he has Shania pull on her nurse hat to walk me through signs of a concussion. Jin doesn't question that it was an accident, though. I got overexcited and tripped. No need to end the séances. No need to whisk me back into the protective custody of my brother.

I tell the others that I'm going to bed, and I reach the top of the stairs before Cirillo comes after me. He waves me into his room, and I almost walk into my own and shut the door, but at the last second, I follow him.

"Did you really accidentally topple the chair?" he asks once he's shut the door.

"Are you concerned for my safety? Or worried about missing a potential physical manifestation for your funding application?"

His lips press into a sour line.

"I don't expect you to be concerned for my well-being, Dr. Cirillo," I say. "But I *am* concerned about how your data is going to be used, so don't expect me to be completely forthcoming."

"Something toppled the chair."

I don't answer. Sure, I feel a little childish, but whatever's happening here is about me, and I don't really care how it affects this stranger's livelihood.

He moves closer, voice lowering. "If we are dealing with a being that can move objects in the physical world, that is a safety concern."

"We already knew that, between the stairs and the bath mat."

"Which were centered on you. As was this one. Yes, I care about my work, but if you are in danger, we need to take action."

"Okay. I'm in danger. Now what?"

He hesitates, as if he still expected me to deny it. It's so much easier when you can just warn someone of danger and then wash your hands of the consequences.

"Should we leave?" I say. "I've been targeted three times. If I told Jin—"

"I don't think that's wise."

Yeah, I'm sure you don't.

He continues, "We have unleashed something here, Nicola. If we leave, we risk inflicting that on others. You need to be aware of your responsibility. We aren't investigating a haunted house. You brought the ghosts with you. You can't leave them behind."

When I don't answer, he presses on, "One of them is your husband. I'm sure of that. We all heard him. He's here, but when we brought him in, something tagged along, something dark."

"You sense two entities?"

He peers at me, but I keep my expression only mildly curious.

"What else could it be?" he asks.

I shrug. "You tell me. You're the expert."

"We clearly heard Anton in the living room, and at the same time, another entity knocked over your chair."

That's one way of looking at it. The other way is that Anton lured them out to target me, but I'm sure as hell not mentioning that to someone who'll put it on a grant application.

"If it's a second ghost," I say, "then you can contact it, right?"

"I can try, but as I've said this doesn't feel like a true ghost. 'Entity' is a better word. A dark entity." He straightens. "I will still try to make contact tomorrow, during our final séance. For now, I just need you to be careful. You're sharing the twin-bed room with Shania tonight?"

"I am."

"Good, then everything should be fine."

No, Doctor, your grudging precautions are not going to stop anything in this house that actually wants to hurt me, but at least you'll get your damn funding.

I can grumble, but I'm not exactly packing my bags, am I?

He's right that if we summoned something dark, I can't walk out and leave it for unsuspecting strangers to deal with. But I also need answers, and I'm not leaving until I get them.

I'm dreaming of Anton. We've flown to Banff for the weekend and hiked up Sulphur Mountain. That wasn't nearly as easy as it'd been when I was young—with less battle-scarred lungs—but I did it, and I'm damn proud of myself.

We've found a quiet spot to rest and enjoy the view, and we're celebrating with a mini bottle of champagne.

"You know what I love about climbing mountains?" Anton says. "The sense of accomplishment. I could have taken the gondola up for this view, but I did it the hard way."

"Uh-huh."

"Okay, it was harder for you. Which means you get this first."

He passes over the champagne, and I drink straight from the bottle.

"Also, if we took the gondola," he says, "we'd be enjoying this view with a hundred total strangers."

"And security guards telling us we can't drink."

"True." He stretches out his legs. "I think I'm going to keep you, Nic."

I snort. "Good to know. Do I have a say in that?"

"I suppose you should."

"Uh-huh."

He twists to face me. "Any chance you'd be interested in making it official?"

I lift my brows.

"Marry me, Nic."

I stare at him. Then I laugh. "I'd blame the champagne, but you haven't had any. The altitude then?"

He puts out his fist and opens it. On his palm is a band studded with diamonds.

"Shit," I say.

"Uh . . . not *quite* the response I hoped for."

I set down the bottle and face him. "You know marriage isn't an option, Anton."

"Why? Because of the three other husbands you have tucked away? I'm good at sharing, and they seem the quiet sort."

I sigh.

"You mean because of the CF," he says.

"Yes, because of the CF. I won't be climbing mountains in a few years."

"So? I don't need to climb mountains. I need to be with you."

I turn to face him. "Wait until I'm bedridden, praying for a transplant that might not even work. And that's if I get one, which I probably won't because it should go to someone younger."

He meets my gaze. "I. Don't. Care."

I open my mouth to protest, but he leans toward me, locking eyes.

"If you're in that bed, Nic, I want to be sitting beside it. No, I want to be on my feet, advocating for you, and when it's too late for that, I'll be holding your hand until the end."

My eyes prickle. "That sounds very romantic, but the reality—"

"The reality is that I know what I'm getting into. I've done my research, and I understand."

"We've talked about moving in together."

"Sharing a condo says I'm just hanging around until the first sign of trouble. That isn't what I want." He lifts the ring. "In sickness and in health."

"I . . ."

"If you don't want to marry me, say so. I'll survive. Maybe. Hopefully."

He gives me puppy-dog eyes, and I knock my shoulder against his.

"Can we talk about it?" I say. "I want to be sure you really do understand everything that's going to happen to me. This can't be a grand romantic gesture, Anton. Proving your love by caring for a woman with a terminal condition."

"If you felt, for one second, like I was martyring myself, you'd pack my bags and kick my ass out, no matter how sick you were."

"I would."

"This isn't a grand gesture, Nic. It's a hope." His face comes to mine. "A hope that you'll grant my wish, and let me have you for as long as I can, right down to the last second."

I lean in and kiss him, and relief floods me. A relief that comes from my current self, reliving that dream.

In it, I look at Anton, and I am absolutely certain I am not misremembering. No smooth-talking con artist proposed to me that day. It was my Anton, as sweet and awkward and goofy as he'd been as a teenager.

I know people can do horrible things and their loved ones never have a clue. But in my gut, I cannot look back on this Anton and see a boy who murdered a teenage girl.

Does that mean he *couldn't* have done it? Not unless he wasn't in his right mind. Not unless he had literally been possessed, and was left only with the most subconscious awareness that he had a reason to feel guilty about Patrice and Heather.

Is that the answer? I don't know. What I do know is that it's not just my gut that believes him, but my brain.

What reason would a sociopathic Anton have to marry me? He had his own money. He wasn't getting any of mine even after I died, and he made sure of that himself.

I brought nothing to the marriage except my cantankerous self and a whole lotta baggage, and he gave me the best years of my life.

Tonight something toppled that chair. In my dreams last night, Anton did that to me in the cafeteria. That should mean it was him . . . except he'd never done anything like that even in play. Oh, some guys could. They'd pull a jerk move like that and then claim they were just goofing around, like they would with their friends. But that had never been Anton's style. Not tipping chairs, not poking at me on a staircase, not moving a bath mat under me.

Did I do it to myself? Echoing the dream?

Something nudges at me. Someone who did once topple a chair I was in. Goofing around. Acting like it'd been a mistake. Saying they only meant to startle me.

Who did that? I tug at the memory, but nothing comes and instead the proposal dream returns, Anton and me in that forest. I let myself drift, enjoying the peace of the mountainside and the relief of knowing—

I freeze.

This isn't the mountain forest.

It's the forest where Heather died.

No, I don't want to be here. Take me back to—

A twig cracks. As I turn, I glimpse Heather's body through the trees. She's on her back, with her stomach split open, guts snaking out.

I turn away sharply.

Wake up. I want to wake—

Another twig crack. I glance over to see a figure slipping through the trees.

The figure is a bit taller than me. Slender, dressed in jeans and a corduroy jacket with sherpa lining. Work boots.

I force my gaze up, over the open jacket and the Nirvana T-shirt, up to the curling dark hair and the Roman nose and the green eyes.

Anton stands there, staring at me. My gaze drops to his hand. He's clutching a knife, the blade slick with blood.

No.

That is *not* what happened.

Yes, twice that night I heard something and saw a shadowy figure, but it wasn't even enough to make out size or shape. I did not see Anton.

The dream rewinds, and this time, it's correct. I only catch movement and think I spot a shadow in the forest.

The scene replays, and I grit my teeth. Fine, I'll play the memory through. That's obviously what my subconscious wants.

I head for the path, moving as carefully as I did that night, not wanting to alert whoever I'd seen in the forest. I make it into the woods. I'm walking, so slow and measured—

The rustle of undergrowth.

I wheel. The figure is right there.

That's not what happened. Keep going.

I can't move. I'm transfixed by that figure. My feet turn against my will, and I take a step and then another. The dark shape stays where it is.

I just need to get closer. See who it is.

Another step. Another—

The figure lunges, and a face flies from the darkness. The same face I saw in the online photograph earlier.

Roddy Silva.

His eyes meet mine, and his lips twitch in a quarter smile. "I will cut you open, and I will gut you."

I turn and I run, even as the grown-up part of my brain screams that this is a dream. I never saw Roddy. Roddy never chased me.

Only he's chasing me now, and I'm running for my life, and I can't breathe. I can't *breathe.*

I try to go faster, but my lungs are on fire, and his pounding footfalls are getting closer, and I can feel him there. Right behind me, and I'm going to die. He's going to stab me because I can't run any faster. My lungs will burst, and I will fall, and he will rip me open, and I won't even be dead when he does it.

Heather had been alive when I found her. She'd been alive when someone gutted her—

There's something ahead. Someone on the path.

Patrice! Yes, Patrice is here.

Oh, thank God.

I give one final burst of speed. Here is my salvation. Get to Patrice.

She isn't lying on the ground, though. She's sitting in a chair, head forward as if she'd fallen asleep there.

She lifts her head weakly, her eyes struggling to focus.

"Janica?" she says. "W-what are you—?"

I find one last burst of energy, running full out . . . and I grab the back of the chair, yank it over, and keep going. Behind me, Roddy snarls in victory and Patrice screams the most bloodcurdling scream and then . . .

And then I can breathe again.

Roddy is killing Patrice, and I am safe.

TWENTY-SIX

I wake on the bedroom floor, fighting with a sheet I dragged down with me. I struggle free and sit up and lean forward as I catch my breath.

What the hell was that?

A nightmare, Nic. They take little bits of reality, weave them with our doubts and fears, and throw them back at us.

But it felt real. It felt like something I was remembering.

It's not.

But . . .

I rub my face, climb back into bed, and wait for my breathing to slow. Then I do what my brain does best. I analyze.

None of that happened. I did not see Anton that night. I certainly did not see Roddy. And I definitely did not sacrifice Patrice so I could escape. And if I want proof of that, well, Patrice didn't die, did she?

It was a nightmare.

So why does it feel so real?

Because it's the middle of the night, and you're in a haunted house. Oh, and the reason it's haunted? Because you brought your dead husband and all your fucking past baggage with you.

Well, I do always overpack.

I bite my tongue against a hysterical laugh. Then a sound comes. The slow creak of footsteps in the attic. I go still and listen.

Thump. Thump. Thump.

I roll over and startle when I nearly fall out of the bed again. I'd forgotten I was in a twin now. Shania is across the room, in the other bed, her back to me as she sleeps soundly.

Seeing her, I have to bite back another laugh.

To sleep soundly in a haunted house because, as far as you know, it's only haunted by your new friend's loving husband, and if she ever suspected anything worse, tonight's séance proved her wrong.

Thump. Thump. Thump.

I flip over again, hands to my ears. There's no one in the attic. It's locked.

As if in surrender, the sound stops, and I breathe again, sinking into the pillow. Minutes tick past. Shania tosses in her sleep. Did she hear it, too?

Creak. Creak.

My heart thuds as my gaze moves to the head of my bed. That's the sound I heard last night. The ghostly echo of the dumbwaiter pulley.

Creak. Creak.

Wait. It's not coming from over my head. It's down by my feet. It must be something else—

No, I switched rooms. That's where the dumbwaiter is now.

I reach for my phone. I'm going to record the sound.

"Nic?"

It's Shania, her voice groggy with sleep. I turn to see her lifting her head from her pillow as she pushes up her sleep mask.

Creak. Creak.

"Do you hear that?" I say.

"Hear what?"

Creak. Creak.

"That."

She peers at me. "I don't hear anything." She blinks hard and her eyes open wide. "Is it Anton?"

I shake my head. "Just the pipes creaking."

She gives a soft laugh. "You really *do* have good hearing." A pause. "Everything okay, Nic?"

"I'm fine. Go back to sleep."

She lowers her eye mask and lies back down, and within minutes, the soft sound of deep breathing fills the room.

I lift my gaze to the ceiling.

No more footsteps.

Also, no more creaking "rope in pulley that doesn't have a rope."

I sit up to think. Then I see Shania. I need to let her sleep. No, mostly, I just don't want her realizing anything's wrong, but also, she should sleep.

I shiver, grab my wrapper, and head out. I can't resist stopping by the attic door again. Still very much locked.

I head for the stairs. I take them slowly, but there's no need. Nothing happens. The house is silent and still.

I walk to the kitchen and start to pour a glass of wine. Then I put the crystal glass aside and take down a plastic patio one instead, just in case something shoves me from behind and I fall, breaking glass that will manage to embed itself in my artery and I'll bleed out on the floor.

"Would that be such a bad thing?"

The words seem to whisper inside my head, and I jump.

Where the fuck did that come from?

Okay, I am *not* in the right mental place for this wine. I open the fridge and take a can of pop, emptying it into a plastic tumbler. There, safe from poltergeists breaking my glass and safe from fueling my muddled brain with alcohol.

I sip the pop and pad into the dining room. Then I keep walking. I intended to sit in the living room, but as I walk, I relax. I move to one of the breakfast-nook windows, struck by the urge to stroll around the garden, only to see a cloud of midges swirling around the yard.

They're back. . . .

I shake my head and settle for strolling around the main floor, which conveniently loops from kitchen to dining area to living room to hall and back to the kitchen.

As I pass through the living room, I'm reminded of the séance. Everyone heard Anton's voice. So why does something inside me balk at admitting it was Anton?

I don't like what he'd said. Same as what Jin and I heard in the sitting room.

That he said he loved you and he was fine?

That's exactly what all these damn con artists have given me—whispers of reassurance from my dead husband. If Anton had one chance to say something, he'd probably crack a bad joke . . . only to realize he should say something meaningful . . . just as he's being yanked back to the afterlife.

Just when you thought you got rid of me, my ghost comes wafting back, like a bad smell. Er, shit! Love y—!

Could Cirillo be faking it for his funding application?

It really did sound like Anton, and the con-artist recordings never have. How could Cirillo do that?

"Nic."

The voice sounds right beside me, and I jump, spilling my pop and nearly slipping on the mess. A whispered profanity follows.

"Anton?" I say.

"—need—stop—doing—"

The words are so faint I can only parse out those few.

"Anton?" I say. "If you're telling me to stop rethinking Heather's death, I can't. I'm sorry. If you have something to say, say it. But you know damn well I'm going to keep thinking and I'm going to keep asking."

"—please—not—"

A hand shoves me from behind, and I fly forward, tripping and stumbling before I catch myself.

"Anton?"

Something flashes in front of me. The barest image, stuttering, like a broken holograph.

Anton.

I *see* Anton.

He's gone before I can blink, but his image stays seared into my retinas. Anton with his eyes blazing in fury, his mouth open as he says something I can't hear. Anton lunging toward me.

And now there is nothing. No image. No sound. The house has gone so silent the quiet hurts my ears.

"Anton?" My voice shakes. "What the hell is going on?"

That was him. You know it was.

But was it really *him*? My Anton? I'd never seen that look in his eyes.

I rub my eyes and take a deep breath. Then I resolutely stride to the kitchen to get a cloth for the spilled pop.

As I clean up the floor, nothing else happens. No voices sound inside my head or outside of it. No shoves. No flickers.

I'm straightening when something clanks to my left. I spin and find myself looking at the basement door.

I pause, still half crouched, straining to listen. Another sound comes from below. A hollow metallic clunk.

I set down the sticky cloth and crack open the basement door.

What am I doing?

I turn on the basement-stairs light.

What the *hell* am I doing?

I open the door all the way. It swings inward, and I pick up the soaked cloth and wedge it underneath. Then I test, being sure it won't close on me.

Close on me when? When I go down the stairs, which no sane person would do in this situation?

I check the lock, being sure it's completely disengaged. Then I grab the railing securely and descend the first step.

Another step down.

Seriously? Who the hell wakes up in a haunted house, gets shoved by an unseen hand, hears noises in the basement, and thinks, "Huh, I should check that out"?

If the house is haunted, I brought the haunting.

Whatever is here—Anton or something else—the threat is to me. Only me.

And that makes it okay? Maybe it really was my subconscious earlier, suggesting death by exsanguination might not be so bad.

I keep descending, listening after each step.

Do you have a death wish, Nic?

Don't be silly. If I did, I wouldn't still be walking this earth. When I set my mind to something, I do it.

I'm going into the basement because that noise could mean Brodie has returned. If so, I'm making sure he gets back to his poor mother.

So I'm going to confront a drug addict?

Better than a vengeful spirit, right?

I reach the base of the stairs. Looking around, I spot the spade Jin had moved here while we searched. I pick it up.

There. I'm armed.

I flick on the light in the furnace room and wheel through the doorway.

No one's there.

As I make my way toward the sleeping bag, I mentally pull up a snapshot of how we left it. Nothing has changed.

I exhale and start to back out.

Drip. Drip.

I go still, my hands readjusting on the spade handle.

Another step back toward the door.

Drip.

That's what I'd heard yesterday. A dripping that went away, and then I got distracted finding Brodie's "nest" and forgot about it.

No, I'd ignored it because it was a dripping sound in a room with a water heater. I figured it was a normal noise.

It doesn't seem normal, though. Could the water heater be leaking?

I maneuver until I can crouch with my back safely to the wall. Then I bend down. There's no water under the heater or around it.

Could the dripping be condensation inside the hot-water tank? Is that a thing?

I'm rising when a rustling comes from outside the room. I freeze and listen. The sound comes again. A faint rustle.

I grip my handy spade and head into the hall. The rustle is coming through the open door into the storage area. I slide closer, reach through, and flip on the light. Something scuttles across the floor, and I stumble back before the sight resolves into a tiny brown mouse running for its life. The critter dives behind a pile of chairs with more rustling, as it frantically looks for an escape.

"Sorry, mousey," I whisper. "You wouldn't happen to have seen a ghost down here, would you? Or a part-time gardener?"

It doesn't answer.

I return to the furnace room. Back to the water heater to figure out where the dripping—

The spade twists in my hands. Before I can process that, the metal edge drives into my shins. I stifle a howl as I tumble, still gripping the spade. It twists again, and I quickly throw it aside. As it clatters to the concrete floor, my gut screams that I've made a mistake. I should have kept hold of it. Now whatever grabbed the spade can wield it against me.

Except it doesn't. The spade lies on the concrete, unmoving.

I take deep breaths as my mind replays what just happened. Something grabbed the spade—

No, that's not what it felt like.

It felt as if something took hold of *me*. Like I'd been the one ramming the edge into my shins.

That doesn't make sense.

"Doesn't it?"

The whisper seems to come from inside me and all around me at the same time.

I scuttle back against the wall, ignoring the throbbing in my shins.

"You did that. You did it to yourself."

I squeeze my eyes shut. I'm hallucinating.

"Why are you still here? You should be dead by now."

My head whips up.

"Anton is waiting. Isn't that what he said? What are *you* waiting for?"

I blink hard, my terror hardening to anger. When my story came out, I read comments of people praying Anton's words wouldn't lead me to do something "drastic" . . . while their tone said they were kinda hoping for that *Romeo and Juliet* ending. People speculated on how long it'd be before I joined him, whether in his final moments he'd seen how little time I had left.

That old anger propels me to my feet. At the last second, I remember the spade, but it hasn't moved. I still jog out of that room and shut the door.

As I do, another door slams somewhere above me.

Someone must have heard my yowl of pain. Or the clatter of me throwing the spade.

I look up the stairs and . . .

The basement door is shut.

That isn't possible. I wedged it open.

I stride up, too angry to be freaked out.

It's completely shut, and the cloth is nowhere to be seen, which is impossible because I'd wedged it from this side of the door.

Someone took the cloth and locked me in the basement.

I hurry the rest of the way, grab the knob, twist, and . . .

The door flies open. I scramble out and see the cloth behind the door.

So now what?

How about jumping in the car and leaving?

I shake my head. I'm the only one in danger, and I haven't experienced anything worse than a dull spade to my shins, which didn't even break the skin.

If whatever is here wants to talk to me, I'll be in the living room, enjoying my first coffee of the day as I figure out what to do about this.

TWENTY-SEVEN

I decide to tell Cirillo what's happening. Yes, I don't trust him not to use my story, but it's not as if he's planning to sell movie rights. He's the expert. He'll know what to do.

I don't get a chance to talk to Cirillo. Before breakfast, he's in his room working, coming down only for a coffee and then heading back up before I can get to him. I consider knocking on his bedroom door, but it's six in the morning.

Everyone convenes for breakfast, which means I have no chance to speak to him privately then. After we eat, Jin has to leave and before he does so, he needs—apparently—to be really, really sure that I'm not going to start the last séance without him.

I agree, and I mean it. Yes, it'd be easier to do the séance without Jin. I could tell Cirillo enough about my past to explain why I need to ask Anton about someone named Roddy. But I have enough common sense—and self-preservation—not to do it without Jin around. I don't trust Cirillo to stop the séance if things go wrong, and Shania will trust my judgment. In short, I need someone who can and will stop me, even if answers are dangling right in front of my nose.

I don't walk Jin out. The bugs are back, not as bad as they'd been at the height of their invasion, but enough for me to hand Jin my keys and wish him a safe journey . . . and then slam the door shut behind him as he races to my car.

Once he's gone, I find Shania in the kitchen, cleaning up. Cirillo has retreated to his room again.

I do my nebulizer therapy and then put on my vest. If Cirillo doesn't come down by the time I'm done, I'm going up.

I'm in the sitting room, hooked up to the vest, trying to concentrate on my book. I hear Shania in the hall, and I wait for her to enter, but she backs off. She must realize where I am and decide to leave me alone, in case Anton reaches out.

In case Anton reaches out.

After last night, I have no idea what to think. So much is happening and so much of it is contradictory that my puzzle-loving brain has thrown this aside as unsolvable.

Temporarily unsolvable, I should say, pending either more data or more caffeine. Anton used to buy me books of logic puzzles, and some that definitely fell into the too-challenging category, but I never gave up. I just set them aside. That's what I've done here. Set aside—

"Nic?"

My head jerks up.

I look around the room. The voice seemed to come from behind my head.

"Hey."

The word is a whisper, as if we're someplace quiet and he's trying to get my attention. But it definitely sounds like Anton's voice, coming from my left this time.

"Anton?"

The whisper comes from behind me again. "I love—"

There's an odd popping noise, and the voice stops. Then another pop, louder.

"It's okay," Anton's voice whispers to my left, but I ignore it now, my brain fixated on that double pop. It sounded mechanical.

I turn off the vest and remove it. I've never heard it make that sort of noise, which doesn't mean it couldn't, but the sound seemed to come from behind and above me.

Setting the vest aside, I look at the wall behind where I'd been sitting. There's a bookshelf covered in bric-a-brac, including two dolls. I take down the dolls first and turn them over. Nothing.

I tear that damn shelf apart looking for the source of the sound, and I don't find anything. Then I plunk down on the recliner with more force than necessary and re-situate myself as I had been.

I close my eyes and mentally replay the sound. It came from behind and above, yet I've emptied the bookcase and . . .

I gaze up and find myself looking at a vent.

I stand on the recliner seat, but the vent cover is still a foot from my hands. That means doing some fancy—and risky—footwork, and it's only once I'm balanced on the recliner arms that I remember I'm in the house with a ghost that likes to shove me.

I steady myself, reach up, and pry out the vent. It comes free with a pop that makes me stagger backward. Something drops out and bonks me on the head. I get down from the recliner and find the offending object on the floor.

It's a miniature speaker, the sort that I know—from my séance experiences—will have a battery and an MP3 player. When I first found one at a séance, I looked it up online and found a similar model being sold for Halloween costumes and haunted houses. A tiny speaker and player, with a motion-sensor trigger. This one looks more elaborate. Judging by the Bluetooth symbol, it can be activated that way, too.

There are three tiny buttons on the side. I press one, but nothing happens. That's when I see duct tape over a light, and I take it off to see that the light is red. That was the popping sound I heard—the speaker broke.

I look in the other direction from which I'd heard Anton's voice. Sure enough, there's another vent, this one a cold-air return. I remove the cover and find another microspeaker. When I pull the tape off this one, the light is green.

I hit the first button.

"Hey," Anton's voice says.

It takes a moment before my trembling fingers can hit the button again.

"Everything's fine," Anton says.

I hit it again, and there's a soft laugh. Anton's laugh. Another push, and he murmurs, "I love you, Nic."

I collapse onto the sofa as something inside me shatters.

Something inside me? No, I know what's shattering.

Hope.

This is what I'd heard. All the times in this house that I thought I heard Anton, this was what I was really hearing. His recorded voice.

But what about that time in here when he startled you, when he apologized? What about when you couldn't quite make out what he was saying, like last night?

I push that aside. I have the answer here in my palm, and anything else was either more recordings or my imagination adding to the repertoire because I'd been so sure he was here.

Hey.

Everything's fine.

I love you.

The tears come then, hot tears streaming down my face. I wanted this so bad. Even if I'd doubted, had felt that this wouldn't be what Anton would say, I'd still hoped.

I push the thought away and angrily swipe at my tears. I play the speaker again. That's Anton's voice. I'm sure of it.

Where the hell would Cirillo get recordings of Anton's voice?

Not Cirillo.

He'd been too excited at hearing these recordings.

Shania? No, she wouldn't have access to Anton's voice, and certainly not clips where he whispered that he loved me.

I hit the button again and put the speaker to my ear. When I do, there's a slight hitch between "everything's" and "fine," as if two clips were stitched together. The "hey" is clear. The laugh is clear. So is "I love you, Nic," but there's something about the way he's saying it . . .

Anton's voice is low and rough with emotion. I've heard him say it exactly that way. But where . . .

Our wedding video. Signing the register. Anton leaning over my shoulder, telling me he loved me.

There's only one person who could have done this. The guy who always joked about being in the AV club at school, who videotaped every family event for posterity, from my wedding to birthdays with my niece and nephew. Endless footage to comb through and find the bits he needed to re-create Anton, reassuring and loving Anton.

I remember that night in here with Jin. How we'd both heard Anton. Then he had me close my eyes while he left notes where he'd heard the voice. While he'd removed the speakers that created the voice.

Jin had only been the first to hear Anton when he allegedly heard him laugh, which no one else had. For the recordings, he must have triggered them and then waited, only chiming in after others had. Making sure I didn't think it was suspicious that my skeptical brother-in-law was always the first to hear Anton.

Before Jin left, he'd insisted we wait for him before doing the last séance. Because it's hard to stage a show when you're a hundred kilometers from the stage. Oh, this little performance would be easy enough, but the real show needs him.

Jin has spent the last eight months running intervention with my séance obsession. He knew I was going through hell, unable to stop myself, and he'd been there to help me stop.

Or had he? Libby had been the one truly running the intervention. Jin had just tagged along for moral support.

Still, he knew what I'd been through with endless con artists pretending they'd made contact. So after all that . . . he sets it up to seem like Cirillo contacted Anton?

I don't understand.

The whispers from last night come back.

Why are you still here? You should be dead by now.

Anton is waiting. Isn't that what he said? What are you waiting for?

My stomach twists. Could those have somehow been Jin?

I'd heard a noise in the basement and gone downstairs, where I heard a rustling that turned out to be a mouse, and I forgot the clangs that originally caught my attention.

That mouse wasn't responsible for the clangs. Or for the dripping that held my attention while Jin could close the door upstairs and activate the recording.

A recording of someone urging me to join Anton. To kill myself.

Or not even a recording, but Jin himself, using his tech to disguise and throw his voice.

I rub my face. No, that's ridiculous.

Is it?

He's playing me clips of Anton's voice, his laugh, his reassurance, his love.

I'll be waiting.

Anton is right there, on the other side, waiting. Hear his voice? Remember how much you loved him? You want to be with him, don't you?

I rub my face harder. That makes no sense. What would Jin have to gain by my death?

Money.

I don't know my brother's financial situation. He refuses to discuss it, which tells me it's not as good as my own—he doesn't want me feeling bad about inheriting my parents' estate. I know that I make more, and my take-home pay is significantly more, since I don't have dependents.

Libby might be a clinical psychologist, but she works for a hospital, which means she's not bringing in private-care-level income. Neither is Jin.

My brother isn't struggling financially. If he were, I'd be there to fill the gap. But Jin isn't Keith, and there's a million-dollar jackpot waiting for the death of someone who has lived longer than anyone expected her to.

More than a million now, with my personal estate doubling after inheriting from Anton. After Anton's death, I changed my will. All the remaining trust goes to Keith, as our parents wanted, but now so does half of my estate, with the rest still divided between his two kids.

It's a lot of money. And the only thing standing between it and Keith is me.

The only thing standing between it and *Jin* is me.

Am I honestly thinking Jin would try driving me to suicide to cash in? That's ridiculous.

Is it?

I've already been questioning whether my husband could be a sociopathic killer. I've been telling myself that no one ever really knows anyone, and Anton has only been back in my life for a few years, and am I really sure he couldn't have killed Heather?

Now I'm refusing to believe something horrible of someone I've known for less time? Yes, Jin and I are close, but I don't know him as well as I knew Anton, so if I'm questioning my husband . . .

If I'm questioning my husband, maybe it's a sign that I need to get the hell out of this house. Stop this bullshit and leave.

I can't leave because Jin has my damned car.

I sit there, staring down at the speakers, and then realize a fundamental truth. Jin is not dead. So, unlike my deceased husband, I don't need a séance to ask him what the hell he's doing.

I grab my phone and call. After six endless rings, it goes to voicemail. I frown down at the phone. Unlike my brother, Jin always answers while driving. Keith won't, nor will he learn how to use Do Not Disturb while driving, and I swear sometimes he does it just to piss off his tech-savvy little sister.

Jin must be on the line. Not to Keith, who would give him shit for talking in the car, even over Bluetooth. But if it *were* Keith on the other end, Jin would swap calls to tell me. It must be work.

I should wait patiently, but I just found out that my brother-in-law—and one of my best friends—faked my dead husband's voice on a recording. I don't give a shit about being patient or polite.

I call again. Again it goes to voicemail.

I text, but the message sits there, delivered but not read. As I stare at it, I reconsider whether I really want to speak to Jin right now. I can't read his body language over the phone. This might be a conversation best held in person.

I turn the speakers over in my hand. Then I flip my phone to the notepad and start a list of everything I've experienced that I suspected could be Anton.

Next I go through the list and remove every voice that was definitely recorded.

I sort the rest of the list into things I thought were Anton and the rest.

Without those recorded reassurances, the Anton list is short. A few utterances, and one physical manifestation, where I thought I saw him lunging at me last night.

The only things that others experienced were those recordings, meaning the rest could be my imagination. If there's any chance those things *were* Anton, none of them are clearly positive in nature. And for all the times I thought I heard him, there are none where I can say, beyond any doubt, that it wasn't another recording.

Cirillo thought we had two entities here: Anton and some darker force. I'd worried that the darker force *was* Anton, and the only thing arguing against that was the quiet reassurances . . . which were fake.

But without those, there's also no corroborated evidence of Anton at all. Cirillo was basing "Anton is here" on those recordings.

Now I really need to speak to Cirillo.

TWENTY-EIGHT

I'm not going to accuse Jin, but Cirillo has to know about the speakers. Basing his funding application on fake data could cost him his career. He can help me sort through the evidence and determine what is legitimate. Because some of it *is* legitimate, and whatever Jin has done, there's no way he's responsible for the invisible hands that have pushed me or pulled rugs from under me or slammed a spade into my shins.

I tuck the speakers into my pockets. I don't want Shania seeing them until after I've spoken to Cirillo.

I can hear Shania tapping on her laptop in the breakfast nook, so I sneak around the other way, and pause in the kitchen. No sign of Cirillo, not even an empty mug by the sink. He must still be upstairs.

I climb to his room. The door's closed. I knock. No answer. I knock again.

"Davos? I need to speak to you."

Still nothing. I gingerly take hold of the doorknob. It goes a quarter turn and stops.

Locked.

Okay . . .

The locks on these doors have been changed since the house's bed-and-breakfast days, when each guest required a secure room. These are simple privacy locks, the sort intended to keep your kids from barging in.

I knock again, louder. Worry slides in to replace the annoyance. I keep telling myself that everyone else is safe because the ghost only targets me. Again, that's a logical fallacy. The ghost has only targeted me *so far.* There's no reason why it couldn't go after the others.

I fetch a pen from my room and take out the refill. Then I knock again before putting the slender cylinder into the hole and popping the lock.

The door opens. I push it one inch.

"Davos? It's Nicola. I'm coming in."

No answer.

I open the door another couple of inches. His room doesn't have an attached bathroom, so he can't be in that. I can see the bed and small desk, and he isn't at either.

I step inside. The only place I can't see is the floor on the other side of the bed and desk.

I check the bedside first. No signs of him there. I turn around where I can see the spot behind the desk. He's not there either.

My gaze goes to the window, as if a forty-year-old professor is going to exit that way.

This makes no sense. If the door can only be locked from the inside . . .

Wait. If I was easily able to open it, there's no reason Cirillo couldn't lock it behind him and then use something to pop it open. That's the only way to have a semi-secure room.

Mystery solved.

I hurry toward the door. I want to relock it and get out before he returns. I don't relish explaining why I broke into his room. Yes, I was concerned, but I'm not sure my brain is a good judge of reasonable behavior right now.

I'm passing the desk when a notebook snags my attention. I might be a techie, but I do appreciate a fancy notebook. I've even been known to buy them, on the off chance that I'll suddenly decide to start taking longhand notes. The book is gorgeous. Leather-bound by the looks of it. I find myself reaching to open the cover.

Um, weren't you leaving? Quickly?

I just want to see this. Such an expensive cover on a disposable item seems a waste. Also, the book has a lock. It reminds me of the diary I had as a child, only this is a real lock, one that can't be picked with a fingernail. It's been left half latched, as if it didn't quite catch when he shut it.

I wriggle the locking mechanism open, flip the cover, and give a nod of satisfaction. This isn't a disposable notebook. The leather-bound exterior holds a removable pad of paper.

So now I'm at Cirillo's desk, having broken into his room and opened the notebook he accidentally left unlocked. As long as I'm piling on faux pas and misdemeanors . . .

I flip to one of the latest pages.

NL is not an easy woman to work with. She's argumentative and fixated on disbelieving her own experiences. I'm not sure why she hired me. I know she has a history of uncovering fraudulent mediums, and I've begun to suspect I've been set up.

I snort. *You're worried about being set up?* Now he knows how I feel when I'm questioning *his* motives, feeling misled.

That page is about five from the end, shortly after he arrived and before stuff really started happening. He soon lost his skepticism.

This might be the most complex haunting I have encountered, as well as one of the most definitive. There is no doubt that there are entities here. We have successfully summoned AN, but he seems to be trapped on the other side of the veil. There's a second entity as well, a darker force that I can't pin down.

I need to push NL further. Both entities are clearly focused on her. I realize it may be unethical to push her when I have doubts about her safety, but I will keep a close watch on the proceedings. NL herself might be difficult, but she is at the center of a compelling story.

I believe I finally have the cornerstone of my book. Sid has argued that he can't sell it without a strong central narrative to hang my research on. I have fought that, but I finally understand what he means. My experiences and research are interesting and important, but a mainstream audience requires more, and with NL's story-the background and the séance results-I think I have it. Sid agrees.

I reread that last paragraph. Then I skim for a sign that I have misinterpreted, and that Cirillo is *not* using my séance—a *private* engagement—for a *book*.

The following pages only make it clearer, as the asshole tap-dances around the fact that he is milking my tragedy—and endangering my safety—to get a damned book deal.

He's planning to profit off what happened to me, off what's happening here.

He's willing to push me past the point of safety for a better story.

Hey, if we're lucky, the entity will kill Nicola, and I'll get to write a tragic romance of a woman who dies at the hands of an evil entity accidentally summoned while she's desperately trying to contact her husband.

Aww.

I tried to convince her to end the séances when they got dangerous, but she refused. I think she hid the worst of it from me. It was almost as if she wanted to join her husband. How sad . . . and yet heartwarming at the same time. A satisfying story of lovers reaching across the divide to reunite.

Could that have been Cirillo I heard last night? Telling me to end my life?

By this point, I have no fucking idea. I only know that this asshole has set me up. I kept telling myself that he'd stop if things got too dangerous. Hell, he insisted he would. But here I have the proof of his lie. Whatever we've summoned *is* dangerous, and he wants to push harder.

Time to pull the plug on this. My brother-in-law has staged at least half this damn summoning, and my medium is ready to shove me into traffic to get a story from it.

If there's any consolation, it's that Cirillo is going to be livid when he realizes how much was faked.

I shut the book and stalk from the room. When my phone buzzes, I barely glance at it.

Keith. Figures.

I send it to voicemail. He texts.

Keith: When did Jin leave?

Really, Keith? This is not the time. I almost ignore the text. Then I remember what Jin has done, and my stomach plummets.

I'd forgotten what might be the most important part of that equation: my brother. I just discovered that his husband . . .

I'm not sure what Jin's motive is, but he's betrayed both of us, and goddamn it, my brother loves him.

Fuck.

> Me: Just after nine.

Keith: Have you heard from him?

> Me: No.

**Keith: We were supposed to grab coffee before his
meeting. I've been waiting for thirty minutes**

> Me: Toronto traffic?

Keith: He's not answering his phone or texts

Shit.

I don't tell Keith that Jin didn't answer my calls and texts either.
I don't want to worry him, and the one who's really worried is me.
Is Jin avoiding us? Is there some kind of setup here that I don't see?

> Me: Maybe he finally listened to you and shut off his phone
> while he's driving
> Me: Or he didn't plug it in properly last night and it's dead

Keith: Yeah, I'm mother-henning again, aren't I?

> Me: Cluck-cluck
> Me: I'm sure he's fine

Keith: I'll chill. Talk later?

I send a thumbs-up, and I'm just glad this conversation is by text; if
he could hear my voice he'd know something was wrong.

I can't think about Jin right now. If I suspected he was any threat to Keith, I'd stop whatever I was doing and deal with that first. But I don't see any possible motive for those recordings that would involve hurting my brother.

Unless that's his ultimate plan. Drive me to suicide and then kill my brother for the money.

I press my fingertips to my temples. I'm losing my mind. I really am.

And what if that's not hyperbole? What if something really *is* wrong with me?

First I suspect Anton could have murdered Heather and framed Patrice. Then I think Jin is trying to drive me to suicide to claim Keith's inheritance. Finally, I convince myself that Cirillo is stealing my story for a book.

Except I know the part about Cirillo is right. I read it upstairs.

Am I sure? If I really were spiraling into some kind of mental break, couldn't I have hallucinated that?

I rub my temples.

I know what I saw.

Just like I saw Anton's ghost last night? Saw my husband's spirit lunging at me, his face twisted in rage? Like I'm sure that spade twisted in my hands and rammed into my shin?

Just like I'm sure that basement door swung shut after I propped it open?

Just like I'm sure someone tried to push me down the stairs and yanked out the bath mat?

Yes, damn it. I *am* sure. If my imagination is edging into paranoia, that only applies to my fears about Anton and Jin. The rest is real, and if the rest is real, then can I be blamed for spiraling into wild theories about my husband and brother-in-law?

I'm forcing myself to question two people I love because whatever is happening here, it's bad, and I need to consider even the ugliest— and most outlandish—possibilities.

I reach the main level. Shania is still in the breakfast nook. When

I walk into the kitchen, it's so dark that I think someone has pulled the blinds. Then I hear the buzzing. I hadn't noticed it before now. Maybe I'd gotten inured to it the other day, and when it returned, I just didn't notice.

Beyond the kitchen windows, the world is dark with a swarm of midges thicker than I've ever seen. I have to walk to the window to be sure of what I'm seeing. It is literally black outside the window.

Is that actually the bugs?

Yes, I can hear them, and I can see a few on the glass.

But are you sure that entire roiling swarm is midges?

What the hell else would it be?

Why aren't the others noticing this?

I walk into the living room. Beyond it, I can see the back windows, and they're just as dark. Yet Shania keeps working away in the breakfast nook.

Am I hallucinating?

Where the hell is Cirillo?

I rub my temples and ignore the bugs. Shania will be working with her headphones on and she's probably pulled the blinds against the screen glare.

Now find Cirillo.

I'm passing the basement door when I catch a noise. I'm not even sure what it is—just something in the basement.

I ease open the door. It's dark below, the lights all off. I'm standing at the top of the stairs, head tilted to figure out what I heard.

I'm reaching for that light switch when I stop. It's *not* completely dark down there. My eyes have adjusted enough for me to see light shining from under the closed furnace-room door.

A door I left open last night.

TWENTY-NINE

I consider, and then I back into the kitchen and grab a steak knife.
I don't want to bump into Brodie Kilmer high on something and
hiding in our basement.

With the knife in hand, I quietly descend the stairs. At the bottom,
I take a moment to listen at that closed door. I'm definitely hearing a
person moving about inside.

I ease the door open a crack. Then I peer in to find myself looking
at Cirillo's back as he bends to examine something.

Why the hell is Cirillo down here with the door shut and the
stairway light off?

I remember last night, what happened to me down here, the voices
I heard.

I'd wondered whether it could have been Cirillo and then brushed
it off as paranoia.

Before I can back out and think this through, Cirillo turns, as
if sensing the open door. He gives a start. I push it open and walk
through.

"What are you doing down here?" I say.

He starts to casually push his hands into his pockets, and then realizes he's holding his phone, and settles for leaning against the wall.

"I heard something last night," he says.

"Last night?" *And you came down at almost noon to check it out?*

As if hearing the unspoken part, he says, "I'd forgotten all about it. I woke around four hearing something, but I was so tired that I fell back to sleep. I was getting a coffee when I passed the basement door and came down to investigate."

Shutting the door behind you. Turning off the light at the bottom of the stairs. Shutting the next door behind you, too.

"Well, if it was four in the morning, that was me. I went to the kitchen for a glass of water, thought I heard something, and investigated. Turned out to be a mouse."

"Ah."

"While I have you, though," I say, "I've been trying to speak to you about something. One thing that kept me up last night was that talk about using my story for your grant."

He exhales in a slow hiss through his teeth.

NL is not an easy woman to work with.

"It will be anonymous," he says. "You have my word on that."

"I know, but I've decided I need more. I'm having an agreement drawn up."

He stiffens. "An agreement?"

I give a dismissive wave. "It's nothing, really. Just protecting both of us. It says that if my story is used for funding, all names and locations will be changed."

He relaxes. "Of course. I can do that."

"Great. My lawyer is working on it now."

"Yes, of course. Whatever makes you feel more comfortable, Nicola."

I turn back toward the door and then stop. "Oh, and she's putting in something about limiting the use of my story to research and associated funding. Not my idea. She's just covering all the bases. Making sure you don't do something like sell book or film rights." I laugh. "I told her that was silly, but you know lawyers. We pay them to be thorough."

Call me a petty bitch, but I bask in the frozen horror that seeps into Cirillo's face.

"Davos? Are you okay?"

"Y-yes. I . . ." He gathers his professorial dignity and lifts his chin. "I just realized that I am going to need to place a call myself. You are correct about lawyers and their thoroughness, and mine will insist on seeing that agreement before I sign it."

"That's fair."

He lifts his phone and begins to tap. "I'll let him know, but I warn you that he is much too busy to get it done on such short notice."

"Really? Shit. Well . . ." I gnaw my lower lip. "Maybe you can make it a priority? We can't hold our last séance until it's signed."

"What?"

I give a rueful scrunch of my nose. "Yeah, my lawyer is a real hard-ass. She's furious with me for even starting this without a proper agreement. She's warned that if I proceed without a signed contract, she's dropping me as a client because she can't be held responsible for what happens if I proceed against her advice."

Thank God my lawyer is my former university roommate, who really will be able to squeeze in this agreement today . . . and won't give me shit for putting words in her mouth.

I relish the look on Cirillo's face and then, because I truly am the most petty bitch ever, I add, "Maybe skipping the séance is for the best. I'm starting to think this isn't safe for me. I've heard from Anton. I know he's fine. That's what I wanted."

"B-but you can't leave it like this," he says. "You've unleashed something here—"

"Pretty sure I'm not the one who summoned it. When I say I can't proceed, I don't mean you can't finish up. I just can't be here. I'm—"

He turns sharply, and my brows shoot up as he directs his glare into the room at large.

"Did you hear that?" he says.

I resist the urge to cross my arms at the obvious distraction.

"A dripping sound," he says. "I heard it just before you came down."

Okay, *that* gets my attention.

"I heard it last night," I say. "I can't find it, though. I thought it was the hot-water heater."

"It's not. The sound is too sporadic for me to get a fix on it."

Part of me wants to brush this off, so I can go place that call to my lawyer. Yet another part can't help but be drawn into this most minor of mysteries. Sure, a random drip is the least of our concerns, but it pokes at me, and if we can solve it together, I can keep Cirillo from knowing I'm pissed off . . . until I want him to know it.

I look around. "I investigated the water heater and the furnace. Neither seems to be dripping. Same with the pipes."

"And I looked for any moisture on the floor. There's nothing. We aren't below the main-floor bathroom, so that isn't the answer. I can't—"

He stops. "There, did you hear it?"

I only lift a finger for quiet. It was a single drip, one that seemed to come from my right. I'm starting to move in that direction when another drip sounds, this one loud enough for me to pinpoint.

"The old furnace," I say. "I didn't think to check that."

Cirillo frowns. "Because it clearly hasn't been used in decades. What would be dripping in that?"

I shrug. "Furnace oil? Condensation?"

I move closer for a better look. It really is a monster of a machine.

"There's a service door there," Cirillo says as he points at a metal hatch on the side.

I shake my head. "That's for wood."

"It's a wood-burning furnace?"

"Combination oil and wood. Anton told me about it. After his grandfather died, it was his and his brother's job to chop wood when they were here. His brother paid him to do it for both of them."

I walk over and take hold of the lever. "You open this and put in the wood." I turn it, surprised to find that it moves easily. When I yank open the metal door, something drops inside. I fall back with a yelp and then give a short laugh.

"Yep, I'm a little jumpy," I say.

Cirillo doesn't answer. I frown over to see him staring through the wood-loading door. I follow his gaze in and see what looks like a shoe inside the furnace.

I reach to pull it out . . . only to go still. It's not a discarded shoe. It's hanging . . . down. Hanging off what looks like a leg.

I stagger back, hands flying to my mouth.

Cirillo whirls on me. "You just happened to know how to open that, Nicola?"

"W-what?"

I drag my gaze away from that hanging foot and stare at Cirillo, his ice-cold gaze fixed on me. I take a slow step backward, and my hand moves toward the steak knife in my rear pocket.

There is a foot in the furnace. A *leg* hanging down from somewhere in the dark depths, and Cirillo is glaring. At *me*.

"W-what's going on?" I say, resisting the urge to back up again.

"That would be my question." His gaze locks on mine. "Do you want to know the real reason I came down here, Nicola? Yes, I heard something last night. But I suspected it was you. I've begun to suspect you've been doing many things. Last night, you were the only one who didn't run into the living room when we heard Anton's voice . . . and you should have been the first. You lured us out so you could knock over your chair and pretend it was a ghost."

I can't form a response. His words don't make sense. There is a foot—a *foot*—dangling inside the furnace, and he's accusing me of pretending a ghost knocked over my chair.

"You're the only one experiencing the physical manifestations," he says. "We've heard Anton's voice, but those could be recordings. The rest is all you."

I wave toward the foot because it's all I can think of to do.

"Do you really expect me to fall for that?" he says. "No, silly question. You *do* expect it. You swing open that furnace door and down falls a mannequin leg, and I'm supposed to run screaming from the basement, giving you time to hide it and then claim it was a ghostly manifestation."

Footsteps pound on the stairs, and Shania comes running in.

"What's going on?" she says. "I heard—"

She sees the open furnace door and frowns, and I dart forward to shut it, but it's too late. She backs up, hands clapping to her mouth.

"It's fake," Cirillo snaps. "Are you happy now, Nicola? Doubled your audience? Too bad your brother-in-law isn't here to see it. No, wait. That's intentional. You waited until Jin was gone. He's an intelligent man who knows you well enough to see through your tricks." Cirillo advances on me. "Those mediums you visited, they didn't set you up, did they? You set yourself up."

I open my mouth, but I can't form even a strangled protest as my brain struggles to make sense of what he's saying.

He continues, "When you contacted me, you expressed your discomfort with all the attention your situation brought. But that was a lie. You *enjoyed* it. And if one of those mediums managed to contact Anton, it would be over. So you had to keep making them look like charlatans. The poor grieving and sick widow, taken advantage of, over and over again."

I start to hear what he's saying. What he's accusing me of. Anger sparks . . . and then I remember I have those speakers in my pockets, and I have to resist the urge to slap my hands over them, like a child trying to hide the evidence.

"I'm not sick," I say with as much calm as I can muster. "I have a chronic illness. I *am* a grieving widow, and maybe I've made mistakes, but no one who knows me would ever suspect I set this up to draw attention to myself."

My gaze goes to Shania, looking for confirmation, but she's frozen with such uncertainty on her face that my stomach twists.

"Shania?" I say.

She can't meet my gaze. "You used to fake these, Nic."

"What?"

"When I went to that first medium with you, I was shocked by how quickly you saw through the tricks. You told me you used to set them up."

"When I was a *child*. At sleepover séances in middle school, I faked things because that's what the other girls wanted. It was a game."

I look from Shania to Cirillo. "I did not fake this. Any of this." My gaze locks on Cirillo. "You said I lured everyone out upstairs to pretend a ghost toppled my chair over. But I never said that."

"You didn't need to," he says. "That's part of the act. You're the first to insist it could all be your imagination, so no one can think you're jumping to conclusions . . . let alone staging it yourself. Are those even your husband's ashes in that box, Nicola?"

The anger ignites. "*Excuse* me?"

"Something is wrong with this summoning. We keep hearing Anton, but he's just throwing out random sound bites. No matter how hard I focus on him, something is wrong. Whose ashes are in that box?"

My vision clouds red with rage. He is accusing me of tampering with my husband's mortal remains to keep milking . . . What am I milking? What would be the point of all this?

My rage freezes.

What would be the point indeed.

He's accusing me of something so heinous, I'll forget everything else.

That is the point.

My jaw clenches, and I need to force myself to get words out. "There is a foot in that furnace, Dr. Cirillo. You stand here accusing me of staging it, but you haven't made a move to prove that."

If Cirillo hasn't been eager to prove the foot is fake, does that mean *he* planted it?

I start to step toward the furnace. Then I stop.

"I need something to hold it," I say. "If it is fake, I'm not leaving fingerprints."

"For fuck's sake." Cirillo strides toward the open door, reaches in, and grabs the shoe. He yanks it, hard, and it comes off in his hand, and he staggers back.

"Nice try," I say. "Let me guess. The fake foot is stuck, and you need me to run upstairs and get something to help pull it out. No, now you'll need both me *and* Shania to go upstairs, though I'm not sure how you'll convince us of that."

The look he shoots at me is so full of hate that my insides stutter. My first thought is: *What have I done to him?* My second thought? *I know what I've done.*

By insisting on a legal agreement, I've called his bluff, and that's where his focus is. On the bitch who is trying to ruin his shot at a book deal.

There's a foot hanging out of that furnace, and he's decided I put it there because he's too incensed to realize that makes no fucking sense.

And now I'm doing the same thing. There is a foot hanging in that furnace, but I'm ignoring the implication because I've bought into his narrative. Someone must have put a fake foot in there. Anything else is . . .

"Davos?" I say, my voice breathy as he turns back to the furnace. "I . . . I don't think—"

He's already at the door, leaning in to grab that foot and show me that he's right and I'm wrong, and I probably did this whole thing for attention because that's what people like me do. Tragic widows. The chronically ill. We get a taste of attention, and we want more.

He grabs the foot, and then staggers back with a strangled shriek, and with that noise, I know what has happened. He grabbed the foot, expecting plastic, and touched flesh. Cold flesh.

Jin.

I shove past Cirillo, clawing and scrabbling to get to that furnace.

Keith said Jin hasn't shown up and I can't get ahold of him, and when he left this morning, he was wearing running shoes and—

There is a sound in the furnace. A slow, sliding sound. Before I can get to the furnace, something falls from its depths.

The first thing I see is blood. Clothing and skin bathed in blood, and I'm slammed back twenty-two years, turning over Heather and seeing what had been done to her.

The images crash together into a single picture, a body splayed with the chest sliced open from throat to sternum, intestines spilling out.

I squeeze my eyes shut for a split second before I hear Shania screaming and realize she's been screaming all along.

I force my eyes open. I see a hand. I see a knife clutched in the hand, and I see Patrice lying on the forest floor, reaching for a bloody knife—

Stop! Stop!

I let out a snarl of frustration and shake away the memory, but when I open my eyes, that is what I do see. A hand clutching a knife. A pale white hand that is not Jin's.

I drag my gaze along that arm and . . .

And I was not imagining things. I was not letting the past shape the present. I am looking at a chest sliced open, intestines spilling, and a bloodied hunting knife clutched in the corpse's hand as if . . .

As if what? They sliced themself open and crawled into the fucking furnace?

That's when I finally look at the face. It's a young man, and Mrs. Kilmer's words come back.

He's five foot ten and a hundred and sixty pounds. Short light brown hair and blue eyes.

"Brodie," I whisper.

We've found Brodie Kilmer.

THIRTY

The moment I see the body—and realize who it is—I run for the door. Cirillo leaps into my way.

"Where do you think you're going?" he says.

I stare at him. "To call the cops, obviously."

"You can place the call from the basement, Nicola."

"I could if I had my damn phone." I go to pat my pockets for emphasis and then remember the speakers and steak knife and stop.

"Fine," I say. "You call them."

Cirillo only eyes me, and there's a moment where I feel like I must be dreaming because none of this makes sense. There's a body lying a few feet from us. A *mutilated corpse.* The obvious next step is to call the police. Yet Cirillo stands there, eyes narrowing, as if I've suggested we stuff poor Brodie back into the furnace.

He must be in shock.

"We need to call the police," I say slowly.

"You were running from a crime scene," he says.

"What?"

"You don't think this *is* a crime scene?" He steps toward me. "Are you going to tell me the boy did that to himself?"

"No, obviously it's murder. That's why we need to contact the police."

He only watches me with those narrowed eyes, and a chill creeps up my spine. Over the last few days, I've wondered whether I'm losing my mind. But now I'm the one doing the sane thing, and if Cirillo is stopping me, then either he's lost it . . . or he's responsible for . . .

I look toward Brodie's body, and carefully inch my hand toward the steak knife in my back pocket.

"That's how you found Heather and Patrice, too."

I freeze, following the voice as if it comes from nowhere. As if I've forgotten there's someone else down here with us.

"I looked up the story, Nic," Shania whispers. "That's what I was doing upstairs. You gave me enough to look it up, and I had to know." She looks at me. "You found Heather, nearly dead, with her . . . her stomach ripped open. And you found Patrice lying on the forest floor, injured and holding a hunting knife. Right, Nicola? Or it's Janica, isn't it? Your real name is Janica."

"*Real name?*" Cirillo wheels on me. "What the hell is going on?"

"What's going on is we have a dead body," I say as calmly as I can, enunciating each word. "One of you needs to call the police. I am not trying to leave. I will stay right here until they arrive and answer all their questions. Just—"

"I want to know what Shania is talking about," Cirillo snaps.

Seriously? There is a mutilated corpse so close I can smell *it, and you're worried about—*

I stop the thought and speak again, just as calmly. "Call 911, and then I will explain—"

"It happened when Nicola—Janica—was in high school," Shania cuts in. "Back when she knew Anton."

"Holy shit, are we really doing this? There is a murdered—"

Cirillo blocks me as Shania keeps talking.

"Nicola and her two friends were holding séances in the forest," she says. "Something went wrong. Anton was there—Nicola admitted he and his friends staged a haunting. Then one of the girls ended up like this."

She waves at Brodie, and I can gnash my teeth at this sudden betrayal, but she's in shock, and all she can think is that this dead boy has been killed like my friend from twenty-two years ago.

I've been wondering whether my husband had something to do with that, so I can't really blame Shania for wondering whether I'm responsible for this. She barely knows me.

The problem is that a *corpse* just fell from the furnace, the badly mutilated corpse of a missing young man, and the very obvious next step is to call the police. But that's me, thinking logically even in my shock. Now the *logical* thing for me to do is to answer their questions so we can make that phone call.

"Yes, we held two séances," I say. "Anton and his friends staged a haunting at the first, acting as if we'd conjured the ghost of a young man who killed his girlfriend. Patrice thought she was possessed by that young man."

Shania tries to jump in, but now I'm the one speaking over *her.* "Patrice insisted on a second séance to fix it. At the time, I didn't know the boys faked the haunting. I didn't know what happened. But I thought if it was all in Patrice's head, we only needed to convince her we'd fixed it. Instead, Heather ended up . . ." I look at Brodie's body and can't get the words out.

Shania says, "Then Nicola claimed she stumbled over a blood-covered Patrice lying in wait, with a knife in her hand. Patrice chased her out of the forest."

"No," I say. "I found Patrice lying *beside* a knife. She had blood on her. When she started to get up, I ran. The police came. Patrice was arrested and . . ." I swallow. "She was remanded to a mental institution."

"While you got to walk away, change your name, and lead a happy new life with the guy who started it all," Shania says. "The guy who made Patrice think she was possessed."

The venom in her voice startles me.

I say, quietly, "I hope that's not what happened. It really was just a prank—"

"Boys being boys."

"I never said that." I keep my voice level. "I'm not defending what they did."

"What about what you did?" Shania says.

My shoulders tighten as guilt rolls over me. "If you mean changing my name, I was young and convinced that everyone knew who I was after the news stories. If you mean the séances, yes, obviously I regret not doing more to stop Patrice and Heather."

"I mean this." Shania jabs a finger at Brodie. "We found him exactly the way you found Heather and Patrice. Sliced open with a bloody hunting knife in his hand."

I don't say that's not how I found either Heather or Patrice. She's conflating the two because she's freaked out, and she's drawing parallels because there *are* parallels.

I don't know what's going on. I can't wrap my brain around it. Maybe that's why my mind keeps screaming at me to call the police.

Call the police. Let them deal with it. Get out of this house. *Now!*

I didn't kill Brodie. I cannot imagine Jin or Shania or Cirillo killed Brodie. But there is something in this house, something that knows me as Janica, and I don't know if it's Anton or Roddy or Anton possessed by Roddy—

Stop. Focus.

Call the police. Let them deal with it. Get the fuck out of this house.

"You think I had something to do with this." My voice is flat as I push any hint of outrage from it. "Okay. That's for the police to decide. I'm not trying to escape. I'm not even insisting on being the one who makes that call. I will sit over there." I point. "I will wait for the police to arrive after one of you calls them."

That's reasonable, right? It's the most fucking reasonable thing anyone could possibly say when accused of having sliced open a young man whose body lies a few feet away.

In fact, it's probably too reasonable, even for me, which means I'm in shock. But the point is that I'm not running for the door. I'm not insisting on using my own phone, so I could escape while I'm upstairs getting it. I'm not insisting on making that call, so I could fake it. And I'm not asking how the hell anyone could think I'd do something like this.

I might be shaking inside. I might be freaking out and trying so damn hard not to panic, but outwardly I am calm and I am reasonable.

"Nicola didn't do this," Cirillo says.

My breath catches.

Dear God, is someone else here being reasonable? Hallelujah.

He continues, "Either way, though, it's obvious why she wants us to call the police."

Because there's a dead body in the room? A mutilated corpse that was stuffed in a furnace? I have to bite my cheek against the wild urge to laugh at the absurdity.

"She wants us to call the police because she knows she'll get away with it."

"What?" I pivot to face him.

Cirillo says, "Anton was there for those teenage séances. He orchestrated the fake hauntings."

Shania nods.

I fight against the surge of howling frustration and resume my role as the voice of reason. "Anton was only at the first one. His friends wanted to play a prank, and Anton went along to keep them in check. They were all at a movie when Heather died."

"Are you sure?" Shania says. "That's easy to fake. Just buy tickets. Maybe they were setting up an alibi."

"Anton didn't kill—"

"Even you suspected he might have been involved."

My mouth opens in protest, but she barrels on. "I caught you looking up the case yesterday, and you confessed your fears. Dr. Cirillo thinks we have two entities—Anton and something dark. You're afraid Anton *is* the something dark."

"I considered it . . . and dismissed it."

"Conveniently," she mutters, and part of me wants to laugh. Ever since I've known Shania, I've wanted her to be more assertive, more confident. Now she is . . . and it's at my expense.

I can be hurt, but I understand. She read the details of my past online and then found Brodie murdered in a way that matches my friend's horrible death. At the very least, I'm the kind of woman who marries a sociopath and tries to cover for him.

Cirillo nods. "All right then. That confirms my suspicion. Why is Nicola so eager to call the police?"

"Because there's a fucking—" I begin.

"Because she knows she can get away with this," he says again. "No one is going to believe a terminally ill widow sliced open this boy. And no one is certainly going to believe a ghost did it."

"Why would Anton's ghost do this?" I wave at Brodie. "Why would I do it? If there is something here and if it killed this boy, then it's not my husband. I'm not even sure it's human. Maybe it's Roddy Silva—"

"Who?" Cirillo says.

"The other young man she mentioned," Shania says. "The one who killed his girlfriend twenty years before her friend, Heather, died. Roddy Silva murdered his girlfriend in the same way and then took his own life and was found holding the knife. Like that." She points at Brodie.

He wasn't found like that, but again, I won't nitpick.

"Also?" Shania says. "Roddy was Anton's uncle."

Cirillo rubs his temples. "So we're dealing with generational homicidal madness. But Nicola? If you swear those ashes upstairs belong to Anton, then that is who I've summoned. Not this Uncle Roddy. Not some random ghost. Your husband. Anton. Who seems to have murdered this Heather girl when he was alive and now, as a ghost, he has murdered Brodie Kilmer."

"You said ghosts can't seriously harm the living."

"Obviously I was wrong. Now whatever the story, you know the police won't listen to nonsense about homicidal ghosts. That's why you want to call them, and that's why we are not letting you."

"We have a dead body. A murdered young man—"

"And I can get his story. From him."

I go still. "What?"

Cirillo waves at Brodie. "I had you bring Anton's ashes because it provided the best way to contact him. This is even better. I'll summon Brodie and ask what happened to him."

I stare. He's kidding, right? Oh, I can tell by his expression that he's not, but that only means he's lost it. Seeing Brodie like that has shattered all semblance of common sense, and he's spiraling into a delusional world where contacting a murdered man's ghost is the very definition of reasonable.

No, not reasonable. There's something in his eyes, like he's spotting that golden ring dangling in front of him again.

He sees a story. A marketable story even better than the one he has, because in this one, he becomes the hero.

In the middle of a series of séances, Dr. Davos Cirillo discovers a horribly mutilated corpse . . . only to learn it matches a corpse from the grieving widow's secret past. He has no idea what to make of this, but the solution is clear. He must reach beyond the veil to the one person who can answer this most unanswerable question.

He must summon the dead man's ghost.

Will anyone reading such a story pause to wonder why Cirillo didn't call the police? Not if he spins it right, and certainly not if he actually makes contact and solves the murder.

All I know for sure right now is that I do not want to contact *anything* in this house. Because whatever killed Brodie is waiting for nightfall. Waiting for the next séance.

I look at Shania. She might be confused and in shock, but even she knows we need to call the—

"Agreed," she says, and her eyes glint in a way that makes me do a double take. "Contact Brodie's ghost. Find out what happened."

"Are you—?" I stop myself before saying anything to set them off. Instead, I speak slowly. "We need to call the police. Even if Brodie could tell us anything, we can't do a séance right now. Whatever killed him is here, and if we summon it—"

"You aren't going to stop, are you, Nicola?" Shania's voice has gone ice-cold. "You'll say anything to keep us from getting these answers. Well, the only ghost I've heard was Anton."

"That wasn't Anton," I blurt. "Jin set it up."

I pull out the speakers. Something clatters to the floor, and everyone stops to stare at it.

The steak knife.

They don't say a word. They just look from that knife to me, as if all their questions are answered.

"It's a steak knife," I say. "From the kitchen. I grabbed it when I heard someone down here because I thought it was Brodie. This is what I wanted to show you." I lift the speakers. "Jin was playing recordings of Anton's voice, spliced sound bites. I found these in the sitting room."

Their gazes turn to the speakers. Then Shania's gaze goes from the knife to the speakers to me, and she says, "How could you, Nicola?"

"W-what?"

"You've been setting up speakers, just like Dr. Cirillo said, and you're showing us the proof and blaming *Jin*. Your brother-in-law? Who came here to support you?" She shakes her head as she lowers her gaze, her voice going thick, as if with tears. "I don't know you at all, do I?"

Goddamn it! That's why I didn't want them finding the speakers in my pockets. But in my panic, I dove in.

Did I really think they'd believe me?

"Anton's not here," I say. "Whether you think I set these up or not, someone did." I hit the button and the recording starts. "This is what we heard. Not Anton. Whatever is here—?"

"Stop talking, Nicola," Shania says. "Just stop talking."

"No, I am going to *keep* talking until someone listens."

Cirillo moves toward the stairs. "Shania, please watch Nicola while I fetch my equipment for the séance."

"Like hell," I say, rocking forward. "If you two want to contact Brodie, be my guest. I am going upstairs and calling the police—"

Cirillo steps into my path.

I glare up at him. "Get the hell out of my way—"

The blow comes from behind. It slams into the side of my head, and I reel, half from the blow and half from the shock of it.

Woozily, I turn to see Shania with the spade, and I somehow don't make the connection. Shania wouldn't hit me, not with a spade of all things. It must have been the ghost. It's here, and it struck me and—

Shania swings the spade into the side of my knee.

I dimly hear myself gasp "Shania?" as I topple.

"There's rope in the next room," Shania says. "Grab it. We're going to need to tie her up. Find something to gag her."

Silence from Cirillo as I start to rise, still dazed from the blow to the head and the shock of what's happening.

"She's not going to let us do this," Shania snaps at Cirillo. "She's going to escape. She killed that boy. We both know she did. We need to detain her and contact his spirit."

I'm on my knees. Cirillo isn't answering. He's in shock himself. He's realized this goes too far, that something is wrong with Shania.

I catch a glimpse of her face, the look on it, and for a moment, I don't see Shania. I see Patrice in the forest that night, the emptiness in her gaze that had stopped me cold, made my gut scream something was wrong.

Something was wrong with Patrice.

Now something is wrong with Shania.

Something is *inside* Shania.

I push up, my hands outstretched to ward off another blow, but when it comes, it's from behind. Cirillo knocks me to the floor, and before I can process that, I'm flat on my stomach with my arm twisted behind my back.

"Get the rope," Cirillo says. "We'll do the séance quickly and then call the police to arrest her."

THIRTY-ONE

When Anton died, I spent the next twelve hours in denial. I completely refused to accept what had happened.

After Heather's death, I started dreaming about the deaths of people I loved. My mother. My father. My brother. For ten years, anyone who came into my life died in my dreams. That faded until my parents *did* die, and the dreams returned. Keith died over and over. Libby died. Their kids died. When Anton entered my life, it was his turn.

I would wake from those dreams sweating and shaking and gasping for breath, certain that the one who was really dying was me, that my lungs had finally stopped working. Then my heart would slow, and I could breathe, and whoever had died in my dreams was alive, and the relief of that brought me to tears.

Everyone in my life—from my family to my friends to Anton— got used to those days when the Nicola who routinely forgot birthdays suddenly showered them with gifts and attention and random acts of kindness. To them, it was just a personality quirk. I only ever told Anton the truth, because as the guy sharing my bed, he couldn't help but notice that my overly attentive days came right after sweating and shaking nightmares.

So when my husband really did go from planning a trip to Iceland to taking a trip to the morgue, I declared it another nightmare. It had to be. Oh, I went through the motions, acting as if he'd died because that was part of the routine. But it was all an act as I waited to wake up.

So now I am in a situation where I should be telling myself it can't be real. Bound and gagged by Shania? In a basement where a young man has been murdered? While a parapsychologist prepares for a séance to contact the dead man's ghost and ask what happened?

That's clearly a nightmare, and part of me should be shaking my head in disbelief while the other part waits to wake up.

But I know I'm awake.

However unreal this is, it's happening.

Something is wrong with Shania, and Cirillo doesn't see it because he's barely seen her. I realize that now. Over the last few days, his focus has been mostly on me. I'm both his client and the nexus of the haunting. I'm also a pain in his ass, a woman who could be his salvation or his downfall, depending on my whim.

He's noticed Jin, too. Jin is a man, and he's about the same age and a fellow professional. Jin has been worthy of notice.

But Shania? Quiet and docile Shania hasn't really crossed his radar. She's like one of his students, hovering on the periphery. I don't think they've even had a one-on-one conversation.

Cirillo hasn't noticed her normal behavior, so he doesn't realize how out of character this is. All he cares about is that she's on his side. Better yet, she's suggesting very convenient things he wouldn't dare, like binding and gagging the person most likely to fuck this up for him.

Can't accuse a guy of hitting a woman when it was another woman's idea. That's how the law works, right?

I don't bother with Cirillo. It's Shania I appeal to. Either somewhere inside, she'll hear me, or Cirillo will realize this isn't her normal behavior and snap out of it himself.

I don't just lie there and talk either. I fight, but Cirillo has my arm in a hold, and I can tell my wrist is going to snap if I keep struggling. I'm still dazed from the blow to the head, and I keep eyeing that spade, knowing Shania will be quick to use it again. I also eye the steak knife five feet away on the concrete floor. They're both ignoring that . . . for now. But it exists, and the knife I brought to defend myself could be used against me.

Maybe I shouldn't care. Maybe I should fight like hell and take any risk to escape. But even as I see the look on Shania's face, part of me whispers that I could be mistaken. Maybe she's just scared, thinking I really did murder Brodie. Or angry, fearing I'll escape justice.

What matters is that they are about to conjure a dangerous spirit. And yet somehow, while I'm aware of that, I cannot help worrying about Shania. I don't want to hurt her, and in the end, while I do fight, I don't fight enough, a fact I don't fully comprehend until I'm bound and gagged and helpless . . . and they start trying to contact Brodie's spirit.

Cirillo has brought his equipment downstairs. He's set it all up and then arranged a séance setting using everything in this room that belongs to Brodie, including the young man's mutilated corpse.

Cirillo doesn't move the body. It's still half outside the furnace, intestines dangling, and Cirillo has set up his séance materials around it. There's an obscenity to the tableau that makes it look like a ritual sacrifice, and when I realize Cirillo's just going to leave Brodie like that, I stare in horror.

They have a mutilated corpse hanging out of a furnace, and Cirillo has carefully arranged his séance shit around it, as if Brodie's body is mere stage dressing.

Cirillo has left Anton's belongings upstairs. But when Shania runs upstairs, she returns with the cremains box.

"You forgot this," she says.

Cirillo frowns. "Why would we need that?"

Shania pauses, staring down at the box. "Oh, uh, right. Sorry."

"Just put it aside," Cirillo says with some impatience.

She nods and tucks the box just outside the furnace-room door. Then Cirillo beckons her over. They each kneel on one side of Brodie's splayed legs, and I shout at them against my gag, unable to believe they can't see what this looks like.

That is a young man's body. His *mutilated* body that they're treating like a fucking *centerpiece*.

"Brodie Kilmer," Cirillo says. "If you are still nearby, I invite you to join us."

Cirillo pauses, and Shania glances over, but he ignores her and keeps his focus empty.

"Brodie," he says. "I know what happened to you was . . ." Cirillo trails off, as if searching for words, and I clamp my jaw to keep from laughing hysterically into the gag.

I know what happened to you was bad.

Er, really bad?

Er, horribly bad?

"Terrible," he says finally. "And also terrifying. I cannot begin to imagine the pain you endured. The pain and the shock. I am sorry for that, but—"

"But"? Really? How the hell can anyone with an ounce of compassion end that sentence with a "but"? This kid was *ripped* open. He lived long enough to see his insides, and I know that because—

Heather's face flashes, and I start to shake.

Cirillo is still talking. "But I fear we need to speak to you. You want to find who did this, and so do we. Tell us who did this to you, Brodie. We are listening, and we will see justice done."

Shania's gaze flickers my way, the hate in her gaze chilling my blood.

Something must be wrong with her. That was the obvious answer to what seems like a complete transformation of character, but I realize this could just be her reaction to a betrayal. She trusted me, and I've turned out to be a vicious killer.

Is that what she believes?

I thought my dead husband might have killed Heather, didn't I?

Did I? Or was I just protecting my heart and my pride by refusing to blind myself to a possibility?

Is that what Shania is doing?

"Brodie Kilmer," Cirillo says. "If you are there—"

The candle flames waver.

Two beats of silence pass.

"Is that you, Brodie?"

The flames flicker more, one sputtering out.

When Cirillo relights it, his fingers are trembling, and he has to try twice. Then he looks overhead. Checking for a heating duct or anything else that could affect the flame. He lifts the candelabra to move it . . . and all the flames sputter out.

"Thank you, Brodie," Cirillo says in a reverent tone. "I understand that you seem to be with us. I am going to ask you a question, and I hope you do not take it as a sign of disrespect. I must be sure who I am speaking to. I am going to relight these candles."

Cirillo does that. "Now, I will ask a series of questions, with two possible answers. If it is the first, snuff out this candle." He points. "If it is the second, snuff out the other. I know you attended a local high school. Was it—?"

Both flames go out.

When Cirillo speaks, it's with such exaggerated and patronizing patience that I truly feel sorry for his students. "Let's try that again, Brodie," he says as he relights the candles. "I will ask a question—"

The flames go out.

"I understand you may be offended by me quizzing you, but I must be sure who I am speaking to." Cirillo lights them again. "One question should be enough. Let's—"

The candelabra flies straight into Cirillo, who scrambles back, smacking at his clothing as if he'd been hit by a fireball.

Cirillo takes a deep breath, centering himself and very deliberately uprighting the candelabra, only to have it fly at him again.

"Maybe it's not Brodie?" Shania's voice is hesitant, more like herself now.

When Cirillo turns on her, she shrinks back under his glare.

"Could it be Anton?" she says. "Maybe he really is here? Maybe . . ." Her gaze moves to the door, where she left the cremains box. "I'm sorry. I don't know what I was thinking. Should I take that back upstairs?"

"Anton Novak?" Cirillo's voice is harsh now. "If that is you, then you can see your wife. If you are upset about our treatment of her, then perhaps you should step forward and speak to us."

Dear God, does this asshole really think that's the way to talk to ghosts? Like they're misbehaving children?

What do you have to say for yourself, young man?

Cirillo continues, "I thought that because you made the candles flicker, that was how you wished to communicate. If there is another way, please use that, whether you are Brodie Kilmer or Anton Novak. We wish to speak—"

Brodie's legs begin to shake, jerking up and down. Shania scrambles up with a shriek. Cirillo is on his feet, backing away before stopping himself.

"Is he . . . ?" Shania says as the legs continue to twitch.

Cirillo doesn't answer. It's not Brodie's body moving. It's someone moving his body, plucking at his jeans legs and jerking them up and down. Then his intestines start wriggling like there's something inside him.

Or like someone is *reaching* inside him.

Brodie's body goes still and so do Cirillo and Shania.

One footstep sounds, clear and deliberate. Shania yelps, and I struggle against my bonds.

Oh, you just realized now that you need to get out of here?

My gaze flies to the knife. It's only a few feet away from me. I inch backward in that direction. No one notices.

Just keep inch-worming backward until—

I stop as I see what they're staring at. The furnace, where letters have appeared in his blood.

TRIGE

My goddamn puzzle-solving brain stops short like a dog seeing a squirrel. "Trige"? What word starts with . . .

No, those aren't the starting letters. The unseen force is writing backward, from end to start. An A appears, and then a P, and I realize that what I thought was a G is a C.

PATRICE

THIRTY-TWO

Now I truly am stopped cold, staring as everything in me screams that this can't be what I'm seeing. That E must be a K. Patrick. It cannot be—

"Patrice," Shania whispers, and there's an odd note in her voice.

"Isn't that . . . ?" Cirillo turns to me. "Isn't that the name of the girl who supposedly murdered your friend?"

Does he actually expect me to answer? I'm bound and fucking gagged.

"It is," Shania whispers. "Patrice Jones. Nicola had Patrice committed to a mental hospital for a murder Nicola committed."

I writhe and try to speak, but only muffled grunts come out.

"Is Patrice . . . dead?" Cirillo asks.

"Two years ago," Shania says, her tone oddly empty. "She died in that hospital."

I go still. I hadn't been able to find that online.

How hard did I look?

Not hard enough. When the answer hadn't come up immediately, I told myself there was nothing new in the case and moved on, presuming Patrice was still alive and in custody.

So what am I saying?

That Patrice is here?

That her ghost is here?

That's not possible. How the hell would Cirillo have conjured Patrice?

Does it matter?

"Patrice Jones?" Cirillo says slowly. "Am I speaking to Patrice Jones?"

The footsteps start again, as slow and deliberate as before.

Like upstairs, during the séance, when footsteps had circled me. Like the ones in the attic, circling above my head. I'd heard others in the sitting room, but they'd been normal steps. This is a taunt, a tiger circling prey.

As I hear those steps, any pity or grief inside me crystallizes, and I glare in that direction.

Cut this shit out, Patrice.

If you have something to say to me, say it.

God, I'm as bad as Cirillo, aren't I? Worse even. Instead of shaking my finger at a misbehaving spirit, I'm challenging one that seems to have . . .

My gaze goes to Brodie, and I swallow.

Patrice did that. Not Anton. Not Roddy.

Patrice killed Heather, and she killed Brodie, and maybe I should be backing away in terror, but all I can feel is fury.

I spent twenty-two years doubting what I saw that night.

Twenty-two years thinking I might have helped commit an innocent girl to a hospital for the criminally insane.

She did it, though.

She killed Heather.

Who toppled my chair once as a "joke"? Patrice. I remember it now. It was shortly after we met. Oh, she'd said it was an accident—she only meant to tilt it—but it was a test. Would I put up with her shit? Apparently, yes.

The footsteps stop right in front of me. I'm very aware then of the fact that I am on my knees, hands bound behind my back.

I am kneeling at her feet, defeated and trussed up like a goddamn offering.

I shift, trying to stand, but I'm not that limber. I'm stuck on my knees, looking up—

My nostrils pinch closed. I jerk back, but the grip is tight, and that initial startle of surprise turns to confusion.

And then I can't breathe. One second I'm trying to figure out what the hell is going on, and then I can't breathe.

My mouth automatically opens for oxygen . . . only it can't get any. There's duct tape over it.

I still don't panic. It's just something—Patrice?—pinching my nose shut. An annoyance, an insult even. Mocking me.

I jerk back, but it's as if a vise grabs my head, pinning me in place. As my lungs begin to burn, actual panic sets in.

I can't breathe.

No, this is silly. Patrice is just holding my nose to mock me.

Pull away. Yank backward. Rip from her grip.

Only I can't. Something pins me there, keeping my head firm, my nostrils closed.

I can't breathe.

Oh God, I can't—

Hello, Janica.

I freeze. It's the voice I heard last night, the one that seems both inside my head and out of it.

The voice continues.

Remember Sandy's party? When you drank too much punch, not knowing it was spiked? You were always fun when you had a little to drink, but when you had too much? That's when I saw the real Janica. Sad and scared Janica. You started crying and babbling about how you were afraid to die, how you couldn't stop thinking about what it might be like one day, when your lungs gave out and you couldn't breathe.

The voice slides through my ear, straight into my brain.

Is it everything you imagined, Janica? I hope so. I hope you die in tears and terror, and I hope your last thought is regret. Regret for betraying me.

I can't answer. Can't think. My lungs burn and my vision clouds, and I am going to die.

I can't breathe, and I am going to die.

You knew what happened to Heather wasn't my fault. You knew I couldn't have been in my right mind. You were my friend. You should have protected me, made something up, told them you saw a stranger in the forest.

I can't see. Everything is dark, and my lungs are on fire, and why can't I break free? She's pinching my nose. Such a simple thing. I just need to jerk away, but I can't and I am going to—

"No!" Shania screams, and my heart leaps.

Oh God, thank you, Shania.

Hands wrench me away from Patrice. Surprisingly strong hands, ripping me from Patrice's grip and then yanking the duct tape from my mouth. I double over, gulping breath.

Shania is still screaming. Still screaming "No!"

I shake my head to tell her I'm okay. Then my vision clears, and I see her running at me, the spade in hand. I manage to fall to the side before she reaches me, but she's not aiming for me. She's aiming behind me. At the person who really did free me from Patrice's grip.

Cirillo lets out a sound, half anger and half shock. I twist to see him almost dodge the spade, the blade skimming his shoulder. He grabs it in both hands and wrenches it from Shania.

"What the hell are you doing?" he shouts. "It was trying to *kill* her."

"*It* is Patrice Jones," Shania snarls, hands out as if she's still holding the spade. "*It* is a friend Nicola betrayed. *It* is a woman who died in a mental ward because of Nicola."

I struggle to find my voice, and when it comes, it's a raw croak. "No, Shania. I don't know what you read online, but I told the court exactly what I saw that night. Nothing more. I never said I saw Patrice holding a knife. I never said she killed Heather."

"Liar!" she spits at me. "You are such a *fucking* liar."

Cirillo says nothing, but I can feel him behind me, cutting at my bonds in silence, letting Shania rave while he gets me free.

"I'm not lying," I say. "Read the trial transcripts."

"I know the truth. I didn't read that story online. She told me. She told me *everything*."

I got still. "Patrice? Has her ghost been talking to—"

"Her ghost?" Shania's high-pitched laugh rakes down my spine. "You're so self-absorbed you never look beyond your own little life. I tested that when I told you my sister died of an infection. If you gave two shits about Patrice, you'd know she died two years ago of a staph infection. A simple cut on her hand. That's what killed her."

I stare as the pieces try—and fail—to jam together. "You're . . . ?" I shake my head. "No. Patrice had a brother, but you're too young to have been him."

Her shoulders convulse, as if I struck her. Then her face twists. "You lying bitch. Don't pretend Patrice didn't tell you about me."

I rack my brain for any memory of Patrice mentioning a much younger sibling. Then it comes. Something she said once when Heather and I invited her to the movies.

Can't. Gotta look after my mom's new brat.

Patrice's parents had been divorced, and she spent most of the school year with her father and his second wife. Her mother had remarried and had a baby.

A baby who would have been about thirteen years younger than us.

"I'm sorry, Shania," I say, voice soft. "I forgot Patrice had a much younger sister. She absolutely did talk about you. And I'm sorry if she felt I'd done something to her, but please read those transcripts. I—"

"You murdered Heather. That's what Patrice said." She looks around the room. "Patrice? I know you're here. I brought you here to make this right."

Cirillo leans toward my ear. He's been silently working on my bonds, and when I glance at the floor, I see the steak knife is gone.

"Keep her occupied," he whispers. "Just keep talking."

"Shania?" I say. "You want Patrice to confront me. I get that. You've summoned her—"

"Me? I didn't summon her. Dr. Cirillo did." Her lips curve in a smile. "Who do you think is in that box, Nicola? Not your sainted husband. I dumped his ashes in the trash back at your condo. I swapped out the ashes after convincing you to bring them here."

I blink, and the world seems to slow as I process what she said. As I struggle to fully comprehend what she means. When I do, something inside me shatters.

Two minutes ago, I truly thought I was about to die, but this is what breaks me.

How many times had I told myself it wasn't Anton in that box? It's not, but that box represented my final promise to my husband. A promise that I'd find a place for his remains to rest. I would protect them. I would look after them.

And Shania dumped them in the trash.

She *threw* my husband's *remains* into the *trash*.

I can regret not being careful enough, but I *was* careful. The only thing I regret is that I ever suspected Anton of killing Heather. If there was any doubt left, it disintegrates as my entire body shatters in grief.

Shania threw his ashes in the trash. That wasn't anger or revenge. It was simple disdain and disrespect for a man she'd never known. She disposed of his bodily remains so she could put her sister's ashes in his box and sneak them into Anton's séance. In hopes that Cirillo would summon Patrice instead.

The grief itself disintegrates, consumed by a red-hot explosion of rage. I lunge at Shania, but my legs aren't free yet, and I writhe and snarl as Shania only watches me. Then she goes still, and her gaze flies behind me.

"What are you doing?" she says to Cirillo.

She stomps toward him. "What the fuck are you doing?"

Cirillo cuts the last of the rope around my ankles and scrambles to his feet, his setting jaw nearly hiding the fear in his gaze. "That's what I need to ask you, Shania. I don't know what the fuck *you* are doing, but it ends here. Nicola and I are leaving, and—"

The steak knife twists in his hand. That's all it does. It doesn't fly dramatically from his grip. It just twists and flicks . . . and his wrist opens in a gush of blood.

THIRTY-THREE

For a second, we all freeze. Even Shania goes still, her eyes wide, the young woman I knew evident in her horror. I recover first. I run for Cirillo as the steak knife falls from his hand and clatters to the concrete floor. He's still standing there, as if he must be imagining the gash across his wrist gushing blood.

I grab the rope that had fallen from my own wrists, and I wrap it around Cirillo's upper arm. He doesn't react even when I pull hard enough that he should gasp. He's frozen in shock. I'm still pulling the rope, trying to get it as tight as I can to cut off the blood flow when, out of the corner of my eye, I see the knife fly up.

I stagger back, but it doesn't come for me. The blade strikes Cirillo's other wrist, laying it open to the bone. I grab for the knife. I can't think of anything except stopping it, and my fingers clamp down on the blade, metal slicing into my fingers. With my other hand, I grab the handle and grip it tight. Then I dive for the rope.

Tie off the wounds. This is how my brain copes with what has just happened. Practical action. Get the knife away from Patrice. Cut off the blood flow to Cirillo's wrists.

I'm grabbing the rope when Shania screams, and I look up just as the spade swings toward Cirillo's head. I lunge, but I don't get to him in time, and he goes down. Blood flies from his second wrist, arcing through the air as he falls.

I scramble over and get the rope around his other upper arm. I'm still pulling when Shania screams again, this time an endless "Nooo!"

I remember the last time she shouted that. When I thought she was trying to stop Patrice from killing me. I'd been wrong then, and so I ignore her now, certain that scream is for me to stop trying to save Cirillo. But when I hear her running footsteps, I twist, ready to fend her off, and her gaze is over my head. I look up to see the spade there, blade down . . . right over Cirillo, who is on his back, staring blankly and shaking with shock.

"Patrice!" Shania screams. "No!"

I vault up, hands rising to knock the spade blade off course, but I don't get to it in time. It slams down onto Cirillo's neck and keeps going until it hits the concrete with a thwack . . . and Cirillo's head rolls away.

I stare, frozen in mid-leap, my gaze on his head . . . which is no longer attached to his body. Which has rolled to the side and is facing me and he blinks and oh God, he blinks. His eyes roll up to mine and there is one unbelievable moment of sheer horror before the life goes out of them, and I am staring at Cirillo's severed head while blood spouts from his torso.

"Oh my God, oh my God, oh my God." That's Shania, her voice rising, and I stare at Cirillo, my brain still comprehending what has happened, her shrill voice a distraction when I am trying to figure out—

And then it hits. What has happened.

I spin on Shania, spittle flying out with my words.

"What the fuck did you expect?" I snarl.

Her gaze rises to mine, her eyes wide and unfocused. "W-what?"

"You unleashed your psycho sister's spirit. You brought her here. You did this. What the fuck did you expect, Shania?"

She shakes her head dully. "No, Patrice never hurt anyone. You let her go to prison—"

"Yes!" I shout. "I let her go to prison. That's what she's angry about. That's what she was saying when she was suffocating me. I betrayed her by letting her go to prison. Not because I lied. Because I told the *truth*. Your sister killed Heather, and I didn't lie for her. That is how I betrayed her. By telling the truth, and even then, I never accused her. If you'd read the fucking transcript, you'd know that I never said she killed Heather. I was never even entirely certain she had until five minutes ago, when she told me she did."

"N . . . no . . ."

"Are you really saying she didn't do this? Look at him!" I jab a finger at Cirillo. "She did that." I point at Brodie, still half out of the furnace. "She did that. She is fucking *evil,* and you brought her here."

Shania collapses as if her strings are cut. Her knees give way, and she goes down.

"No," she whispers. "She said she didn't kill Heather."

"Because she's a fucking *psychopath*. What did you expect her to do? Tell the truth?"

Shania's head drops, sobs ripping through her. I hesitate one heartbeat. In spite of everything she's done, my instinct is to help. But I can't do that. Patrice cut off Cirillo's head with a goddamn spade. Am I standing here waiting for my turn?

Steak knife clutched in my hand, I run, my gaze on the door. Get upstairs. Grab my phone. Get out and call for—

Shania's head jerks up. I skid sideways, thinking she's about to come at me, but she only sits there, her head jerking unnaturally from one side to the other.

Go. Forget her and run!

Yet my gut tells me *not* to run. Do not make any sudden moves. I sidestep to move around Shania, whose head keeps swiveling left to right.

One more slow step—

Shania leaps to her feet lightning fast, and in a blink, she's blocking my path. My grip tightens on the knife as I try to swing past, but she's there before I can.

"Hello, Janica," she says, her voice pitched an octave lower. "Thank you."

I should stare, confused by Shania switching to that name, by the change in her voice. But I look into her eyes, and I am not confused at all.

"Hello, Patrice," I say.

"Not going to ask why I'm thanking you?" She doesn't wait for a response. "I couldn't get in. The brat's anger was a wall against me. But you broke down that wall, and now I'm here."

She takes a slow step my way. I keep my hand lowered, knife held so tight blood drips from my cut fingers.

"Like that night in the forest," Patrice continues. "My defenses were down, and she got in. That's what it takes. Readiness. And blood, of course."

My gaze goes to the pool of blood beside Cirillo.

"Not that kind," she scoffs. "You were always so literal, Nic. *Shared* blood. That's the key. I lowered my defenses that night, and I read the incantation from her book, together with the wine and the mushrooms, and she got in."

"The mushrooms were fake."

She lets out a sharp laugh. "Really? That's your response?" She shakes her head. "They say I lost my mind, but you were never in your right one. Always a little bit odd, weren't you, Nic. Got a computer where your brain should be. No wonder Anton fell for you. He was just like you. A little bit off. A little bit weird. Cute, but not quite right in the head."

My eyes narrow, and she laughs.

"Don't like me insulting your Prince Charming? I can insult you, but not him? How sweet." She tilts her head. "Did you really think he could have killed Heather? He barely tagged along for the haunt-ing." Her hand flies to her mouth. "Whoops. You didn't know about that? Cody and I set it up." She flashes her teeth. "Good practice for haunting you."

She wants me to be outraged. Or shocked. Maybe even curious.

Oh my god, you were the one making those scary footsteps in the attic! Making the dumbwaiter creak! Did you do the newspaper and the blood hal-lucination?

Instead, I say, "You helped Cody spook your friends?"

She shrugs. "He wanted to scare the shit out of you and Heather, so I let him."

"You let a guy terrorize your friends because he *wanted* to?"

"Again, you focus on all the wrong things."

"No, Patrice, I don't think I do. I don't know what that bullshit was about 'her' getting into you, but *you* killed Heather. You snapped. You needed help. I'm sorry if you didn't get it before you slashed open your best friend—"

She lunges at me, exactly when I expect it. I dart to the side and race past her. I make it to the door. Yank it open and barrel through. My foot strikes something on the floor.

The box with Anton—

No, not Anton's ashes. Patrice's. As I race for the steps, I kick the damn box out of my way. Patrice's cremains scatter, and I feel a surge of vindictive satisfaction.

I reach the steps. Patrice is right behind me. I'm on the stairs, sprinting up—

Patrice grabs my foot and heaves, and I fall, my chin hitting the step so hard I bite my tongue, and blood fills my mouth. Dazed, I try to scramble up, but she slams my injured hand into the step. Then she has her fingers in my hair, and she's pressing my throat against the step edge, cutting off my breath. I flail . . . and there's a smack as the steak knife slaps the stair.

I'm holding a fucking knife.

I jam the blade backward. I don't know what I hit. I only care that Patrice screams and releases me.

I scrabble up the stairs and slam the door and lean against it. Patrice pounds on the door, but I have it shut. For now.

I just need a moment. Blood fills my mouth, and my hand blazes with pain, and I just need a moment.

As I heave breath, I map out my escape. My phone is . . .

Where is my phone?

Holy shit. I can't remember where I left it.

I should have grabbed Cirillo's.

Off his headless corpse?

Forget the phone. What the hell am I going to do with it anyway? Notify the cops and then sit in the living room and wait for them to arrive? Even the time it takes me to call will be too much.

I need to get as far from this house as possible.

Get someplace safe and then summon help.

Just go. That's all I can do. Get out the front door—

No, the front door is both locked and bolted. The back door is unlocked. That'll be faster.

As I flex my stockinged feet, I remember Shania talking about Cirillo wearing his shoes inside. Really wish I'd done the same. I reach down to pull off my socks.

Patrice still pounds at the door, but I pay her no mind. Maybe she's right that I'm a little "off." A little too hyperfocused. Doesn't matter. I can ignore her pounding and screaming as I wiggle my toes and direct my attention toward the back door.

I plan my route. Out the door. Onto the patio. Turn left. Get out of the garden. Head down the road. Mrs. Kilmer—

My brain stutters as I remember Brodie. I push that aside.

Mrs. Kilmer's house is the first one. Do I stop there or continue to town? I'll figure that out on the way.

My bare feet grip the floor and propel me along. The basement door swings open behind me. Running footsteps follow. Then a curse and a yelp, as one of her feet slides on the hardwood.

At the door. Twist the knob. Yank it open. Race out—

I run straight into a cloud of midges thicker than fog.

That's not natural. No one can tell me this is natural.

Doesn't matter. I know the way. I turn left and count off my paces, estimating when I can turn left again—

My foot hits something soft and solid, and I nearly fly over whatever blocks my path. I manage to grab the side of the house for balance, and I'm staggering over the obstacle, ready to keep going when I see what looks like an outstretched hand, barely visible through the swarming bugs.

There's a body on the garden path.

It's Jin.

THIRTY-FOUR

I drop to my knees beside Jin. His eyes are closed, his nose is broken and bloody, his shirt is ripped.

My hand flies to his chest, and I nearly collapse in relief when I feel a heartbeat. He's unconscious, though. Unconscious and battered on the garden path.

How is that possible? I saw him leave. Watched him drive away.

Did he come back? Was the leaving a trick? He pretended to leave and then returned—

No. Keith was expecting Jin, which meant he really was heading to Toronto. He must have returned for something and found the front door locked, so he came around the back.

A twig cracks. My head jerks up, and I remember Patrice. She'd be out here by now, and she's searching for me because the damn bugs mean she can't see, and I've stopped running so I'm not making any noise.

I grab Jin's shoulder. I need to wake—

I remember Cirillo's decapitated corpse.

That's what happened when someone got in Patrice's way. When someone came between Patrice and me.

I need to lure her away from Jin.

I carefully check Jin's pockets. My keys are there, but his phone isn't. Where is—?

The bugs clear enough for me to see the cell phone near his outstretched hand. As I reach for it, I stop. Beside Jin is a broken paving stone flecked with blood. That's what hit him. Someone used it to strike him over and over—

I push the thought aside and pick up the phone. It's working but locked. I can still call 911, right? When I can't remember how to do that, I send up a silent apology to Jin and try to unlock it with his face, but that doesn't work.

I take the phone and keys. I also take that paving stone, because I'm not leaving a weapon for Patrice to use on him.

With the keys and phone in my pocket, the stone under my arm, and the knife in my other hand, I veer out into the gardens. Or I think I do. I can't see a goddamn thing with these bugs.

That first day with the midges, I'd chastised myself for not being able to ignore them. Now they're all over me, hitting my eyes, crawling on me, being inhaled with every breath . . . and I don't care. I do not care if every orifice in my body is crawling with midges. I don't care if I'm shitting midges for weeks. I just want to live.

I've said before that I don't want to die, that I was furious at any insinuation I should join Anton, but it was only today that I realized it's not just that I don't want to die. I want to *live*.

Patrice almost killed me in the basement, and now she's stalking me, waiting to do it again, and I will not let her.

I want to live.

I'm sorry, Anton. I'm sorry if you are *waiting, and I'm dragging my heels getting to you. I'm not ready to go. Nor am I ready to just surrender and wait for death to catch up.*

I keep moving. When I think I'm far enough from Jin, I set down the paving stone. Then I take a few more steps and squint through the bugs. I need to make noise. I want to lure Patrice in this direction and then run—

Something swings at my head. I don't even see what it is. I only see the bugs part as something comes at me. I dodge and trip and catch myself . . . and a voice laughs in the darkness.

"Cut this shit out, Patrice," I say. "You know I'm going to win. I always do. I'm the one who got away. The one who escaped and changed her name and lived a damned good life, while you rotted in a mental hospital. Couldn't kill me then. Can't kill me now."

I'm taunting her. With every word, I look from side to side, waiting for her to give herself away.

Instead, she laughs again. Then she says, "Not Patrice."

I spin toward the voice and step backward. "Fine. You aren't Patrice. What would you like me to call you? Evil Patrice? Patrice spelled backward?"

"You *do* think you're clever. Got it all figured out, don't you, girl?"

I keep my gaze fixed in the direction of her voice as I fish out the keys and plan my next steps.

Run to my right. Around the house. Hit the key fob. Climb in.

"Don't want to talk?" she says. "Not as much fun when it isn't your old friend Patrice."

I break into a run. I've got the knife in one hand and the keys in the other with my finger over the unlock button. I'm running as fast—

"Nic!" The voice comes from right in front of me, and someone materializes. A figure waving his arms madly. "Stop!"

The voice is muffled, even though he's right there.

Anton.

I see *Anton*. He's indistinct but waving his arms, mouth open as if shouting words I can't hear. I slide to a stop, and my foot slips, taking me down to one knee as my brain screams that I can't stumble, can't fall, must keep going, just keep running—

The crash of waves.

I hear the crash of waves . . . right below me. The bugs clear enough that I can see my bare foot . . . at the edge of the cliff.

"Anton?" I whisper.

I look up, and he's speaking, but I only catch one word in five.

"Don't—go—run—"

I might not know what he's saying, but I can understand the gist of it.

Don't run off the fucking cliff, Nic.

My eyes fill with tears.

"You always have my back, don't you?" I whisper.

He shakes his head, his face filled with anger and frustration, because he can't truly have my back. He's stuck somewhere between here and there, and this is all he can do, half appear and half speak.

"It was enough," I murmur.

He shakes his head again. Then his gaze goes over my shoulder, and it contorts into the rage I saw last night.

That *was* Anton. I thought it couldn't be because I'd never seen him like that. I could not imagine him being that angry and certainly not at me.

But it's not directed at me.

I spin just as Patrice runs at me. I dive to the side before she shoves me off the cliff. When she wheels, there's something in her hand. Something big and sharp.

She lifts a pair of pruning shears, and her gaze goes to the little steak knife in my hand. Her lips curl in a half smile, half sneer.

"I win," she says.

A flicker of movement as Anton runs at her. She quicksteps back and frowns at his indistinct ghost.

"Roddy?" she says.

"Get—fuck—" he says, his voice cutting in and out.

Patrice laughs. "Not Roddy, but you must be related. Just as cute . . . and just as useless."

Not Patrice.

That's what she said.

She got in.

That's what Patrice said.

Shared blood.

Someone who knew Roddy and also shares blood with Patrice.

"You're Patrice's aunt," I say. "Lori."

She turns away from Anton's ghost, now nearly invisible as he tries to mouth something.

"Finally figured it out," she says.

I try not to look at those pruning shears. Instead, I focus on my escape routes. The one to my left is tempting, in a Thelma-and-Louise kinda way. Grab Lori and pull her over the cliff before she can hurt anyone else. But I doubt I'd survive the fall, and I kinda want to survive.

I need to get my bearings. We're not in the spot where I usually look out, and with the damned midges, I can't see anything. I wouldn't even have noticed the cliff edge without Anton's warning.

I need to catch my breath, too. My heart pounds, adrenaline slamming through me, and I need to push the panic aside and focus.

Keep her away from Jin. Get to the car. Call for help.

"Patrice said you got in," I say. "Her defenses were lowered, and you got in."

Lori's face twists. "I made a mistake. Once you're in, you can't get out. I was trapped inside her for twenty fucking years, and when we finally get out, what does she do? Drags us into *this* sniveling brat."

The cliff edge is uneven. I need to remember that. I can't run along it or I won't see where it curves in.

Keep her talking while I think.

"Was it the book?" I say. "Patrice found a book of witchcraft. She said she read the incantation from 'her' book. Your book."

"Oh my god." Lori's eyes round. "That must be it. The evil book is responsible—" She breaks off with another sneer. "You want a simple answer so badly, don't you, girl? It was the book. It was the wine. It was the drugs. Patrice let me in because she wanted me in.

She killed that girl because she wanted to. But then she had to blame someone else. Blame you. Blame me."

"Samantha and Roddy. You—"

"That was an accident."

I strangle out something like a laugh. "You sliced Samantha open—"

"Roddy had been messing around with me. Promised he'd dump that simpering cow. Then at the bonfire, he tells me he changed his mind. When I demand an explanation, he stomps into the forest, and she goes after him. So I followed. I caught up with Sam, and she said Roddy told her everything and she forgave him."

That sneer, twisting her entire face now. "She forgave *him*. She didn't forgive me. He started it, but somehow it was my fault. We fought. I shoved her, and her head hit a tree. Then Roddy comes running. Accuses me of killing her. He's waving his hunting knife around—who carries a hunting knife to a bonfire? I took it to stop him."

"You *slit* his *throat*."

Lori shrugs. "Which stopped him. That's when I remembered the old stories we'd tell around the bonfire, about a couple who died in that forest back in the fifties. Killed by a guy with a hook for his hand. The guy had his throat slit. The girl was found in a tree with her guts hanging out."

"So you staged their bodies."

"It was a bugger getting her in that tree, I tell you. I couldn't drag her very high. Then I slit her open like Dad taught me to do with deer. Turned out she hadn't actually been dead but . . ." She shrugs. "She was after that."

I set my jaw against my outrage. She *wants* that outrage. She feeds on it.

She's right that I want answers. What made Lori brutally murder her best friend and her secret boyfriend? What let her possess her niece? What made her niece slice open *her* best friend?

Patrice died of an infection, and that is bitterly ironic in its truth. Infected by her aunt, Lori. Had Lori herself been infected by someone farther back in the line, a shadowy threat woven into endless Russian dolls, some ancestor into Lori, Lori into Patrice, Patrice into Shania?

A book of witchcraft *is* too simplistic an answer, and it's more effect than cause. Something dark lived inside Lori, and she fed it with more darkness, shoveling it in until it exploded.

That same dark thread wove through Patrice, drawing her to the book, luring her to the forest even as she thought she was in control, staging a fake haunting with Cody.

Lori slid into Patrice and goaded her to horrific violence. Both of them ended up in a psychiatric hospital, Lori as the permanently traumatized alleged innocent bystander and Patrice as the convicted killer who had apparently spent her time weaving tales of deceit and betrayal. Tales she fed to her little sister.

"But why Heather?" I ask. It's a pointless question, and that's why I ask it. More distraction with a question that doesn't have an answer.

Heather died because Heather had been there, and maybe, in some twisted way, Lori confused her with Samantha, like she'd mistaken Anton for Roddy. I remember that weird fight Patrice started, accusing Heather of messing around with a boy Patrice liked. I remember Heather's utter confusion. Because there was no romantic rivalry. Not between Patrice and Heather. That was Lori and Samantha.

"Why Heather?" I repeat.

"Is that her name?" Lori relaxes back, shears resting against her arm. "That silly—"

I pivot and run.

THIRTY-FIVE

The cliff is to my left. Jin is to my right. I run in Jin's direction and then swerve hard, praying I've laid it out properly in my mind so Lori won't see him.

The midges buzz around me, getting in my hair, my nose, my mouth. I slit my eyes and run. The house should be there. I'm aiming for the west side—

There! A light inside. That's the breakfast nook. Veer more. Keep running.

Keep running? I'm not twenty anymore. Not even thirty. I'm a middle-aged woman with CF whose scarred lungs mean she gets winded while fast walking. My lungs burn like I swallowed molten lava, and my brain screams that I can't keep going, but I bear down and run with everything I have.

The house. I see the house immediately to my right. Then the corner of it. I race around that corner. Around the next one. Then I'm in the front yard.

Where's Lori? I have no idea. Blood pounds too loudly in my ears for me to hear her footfalls, and my lungs hurt so bad I can't focus on anything else. I just run.

There's the front porch. Keep going. The driveway is right there, my car a light-colored shape just visible through the bugs. Hit the key fob.

The alarm should chirp. It doesn't.

I hit it again.

Silence.

I see the back end of the car as I run around it. A Michigan license plate with a rental sticker.

Cirillo's rental.

Where the hell is my car?

I hit the button again and listen for the chirp. Nothing. I look around wildly, my eyes searching for my car through the bugs, my ears straining for some sound of Lori over the whining and buzzing.

Where the fuck is my car? If Jin's here, my car must be, too.

Patrice and Lori killed Brodie and attacked Jin, and they sure as hell didn't move my car afterward.

Wait! I lift my key fob. It has an alarm, right? If I press this red button—

A distant wail sounds. I shut it off immediately—that's a siren call for Lori to find me. But I know which direction to run, and I take off.

Down the drive. Along the road. My car is out here somewhere.

Did Jin leave it down the road on purpose? Hide it and sneak back?

I push the thought away. Right now, Jin is not my concern.

Just get to my damned car. My lungs rattle with each breath, and I know I can't go much farther. Where the hell is my car?

I hit the unlock button again, and I think I hear the car chirp. I keep running, tapping the fob periodically to guide me through the bugs. I'm going downhill now. Why is the car so far—

I nearly collide with the back end. It's stopped right in the middle of the road, the hood facing the other way.

I hit the button again, as if the damn door won't already be open from the dozen other times.

"Ms. Laughton?" a voice calls from the mass of swirling bugs.

It's a trick.

Do not stop. Do not even slow down. Get in—

Through the bugs, a figure appears. It's too solid to be Anton. Too stooped to be Lori.

It's Mrs. Kilmer. "Oh, thank goodness it's you. I can't see a thing with these bugs." As she walks closer, she waves a hand in front of her face. "I've never seen anything like it."

"Get in the car," I say, reaching for the driver's-door handle.

She stops short. "What?"

Oh, right. This poor woman doesn't know I'm running from my young housemate, now possessed by the murderous ghosts of her relatives. I swallow the hiccuping laugh bubbling up in my throat.

Don't snap at her. Don't bark orders. She has no idea what . . .

No idea what happened to her son.

My insides clench, pain ripping through me, sympathetic agony for what this poor woman is going to discover.

I shove it back and say, "Please get in the car, Mrs. Kilmer. There's been an accident at the house." That wild laugh threatens again. *An accident? That's one way of putting it. Horrific double murder is another.* "Please get in the car. I'll explain as I drive you home."

"Oh. All right. Thank you. Something is really wrong with these bugs. I've never seen—"

"Mrs. Kilmer? Ma'am?" I'm overly polite as I struggle to keep my voice steady. "It's my CF. I can't breathe with these bugs. We need to get in the car now."

Her eyes widen and she murmurs, "Oh, of course."

"Nic!" Anton's voice sounds right beside me, as if he's shouting in my ear.

I jump and look around wildly, but he could be standing a few feet from me and I wouldn't see him through the bugs.

He's warning me to move faster, that the longer I stand here talking to Mrs. Kilmer, the more time I'm giving Lori to find me.

I yank open the driver's door. Mrs. Kilmer turns to go around to

316 ≈ KELLEY ARMSTRONG

the passenger side. Then she stops, and her eyes go even wider, her mouth opening in an O of surprise.

Anton shouts something, words indistinct and garbled but frantic.

Mrs. Kilmer staggers forward, and I release the door to grab her. There's a wet, ripping sound, and her body convulses, head thrown back, mouth open.

Something flashes silver amid the swarming fog of bugs.

The pruning shears.

The shears ram into Mrs. Kilmer's back again, the tips appearing. Then the blades start to open, and Mrs. Kilmer screams, a raw, animal sound.

I let go of Mrs. Kilmer and punch my fist into the swirling bugs. My hand strikes flesh. I grab the steak knife from my pocket, and I lunge at the figure lost in that swarm of bugs. I stab and stab again.

I feel the knife make contact. I can't hear anything over Mrs. Kilmer's screams, but the blade comes back bloody and I keep stabbing, moving toward whatever—whoever—I am stabbing, and that's when I realize I cannot see who I'm stabbing.

I don't care. I am stabbing whoever just rammed pruning shears into an innocent woman and *opened* them. I keep stabbing until I see Lori's face twisted in pain and rage.

"Can't get out, can you?" I say as I yank the steak knife back again. "You're trapped in there, and I hope this—"

"Nic?" It's a small voice, as if coming from deep within. A soft sob follows. "Nicola?"

I hesitate.

"Nic?" Tears brim in her eyes, and I don't see Lori anymore. I see Shania.

I stay where I am, knife raised, blood dripping. I search Shania's gaze for a sign that this is a trick to make me stop. I don't see it.

So what am I going to do now?

They're in there. Patrice and Lori. I know they are, and they aren't going anywhere.

I can't save Shania.

Shania had been ready to watch me die. She'd set me up from the start. She threw Anton's ashes into the trash, and I want her to pay for that.

But that makes it worse, doesn't it? I want her to pay, and so if I slam this blade between her ribs, is that why? Not to save my life or to protect Jin, but to make Shania pay?

"Nic . . ." Anton's voice whispers from somewhere behind Shania, who's doubled over, sobbing and retching as she clutches her bloodied chest.

"I don't know what to do," I whisper to Anton.

He appears then, as clearly as I've ever seen him, his face drawn in a sad smile.

"I'm sorry," he whispers.

My own tears rise. "No advice?"

That sad smile quirks at the corners. "Did you ever take my advice? Anyone's? You'll do what you need to do, and it'll be the right thing."

My eyes fill. "I miss you."

His mouth opens—and Shania lunges at me, howling as she smashes both fists into my chest, pushing me back. I raise the knife, but she just keeps coming, face contorted with rage.

"We aren't going to stop, Janica." It's Patrice now, snarling. "I *will* kill you. I swear I will."

I slash the knife. It catches her outstretched hand, but she only shoves me again, harder. Then something flickers behind her eyes. A flash of horror from Shania, quickly replaced by Lori's death's-head grin.

"We aren't stopping, girl," Lori says. "We will kill you. We will kill your friend back at the house. We will kill anyone who comes to find you."

Another blow, this one slamming me into the car. My foot hits Mrs. Kilmer's outstretched hand, and when I look down, Lori grabs for my knife hand, but it's a half-assed swipe, as if she's not actually trying to grab it.

Because she's not.

In that moment, the world seems to creak to a halt. The blood stops pounding in my ears. My adrenaline ebbs. Even my breath returns, clear and even.

I understand what Patrice and Lori are doing . . . and I lift my hands over my head.

"I'm sorry, Shania," I say. "If you're in there, and you can hear me, I truly am sorry. You thought I was responsible for what happened to your sister. I understand, and I forgive you. I only hope you can forgive me for this."

I draw back the hand with the knife, and victory flares in Lori's eyes. She sees the end coming. She sees freedom coming. The freedom to bide her time and return when she can, called forth by another family member with this darkness weaving through them.

"I'm sorry, Shania," I whisper. "I really am."

I plow my hand into her stomach. Lori throws back her head, her agonized scream almost ecstatic. With the pain comes freedom. A knife in her gut—

I see the moment where she realizes the truth. Where her head whips up, eyes widening, gaze going to the knife in my left hand . . . while my right punches her stomach a second time.

Lori falls backward, and I pounce on her. I jam the knife into my back pocket and flip Lori over and then pin her like Cirillo did to me. She fights like a wild thing, all gnashing teeth and howls of rage. She wants me to kill Shania. Kill her host. If I do, I release her. I release Lori, and I release Patrice.

This is the horrific thing I am doing to Shania, and it might even be worse than killing her. No, it *is* worse. I am sentencing her to the fate of her aunt and her sister.

"I am sorry, Shania. Truly and utterly sorry—"

"Nic!"

This time, Anton's shout has me whirling, knowing it's a warning and—

Tires roar on pavement. A car is speeding up the road, and the driver can't see us with the bugs.

I grab Shania and roll as fast as I can. Brakes scream. Tires appear right where my head had been. A door squeaks open.

"Nicola!"

That voice. That wonderful voice.

I'm sorry, Anton, I adore you, but this is the voice I want to hear right now.

Keith appears, his face frantic. He sees me pinning Shania down.

"Call the police," I say.

He hovers there. I open my mouth to start explaining, but before I can utter another word, my brother—my wonderful brother—nods and pulls out his phone and makes the call.

THIRTY-SIX

The bugs are gone. Maybe that's the last thing I should be thinking, but it's all my brain can process as I sit in the front yard, police cars in the driveway, ambulance out front. In everything that is happening—one person injured, three horribly murdered, the alleged killer ranting about ghosts and séances—I have been forgotten, and that is exactly what I want. A few moments to sit and stare at half-dead midges crawling on my jeans.

Keith is with Jin. I insisted on that. My injuries are minor, and Jin's are not, though the paramedics say he's stable.

I sit there, watching the midges die, and my mind is empty. Blessedly empty, my body equally empty, drained of adrenaline, only retaining enough energy to keep me upright.

I will need that energy. From experience, I know what happens next. The police will remember me—the only lucid survivor—and I will spend hours in questioning, praying it doesn't end in a jail cell. But I can't bring myself to care about that right now.

I'm safe. Jin is alive. Everyone else . . .

"Nic."

When the whisper comes, it might be the only thing that could pierce my shock and exhaustion. I follow it to see the faintest outline of Anton. Even without the bugs blocking him, he's barely there, pulsating as if he's already fading back to the other side.

"I'm sorry," he says.

"I think that should be my line."

He crouches in front of me. "I can't stay."

My eyes fill. "I know. I shouldn't have called you—"

One finger rises to my lips. "Shhh."

I nod, tears spilling out.

"I didn't get a chance to finish," he whispers, his voice barely there now. "At the roadside. When I said I'd be waiting."

I look up. I can just make him out.

"What I was trying to say is . . ." He comes closer. "I'll be waiting. But don't be in any rush to join me." He looks into my eyes. "I'm not going anywhere."

I choke out a sobbing laugh, and I swear I feel his lips against my forehead. And then he is gone.

I'm in the hospital for observation. I don't need it, but sometimes people—even doctors—can get overcautious when they hear you have CF. I've just suffered a trauma and . . . who knows? Better safe than sorry.

I'll argue tomorrow. Argue with the doctors. Argue with Keith. Convince my poor beleaguered brother that I can go home. Or, if he insists, I'll go home with him for a day or two.

The police have their story. A version of the truth, where we'd been conducting a séance to contact Anton, and Shania swapped out the ashes, hoping to contact her sister instead. She thought we had, and she believed she was possessed by the spirit of her sister, a madness that led her to murder.

When I'd explained, I could feel their gazes on me, the weight of them throwing me back twenty-two years to the detective who'd said, in all seriousness, that this was what came of messing with dark forces. But he hadn't been entirely wrong, had he? He just didn't have the whole story, where the "dark forces" were a very specific sort, shadow tendrils that ensnared a family.

They'll still need to investigate, of course. But the evidence will support my story, which Jin can corroborate as much as possible.

As for what happened to Jin, he'd set out that morning only to have my car die a few hundred feet from the house. When he couldn't get it going again, he'd fought his way back to the house through that fog of bugs, and been attacked by something in it.

Did my car coincidentally die before Jin could escape? I doubt it. Same as I doubt that was just an unusually dense swarm of midges. Whatever "dark forces" had been present, they'd tried to make damn sure we couldn't flee.

I've pieced together the rest as best I can. It seems Shania saw the story of Anton's death. She'd already been living and working in Toronto, and that article launched a plan of revenge. She inserted herself into my grief-counseling group where—after a few sessions—she'd requested me as a mentor. Had she always hoped to use the séances to contact her sister and unleash her on me? Had she been working up to that? I won't ever know all the answers, but when I invited her to join our week at the lake house, she saw her chance, though I don't think she ever imagined anything like what actually happened.

Shania is undergoing assessment now. I know what will happen. The same thing that happened to her sister and aunt. She will spend her life in a mental hospital, and the horror of that will never leave me.

Patrice blamed me for putting her in an institution. I can argue that Shania put herself there when she sentenced me to death at Patrice's hands, but that's not entirely fair. I chose to let Shania live, and that was no mercy. No mercy at all.

When my hospital room opens, I expect to see Keith. Instead, Jin slides in.

"Hey," I say, rising to sit. "Up and around?"

"I heard you found the speakers," he says.

I go still, and then I nod.

His face falls and his head drops. "I'm so sorry, Nic. I only wanted to give you closure and reassurance. But it was a patronizing thing to do, especially to a friend."

"Yep."

He looks up with a wan half smile. "Not going to tell me that my heart was in the right place?"

"Oh, I know it was, but it was still patronizing, and I would be furious if I didn't feel guilty being angry at a guy who was beaten with a paving stone."

"By a vengeful ghost. Don't forget that part."

I reach out and squeeze his hand.

He pulls a chair up to my bed and sits. "I'm sorry for all of it, Nic. For Shania and Brodie and Mrs. Kilmer and Dr. Cirillo. For what you had to go through, both twenty-two years ago and what you went through now. But I'm also sorry for what you didn't get. I really did hope we'd contact Anton."

I could tell him the truth. Maybe I should. But it feels too private, too personal. Like the moment at the roadside that should have been just between Anton and me, only it wasn't. This can be.

"I know he's there," I say. "I know he's waiting. And I know, if he could make contact, he'd kick my ass and tell me to start living again."

Jin's gaze meets mine. "He really would, Nic."

I turn away as I nod. "His life was cut short, and I will never stop raging at the universe for that. We had plans, and he's gone, but those plans don't need to die with him. They just need to change a little."

I look over at Jin. "Lucy has always wanted to see the northern lights. What would you say to a family cruise to Iceland? You, me, Keith, Libby, Hayden, Lucy . . ."

His brows rise. "A cruise with all of us? Are you sure?"

"Absolutely. A celebration. No expense spared." I smile. "My treat."

ACKNOWLEDGMENTS

My main character, Nicola, has cystic fibrosis, which I do not have, meaning I needed help with this aspect of the story. I found it with K. Vargas, who patiently answered all my questions and read the manuscript to ensure I represented Nicola and CF as best I could. A huge thanks for that and, as always, any remaining errors are mine alone.

ABOUT THE AUTHOR

Kathryn Hollinrake

Kelley Armstrong is the author of more than fifty novels, most recently the Rip Through Time mysteries and a horror novel, *Hemlock Island*. She lives with her family in Canada.